D1599911

Acclaim for Suzanne Adair

Paper Woman
winner of the Patrick D. Smith Literature Award:

"A swashbuckling good mystery yarn!"
—The Wilmington Star-News

The Blacksmith's Daughter
"Adair holds the reader enthralled with constant action, spine-tingling suspense, and superb characterization."
—Midwest Book Review

Camp Follower
nominated for the Daphne du Maurier Award and the Sir Walter Raleigh Award:

"Adair wrote another superb story."
—Armchair Interviews

Regulated for Murder
"Best of 2011" from Suspense Magazine:

"Driven by a desire to see justice done, no matter what guise it must take, [Michael Stoddard] is both sympathetic and interesting."
—Motherlode

A Hostage to Heritage
winner of the Indie Book of the Day Award:

"Suzanne Adair is on top of her game with this one."
—Jim Chambers, Amazon Hall of Fame Top 10 Reviewer

Books by Suzanne Adair

Mysteries of the American Revolution
Paper Woman
The Blacksmith's Daughter
Camp Follower

Michael Stoddard American Revolution Mysteries
Deadly Occupation
Regulated for Murder
A Hostage to Heritage

Deadly Occupation

Suzanne Adair

A Michael Stoddard American Revolution Mystery

Deadly Occupation
Copyright © 2015 by Suzanne Williams
Raleigh, North Carolina

ISBN: 978-0988912939

Excerpt of *Regulated for Murder* © 2011 by Suzanne William

Map of Southeast North Carolina 1781 © 2015 by John Robertson and Suzanne Williams

Acknowledgements

I receive help from some wonderful and unique people while conducting research for novels and editing my manuscripts. Here are a few who assisted me with *Deadly Occupation*:

The 33rd Light Company of Foot, especially Ernie and Linda Stuart

Marg Baskin

Ada Brown

Dr. Jerry C. Cashion

Margaret Coin

Conni Covington

Robert M. Dunkerly

Mike Everette

Don Hagist

Nolin and Neil Jones

John Robertson

Susan Schreyer

Diane Vallere

Special thanks to Ava Barlow for cover photography; to Ava Barlow and Jenny Toney Quinlan for cover design; and to Ashleigh Crawford for interior design.

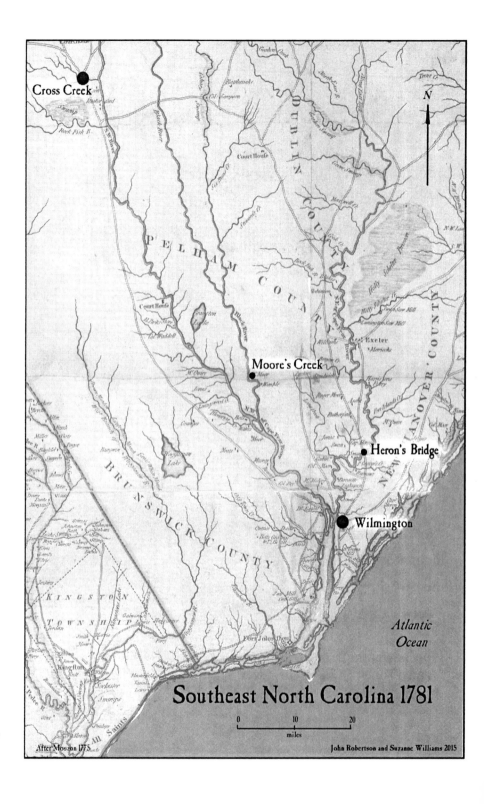

Cross Creek

N

DUPLIN COUNTY

PELHAM COUNTY

Moore's Creek

NEW HANOVER COUNTY

Heron's Bridge

BRUNSWICK COUNTY

Wilmington

KINGSTON TOWNSHIP

*Atlantic
Ocean*

Southeast North Carolina 1781

0   10   20

miles

After Mouzon 1775

John Robertson and Suzanne Williams 2015

Chapter One

WITH A NOD of approval for the sergeant, Lieutenant Michael Stoddard clasped his hands behind his back and faced the thirty soldiers where they stood on the sand-and-shell road. Each man in the two parallel lines before him was clear-eyed, his chin up and shoulders squared. Red wool coats had been brushed out and buttons buffed. Even in the dull winter dawn, every musket looked clean.

It was a fine day, indeed, for the Eighty-Second Regiment to occupy Wilmington, North Carolina, and these men were ready for it.

"Men, we'll be marching out shortly, as soon as Captain Barkley heads upriver with the galleys." A column of soldiers stomped through a drill behind Michael. He elevated his voice through the clank of muskets and equipment. "Here's how matters stand. A deputation of civilians met Major Craig last night and gave him their articles of surrender. He rejected their terms. Any residents remaining in Wilmington when we arrive will be considered our prisoners of war, at Major Craig's discretion."

The din from the drill faded. Over the shoulders of his men, Michael saw a ship's boat from the transport that was anchored in the middle of the Cape Fear River reach the bank. Infantrymen disembarked from it onto North Carolina soil and trotted up for inspection with another sergeant. He paced to allow him to make occasional eye contact with the men before him. "Scouts report that the regiment's presence has thrown the rebels into confusion and panic. The leaders of these 'patriots' have fled the area, some with little more than the clothing on their backs. Less than a day ago, the militia commander, Colonel Young, evacuated his garrison from the barracks in town. Yes, surprising as it sounds, the rebels appear to have been caught off-guard by the Eighty-Second's arrival."

From the corner of his eye, Michael saw that a scout who'd been present at last night's meeting, a free Negro called Teal, was conferring with Captain

Pitcairn, his gestures animated. Michael returned attention to his men. "We've learned that Wilmington is home to many merchants who are not sympathetic to the rebel cause. Perhaps the occupation will proceed more smoothly than what we'd expected when we sailed from Charles Town. However, I don't need to remind you lads to keep your wits about you. You can imagine what we'll find when we arrive in Wilmington at the end of today's march. Sullen and hostile townsfolk, and special 'gifts' that the militia left behind, like spiked cannon and traps set in the barracks. Don't delude yourselves into believing that we've seen the last of the rebels, just because they ran like rabbits—"

"Mr. Stoddard!" called Pitcairn. "A word with you over here immediately!"

After another nod to the sergeant, who stepped forward to address the men, Michael strode for the captain and scout. While he traversed the distance between them, he squinted at the overcast sky to the southeast. Was that a thin column of smoke rising? Hard to say against the clouds. He didn't smell smoke—but the breeze was coming from the west.

After exchanging a salute with Michael, Pitcairn jutted his chin to Teal, who was carrying a rifle. "Tell Mr. Stoddard." His nose red, the captain sneezed into a handkerchief.

The scout's hunting shirt was rumpled, and his face was sweaty, as if he'd been running. "I have come from the estate of loyalist merchant Mr. Farrell one mile distant from here. This very moment, about twenty men on horseback are attacking the estate." He swiveled, pointed to the southeastern sky, and added in his melodious-accented voice, "They have set one of the outbuildings afire. You see?"

Yes, that *was* a column of smoke. Michael addressed Teal. "Are these men from Colonel Young's militia?"

"I do not believe that they are—"

"Even if they were, it wouldn't matter." His voice gravelly, Pitcairn cleared his throat. "I've just watched those soldiers pass inspection, Mr. Stoddard. Excellent work. They're more than a match for rebels."

It sounded as though Pitcairn wanted him to run some men out there and take care of those marauders. Michael swelled his chest. "Orders, sir?"

The first portion of Pitcairn's cough missed the handkerchief. "Bloody head cold. Take ten men and follow Teal back to the estate. Render assistance to the King's Friends and drive off the perpetrators. Any captives will be marched to Wilmington with the regiment and imprisoned there."

Michael frowned, certain he'd misunderstood. "*Ten* men, sir? Teal said there were twenty mounted rebels. Surely all thirty men—"

"It isn't a pitched field battle. They aren't Continental dragoons. They're just rabble on horses." Pitcairn sniffed, propped a fist on his hip, and waved the handkerchief once. "Stand your ground with your selected ten, give those rebel scum their first taste of the King's might, and the miscreants will run away. They *always* run away. You know how it is."

True, untrained civilians ran from the sight of bayonets. Often militiamen did, too. But Michael was reluctant to discount the level of danger. His lips pinched.

Pitcairn scowled at him. "Do you understand your orders?"

"Sir." Michael's chin came up.

"Good. Send the remainder of the men over to me directly. I'll put them to work. Step lively now. Dismissed." They saluted. The captain turned his back on Michael and Teal and, after a moist sneeze, headed for another group of infantrymen.

A sinking feeling in his gut, Michael stared at the captain's retreating back, then swung his scrutiny to the men farther north on the road. Jove's arse! Surely he and ten infantrymen hadn't just been assigned a Forlorn Hope? He expelled a hard breath that converted to white fog in the chilly air. "Come along, Teal." He stalked toward the men.

The Negro caught up within one step. "I expected him to give you more soldiers, Mr. Stoddard. Infantry versus cavalry, you know."

In a corner of his mind, Michael recognized that Teal spoke with an accent he'd never before heard on any slave, whether captured African or American-born. He pushed the curiosity to one side and focused on the problem that loomed. Those might be untrained rebels attacking the Farrell estate, however Sir Isaac Newton's Laws didn't favor combatants on the ground over those astride charging horses unless they leveraged themselves shrewdly.

"Teal, tell me more about those rebels. What weapons do they have?"

"I do not think all of them are armed, sir. A few men fired pistols into the air. Their leader had a sword. Two or three carry muskets. And many of them look drunk."

Drunk at dawn on Sunday morning—that must've been quite a jollification the night before. None of the infantrymen was drunk. That improved their odds a bit—but not enough to take the edge off Michael's wariness. "How about the terrain between here and there? Is there a track of some sort?"

"Yes, sir, you will find a drive starting at the big mulberry tree back there. The drive will take you to the estate. The land is flat, much like what you see around here, and trees and brush surround the drive. It all thins out closer to the buildings."

"Thank you." Hmm. Sneak up on the rebels? Draw them out? Chase them off?

"You are welcome. I hope you can save the lady of the house."

Ice shot up Michael's back, and he swiveled his head to stare at the scout. "Are you speaking of Mrs. Farrell? What's happened to her?"

Teal shrugged. "Nothing yet. But the rebels were hollering for her to come out of the house."

"Why were they asking for her? Are they acquainted with her or her husband?"

"I do not know, Mr. Stoddard."

Hairs on the back of Michael's neck prickled. Was there more to this story than a random rebel attack on the property of a loyalist? With another brief press of his lips together, he made his strategy decision. Intimidate the rebels, and draw them away from the buildings so they didn't set anything else afire or hurt the lady.

They arrived at the group of soldiers, and Michael went over to stand beside the sergeant. "Lads, we've received a report of mounted rebels attacking a loyalist's estate one mile to the southeast. Who of the King's finest will accompany me on reconnaissance and run those whoresons off? Step forward two paces if you will."

With a rattle of muskets and cartridge boxes, every man stepped forward two paces. Again, Michael sighed, hard. He'd been transferred to the Eighty-

Second while the regiment was garrisoned in South Carolina. By now, he knew the names of most soldiers and a little about each one. All but one man before him was a combat veteran. Decisions, decisions. "On the double. Rollins. Ferguson. Buchanan. Lindsay. Jackson. Wigglesworth. Stallings. Henshaw. Stone."

That made nine soldiers hustling toward him. He needed one more. He eyed a recent recruit from Nova Scotia, the only six-foot-tall man in the squad. And as he considered the interesting role that Nick Spry had reportedly played in a scuffle the night before, the back of his neck felt tickly again, a hunch that eighteen-year-old Spry, who'd not yet seen combat, would prove helpful during the engagement this morning. "And Spry. The rest of you report to Captain Pitcairn."

***

The packed-dirt drive was wide enough for a carriage and flanked by longleaf pines, live oaks, and an occasional leafless mulberry. Wiregrass and prickly pear carpeted the brackish wilderness beyond the drive—ubiquitous, as far as Michael could see, in the landscape of the Cape Fear. But the last thing he wanted was for those twenty rebels on horseback to perform some sort of envelopment upon his ten infantrymen in all the cacti and crushed shells. To keep the patrol alerted of any rebel sentries or scouts, he sent Teal up ahead and had Spry fall back.

The patrol jogged southeast. Sounds from the regiment quickly faded, screened out by the foliage. After they'd clanked along for about seven minutes, Michael caught whiffs of burning building and heard the distant shouts of men engaged in dark revelry. He and his men rounded a tree-shadowed bend to a straight stretch. From about seventy-five feet ahead, Teal was closing the expanse between them at an open run, eyes wide with terror, arms pumping. "They have seen me!"

From somewhere beyond the scout, Michael heard the thud of approaching horses, and the shout of a man: "Run down that colored rat, boys!"

Hoping that partial shadow would enhance the menace his patrol posed, Michael ordered the nine soldiers to halt, form a line across the drive at the bend, and fix bayonets on their loaded muskets. He exhaled a quick breath that did nothing to settle the flutter in his gut. "Make ready!" At his command, the patrol became a wall of red in the gloom, the vertical line of each musket extended upward by almost two feet of sharp, metallic hell.

Half a dozen rebels on horseback trotted into view around a curve one hundred feet down the drive. The man in front spotted Teal and snarled. "There's the spy!" He kicked his horse in the sides and picked up speed.

The men with him followed, and one roared, "Yee-aww, we got our rascal now!"

Christ Jesus! Those men were going to trample Teal if the patrol didn't intervene. "Present!" Michael bellowed, his right hand balled into a fist at his side, his left hand clenched around the barrel of his loaded fusil. Each redcoat swiveled to cock and aim his musket, all movements smooth and synched. Not a man quailed.

Teal yelled something that sounded like "*allahuma thabetna*" and dove into the brush.

The rebels' eyes bugged on the patrol. "Whoa! Shit! Stop!" screamed several at the same time. The charge degenerated into a tangle of swearing riders and snorting horses about sixty feet away. After they finally got themselves reined about, they retreated up the drive as fast as they could get their mounts to go.

They vanished around the curve, and Michael heard their yells: "Redcoats— dozens of 'em! Get out of here! Save yourselves!"

Dozens. Michael smirked and ordered his men to stand down and remove bayonets. The flutter in his gut faded. He let out a breath of relief. Had those riders decided to charge his patrol from so close, his men could have been run down.

"Did you hear those cowards?" Jackson laughed, short. "They thought we looked like dozens."

Henshaw guffawed. "Maybe the regiment will number a thousand by noon."

"And all the rebels in North Carolina will surrender." Stone grinned.

For a moment, Michael watched Teal crawl from his hiding place and stand in the drive, head turned in the direction that the mob had fled. No doubt the scout was shaken after that experience. He listened again for the rebels. No longer pitched with revelry, those fading shouts were tight with panic and fear.

Michael said to Stone, "I wouldn't wager on their surrender if I were you, lad. Those were only pathetic wasters. Don't mistake them for the trained, tough rebels in these parts. And let's not forget our duty here. Make certain those scum are gone and the King's Friends are safe."

That was when he realized that he was missing one man. His gaze made a circuit of the patrol. "Where's Spry?"

A trip back around the bend rewarded him with the sight of the blond recruit strutting toward them, musket in one hand, waving the other arm to get their attention. To Michael's query about more rebels, Spry shook his head and halted thirty feet up the drive. "All quiet on this end, sir. But I found something back there that you ought to see."

For now, the rebels were gone, so after Michael motioned for Teal to catch up with them, he and the men followed Spry northwest about forty feet, where the recruit pointed out a one-inch thick piece of wood, three-feet squared, lodged firmly in the sandy soil not far off the east side of the drive. While everyone watched, Spry lifted one side of the wood. Metal squawked: hinges. The square of wood covered the entrance to a manmade underground tunnel.

A shallow tunnel, only about three feet deep from what Michael could tell. Any deeper, and it might fill with water. A couple of dead leaves and a little sand spiraled down into the gloom. Having opened the cover all the way, Spry straightened to his full height and grinned with white, horsey teeth.

Michael studied the maw below him, then lifted his gaze past it to the trees, as if to see beyond them. Where did the tunnel lead? And for what purpose was it used?

Judging from the small mound of dead leaves around the hole, the board must have been covered with forest debris earlier and thus disguised. So how did Spry find it? He studied the recruit in appreciation of his observational skills. "The rest of us walked right past this thing earlier. How is it that you spotted it?"

"Sir. As I passed by, a couple of squirrels chased each other across it." He shrugged. "Their thumping around on it made a sound that was wrong for the natural forest. Hollow. Like a board covering a hole. So I investigated."

Buchanan muttered, "That's bloody amazing, Spry."

It was beyond amazing. Michael wondered how many of the other men with him would have followed up on such a subtle stimulus. He wasn't sure that *he* would have done so.

Teal moved in beside him, nodded at the hole, and said, "Ah. Of course."

Michael frowned at him. "This is familiar to you?"

"I have seen a few tunnels like it, Mr. Stoddard."

"What can you tell me about it?

"Tunnels like these are used for escape, sir. I suspect that this particular one goes to a hiding hole below the Farrells' house."

"Escape—hiding hole? Wait a moment." Michael turned to face him fully. "Escape tunnels farther inland are tall enough for an adult to walk hunched over. But from what I can see here, this tunnel is only about three feet tall. The only way an adult could pass through there is on hands and knees." He gestured to the east. "And how far away is the house from here—a quarter mile? Are you saying an adult would crawl that distance to escape?"

Teal held his gaze. "Those who are desperate would do so, sir. For five years, rebels have controlled North Carolina. On occasion, they persecute loyalists. Some loyalists built escapes for themselves and their families."

The scout nodded to the bend in the road where all of them except Spry had narrowly avoided a skirmish. "It is not so difficult for me to sympathize with persecuted loyalists." He regarded Michael again. "If I had to do so, Mr. Stoddard, I would crawl on my hands and knees a quarter mile to escape being captured by scoundrels like those back there."

A little chill slid down Michael's backbone. He could imagine what would have happened to Teal if he'd been overtaken by those riders. He nodded to the Negro. "Your point is well made."

After another glance down the tunnel, Michael replaced the cover, brushed sand off his hands, and surveyed his patrol. "All right, lads, let's move along to Mr. Farrell's house and ensure that he doesn't need to use this tunnel. Teal, you're up front again, but don't get so far ahead this time. Spry, stay behind."

The nine infantrymen and Teal headed down the road. For a moment, Michael hung back and paced himself beside the recruit who was three inches taller than he was and a good forty-five pounds heavier. Again he thought about the incident last night. Coop up several hundred men in the belly of a transport ship, toss them around for three days in a storm—and the result when the ship stopped rolling wasn't always gratitude. "Spry. Tell me about the fistfight."

"Sir. It was quickly resolved. I regret that such a trifling matter was even brought to your notice." Spry kept his gaze forward.

Michael had looked over the recruit's face during squad inspection. No black eye, split lip, bruises, or cuts. "Captain Pitcairn has dispensed disciplinary measures on those men. What I want to know is how you managed to step between two pairs of swinging fists and stop the fight without being drawn into it yourself."

The corner of Spry's mouth crimped. He was holding back another grin. "Well, sir, it helps to be larger than either of the men who are doing the fighting. Gets their attention, you know."

"I'm certain it does."

"And I suggested that they save their enthusiasm for the rebels. Sir."

Michael gave a quick smile. "Well done, lad."

"Thank you, sir." Spry's big teeth shone.

As Michael quickened his pace to catch up with the rest of his men, he pondered. Later that day, when they arrived in Wilmington, Spry would be one of many men put to work at menial tasks such as digging latrines and building redoubts. It was guaranteed work for privates. Good, honest labor for the average soldier.

Except that the recruit from Nova Scotia wasn't the average soldier. In the few weeks that he'd been with the regiment, Spry had figured out what motivated seasoned fighters who were forced to sit idle in a garrison while they awaited their next assignment, and he'd used that to neutralize aggression.

Not to mention the fact that his observational skills were astounding.

Spry would be wasted on all that good, honest labor. Michael, who'd joined the Army at the age of seventeen, a year younger than Spry was, had nine years of service to His Majesty on American soil, and he'd seen how the machine worked. If Spry had unrealistic expectations about what the Army could do for him, its hulking orthodoxy would grind down that ambition.

Still, every now and then, special assignments became available within the Army for astute, deserving men. Michael resolved to keep his eyes and ears open for one of those assignments on behalf of Nick Spry.

Chapter Two

WHEN THE PATROL reached Farrell's two-story house, the torched outbuilding, mostly burned down by then, was the only sign of the rebels' visit. A gentleman in his early forties wearing spectacles and a fine suit of lace and medium-blue velvet met Michael on the front porch and introduced himself as Farrell's brother-in-law, Carlisle. He thanked Michael for driving off the bandits. Michael declined his offer of brandy and inquired after the safety of the household, especially the lady.

"Those rebel beasts—of course, we were all quite frightened." Carlisle flattened his lips together a moment while he cleaned off his spectacles with a handkerchief. "It's good of you to inquire about my sister. Before your fortuitous arrival, those villains were calling for her. It would have terrified any lady." Carlisle replaced his spectacles and handkerchief and smiled at Michael. "But fortunately Alice isn't here. She and Richard—that's Mr. Farrell—drove to Wilmington yesterday for a few days. They own a tobacco shop in town."

Michael took silent note of the information about the tobacco shop. "So those scoundrels didn't know that the Farrells weren't here. What business did they have with your sister?"

The fellow spread his hands. "I have no idea, sir. Rebels excel at random attacks just like this one. The past five years haven't been easy for the King's Friends here in North Carolina. I'm sorry to tell you that this isn't the first time rebels with dishonorable intent have sought out loyalist ladies."

Michael sighed. The backcountry of North Carolina sounded as chaotic as that of South Carolina. How many more loyalist estates would be attacked before the Crown restored order? "Who among those rebels did you recognize, Mr. Carlisle?"

"Why, none of them, sir. I live in New Berne and came here a few weeks ago to visit Alice and her family." His smile enlarged, and he rubbed his palms together. "*And* to take advantage of the clear winter nighttime skies here. I have just completed building my fifth telescope and have been dutifully recording my discoveries of binary stars with it—and studying the parallax of stars in one particular quadrant of the sky. Possibly sir, yes, possibly I may have found another primary planet in our solar system. At the very least, it's a comet. Is that not exciting?" Behind his spectacles, Carlisle's eyes gleamed.

Michael blinked and heard the yawn of a soldier out on the lawn. A man with Carlisle's interests wouldn't know the local rebels. During daylight hours while most people were up and about, socializing, he'd be sleeping off his stargazing. "Yes, well, good luck with your astronomy endeavor, Mr. Carlisle."

"Thank you. Naturally, if it is a planet, we shall have to name it after a Roman god or goddess. Diana or Vulcan, perhaps." Carlisle wiggled his eyebrows and pressed his forefinger to one side of his nose. "But likely not old Bacchus." His expression sobered. "Please, Mr. Stoddard, when you reach Wilmington, do look in on my sister and make sure she's safe."

Depending on Michael's assignments after they reached town, that request might take him a few days to fulfill. He nodded. "I will, Mr. Carlisle, as soon as I'm able."

***

A cold sprinkle fell on the patrol during its return to the landing site. Yorkshire-born Michael was happy to ignore it. He was no longer stuck in frontier Georgia, where he'd been garrisoned the previous summer. Cockfights and drunken brawls had been a staple of Saturday night entertainment in the village of Alton.

Plus he'd heard a rumor that Major Craig had checked into his background right before the regiment sailed from South Carolina. Craig had taken a personal interest in him, eh? Well, those inquiries weren't about Michael's courier assignment in December, his cover for a personal mission of dark justice that had fallen apart. No one knew his true motive for taking that assignment—with the possible exception of a double spy in South Carolina. So Michael's fortune had greatly improved, and a little rain didn't bother him at all.

While the patrol had been on Farrell's estate, the remaining men of the regiment were brought ashore, and Captain Barkley and the galleys headed upriver. Companies were positioned on the road for the march northward. Michael disbanded his patrol and made a brief report to Captain Pitcairn about the favorable outcome of the morning' activity. The captain's handkerchief muffled his acknowledgment.

Musicians kept the regiment tramping along in step on the flat, straight road. Late morning, the drizzle stopped. The sky cleared rapidly to a dazzling blue. Although the late-January sun failed to take all the bite from the air, the wind calmed.

On horseback and afoot, the regiment's scouts came and went. They kept the Eighty-Second informed of rebel scouts and militiamen who monitored their progress at a distance, not challenging the soldiers. Around noon, two scouts rode in from the north to confirm that Wilmington was defenseless. They also reported that the civilian men left behind planned to meet the regiment south of town and surrender their arms. The news whisked the buzz of good spirits among infantrymen and artillerymen.

Michael spotted Teal and waved him over, having thought about his accent and the words he'd uttered in another language when he'd jumped into the brush to escape the rebels. As soon as the Negro matched his stride, he said, "Teal. Is Teal your true name?"

The scout's eyes widened on him, then he looked ahead. "My true name is Tasheel bin Rasul."

Michael felt his eyebrows rise. Teal was a Mussulman. "Where is your home in Africa?"

"I am not from Africa. I am from Mokha, on the Arabian peninsula, where I exported coffee for my grandfather's prosperous business." A snort of mirthless laughter escaped the scout. "And I got from Arabia to America the way most of us find our way here."

The slave trade. Michael swallowed down a bitter taste in his mouth. "Mokha? I thought most of the slave business was out of Africa."

Teal didn't speak for a moment. Then, after a glance Michael's way, he spun a story about being kidnapped five years earlier and sold into slavery by a competitor who lusted after a greater share of the coffee export market as well as both of Teal's wives. Teal was transported across the Red Sea, then loaded aboard a caravan headed north to Egypt. Every time he made effort to contact his family, he was beaten. Slavers changed his name to "Teal" fearing that Tasheel bin Rasul would be too difficult for his new master to pronounce.

Half a year later, on a plantation in South Carolina, his command of English was good enough for him to explain his circumstances to the owner of the plantation. For proof, he transcribed the first *sura* of the Qur'an in Arabic and offered to translate it into English. His version was similar to a translated copy of the Qur'an owned by a friend of the plantation owner. It corroborated Teal's story.

His master wrote to his grandfather in Mokha, then freed Teal when he received a joyful response. Teal worked as a scout in the Carolinas to earn his passage to England. From there, his grandfather would pay for his return to Mokha. In Teal's absence, his grandfather had kept his wives safe for him, as both had borne twins after the abduction. And the blackguard who'd had him abducted had fled to the Arabian Desert bearing the sentence of death.

Captain Pitcairn called for Teal then, and Michael sent his gaze forward rather than allow it to follow the scout. *Two* sets of twins? Ye gods. Surely the Negro was stretching that part of his tale. Mussulmen were cunning storytellers, and the time that Teal talked had flown by. Portions of his tale sounded like the wild adventures found in a book called *The Arabian Nights' Entertainment*. But wherever the truth lay, Teal had clearly endured much on American soil and deserved to go home.

★★★

Mid-afternoon, the final man from the column of civilians that had marched out and met the Eighty-Second took his place in the front row of the civilian group. He set his rifle, ammunition, and powder horn on the ground before him, then straightened. Like each of the craftsmen and merchants who'd marched with him from town and lain down their own weapons, his wide-eyed gaze hopped around six companies of soldiers turned into a sea of scarlet by the sun. Like each of the townsmen before him, he gulped, and his shoulders hunched.

Michael knew that every one of those civilians was anxious, even resentful. He suspected that the rebel "governor," his cronies, and officers in the Continental Army would label all one hundred and ninety-eight civilians "cowards" and mock them. However he was grateful that they'd had the courage to surrender themselves to the regiment. Instead of watching the Eighty-Second sack and burn their homes, these men would be paroled and return within a day to their businesses and families.

The Eighty-Second got right to work. Soldiers set up a temporary camp south of town, took charge of the two batteries used to guard Wilmington, and cleaned up the welcome that the rebels left in the barracks: overturned cots and chairs, piles of cow dung and fish offal, and buckets of piss. Not that the rest of Wilmington smelled better than the barracks: the town was situated on the Cape Fear River, and its primary industries were the manufacture of naval stores such as tar, turpentine, and lumber.

Next morning, Monday, the twenty-ninth of January, the regiment confiscated tax records hidden aboard a boat northbound on the river. Alas, Michael wasn't assigned that mission. Major Craig was eager to march ten miles up the Northeast Cape Fear River to "Heron's Bridge," where Colonel Young had established his post, so he could capture rebels and confiscate provisions and ammunition. So Captain Pitcairn gave Michael and two privates the insipid task of impounding wagons to support Craig's expedition, set to leave the following afternoon.

Tuesday morning at reveille, Michael awakened with a runny nose. Every time he inhaled the whistling cold morning air inside his tent, the back of his throat felt like a cat had sharpened claws across it. Coop up several hundred men in the belly of a transport ship, and yes, some of them were bound to get head colds. Maybe Pitcairn had given him *his* cold.

Illness, however, was the least of Michael's worries. He and the privates had found only four dilapidated wagons for Major Craig's venture that afternoon. The lack of wagons wasn't normal in a town the size of Wilmington. Civilians were withholding information about it, and from the bitterness in those surrendered men's eyes on Sunday, he knew he wouldn't find out where the wagons were by throwing his weight around.

After morning parade, he visited the wainwright's shop. A little bell over the door jingled when he let himself in. Three men stopped conversing behind the counter to stare at him for several seconds. Then the oldest man, a stocky fellow, pasted on a smile and came forward. "Good morning, Lieutenant—er, Captain—"

"Lieutenant Stoddard." Ugh, he sounded awful, as if he were talking through a nose packed with lint.

"Mr. Stoddard. A pleasure to meet you. Welcome to my shop." The man clasped his hands before him. "My name is Smedes."

"It's a pleasure to meet you, too, Mr. Smedes."

"How may I be of assistance, sir?" The wainwright's gaze made furtive darts past Michael's shoulders. He wanted to escape.

The head cold had annihilated Michael's sense of smell, a minor miracle in a town that stank of tar and tidal debris. Nevertheless, the men reeked of apprehension and mistrust. They needed a carrot, not a stick. He coughed into his fist and allowed his arms to hang easily at his sides. "The regiment will be hiring reliable civilian contractors for occasional projects." That much was true. "For example, next month, we'll need someone to build us a few wagons with modifications." That part was balderdash, and maybe Smedes wouldn't press for details about the "modifications." Michael glanced over what he could see of the shop, including the two young men behind the counter. "You've two apprentices, eh? What sort of work do you take on here, Mr. Smedes? And how many projects can you manage at once?"

The wainwright's shoulders relaxed when he realized that Michael's visit was about business opportunities. By twenty minutes later, Michael had met the apprentices, received a tour of the shop, and seen three works in progress that exemplified the professional quality of craftsmanship found there. He'd also learned that Colonel Young and his militia had seized all the good wagons in Wilmington to evacuate their supplies last Saturday, same day that the rebels' Committee of Safety had fled town.

When Michael left the shop, Smedes and his apprentices were wearing genuine smiles of confidence that their business stood to profit from the occupation. Out in the dirt street, Michael dropped his smile of cordiality, dragged a soggy handkerchief from his waistcoat pocket, and honked into it. The cotton of congestion expanded through his head. Eyes watery, he shoved the handkerchief away and stared north toward Market Street through the faint, blue haze of wood smoke.

No doubt Colonel Young and his men were thumbing their noses at the British after leaving them four vehicles unfit for firewood. Where the deuce was Michael going to find wagons? So much for improving his fortune.

"Mr. Stoddard, sir!" Private Ferguson was trotting south on Front Street and waving at him. He saluted when he reached Michael, then took a few seconds to catch his breath. "Major Craig wants to see you immediately, sir. His headquarters at Third and Market Streets."

"Thank you, Ferguson." No wagons for the expedition, and Craig wanted to see him immediately. Shit. A dull ache germinated in his gut, as if the biscuit he'd eaten for breakfast fused to glass.

Ferguson frowned at him. "Sir, you don't look so good. Red in the nose, and rheumy about the eyes."

When Craig caught the rebels who'd abandoned town three days earlier and taken all the wagons, Michael looked forward to sneezing on them, passing along the head cold, special gift of the British Army. "Excellent. I hope I look demonic."

"Demonic? Er, no, sir."

Of course he didn't look demonic. He looked like everyone's honorable dark-haired, dark-eyed nephew, of average stature, and the reliable sort of fellow entrusted to defend and guard a room full of bosomy, lustful virgins. He dismissed the private, who jogged off to deliver more messages, then strode north for the commander's headquarters.

Haze from wood smoke coated his walk to Market Street and overlaid the regiment's transition from the encampment to the barracks. Residents, their expressions dazed, yielded in the streets to the commotion of infantrymen marching off to drill, and to the rush of the army's civilian retainers, sutlers, and contracted artisans.

At the front door of Major Craig's headquarters, the provost marshal's guard informed Michael that the commander consulted with a courier in the study. Michael trotted back down more than a dozen steps and assumed position in line behind scouts and soldiers. Hurry up and wait.

The three-story wooden house, owned by a prosperous merchant, was elegant enough. But the delay encouraged Michael to evaluate Market Street's mud puddles and the weather-beaten wood and brick of neighboring buildings, taunted him with memories of Charles Town's sophistication. Maybe he'd deluded himself, and Wilmington was just a bigger version of that Georgia village.

In addition to being at the end of the world, Alton had been home to his first murder investigation. His jaw tightened. Yes, a murder solved, and an investigation closed, but no justice served. The killer was a demon that took the shape of an officer in the Seventeenth Light Dragoons, ostensibly serving His Majesty. Michael pressed a fist to his lips.

The courier who'd been in conference with Craig breezed past him. Up on the porch beside the front door, the guard caught Michael's attention and summoned him forward. As Michael passed men in line who'd waited longer than he had, their expressions proclaimed, "Better you than me." In this regiment, when a soldier was bumped to the head of the line, it often meant that he was due disciplinary action from the Eighty-Second's irascible commander.

Those bloody wagons. The sensation of glass in the gut returned to Michael. He stomped up the steps and, inside the house, drew up short of the study's closed and polished walnut doors, his throat burning and head pounding. Then he removed his hat, entered the room, and pulled the doors shut behind him.

At a small table to his right, near the fireplace, an adjutant dipped his quill in an inkwell and scratched away at correspondence. In a stream of sunlight at a front window, Major James Henry Craig glanced at the time on a gold watch, snapped it shut, and replaced it in his waistcoat. Scowling, he pivoted and returned Michael's salute. "I sent three men to look for you this morning, Mr. Stoddard. Where have you been?"

Blast. Barely had Michael stepped into the office, and already the audience was off to an inauspicious start. "Sir." He gulped and winced. Surely a dozen needles were embedded in his throat. "I've been searching for wagons in town to support your operations this afternoon—Captain Pitcairn's orders yesterday."

Craig squinted at him. "Why the devil did he send you on that wild goose chase? There are no wagons to be found here. The rebel militia took them all when they—bah, never mind about the wagons." He swatted his hand through the air. "We shall fetch them all back to Wilmington soon enough." He seated himself behind a longer table littered with letters and other documents, the broad span of his shoulders disguising the fact that he was several inches shorter than his lieutenant, and motioned to one of two ladder-back chairs opposite the table from him. "Sit. We haven't much time."

The major obviously had something on his mind other than wagons. Unsure whether to feel relief, Michael took a seat. Thirty-two-year-old Craig studied him, eyes keen, and facial features sharp, as if carved from ivory. Then he rested his palms on the surface of the table and pushed forward, shoulders beefy. "This afternoon, when I march out with most of the men to engage Colonel Young, you shall remain in Wilmington."

Surprise prickled Michael's soul, raised his chin. "Sir?" Was he being left behind as acting commander? A little bubble of elation swelled in his breast.

"I'm relieving you of your usual duties."

The bubble deflated. Michael forced himself to continue sitting straight while his mind raced. This was some sort of disciplinary action. He must have angered an officer, or flouted a regulation, or—

Wait a moment. Had someone recognized what he was really about when he'd volunteered to run those dispatches from Charles Town to the Carolina hinterlands back in December? His pulse jerked a few beats. Damnation. Had he been reported?

Chapter Three

MICHAEL'S JAW CLENCHED. Craig had merely to *suspect* his intention, and—Michael jerked a glance over his shoulder. No detachment of the provost's men crowded the study's entrance, waiting to take him into custody. The doors remained closed, and the adjutant continued scratching out correspondence. Nevertheless, when Michael straightened in his chair and faced forward, he braced himself for an interrogation over his motive for running those dispatches.

Craig eased back in his chair, palms upon the table. One forefinger idled. Beneath it, a piece of paper skittered about on the table's surface like a trapped mouse. "When I arrived in Charles Town at the beginning of this month, I read Captain John Sheffield's letter attached to your file."

So Craig *had* taken a personal interest in his background.

But there was a letter from *Sheffield* in his file. The inside of Michael's mouth tasted bad. He swallowed and grimaced.

Craig made a quick nod at Michael's expression. "Yes, I took note of that vile business at your post last summer in Georgia, the Spaniard's torture and murder."

How much had Captain Sheffield detailed in his letter? Michael doubted he'd reported the truth. Lieutenant Dunstan Fairfax had tortured the Spaniard to death, slowly, for his own entertainment. Yet he'd never been apprehended for his crime, never been arrested. That thing in the uniform of a lieutenant in the Seventeenth Light Dragoons had been born into the aristocracy, but it wasn't human.

"You solved the murder."

"Sir." Yes, he'd solved it. Then Sheffield had spun balderdash over his findings and lied to conceal Fairfax's evil.

Worse than Fairfax's depravity with the Spaniard was the problem that he didn't confine his sport to the Crown's enemies. Michael caught himself massaging his throat where the tip of the monster's dagger had teased out blood. Sweat sprang to his forehead. He yanked his hand away, then stuffed the splinter of horror into the depths of memory.

From the direction the discussion was taking, it seemed that Craig didn't know that Michael had acted as a courier in hopes of tracking down Fairfax in the backcountry and quietly delivering the justice that the fiend had so smoothly escaped. Thus Michael's secret was safe. Nevertheless, anxiety continued to thrust against his ribcage from the inside. He'd been relieved of duty and earned disciplinary action, a black mark on his record. Why?

"Lieutenant, let's talk a moment about justice."

Justice—bah. Michael fought to keep a sneer off his face as he recalled Sheffield's version of "justice." *I shall do nothing about your findings, Mr. Stoddard. The victim was an assassin, an enemy of the Crown...Mr. Fairfax will be leaving Alton within a few days. Good riddance to him.*

Michael and Sheffield hadn't agreed on that point. At all. In the letter attached to Michael's file, Sheffield must have reported Michael's defiance, the way he'd argued with his commanding officer over Sheffield's insipid official statement, a lie that soothed Alton's civilians as well as the soldiers stationed there. Michael must have been relieved of duty because of his insubordination toward Sheffield.

But why had it taken the Army half a year to mete out the disciplinary action? Michael swiped clammy palms on his trousers and struggled to maintain a neutral expression. He waited.

The scarlet of Major Craig's uniform coat seemed to pulsate. On his table, the whisper of papers quieted. "Residents approached me yesterday with concerns about justice." Craig's voice grew rough. "They described a rebel Committee of Safety that carried out justice on a whim, when it felt like it." His palm smacked the surface of the table. "By God, I shall tolerate no foul play while I command this post. While we occupy Wilmington, law-abiding civilians here will be protected from criminal activity. When crimes are committed, competent men will investigate." His forefinger jabbed out at Michael. "And that, Mr. Stoddard, is why you'll remain behind. Based upon Captain Sheffield's recommendation, I'm appointing you as my lead criminal investigator, reporting directly to me."

Michael stared at him. In the first second, shock stiffened his expression. *Lead criminal investigator*—had he heard correctly?

Then euphoria overrode the stuffy, achy head cold, tripped his pulse, and shattered the shock. Craig had indeed said *lead criminal investigator*. This was no daydream. He blinked rapidly. His jaw relaxed. "Sir? Thank you, sir!" Huzzah!

His pulse tracked back on rhythm. Justice, yes. Justice he'd seen denied civilians in America for years whenever rebels lacking experience and competence destroyed the foundation of legitimate government and dabbled at law making.

Justice denied a Spaniard in Alton, and, later last summer, a Dutchman in Camden, and the gods only knew how many others—not because they were enemies of the Crown, but because they'd captured Fairfax's fancy as *sport*. Relief dissipated Michael's euphoria, eased the pressure in his chest. Maybe no one would ever discover his true motive for delivering those dispatches. And maybe someday he'd get another chance, a more refined opportunity, to rid the earth of Dunstan Fairfax.

"Select an assistant for yourself from among the men," said Craig. "Train him."

Michael restrained a grin at the mental image of Spry standing over the secret entrance to the tunnel on the Farrells' estate. Would criminal investigation appeal to him? Hah! He wagered it would. "Sir."

Brooding draped Craig's expression. He fished a few pieces of paper from a portfolio and slid the top sheet across the table to Michael. "Several rebel leaders relocated their wives and families from estates to homes inside Wilmington before they fled the area. Their names and those of their family members are on that list."

Michael sucked in a breath at the top name. "William Hooper. Why would a signer of the Declaration of Independence leave loved ones behind?"

The keenness in Craig's eyes grew calculated. "He was desperate, realizing he couldn't travel quickly enough with them. An agonizing choice he made: trust them to my mercy rather than the mercy of the King's Friends in the countryside."

"Surely he knows we shall arrest them."

"No. Keep an eye on them, but don't arrest these families unless they give us cause to do so."

"Sir." What was Craig's rationale behind such an unconventional directive? Careful to keep skepticism out of his expression, Michael shut his mouth and said no more of the matter. After nine years in the Army, he'd learned when that was useful.

Craig pondered another paper drawn from his portfolio. "If we're to earn the cooperation of this community, key men of the garrison must be accessible to residents. It so happens that a widow on Second Street inquired whether I might board an officer in her home to grant her protection. Her home was apparently broken into twice in November, and the Committee did nothing to help her because she's a loyalist." He passed the paper to Michael. "Here is her direction. It's my decision that you and your assistant shall be quartered with this widow. Her name is Enid Jones."

A roof over his head, a bed to sleep in, and home-cooked meals. Worth the few pennies each week. Michael couldn't resist a grin. "Thank you, sir."

Craig's mouth crooked. "And just so you don't get cocky with such a soft life, I'm assigning you straightaway on two inquiries. Word has reached me of a vicar named Elijah Spivey who established a congregation last month northwest of town. It's called the Church of Mary and Martha of Bethany." Craig's lips twitched. "It's rumored that he has attracted large numbers of ladies into his flock by promising them leadership positions within the church."

Michael snorted. "That doesn't sound like any Anglican church I know, sir."

"Indeed. And the church building is located in an area where there are pockets of rebel resistance. Find out who Vicar Spivey is and whether he's taking advantage of people." Craig's bottom lip flattened, pushed against the top lip. "If he's anything except a legitimate Anglican—and *especially* if he's a rebel advocating sedition as the will of God—arrest him and bring him to jail."

"Sir." Michael maintained an even tone while picturing his older sister, Miriam, fired up behind a pulpit in Yorkshire. Craig's concern wasn't difficult to decipher. Only a few years earlier, Britons had tittered over the image of

American women who spoke out as patriots. But when those ladies united to boycott imports of tea and cloth, the joke was suddenly on Britain: unsold merchandise that totaled thousands and thousands of pounds of lost business. No telling what magnitude of change women could wreak from a pulpit. Especially if those women were zealous Whigs.

"And as to the second investigation, a gunsmith, Gabriel Garrity, on Third Street reported this morning that his wife, Julia, has been missing since Saturday. Here's Mr. Garrity's direction."

How could a man misplace his wife for three days? Michael studied the final paper. On Saturday, Colonel Young's militia and the Committee of Safety fled town.

Craig's scrutiny of him sharpened. "Yes. I wonder whether it's a coincidence that she disappeared the same day the militia and Committee left."

"Wives disappear for many reasons, sir."

"Right you are. A final point about Mr. Garrity. He claims to be neutral in this conflict." A corner of the major's mouth pinched, an accent mark on his opinion of neutrality. "Stay alert."

He pushed up from his chair, followed by Michael. "We've a supply depot to establish and defend here. From Wilmington, we must support Lord Cornwallis's initiatives on the interior of North Carolina." He let out a sigh of weariness. "But as of a few minutes ago, I learned that our mission in the Cape Fear has become even more critical." Craig pressed his fingertips to the surface of the table. "The courier just before you brought foul news. Almost two weeks ago, on the seventeenth, the Continentals and their allies defeated Colonel Tarleton and the Legion in the backcountry of South Carolina. Most of his infantry is lost. Dead or captured."

Michael gaped. How was that possible? When he'd delivered those dispatches less than five weeks earlier, he'd walked through the camp of the British Legion. Tarleton's men had been fit, primed for battle. "And his cavalry, sir?"

"They fared better, but not by much. What this means, Mr. Stoddard, is that the Eighty-Second Regiment stands between His Majesty and chaos. And not just here in North Carolina. So when I return from the infernal distraction of Heron's Bridge within a day or two, I expect you shall have the trifling business of a vicar and a missing wife well in hand, so we can focus on our mission. Any questions?"

"No, sir."

"Excellent. Dismissed."

***

No one answered Michael's knock upon the front door of the two-story brick house on Second Street. He checked the paper that Craig had given him. Yes, he and Spry were at the Widow Jones's residence.

Behind him on the porch, Spry said, low, "A bloody shame about the British Legion, sir."

"Indeed." How much would it damn him to hope that Fairfax had been among the casualties at the Battle of the Cowpens? He turned to face his assistant. "It appears that Mrs. Jones isn't at home this moment, so we..." He trailed off to swivel his head to the left and listen. Out of sight but nearby, a woman was singing. "Come along." He followed the voice.

In the side yard, Spry muttered, "Sir, look at that!" and cleared his throat, a verbal leer.

Michael had no doubt that the full-figured young blonde hanging laundry in the neighbor's back yard had spotted them walking up to Mrs. Jones's front door and started singing to draw notice to herself. He'd found the colonies loaded with laundresses thus endowed, every one of them under the mistaken impression that he'd been born into nobility, just because he was an officer. He blew his nose, almost a futile effort with all his congestion. "Let's introduce ourselves."

"Sir!" Every time Spry grinned like that, Michael could swear he'd borrowed his teeth off a workhorse. But the teeth went with the rest of Spry. The regimental tailors must cringe every time he needed a new coat. Or shoes, good gods.

At their approach, the blonde abandoned the wet laundry and sashayed over, her initial smile for Michael. His heart jumped a few beats. Oh, yes, all that blonde, curly hair, and what a bosomy figure—He caught the sigh before it left his mouth and vented exasperation at himself instead. After nine years, why wasn't he done thinking about Lydia?

Business, he told himself. He and Spry paused on their side of a low hedge separating the yards, swept off their hats, and bowed. He said, "Good noon, madam."

"Molly." Matching Spry, tooth for tooth, with a grin, she smoothed her apron and curtsied. "*Miss* Molly Pepperton, that is."

"Pleased to meet you. Lieutenant Stoddard, at your service, and this is Spry." Molly's gaze lapped the length of Spry, then shot over to devour the epaulet on Michael's right shoulder. He could almost hear her thought: *The large one, or the wealthy one?*

Her torso wiggled, and a partition magically appeared in her tucker, along with about an inch of creamy cleavage. Michael's gaze burrowed there. No reason why he shouldn't enjoy the view. Beside him, he heard Spry's enthusiastic exhalation. Again, Michael reminded himself that this was business. "We're seeking Mrs. Jones."

"She stepped out to market about a quarter hour ago. She should be back any moment." A pretty pout puffed Molly's lips. "I hope there's no more trouble for her, poor dear."

Michael dragged his attention from her lips to her eyes, wagering that Spry's ogle was still buried in cleavage. "No trouble at all. By her request, we're to board with her."

"Oh, how wonderful!" Again, the blonde's gaze shifted between them, and a deep sigh parted the tucker another inch. "She doesn't need more trouble after all that's happened to her. Her beau was murdered back in November by that odious Mr. Badley and Mr. Prescott. Then those two murdered a messenger from New Berne who'd come to tell Mrs. Chiswell that Mr. Badley and Mr. Prescott had altered her dead husband's will to steal his money."

Michael blinked in confusion. "Er, if I might ask you to clarify—did you say that *two murders* happened here, in Wilmington, in November?"

"Three, actually." Molly moved closer to the hedge. "Mr. Badley and Mr. Prescott also murdered the man they hired to murder Mrs. Jones's beau."

Michael stared the laundress, words swept from his throat by the news, and didn't bother to hide his shock and dismay. *Three murders.* Wilmington was as crime-infested as Alton. "Major Craig mentioned only that Mrs. Jones's house was burgled." Perhaps Mrs. Jones hadn't told Major Craig the full story, omitting information about the murders to make sure that Craig believed her.

"Yes, that happened, too. Mr. Badley and Mr. Prescott broke in looking for an unaltered copy of Mrs. Chiswell's husband's will."

Spry found his tongue. "God Almighty!"

The Committee of Safety hadn't just executed selective justice; the Committee had failed the civilians of Wilmington. As soon as Major Craig learned this new information, he'd wield the crime history as evidence of ineptitude in the rebels' government. In comparison, his administration couldn't help but look exemplary.

The laundress's hand pressed to her tucker. "The Committee let Mr. Badley and Mr. Prescott escape. Can you believe it?" She emitted a soft moan and lowered her hand to reveal additional cleavage. "We *need* you."

Spry's countenance brightened. "They *need* us, sir. God save the King!"

If Spry got any more heroic—Michael's laugh turned into a sneeze. When he recovered composure, he saw Molly's up-and-down approval of Spry. One side of her mouth cocked in invitation at the private. "You do look imposing. Unlike those committeemen, who were always drunk or angry."

Michael said, "Thank you for your time, Molly. We appreciate the information."

"You're so welcome." She didn't take her eyes off Spry. The two of them grinned at each other.

Michael curbed his smile. Spry would appreciate the muscles that Molly had developed from wringing wet laundry. Before then, the criminal investigator and his assistant had work to do. "When Mrs. Jones returns from market, please convey our apologies at missing her. We shall return later in the day." He bowed again, then walked behind the private, giving Spry's shoulder a tap in passing. "Come along, Galahad. Let's find the Holy Grail."

Chapter Four

"LIEUTENANT STODDARD, FROM the Eighty-Second Regiment, madam. Major Craig sent me to speak with Mr. Garrity about his wife."

The servant's pale blue eye flitted over him, almost the only feature visible of her through the cracked-open front door of the brick house on Third Street. "The Garritys aren't here."

"Yes, I understand that Mrs. Garrity has gone missing. Mr. Garrity contacted Major Craig to request assistance in locating her." He moved in a few inches, endeavoring to obtain a better picture of the woman's appearance, but she evaded his visual survey, leaving him with the impression of a haggard brunette in her mid-thirties. "I've been assigned to investigate. Where may I find Mr. Garrity?"

Again, the gaze bobbed, this time pausing on Michael's chin. "You aren't old enough to investigate anything."

Annoyance tensed his lips. Surely he was the only twenty-six-year-old lieutenant in the Army with pimples on his chin. "Madam, is Mr. Garrity at home?"

"No."

"When will he return?"

"I don't know."

"Where is he this moment?"

Her eye continued to measure him, and she exuded obstinacy. Either the servant was several cards short of a full deck, or she was covering for Garrity, or both. Behind him, he sensed Spry shifting from one foot to the other on the porch, eager to muscle the door open and sniff around the house, perpetrate that "imposing" reputation earned by their fellow soldiers every year.

But such a tactic had never won an occupying army the cooperation of civilians. Michael pitched conciliation into his tone. "I appreciate your caution. However, Mrs. Garrity's disappearance is an urgent matter. I doubt Mr.

Garrity, *your employer*, would appreciate delay in finding her."

She snapped, "He's at his shop on Front Street." The door shut with a stuffy puff of air.

Michael heard the inner bar slide across. He leaned forward. "Thank you very much. Have a pleasant afternoon."

Time to pay a visit to a gunsmith who'd misplaced his wife. Michael turned on the porch and nodded at Spry to join him. They headed down the front walkway.

Spry outpaced him at first, then paused to let him catch up. "Sir, I don't know. Curtains drawn in the middle of the day, house dark on the inside—I wager Mr. Garrity's pursuing illegal activities in that house."

"If so, why would he ask our help? Maybe the servant was just afraid of us."

"All right, sir, here's a possible scheme. Mr. Garrity murders his wife and hides the body. Then he asks Major Craig for an inquiry to make himself look blameless, throw us off the trail. What do you think of that, sir?"

Michael smiled at the enthusiasm. "And what's Mr. Garrity's motive? Perhaps your imagination was a trifle colored upon hearing accounts of three recent murders in town, as related by a bosomy blonde."

"Yes, sir. Er, no, sir. Suppose Mr. Garrity's a brilliant fellow, the sort who schemes several steps ahead." Spry frowned. "Uh, do most murderers plot that way, sir?"

At his question, Michael felt as if he'd passed beneath a snow-laden branch that dribbled ice water inside his uniform coat and down his spine. He shrugged to dissipate the sensation and settled his stride. "No, *most* murderers don't scheme several steps ahead."

But in a copse of trees near Alton last summer, hours after the Spaniard's corpse was discovered, the russet-haired murderer had sneered down at Michael from the saddle of his gelding. *I've picked over the area well in the last hour. Do let us know whether you find evidence.* Fairfax, assigned to chase rebel spies from Alton into East Florida, had dared Michael to take over the investigation from him. He didn't think Michael had the stones to prove he'd committed the murder.

Michael's swallow scraped over a burning throat. He coughed. "Criminals embody different levels of sophistication and guile. All we've seen is a servant who behaves skittishly. That means little until we've more context."

A gangly, brown-haired lad thirteen or fourteen years of age sprinted from between Garrity's house and that of a neighbor, loped across Third Street, cut over, and in a flash vanished onto intersecting Princess Street, headed toward the river. Spry stiffened and sucked in a breath. "Was that a pickpocket, sir?"

"Hold up, Spry."

Attentive in the direction the lad had taken, they stopped walking. Michael heard no commotion, no sound of pursuit. Spry swiveled his head, awaiting a command.

After a moment, Michael eyed his assistant. "That was no pickpocket. Let's meet Mr. Garrity."

★★★

From the brick, one-story shop on Front Street came the clink of hammer on metal, a smith forging the barrel of a musket or rifle. Spry sniffed the air and grimaced. "This town stinks of fish and tar, sir."

Michael blew his nose again. "Yes. At least this cold is good for something." He stepped onto the porch of the shop. As at the house, curtains were drawn over windows. Was that detail significant? Fog from the cold layered the periphery of Michael's thoughts. Annoyed with himself, he shook his head and reached for the door handle.

The shop door jerked open from within. A sweaty, stout, freckled man with hair an almost incandescent red blocked their entrance, the clack and ring of metalwork behind him. His gaze bounced from Michael's epaulet to his eyes. His expression was impassive. "Lieutenant Stoddard."

Michael doubted that Major Craig had communicated his name earlier when Mr. Garrity requested the regiment's help. At that time, Craig had yet to even speak with him about the position of lead investigator. Spry, one step below him, picked up on the peculiarity. "Hunh, word travels quickly in Wilmington."

Michael turned to the private briefly to mutter, "It was your pickpocket," before he refocused on the man in the doorway. "Yes, sir, Major Craig's investigator, Stoddard. And this is my assistant, Spry."

The man stepped onto the porch, yanking the door closed behind him to shut away some of the noise. "Gabriel Garrity." He jabbed out a paw as gritty as his apron for a handshake. His bloodshot blue eyes assessed Michael from head to toe. Faint derision prodded his upper lip. "I met your Major Craig. I must say, I thought you redcoats would be taller."

Garrity was a bully. Nine years in America had taught Michael to ignore most condescension from colonists. He opened his mouth to respond. Then two thumps shook the porch: Spry stepping up to plant himself behind his commander. Michael watched the way Garrity's assessment of Spry's height drained his superciliousness and replaced it with caution, and he made sure his response was cheerful. "We redcoats come in all sizes, Mr. Garrity."

The gunsmith grumbled and backed half a step away.

"I'm here at your appeal, to investigate your wife's disappearance. I've questions for you." Conscious of pedestrian and wagon traffic on the street behind him, Michael glanced over Garrity's shoulder. "Do let us step inside for privacy."

"Too noisy in there. Got a big job to finish by the end of the week. The porch is as private as it gets right now."

Apparently Gabriel Garrity didn't care what town busybody overheard their conversation. "Suit yourself. Who lives under your roof?"

"My wife, Julia. My housekeeper, Betty Overton, and her son Ben. And myself."

"You reported your wife missing this morning." Garrity nodded once. "When was the last time you saw her?"

"Saturday morning, about seven o'clock." Garrity crossed his arms high over his chest.

"Why did you wait three days to report her missing?"

Garrity glared at him. "Are you a lamebrain? To whom would I have reported? The town government has been in transition since Saturday!"

Yes, there was that. "Why are you certain she isn't visiting a friend or relative?"

He flicked a look to the street. "She'd tell me if she was traveling. Besides, there isn't a friend or relative nearby that she'd visit."

Surprise hiked Michael's eyebrow. "She has no kin in the area, no friends?" Again, Garrity's gaze made that furtive dash to the street, but he said nothing. Michael bent forward an inch, the tingle of suspicion in his pulse. "What is the name of her paramour, Mr. Garrity?"

The gunsmith's hands dropped to his sides. He balled his fists and growled. "Julia doesn't have a paramour." He glowered at Michael. "And if I tell you my wife isn't cheating on me, she isn't cheating on me." He released his fists.

Garrity might have restrained himself this time, but the fuse was short on that twelve-pounder, and Michael knew to defer for later the obvious question of whether Garrity had a mistress. "Where did you last see your wife Saturday morning?"

"She was in the study writing letters. I kissed her goodbye just before I left for work."

To whom was Julia Garrity writing letters, if she had no friends, family, or paramour? Michael realized he was missing clues, courtesy of the head cold. "Interesting that you went to work Saturday. We've reports that during the day, many townsfolk remained at home—not pursuing business, as you were—to stay out from underfoot while Colonel Young and his militiamen were frantically packing up to flee the regiment. That makes you quite the industrious fellow."

Garrity worked his mouth a few seconds, seemed to be forcing back a snarl. "I have no reason to flee from the regiment. Sunday afternoon, I marched out with the rest of the townsmen and laid down my weapons. I've been paroled. And I told you, there's a big job I have to finish by the end of the week."

"Who's your client with the money?"

"Plantation owner south of here. But my business has nothing to do with my wife's disappearance."

Maybe it did, maybe it didn't. Michael felt Garrity's prevarication, and he gritted his teeth. Usually he could cast questions where the fish were biting. But today he and the witness were circling each other. He tried another angle. "How often does your wife visit you here at the shop?"

"Once a week or so."

"How long have you been married?"

"Eleven years."

"How would you characterize your marriage?"

"Affectionate."

How inspiring that after eleven years, the Garritys had an "affectionate" marriage. Michael knew of only two couples with truly affectionate long-term marriages: his parents, and his sister and her husband. "Who in your household saw you kiss your wife goodbye?"

"I didn't take notice. I just kissed her and left."

"When did you return home?"

"Noon. She was gone. I asked Mrs. Overton where she was. She didn't know."

"Who was with you here in the shop between seven and noon Saturday morning?" Garrity shook his head. "No one."

"Well, then, who can vouch that you were here at work?"

"I don't know."

"So you've no alibi for that period of time." Michael tamped down the stab of victory in his pulse. Having no alibi didn't constitute evidence of guilt.

Another glower gripped Garrity's expression. "Bloody hell, you redcoats are no smarter than those Committeemen. You're assuming that I had something to do with her disappearance."

"Did you?"

He gripped his fists again. "No, damnation! Would I have asked for help finding her if I'd hurt her in some way? I'd have to be mad to do that. I love Julia. She loves me."

"Thank you for clarifying that point for me, sir. Has anyone contacted you about your wife since her disappearance?"

Garrity's jaw slackened. His fists relaxed. "You mean like for ransom money? Someone who'd kidnapped her? No, nothing like that. And I'm not a wealthy man."

"You have wealthy clients. A plantation owner south of town gave you a 'big job.'"

Flame-red stubble on Garrity's chin and jaw quivered like bristles on a cornered wild hog. "Stop twisting my words. All I got is my house, my clients, and my shop. I'm not like those greedy pigs, Badley and Prescott, good riddance, stealing other people's money."

Michael knew he wasn't through hearing about Badley and Prescott. They'd created quite a sensation in Wilmington. "If anyone does contact you, make sure you inform us immediately. We shall be boarding with Mrs. Jones on Second Street. Now, describe your wife for us."

"She's thirty-two years old, brunette, hair down to the middle of her back, brown eyes, about four inches shorter than I am. A buxom figure. There's a portrait of her in the parlor."

"What interests does she have?" At the gunsmith's puzzled look, Michael added, "Gardening? Embroidery? Music? Reading? Does she keep songbirds, raise dogs?"

At the mention of dogs, Garrity's gaze broke, darted right. "She—uh, she reads books."

An affectionate, loving wife who had no kin or friends in the area but wrote letters and possibly read books. Either Garrity was without a clue about women, or he'd omitted most of the details of his marriage and wife. Michael had the disheartening feeling that both might be true. "You have children?"

"No, none."

Julia Garrity wasn't a doting mother, either. What did she do all day? Sit in a dark house and wait for her husband to come home from work? "Who is the fleet-footed lad who preceded us from your house to give you advance notice of our arrival? Brown hair, plum-colored coat and tan breeches, about thirteen years old."

Garrity's eyes widened for an instant, then his mouth tightened. "Ben, the housekeeper's son."

Mrs. Overton, of the pale blue eye. "To progress with the inquiry, I require access to the interior of your home to search your wife's belongings. Your housekeeper is uncooperative."

"I'll send Ben back ahead of you with instructions for Mrs. Overton. She's protective of Julia, and you won't get her cooperation unless I endorse it."

"Thank you. I must also inspect your shop. Yes, I understand that you're on a schedule, but you mentioned that Mrs. Garrity visits you at work. I must have a look at the places she frequents."

The gunsmith's freckles stood out, and he swallowed. "Very well. But you wait out here while I first make sure my lads can pause their work to answer your questions." He stomped back into his shop, banging the door shut after him, slamming down the bar.

Spry scraped at one of his molars with a fingernail. "Must be hotter than Hades in there, them working a forge with the windows and door shut. He might be hiding something, sir."

At least Spry's powers of observation weren't mired in the molasses of a head cold. "Keep your eyes open for anything that seems out of place."

The sounds of smith work from within the shop continued. Michael heard men's voices inside. Then Garrity flung open the door, lips snagged in a faux smile. "Welcome to my shop, gentlemen. Come in."

Chapter Five

A BLAST OF heat from the forge inside made Michael's eyes water. His nose ran again, and he barely opened his handkerchief in time to catch a sneeze with it. Six workers in the dim shop with Garrity skittered glances at the soldiers before re-immersing themselves in work.

At the anvil, two men worked with hot iron for the barrel of a musket. Another man cranked a bore through the inside of a barrel. A fourth broached spiral grooves in a rifle. Chips of maple wood at his feet, a young fellow perched upon a stool sanded a stock he'd finished whittling. And at a bench beside him, also sitting, the sixth man installed a lock.

Busy, busy. Weariness hollowed the eyes of each man, even Garrity. Not for the first time, Michael wondered who the plantation owner was and why he needed so many firearms.

He and Spry wandered around. No employee seemed inclined to conversation, each absorbed in his work. When Michael passed near the forge, the fellow at the anvil toed a bucket of jagged metal pieces beneath a table— ostensibly so Michael wouldn't trip over it, but not before he'd recognized the contents of the bucket. "Mr. Garrity, what are your plans for the broken bayonets in that bucket?"

The gunsmith shrugged. "Scrap metal. We melt 'em down, reuse 'em. If they're in that bucket, they're too badly broken to be welded back together."

From the rear of the shop, Spry said, "What's in this room?" and reached for the handle of a door.

"No, no, don't do that!" For all his bulk, Garrity vaulted across the shop just in time to interpose himself between the private and the closed door.

The door vibrated with a bass rumble originating on the other side. Eyes wide, Spry backed away and glanced at Michael. Michael swept his gaze from the door to Garrity and strode for his assistant and the gunsmith.

His back pressed to the door, Garrity rapped the wood with his knuckles, turned his head to the side, and said, low, "Heh heh heh, good Trouble, good lad." Michael reached them, and Garrity peeled his back off the door with a smile. "Nothing but storage in this room, gentlemen. Iron bars, locks, wood for stocks, and so forth."

Michael frowned. "From the sounds of it, there's a rather large dog in your storage room."

"My shop was burgled several times. The Committee did nothing to stop it, so I bought a burglar deterrent, a bulldog. Opened shop one morning back in October and found a man's shoe, a shredded pair of breeches, and blood on the floor. Heh heh heh. I haven't been burgled since."

Michael braced his hands on his hips. "'Trouble?' That's the dog's name?"

"Yah, Trouble." The gunsmith bared and champed his teeth. "Trouble."

The thing on the other side of the door woofed to acknowledge his name. Michael blinked at the door. Had it bowed outward?

"So, gentlemen, have you seen everything you need to see here at my shop?"

Michael queried Spry with his eyebrows, received a brisk nod. "For the time, I believe so, Mr. Garrity."

"Good. I've already sent Ben home, so Mrs. Overton's expecting you. Let me know what you find out, soon as possible."

***

"Who but the devil would name a bulldog Trouble, sir? And set Trouble to guarding iron and lumber?" Spry walked on Princess Street beside his commander to Garrity's house. "I cannot imagine burglars stealing iron and lumber in the middle of the night—and multiple times, sir. They'd need a wagon to transport it. Wagons are conspicuous. If you're going to burgle a business, burgle the shop of a butcher or a silversmith. Someone whose products you can shove beneath your coat."

Spry's deduction prompted a grunt from Michael. "Mr. Garrity might very well be using that room to store the items he mentioned, but I doubt that's all Trouble's guarding."

"So Trouble's guarding new and repaired muskets, right, sir?"

Michael nodded. "If I were Mr. Garrity, I might let Trouble sit upon my business records, too."

After a few seconds, Spry expelled his breath, hard. "Ah, no, sir. You must want us to burgle Mr. Garrity's business records. Well, sir, bulldogs and me have never got along—"

"Spry, relax. Breaking and entering isn't on our list quite yet. No need. Take a moment to think about what we've observed."

While Spry got quiet and did so, Michael observed the way civilians scurried out of their way on the street, expressions ranging from cautious to resentful. Indeed, why should the people of Wilmington welcome the Eighty-Second with open arms? British occupational forces had established a reputation for sweeping through areas and destabilizing local economies. Major Craig had a tough strut ahead of him.

"Sir, back there in the shop, I saw an oak barrel, mostly covered, with cartridge boxes and ammunition boxes in it."

"Excellent. My uncle's a blacksmith. I've watched him repair swords. I think many of those bayonets in that bucket can be salvaged, welded." Michael smiled. "Put all that together for me. See if you reach the same conclusion I do."

"Yes, sir. Muskets, bayonets, cartridge boxes, ammunition boxes." Spry ticked them off on his fingers. "And we know that someone other than Major Craig contracted with Mr. Garrity to repair stands of arms, sir." He grinned. "Poor bugger. No wonder he was nervous when two redcoats snooped in his shop. When do we arrest him for trafficking weapons with the rebels?"

Michael's laugh was interrupted by a coughing fit. When he recovered, he blinked rheumy eyes at his assistant. "Let's first be certain that's what he's up to. Mr. Garrity strikes me as the sort of fellow who could slide out of one charge of weapons trafficking, find a way to discredit evidence against him. If he weasels out even once, he'll learn from his mistakes, get oilier. We may not catch him at it again."

"So you want to play him along, accumulate counts against him, sir?" They turned onto Third Street. Spry's grin swelled. "How do we do that?"

"Surveillance. Boring work, especially in winter, so we need reliable men who'll take care to avoid being spotted and who won't fall asleep."

"I know some fellows who might be up for the job, sir."

"I thought you might." They approached the gunsmith's house. "But let's not lose sight of the goal of finding Mrs. Garrity."

As they stepped onto the porch, the front door creaked open about two feet to reveal an unsmiling, faded brunette in her mid-thirties, owner of two pale blue eyes, her face and hands wraith-thin, one hand clenched about a feather duster. Michael and Spry bowed. She opened the door wider and stepped aside, gaze downcast. They filed past her into the foyer, and she closed the door.

Michael oriented himself visually in the dim, warm interior and noted the woman's vacant expression and a complete lack of dust on the banister. "Good afternoon again, Mrs. Overton. Spry and I appreciate your cooperation." Since Betty Overton said nothing, he added, "With your assistance, we should like to inspect the rooms Mrs. Garrity frequents to determine whether anything is missing or out of place."

"I shall take you to her bedroom first." The feather duster waved at the stairs.

They followed the housekeeper to a second-floor bedroom furnished with a four-poster canopy bed, two padded chairs with footstools, a mirrored vanity, and a couple of polished wooden chests. Velvet drapes drawn over the window and a fireplace of low coals conferred the gloom and warmth of an antediluvian forest upon the bedroom.

Framed oil portraits hung on two walls. At the portrait nearest the window, Michael discerned the workmanship of the walnut frame, also free of dust. His gaze swept over the portrait's subject, a pretty, plump brunette. But when he pushed at the drape to permit better illumination, Betty Overton rushed to him and batted it from his hand. "No! You mustn't open the drapes, Lieutenant.

She'll see you."

Michael faced her, puzzled a moment at the panic pinching her expression. Then a possible explanation occurred to him. The housekeeper must be feuding with a neighbor. "I should like to see this portrait more clearly for just a moment. Your neighbor's prying cannot be omnipotent."

Fear mobilized her expression, and her voice hissed out. "Not a neighbor! The *witch*."

Congestion must have spread to his hearing. Michael jiggled a finger in his ear. "Pardon me. I thought you said something about a witch."

"Not *a* witch. *The* witch." Mrs. Overton's chin finally came up. "She cursed all of Wilmington years ago, before my husband died, decades before you and I were even born. Stay inside and keep those curtains closed, and you'll be protected."

The zealous heat in her eyes baffled him. Did residents of Wilmington still believe in the kind of witches who harmed people? He considered his impression of the housekeeper from their first meeting and skipped his gaze over to Spry, who stood behind her. The private circled a finger near his temple, indicating his judgment of Betty Overton's wits.

Michael re-evaluated her—thin face, bony hands—and wondered about her credibility in her household and among the residents of Wilmington. "Er, thank you for the warning."

"Certainly, Mr. Stoddard. Vicar Spivey preached about the menace of witches on Sunday. Thank goodness he'll soon bring the wrath of God down upon the Whore of Babylon."

Spivey. Interesting. Michael had been ordered to investigate the vicar. Was there more than a fleeting connection between Spivey and the "witch?" And where did he begin questioning a housekeeper with addled wits?

His attention returned to the portrait. "Mrs. Overton, might I have a candle over here? I'd like to see this portrait more clearly."

Her face relaxed. "Of course." She tucked the duster in her pocket, grabbed a candle in its holder from a nightstand, and knelt before the fire. Then she presented the lit candle to him.

He examined the portrait. By candlelight, the woman's lips appeared sensuous and inviting. His gaze strayed to her bosom, then wandered to her willful dark eyes. He couldn't imagine her married for eleven years to Gabriel Garrity—at least not affectionately.

"That's a portrait of my mistress's younger sister, Miss Salome Ward."

Michael thought of his own sister all the way on the other side of the Atlantic, and three nephews he'd yet to meet, and an ache tugged at his heart. The end of November: that was when he'd received his most recent letter from Miriam. He'd written her back right away, his letter full of stories about Charles Town's social scene and a case of arson he'd investigated. Her response must have been lost. Or perhaps his letter had been. Happened all the time. "It must pain Mrs. Garrity and Miss Ward to live far apart."

"But Miss Salome isn't far. Just an hour south. She runs the Ward family farm."

Surprise shot through Michael, and he swiveled to study Mrs. Overton. "Mr. Garrity told me his wife didn't have kin nearby."

She scowled. "He and Miss Ward argue whenever they're together. I don't understand why. I never argued with my brother-in-law. I especially didn't argue with my husband. Because of all the strife, Miss Ward almost never visits us. Hasn't been a guest in the house since—" She paused. "—October."

Michael took a step toward her in hope. "Then it's possible that Mrs. Garrity visited her sister on Saturday?"

The housekeeper waggled her head. "Mr. Garrity sent a messenger to the farm yesterday, asking if Miss Ward knew the whereabouts of his wife. He got a very angry letter from her early this morning, saying that she didn't know where she was, and accusing Mr. Garrity of foul play. That's when he decided to approach Major Craig about the disappearance."

"If the Garritys had a spat, Miss Ward could be covering for her sister, giving her a respite."

Again, Mrs. Overton's negative gesture. "My mistress's portmanteau and valise are still here, and our driver says she didn't take the chair and horse team out Saturday."

Michael studied the housekeeper. From the looseness of her gestures, he could tell that she believed she was speaking the truth. "Does Mr. Garrity ever threaten Mrs. Garrity, verbally or physically?" Mrs. Overton's lips pursed, and she crossed her arms. Ah hah! Michael leaned toward Mrs. Overton. "Has he ever hit her?"

"Husbands beat their wives all the time, Lieutenant. We learn to accept it."

Michael's pulse jumped with revulsion and pity. And with suspicion. His father had never laid a hand on his mother in anger. Neither had Miriam's husband hit her. He squinted at the housekeeper. "Despite your personal experience, most husbands don't beat their wives. When was the last time Mr. Garrity hurt Mrs. Garrity?"

Betty Overton turned her back on him, glided to one of the wooden chests, and opened it. "All my mistress's clothing is in here except for the clothing she wore on Saturday: a pink petticoat, and a cranberry red gown. Shall I pull her wardrobe from the chest for your examination? You're too close to that window. Come away now, or the witch will see you."

Witch, bah. Mrs. Overton's reluctance to answer his questions ignited his determination to get answers. "Is either of the Garritys involved in a marital infidelity?"

She sighed. "I'm the only person on the face of this earth who's ever stayed faithful to my spouse, and look where that got me: widowed, when my son was three."

Michael blew out the candle, set it down, and walked over to her. "With whom are the Garritys romantically involved? Their names, please."

She stared through him, her face vacant again. Frustration escalated inside him. When Betty Overton didn't want to answer a question, she shut down. "When did you last see Mrs. Garrity?"

"Saturday morning, about ten-fifteen."

"Where were you that morning between ten-fifteen and noon?"

"Here, cleaning the house."

"Who can vouch for your presence during that time? Your son, perhaps?"

One shoulder twitched: her dismissal of the idea. "Ben left the house about ten o'clock and didn't return until mid-afternoon. He told me that he'd find out what was happening with the government. I reminded him about the witch, but he's a headstrong young man."

No one who lived under the same roof as Julia Garrity had an alibi for the time of her disappearance. "How was your mistress engaged the last time you saw her?"

"She was sitting in the back yard, near Chipper's grave."

"Chipper?" He narrowed his eyes at the housekeeper. "Who was Chipper?"

"Her terrier. He died in October." The woman shuddered. "I begged my mistress to stay in the house Saturday. Not just because it was drizzling that morning, but because I knew the witch could target her in the back yard. Only inside was she safe. But she didn't listen to me. About an hour later, I looked out, and she was gone. I risked the witch's wrath by leaving the house and searching the yard for her, but my mistress was nowhere to be seen."

Over the housekeeper's shoulder, Michael saw Spry shaking his head. The exasperation in the private's expression must echo that in Michael's own face. How much of Mrs. Overton's testimony was reliable? Clearly he'd have to question other witnesses to corroborate her points.

"Sit a moment, madam." He escorted her to the nearest chair. She sank into it as if bone-weary, and he squatted beside her. "I'm curious about the—er—witch. Tell me of her."

A spark returned to Mrs. Overton's eyes. "Sixty years ago, a sea captain married a French girl from the Caribbean and built a mansion for her southeast of Wilmington. She was seventeen years old, with black hair down to her knees and eyes like storm clouds, and she wanted to live a wild life of balls and parties. But her husband had to return to the sea, for that was his business. She grew angry every time he'd leave her, alone in the mansion except for the slaves."

Oh, no. This was worse than Michael imagined it would be. He saw Spry cover a yawn.

"One autumn, he returned from the sea, and the witch enclosed the two of them all night in her bedroom. In the morning, slaves discovered that the master had vanished without a trace, and his wife had no idea what had happened to him. Five years went by. No one ever saw her husband again, so she remarried another sea captain. Her second husband also refused to live the wild life. He, too, returned from the sea to spend a night in her bedroom and vanished without a trace. So after another five years, she married again—"

"Hadn't the word gotten out among sea captains by then?" said Spry in an innocent tone.

Mrs. Overton glared at him. "Her third husband was a merchant, as was her sixth husband."

"How many husbands has this woman had?" said Michael.

"No one would marry her after the sixth husband."

"I'm not surprised."

"She took paramours after that. Each vanished after being shut up in her bedroom all night." Gripping the arms of the chair, Mrs. Overton leaned toward

Michael. "I've seen the witch. She looks many years younger than I do. She kills men and bathes in their blood to remain youthful. She delights in young, attractive men like you two. Beware her wiles. And surely you must see the great service that Vicar Spivey will render our community when he rids us of her."

If this clergyman truly targeted a woman nearly eighty years old as a witch and intended to persecute her in the name of God, Michael had to stop him or protect her. He stood, chin lifted. "I'd like to meet Vicar Spivey. What is the best way for me to do that?"

Mrs. Overton's hands released the chair arms, and she sat straight. "Take the northwest road toward Duplin County. About a mile after you cross the Northeast Cape Fear, you'll see the turnoff to the left. Follow it several hundred yards. Have a care to remain on the track. The area is swampy. After you round a bend, you'll see the church on your right, and the vicarage is just beyond that. Most mornings, he can be found at work repairing the church building."

"Thank you." Michael recalled that the gunsmith implied that his wife liked to read, but he'd yet to spot a book in the house. "Show me the books that Mrs. Garrity enjoys reading." He stepped back and allowed the housekeeper to rise.

"She reads little. Mostly she sketches. I shall show you." She shuffled to the opened chest, bent over, and poked around in the contents.

Garrity asserted that his wife read books. Mrs. Overton denied it. The lies were beginning to pile up.

Mrs. Overton straightened. "Ah. Here's Chipper's portrait." She walked over and handed Michael a charcoal sketch on paper. Spry closed in for a look.

Chipper's beady dark eyes fixed on Michael, shaggy hair tied back with a bow on his head, mischief and intelligence at work in his face. The terrier's energy reminded him of a little hound he'd had while growing up, a food thief that delighted in scooting chairs around, tools to help him access fresh loaves of bread that people felt were safe high upon tables and windowsills. "Quite a good rendition. Mrs. Garrity clearly has a feel for the medium." Maybe she'd sketched more than Chipper. He returned the paper to the housekeeper. "Have you more?"

From the chest she produced a portfolio full of sketches and handed him a group. One of Chipper lying at the foot of Mrs. Garrity's bed. Another of him perched upon the chair that Mrs. Overton had occupied minutes before. Chipper in the arms of Salome Ward, nestled against her cleavage—oh, lucky Chipper. Chipper claiming a bench in the back yard. Chipper in the lap of Mrs. Overton. Chipper in the lap of Mrs. Overton's fleet-footed son, Ben. Michael lingered on that one, trying to determine why it pulled at him, before he realized from the apparent age of Ben that it had been a recent sketch, and Chipper looked way too hearty to have passed on to the Great Kennel of old age. "How did Chipper die?"

"An accident." Mrs. Overton removed the drawing from his hand and thrust others at him.

Julia Garrity was obsessed with the terrier. She must have been heartbroken when he died. Michael heard Spry's sharp intake of breath and flipped back to a sketch he'd almost overlooked: Chipper on the lap of a man in his early thirties who sat in the chair where Mrs. Overton had sat moments earlier. Michael scoured the man's features: an expensive periwig, lace at his throat, naughty eyes and smile, a broken nose that contributed to rugged handsomeness.

What was he doing posing for a sketch in Mrs. Garrity's bedroom, her terrier in his lap?

Where were the sketches of Chipper sitting in the lap of Julia Garrity's husband, Gabriel?

"Mrs. Overton, who is this fellow?"

The housekeeper's eyes bugged at the sketch, and she snatched it from him, along with the other sketches. "One of Mr. Garrity's customers. I don't know his name."

A client? Maybe at first. But Michael suspected he'd found Julia Garrity's paramour.

Chin obstinate, the housekeeper slammed down the lid on the chest, shutting away the portfolio and sketches. "I must attend my chores, so I must ask you to leave for now."

He wouldn't obtain more information from the housekeeper about the man. But if she knew her mistress was having an affair, so did Garrity. Those secrets kept poorly. Others in town would know of the affair, too. A little thrill quickened Michael's heartbeat. The fellow with the broken nose was as good as named.

"Mrs. Overton, you mentioned a driver. His name?"

"Mr. Mayer."

"Does he live here?" She shook her head. "Who else lives here beside the Garritys, yourself, and your son?"

"No one."

"Besides the driver, who are the other employees?"

"The gardener, Mr. Hiller."

"I would question him, Mr. Mayer, and Ben."

"The driver and gardener have the afternoon off. My son is on an errand to market."

Michael glanced over the bedroom. "Where does Mrs. Garrity write letters?"

"At her desk in the study downstairs."

"We would examine her desk and address book. And see the dog's grave." She stiffened. "Don't worry. Spry and I won't hold you responsible for any aggression from the witch. But we must search the last place where you saw your mistress. You said a bench in the back yard beside Chipper's grave."

Her expression sank into sullenness. "If you insist." She swept from the room. The men exited after her.

Chapter Six

"SINCE YOU SHOWED an interest in Miss Ward's portrait, I thought you'd like to compare it to my mistress's portrait before you examine her desk and the yard." The housekeeper positioned lit candles to either side of a painting on the wall above the fireplace. "The study is across the foyer. I shall light candles for you there."

She curtsied and left. After taking position before the fireplace, Michael studied the portrait, Spry at his side. Julia Garrity possessed the same dark hair, dark eyes, and bosomy figure of her sister, but without the playfulness. The gunsmith's wife appeared guarded and restless, beauty edged out by snappishness.

The word *witch* came to mind. Then Michael berated himself silently. Eleven years of matrimony to a fellow like Gabriel Garrity might wear on even the Virgin Mary.

He and Spry repaired to the study and searched the nooks and crannies of the big, oak desk that dominated the room. They found stationery, quills, ink, blotters, wax, sealers. They found the gunsmith's address book, a house mortgage bill, and letters from people with the last name of Garrity. Absent was correspondence to or from Julia Garrity, as well as her address book.

Spry heaved a sigh and said, low, "Sir, we should have searched in here before looking at Mrs. Garrity's portrait."

Michael rotated his neck to regard the empty door of the study and kept his voice low. "Truthfully I suspect we're about three days too late to find any evidence in this desk. But perhaps the back yard will be more forthcoming with clues. The feather duster seldom ventures there."

She awaited them at the back door, gatekeeper-stern, as if they were setting out to meander the mythical Labyrinth while the Minotaur prowled within. Michael exited the house and, on the back step, squinted in mid-afternoon sunlight. His first inhalation of the crisp outdoors dried his throat and sent him hacking into his handkerchief. While he wiped his tearing eyes, Spry detoured around him.

The housekeeper whispered from the cracked-open door behind Michael. "Over there, on the left, beneath the dogwood tree." She shut the door in haste, a small snick of finality in the air.

Beneath the dogwood tree, on the ground beside a two-person wooden bench, Spry pointed out a marble plaque. Michael read the inscription aloud. "Chipper, Beloved Companion and Dearest Friend, Born 16 June 1777, Died 20 October 1780."

"Poor dog. He wasn't but three years old, sir."

The subdued tone was so unlike Spry that Michael sensed his assistant had also grown up with a dog and grieved its passage. "Mrs. Overton said his death was an accident." Spry regarded the house, and from his narrowed eyes, Michael knew that his assistant also was wondering about the accident. Michael slid onto the bench. "Snoop around the yard. I shall have a word with Chipper, find out what he knows of Saturday morning."

"Sir." Spry wandered off.

A sliver of breeze worked its way down Michael's coat at the neck. He coughed again and made sure the coat was buttoned at the top. Winter-bare limbs of the dogwood stretched above him, a rustle of curled, brown leaves at his feet. *Dearest friend*, Mrs. Garrity had labeled the terrier. Had the gunsmith been angry that his wife considered a dog—not her husband—her dearest friend?

His thoughts circled the impression that no love had been lost between gunsmith and terrier. He imagined Garrity coming home after a hard day at work and sitting in the parlor to relax, only to have Chipper bound in and hump his leg. He didn't fight a smirk at the vision of the stout smith dominated by a fifteen-pound terrier.

"Well, Chipper, here we are." He leaned back on the bench. "Tell me about the last time your mistress rested here."

He jiggled dead leaves with his boots and gazed through slats in the bench at the leaves below. In the dark carpet, something pale winked at him. Frowning, he knelt and flicked leaves aside. His fingers latched onto paper, folded to less than an inch square.

He stood, opened the paper, and read, *Sweet Julia, we do not have much Time. Meet me alone at Eleven, in the usual Place. In haste, your General Greene.* All scripted cleanly, and in an elegant, masculine hand.

Astonishment exploded up his spine. His attention jerked to the upper right corner: *27th January, Saturday, nine o'clock.* "Hullo, Spry! Take a look at this."

The private ambled over and scanned the note. "Huzzah! Where'd that come from, sir?"

"Folded among those leaves down there."

"'General Greene.' Nathanael Greene, the rebel commander?"

"I doubt he'd have planned a rendezvous with Gabriel Garrity's wife in Wilmington three days ago. Our most recent reports locate him deep in the Carolina backcountry."

"Then this is a sweetheart's affectation, sir?"

Michael shrugged. "Perhaps. Search below the bench. We don't want to miss anything."

While Spry scrunched up his six-foot frame and scrounged around, Michael re-examined the note. With the thrill of discovery ebbed, something about it bothered him. He folded it, opened it again, and refolded it. Irked because he couldn't identify what nagged him, he secured the note in a pocket of his waistcoat.

Who had delivered the note to Mrs. Garrity? Why was it here and not on her person? Had she read it and dropped it in the leaves?

No additional evidence came to light, even after Spry raked through leaves by hand and acquired a layer of dust to dull the red of his uniform. They both expanded the search into the surrounding area for another five minutes before Michael called it off. According to his watch, it was after four o'clock. He and Spry needed to discuss the day's findings with some measure of privacy.

Out front, the private dusted off the black trim on his cuffs. "How about Mrs. Jones's house, sir?"

"Later." Molly the laundress might provide too much distraction. Michael drew out his handkerchief and honked into it again.

"Beg your pardon, sir, but you don't look well."

"You aren't the first person to say so today. Must be true. Let's visit that tavern down the street from Garrity's shop."

Spry grinned. "A tavern. Yes, sir. I bow to the wisdom of my commanding officer." After they'd set out east on Third Street, Spry added, "You realize that Mrs. Overton was watching us from between the foyer drapes." Michael had seen the twitch of velvet in the window and grunted in agreement. "Who's she trying to protect, sir? The husband or the wife?"

"Both. But I doubt it's out of love." He had a bad feeling about Chipper the terrier.

They walked south to Front Street in silence, Michael juggling leads that led nowhere. On the morrow, he planned to question Ben Overton and the Garritys' driver and gardener. While he was at it, he'd question the Garritys' immediate neighbors. Maybe they noticed something amiss at the house Saturday morning or glimpsed Mrs. Garrity in her back yard.

He also pondered conjectures and pieced together the most obvious explanation for her disappearance. "Your General Greene" implied that Julia Garrity considered Nathanael Greene heroic. That, in turn, implied that she was at least a rebel sympathizer, and the writer of the note was a rebel who, from his haste, had deserted Wilmington with Colonel Young. So Mrs. Garrity skipped town with her rebel paramour Saturday morning.

If that were true, the regiment hadn't the time, interest, or resources to chase a runaway wife into the heart of a rebel camp and fetch her home to her husband. The puzzle pieces fit tidily until Michael incorporated what he suspected of her husband. If Gabriel Garrity were conducting business with rebels and knew his wife had left him for a rebel sweetheart, he'd be crazy or dimwitted to set an investigator from the Crown on the tail of his income provider. And Michael's impression of Gabriel Garrity was that he was neither crazy nor dimwitted.

Sometimes the obvious explanation wasn't correct.

Who had delivered the note to Julia Garrity? Why had she left behind such an important message, a hefty piece of evidence? Had she been in haste, or threatened, or giddy with excitement? Had she even seen the note? And what was it that nagged him about the note itself?

White's Tavern, located on Front Street just before Market Street, was an unimpressive, two-story wooden building that nevertheless had ten horses hitched to the post by the time Michael and Spry arrived. Michael pulled open the door, and they removed their hats. Close to two-dozen men of varying ages occupied benches around tables. A fiddled melody arched over the low buzz of conversation, pipes pumped tobacco smoke into the air, a backgammon game was well in progress, and fat wood popped in a big stone fireplace.

Spry shut the door. His big voice resonated. "Smells like roasted chicken in here, sir. Come to think of it, I could eat about three roasted chickens."

The hum of conversation diminished, fiddle melody dwindled, and twenty pairs of eyes regarded them. Hair stood on the back of Michael's neck. Two redcoats. Twenty patrons. Matters could quickly become exciting.

A lanky blond man in his early twenties jogged over from the rear of the tavern, shirtsleeves rolled to his elbows, a smudged apron covering the front of his waistcoat and tied about his waist. "Welcome, gentlemen." Without hesitation, he shook the hands of both soldiers. "Kevin Marsh. My sister Kate and I run this place—"

"Get your facts straight, Marsh," hollered a patron. "Your sister's in charge here. *You* do all the running." Men roared with laughter.

Marsh's lopsided grin indicated he took the taunt in stride. "You cannot blame me for trying to sway new customers. And who might you be?" His gaze landed on Michael's epaulet. "Captain—"

"Lieutenant Stoddard. This is my assistant, Spry."

Marsh's blue eyes widened. "Say, you're the one they were talking about, the investigator."

Spry leaned toward Michael. "Told you news travels fast here, sir."

"I'm mighty glad to have the Eighty-Second here." Marsh lowered his voice. "Especially after the shoddy job of those deputies on the Committee." He fidgeted and frowned. "But for how long are you here? The shop owner next door reported seeing the entire regiment march north out of town about four o'clock."

"Well, obviously Major Craig left soldiers behind to fortify town defenses in his absence. He'll return soon. The Eighty-Second is here to stay awhile." Tension left Marsh's shoulders at his words. Michael also lowered his voice. "My man and I have a bit of business to discuss."

"Yes, sir." Marsh jutted his chin toward the rear of the tavern. "No one will disturb you at that table in the corner. I'll bring out a candle for you. And should you need greater privacy, I've a room in the back."

Michael eyed the darkened corner, wishing the table were closer to the fire.

"It will do."

"And drinks? First one is on the house for both of you."

They placed their orders. Spry blazed a path to the indicated table ahead of Michael. Conscious that the military adamantly discouraged jollification between officers and men, they remained standing to conduct business when they reached the table.

Michael crossed his arms over his chest. "What do you think of Mrs. Overton?"

Spry shook his head. "Two sides of a flipped shilling, sir. Crazy one minute, then sane. She knows Mrs. Garrity is having an affair. She's protecting her reputation. Looks to me like Mrs. Garrity ran off with a rebel beau Saturday morning when Colonel Young left town."

Michael leaned against the wall and bit off a groan. His back ached. Hell of a time to start a fever. "I admit that theory holds attraction. But if Garrity's repairing weapons for rebels and knows his wife has a rebel paramour, he'd be an idiot to ask us for help finding her. Surely he realizes that we'd expose his unlawful activity and throw him in jail without fetching his wife home."

"Sir. Maybe he murdered her when he found out she was having an affair. You want a motive? Jealousy is a good one. That still makes him a fool for asking our help." Spry rubbed his chin a moment. "And that means there's a corpse somewhere, sir."

Unlike his raw-recruit assistant, Michael had been through battles, seen men's heads, limbs, and guts blown away, and horses slaughtered. Vomited when a sergeant beside him had his head blown off by a cannonball. Lain awake remembering the screams of agonized men and horses.

But the impersonal brutality of the battlefield paled in comparison to the deliberate, self-serving evil of premeditated murder. He wouldn't have wished Lieutenant Fairfax on any Spaniard, even though Spain was at war with Britain. The image of the dead Spaniard's torment-twisted face and sightless eyes continued to haunt him, a plea for justice.

In Charles Town, he'd solved two more murders: two more corpses examined, two families distressed. The misery of survivors looked the same, whether the victim had been slave or gentry, young or old, Loyalist or rebel. So he really hoped that Julia Garrity had run off with some fellow. He didn't want to have to deal with another murder victim. Or with the survivors. He got the feeling Spry was like-minded.

The private smacked his lips. "Look there, sir. Here comes a wench with our drinks."

Jarred from reflection, Michael studied the approach of a petite blonde bearing a tray with a tankard, wine glass, and lit candle. In her mid-twenties, she wore a lace mobcap and tucker and no apron over her polonaise gown of fine, cocoa-brown wool. The angle of her head and shoulders said, "Commerce."

"That's no wench, Spry." He dislodged himself from the wall. The men bowed when she reached the table.

She slid the tray onto the table with practiced ease. After placing their drinks before them, as well the candle, she tucked the tray beneath one arm. "Good afternoon. I'm Mrs. Duncan, owner of this establishment. My brother and I are delighted to have the patronage of gentlemen for a change." She swept an amused look around the interior.

"It's our pleasure, madam. I'm Lieutenant Stoddard, and this is Spry."

Her blue eyes homed on him. "Major Craig's investigators? Welcome to Wilmington."

"Thank you—" The pleasantry curtailed with a sneeze that Michael just managed to parry to one side. Embarrassed, he fumbled out his handkerchief.

The owner of White's Tavern frowned. "Where'd you come by that nasty head cold?"

"Transport ship, probably. My apologies." He blew his nose and imagined from her expression the negative impression he must have been making all afternoon upon Wilmington's citizens by virtue of his red nose and runny eyes.

"Well. I trust our fare and accommodations will meet your satisfaction." With a formal curtsy, she headed toward a rear door.

Michael sank into his chair. A good night's sleep would probably work wonders on him. He decided their next stop would be Enid Jones's house. "Spry, why don't you find out which of those patrons over there doesn't mind gossiping with one of the King's Finest."

Spry, still standing, lifted his tankard. "Yes, sir. Incidentally, I used to beat the breeches off two cousins at backgammon."

"Then you've my blessings upon a game."

As soon as Spry sauntered for the civilians, Michael reached for his glass and gulped claret, dismayed to remember that his sense of taste had fallen victim to the cold. He propped feet upon a bench and leaned back with his wine to contemplate nothing in particular except how lousy he felt. But another approach of lace and fine brown wool encouraged him to yank his feet off the bench and struggle to his feet with an attempt at propriety.

"Oh, don't bother standing, Lieutenant." Kate Duncan slid another tray upon the table, this one laden with two cups of coffee and a wooden bowl of steaming, yellowish broth. When she set the bowl before him, he spotted rice, carrots, and onions in the liquid. "Cook needs a taster for the first batch of chicken soup."

"I don't know about tasting. This cold and my—my nose—"

"I won't take no for an answer, Mr. Stoddard." She placed a spoon and napkin beside the bowl, and set a cup of coffee within reach. Then, the tray transferred to an adjacent table, she sat back with her own coffee and gestured for him to sit.

She was going to keep him company until he ate the soup. He resumed his seat. "Thank you, madam."

Sensing another pair of eyes on him, Michael glanced at Spry, who swept a toothy grin of approval between his commander and the woman. Michael ignored him and leaned his face above the steam, not of the mood to woo any woman that moment, even Salome Ward of the luscious cleavage, should she walk through the door and fling herself at him.

A quarter of the way through the soup, his nose cleared, and he tasted parsnips, parsley, and pepper atop the chicken. Toward the bottom of the bowl, his back quit aching, and his entire head cleared. He could smell the pipe smoke in the room. "Well, now. My compliments to Cook." He pushed the empty bowl aside. "I predict you'll run out of soup before you close for the night."

"Good." Over the rim of her coffee cup, her eyes twinkled.

He sipped claret, found he could at last appreciate the bouquet, and reassessed the tavern crowd. Spry had plunged into a backgammon game. Additional patrons had entered while he ate—probably about thirty men total in the room by then—and a couple of serving wenches took orders for drinks among them. He reached for his coffee. "Does your husband help you and your brother with the business, or has he his own business?"

"My husband is dead, sir. Almost five years, in fact. He marched into the swamp at Moores Creek Bridge with MacDonald and McLeod and didn't march back out again. Kevin and I have operated the tavern by ourselves since our uncle Alfred White died." She set down her cup and glanced about with her chin up and a faint smile on her lips. "We earn a decent living at it."

She pressed forward on her elbows. Her eyes glittered, and her voice lowered. "I hear Julia Garrity has been missing since Saturday. I hope she's well. Are you investigating her disappearance?"

"We are. Do you know Mrs. Garrity?"

"A little. I mean, I'm not her confidante." She caught her bottom lip with her top teeth.

"What is your impression of her?"

"Vivacious. Glamorous. Talkative. She enjoys pretty new gowns and hats." Her smile stopped short of her eyes. "What woman would blame her for that?"

Michael thought of the bow in Chipper's hair. Did Gabriel Garrity earn enough to keep his wife to her satisfaction? To what ends would he go to maintain her happiness? *I got a big job I have to finish by the end of the week.*

"I see her at the ladies' group sometimes."

"Ladies' group?"

"An informal gathering of three dozen or so wives and widows. Once a week, we meet in someone's home or shop to drink coffee, eat pastries, and chat."

Michael rolled back his shoulders, revitalized. All those wives and widows: why, he'd just gained almost forty potential witnesses in one stroke. Surely at least one woman in the group knew enough about Julia Garrity to advance the investigation. Huzzah!

"But we don't chat about politics. That's one of our firm rules. Some women are neutrals, some are loyalists, and some are Whigs. If we allowed talk of politics, we'd fight as much as the men do." She cocked her chin an inch, as if daring him to differ with her.

He chuckled and knocked back the rest of his wine, musing over how he could find out more about Julia Garrity's infidelity without loading the gossip mill. "I've just begun my inquiries. If a credible lady in your group is Mrs. Garrity's confidante, I will appreciate the opportunity to talk with her."

"*Credible*, hmm." Her eyes sparkled, but her expression remained otherwise bland. "I suppose that any woman prone to the vapors or hysterics just won't do."

He'd fallen right into that *faux pas*. He felt his ears grow hot, and he scratched the back of his neck above his stock, flustered. "Uh, that is, what I meant was, er—"

"I shall pass along your request."

"Thank you, madam. My man and I are boarding with Mrs. Jones. Major Craig would like us to be accessible to townsfolk."

Her keen eye passed over him. "Then I shall direct any messages from credible ladies to the house on Second Street."

She'd let him off easily. He bowed his head to her. More patrons entered, and the noise level increased. Without standing, she pulled the tray off the other table and piled on dishes so she could return to her work.

She seemed to be the *sanest* civilian he'd met all day. "Er, Mrs. Duncan, do I understand correctly that you've been a resident of this area for several years?" She nodded, and in the candlelight, garnets sparked at her earlobes. "Then I've a few questions to ask of you, but I see business is picking up for the evening. When may I inquire back on the morrow?"

Her gaze searched him, but her expression was mild. "Ask your questions now, sir. I don't expect the bulk of the crowd for another half hour."

"My thanks. What do you know of a vicar named Elijah Spivey?"

Instantly her nose wrinkled, and her lips pursed. "A lizard, that one." She leaned back in her chair. "Ten years ago, he was one of those Regulators—a group of mostly farmers who quarreled with Lord Granville's land agents. Soon as Governor Tryon squashed the rebellion, Spivey scampered up to New York. The next we heard of him, he'd bought land and two old buildings northwest of town in December, claiming he'd been in college in New York all that time and become an ordained minister of the Bethanys."

"The Bethanys? You mean the Church of Mary and Martha of Bethany? According to the information I was given, the church is Anglican, and he's its vicar."

"Anglican? Vicar?" Kate Duncan laughed, short and sharp. "If Spivey's Anglican, then I'm a blacksmith. The Bethanys are foot washers, Mr. Stoddard."

He squinted at her and his words emerged slowly: "Foot washers?" No one had ever washed his feet in church.

"Oh." She tilted her head and studied him. "Well, then, you must experience it for yourself. In my opinion, Mr. Spivey doesn't have a congregation. He has a harem."

Michael's eyebrows rose. A harem. So much for promised leadership positions within the church. Major Craig was correct to be suspicious. "When does he give sermons?"

"Sunday mornings and evenings. Wednesday evenings, too."

The next day was Wednesday. Could he round up at least ten soldiers with an interest in growing closer to the divine at a Wednesday night foot washing ceremony? He fought humor from leaking into his expression. "Thank you.

And have you heard of an elderly French witch who lives in these parts and was married to a sea captain?"

"Elderly French witch?" This time when the owner of White's Tavern laughed, the sound was pleasant. "Oh, for goodness sakes. Can that be Esmé Delacroix? She's hardly elderly—in her forties but looks at least ten years younger, a handsome woman with long, black hair. She might be a quadroon. She's originally from Saint Domingue."

Wistfulness drifted into her expression. "Her husband, a sea captain who was half-English and half-French, set her up in a fine home southeast of town with slaves, off the Sound Road. When he was in port, they'd ride to town in a splendid carriage. As a girl, I fancied their secluded lifestyle as idyllic.

"But I haven't seen the carriage for a good ten years. They replaced it with a more practical conveyance." Her mouth crooked. "How like childhood fancies, eh? John Delacroix died last summer while at home and was buried quietly on the property. Esmé has kept mostly to herself since then, although I saw her at the harvest festival, selling two of her slaves."

Amazing how much of the story Betty Overton had contorted. Michael looked forward to a visit with the "witch," just to see for himself all that the Garritys' housekeeper had exaggerated.

Patrons had begun entering the tavern in twos and threes. "Well, Lieutenant, I'd best get this tray back to the kitchen before some of the regulars hail me 'wench.'"

He stood and pulled the chair out for her. "Thank you for talking with me, Mrs. Duncan. How much do I owe you for the coffee and soup?"

She hefted the tray up, an elfin twinkle in her eyes. "On the house, sir. You look a hundred percent better now than when you first walked in. Get yourself a good night's sleep in a warm bed. And find Julia Garrity for us."

Chapter Seven

ON MARKET STREET, proprietors bustled about closing their shops for the day. Michael, walking next to his assistant, said, "This place *does* stink like fish."

"And tar, sir." They greeted soldiers patrolling the street afoot, and after they'd passed, Spry added, "I whipped the devil out of their champion backgammon player at White's."

"Remind me to never engage you at backgammon. And what's the tavern tittle-tattle?"

"Mr. Garrity used to be a regular. It's a good two months since he's been in, sir."

Michael studied the turquoise and vermilion of the twilight sky. "White's has an amiable atmosphere. Why did he quit going? Did he have a spat with the owners? Or a patron?"

"Don't know. Middle of last year, his visits tapered off. Seems to have put forth effort to go primarily so he could carp to other men about how much his wife complains."

"What does she complain about?"

"Everything, sir. She supposedly badgered him to buy her a new hat and cloak back in October. Maybe she henpecked him to quit visiting the tavern."

"Come now, she may henpeck him, but he doesn't strike me as the sort of fellow who'd knuckle under to a wife's demands that he give up a favorite watering hole."

"My impression, too, sir."

Michael pieced in what he'd learned. "What if our gunsmith stopped going to White's because he ran out of money?"

"Sir, how many men would relinquish their favorite tavern, just because they were short?"

"Not short. Pockets empty. Mrs. Duncan said that Julia Garrity flaunts her finery among the ladies of Wilmington when they socialize once a week. Recall the opulence of her bedroom." And what a disconcerting contrast all that luxury made with Gabriel Garrity's coarseness. "I wager that she thrives in the world of parties and balls." Not unlike Mrs. Overton's fictitious witch, he realized with a start. Michael pondered that train of thought some more. Maybe the housekeeper had swapped character traits of the two women in her head, projecting a negative trait from her mistress onto an innocent woman because of her duty to her mistress.

Spry laughed short. "If that's the case, she lives in the wrong town, sir."

"Indeed, our immortal souls are safe here." Sarcasm clipped Michael's voice. "Back in '75, one of the first acts of the Committee was to rid Wilmington of any activities that might encourage the carnal appetites of citizens, such as balls and parties."

"And horseracing, sir." Spry heaved a sigh. "Ninety-nine feet wide, this fine street, yet wasted for years, unused for a decent run."

"Speaking of carnal appetites, we need to round up some lads to attend Mr. Spivey's evening service on the morrow with us."

"Sir." Spry's shoulders slumped.

Michael suspected his assistant would rather be scrubbing his laundry than sitting in a rebel church pew, so he angled toward him and intoned, "I hear that the service features footwashing handmaidens of the Lord."

Spry's initial gape leaked away into a coarse grin. "Been awhile since my feet were washed, sir."

"Then you're probably due for a visit to church."

"Yes, sir!" They turned onto Second Street. "And when do we visit the French witch?"

"Also on the morrow, if we've time." Michael summarized Esmé Delacroix's history for Spry. "And before I forget to tell you, I'm expecting to hear from the circle of ladies with whom Mrs. Garrity socializes, from someone who's a confidante and can resolve the issue of whether she has a paramour. Mrs. Duncan promised to pass the word along to the ladies." They arrived at the brick house of Enid Jones. "Stay alert for any messages delivered here, at Mrs. Jones's house."

"I see candles lit inside. She's home. I should warn you, sir, they call her the Ice Widow. Don't get your hopes up. They say she's still in love with her husband after all these years."

Michael looked from the Widow Jones's house to his assistant and squinted at the taller man. "Spry, what did I say to make you think I intend to court a widow I've not yet met?"

"Not Mrs. Jones, sir. Mrs. Duncan. You know, the blonde with the slender waist and the full lips and the saucy, high set. She brought you chicken soup, sir. She didn't bring *me* soup."

Michael laughed to cover his abysmal and embarrassing oversight. Damn, he must have felt foul indeed to have not noticed features so pleasant to a man's eye. But there was always the morrow, and for the morrow, he wondered whether he could squeeze in a visit to Miss Salome Ward. Now there was a woman whose features he wouldn't forget, not if her portrait had done her justice.

"She didn't charge you for that soup, did she, sir? Ah ha, that's part of her sport. She leads men along until they're heartbroken, never having gotten so much as to kiss her hand."

Michael eyed him with humor before climbing the porch steps. "All because she's in love with a dead man, eh?" Wilmington didn't lack for legends. He couldn't wait to write his sister, Miriam, about the town's personalities.

"That's what they say, sir. Maybe she's waiting on the second coming of Christ or something."

"Looks to me like you're the one's waiting on the second coming out here in the cold. Come along. Let's introduce ourselves to Mrs. Jones."

"I hope she made supper for us. I'm starved, sir."

Michael knocked at the front door. The patter of footsteps approached across a wooden floor, and curtains twitched in a front window. A sturdy-boned, dark-haired Welshwoman old enough to be his mother opened the door. He bowed and said, "We're here to see a Mrs. Enid Jones. She requested boarders from Major Craig. I'm Lieutenant Stoddard, and this is my man, Spry."

A smile flicked the corners of her mouth, and she opened the door wider. "Come in. I'm Enid Jones."

The Welshwoman closed the door behind them, haggardness in her face testifying to a rough several months. A triple murder in Wilmington in November, Molly the laundress had said. Sometime in the next few days, Michael would sit the older woman down and get the full story. He swept a glance around the foyer, where they stood, then into the parlor, where a fire had been lit in the fireplace. Only a couch, chair, table, and mantle clock—reinforcing emptiness, hardship, and sadness. "We appreciate the opportunity to board with you, Mrs. Jones."

"Please call me Enid."

She wasn't the lady of the house. She'd insisted that they use her first name. Enid was a servant. He thought back to their meeting earlier that day with the laundress. Molly had thrown another name into her summarization of November's harrowing events, a Mrs. Chiswell. Enid was obviously her housekeeper.

Chiswell. That name sounded familiar. Michael scanned his memory but was unable to find a connection.

"This afternoon, men from the regiment brought your gear." Enid addressed Spry. "I prepared a servant's chamber out back for you. Your gear is there." She turned to Michael. "And I only have one guest room with a bed, so I had them haul your gear up there, Mr. Stoddard. We haven't much left to us. I hope it'll do right for you."

Although Michael and Spry would provide Enid with protection, as Major Craig had intended, Michael comprehended the Welshwoman's secondary motivation in requesting a boarder. She needed money. "You keep a tidy home. I'm sure all will be well."

Tension eased from Enid's face. "Are either of you hungry? I've a pork stew ready for supper."

Spry supplied his ear-to-ear grin, and Michael said, "We look forward to supper."

***

Just after dawn on Wednesday morning, the final day of January, the aroma of coffee blended with that of flapjacks greeted Michael when he opened his bedroom door. The back of his throat was only a quarter as sore as it had been yesterday morning. Three cheers for chicken soup and a good night's sleep. Now if he could only figure out a way to keep from aggravating his chin when he shaved. He hadn't missed the relief in Spry's eyes the evening before when he'd informed him that his assistance wouldn't be required for his commander's morning shave.

Downstairs he made his way to the dining room—where he surprised Spry in the act of forking a flapjack toward his mouth. At the sight of him, the private shot to his feet as if the seat of his chair had become a bed of live coals. The fork clattered to his plate. "Sir!"

Between them, the chasm of caste yawned again, and Michael wasn't sure which one of them was more awkward with it. He'd eaten supper alone in the dining room last night and assumed that Enid had fed Spry out in the kitchen. But he remembered hearing them laughing together out in the yard, so maybe Enid had invited Spry to eat in the dining room after Michael went upstairs. By protocol, Spry *should* be eating in another room or the kitchen, no question. Had Michael been born into the nobility, he wouldn't be standing in the entrance to the dining room wondering why he felt ambivalent and aggravated—and not necessarily at Spry or Enid.

In truth, he had far more in common culturally with Spry than he had with the officers born to the aristocracy. And the peculiar nature of the assignment— two soldiers investigating criminal activity, exchanging ideas, endeavoring to draw conclusions as a team—encouraged the blurring of distinctions between him and his assistant. The better part of his discomfort came from the pressure of "rules," not Spry's presence at the dining table. He'd worn the Army's neck stock for nine years, and sometimes that collar chafed.

He walked to the table and sat at his place from the night before, where a steaming cup of coffee awaited him. "Resume your seat and finish your breakfast. I shall make certain that Enid knows to feed you out in the kitchen except when I need you at the table with me while we discuss an investigation."

"Sir." Spry lowered himself to his chair, swabbed his mouth with his napkin, darted another look at Michael, then attacked the final flapjack.

Yes, that felt better. But Michael knew he couldn't afford to relax the rules too often. Few in the Army condoned hugging the fringes of orthodoxy in such a way.

When he took his first sip of coffee, a shudder of delight rippled through him. Enid's coffee bore almost no resemblance to the Army's brew. Spry said in a subdued voice, "Maybe having a mother hen won't be so bad, sir."

"Mother hen?" Michael raised eyebrows at him.

"You'll see, sir."

"How many flapjacks have you eaten?"

"Lost count, sir. Eighteen, maybe twenty." The back door squeaked open, heralding Enid's return. Reluctance permeated Spry's tone. "This next batch is yours. Sir."

"Of course it's mine."

The housekeeper breezed in with a plate of flapjacks. "Oh! Top of the morning, sir. Here you are."

Looking not the slightest bit apologetic over the seating arrangements, she placed the flapjacks before Michael and slid a jar of brown cane syrup closer to his plate. A softened blob of butter crowning the stack of flapjacks slipped down the side. The sugary, hot aroma ripped his appetite loose, and he reached for his fork.

"Just one moment." The housekeeper, scowling, slapped her hand to the table and trapped his fork. "What happened to your chin? Pimples? Bah, it's all that grease and biscuits the Army feeds you men."

Spry sat back, rubbed his belly, and grinned at Enid. "I like grease and biscuits."

Michael's stomach made a noise like a bear with an earache. Enid released his fork and straightened. "I've just the thing for you."

After she sallied from the dining room, Spry whispered, "Mother hen. Sir."

Not wishing to speculate on what remedy the Welsh had concocted for pimples, but intuiting that it wouldn't be pleasant, Michael tore into his flapjacks. Spry rose and became absorbed in something just outside the window, in the neighbor's back yard. Michael had managed to scarf down most of the food when Enid returned bearing a rectangle of linen on a small plate. "Press this onto your chin." She extended the plate.

Michael set down his fork and picked off the piece of linen. The last second before he slapped it to his chin, he smelled witch hazel and some underlying blend of herbs. Then every pimple exploded in fiery agony. "Gah! What the blazes is in this?"

"You don't need to know. Ah ah, hold it on your chin longer. That's it. Twice a day for a week ought to do you some good. And don't go touching your face afterwards."

She left a minute later, taking the linen rectangle from hell with her. Michael dove back into his breakfast, despite his chin feeling like a practice field for grenadiers. The fact that Spry was still looking outside the window instead of at him reinforced his impression that the lower half of his face had melted.

Then he heard a woman singing "Johnny's Gone for a Soldier" just beyond the window, and Spry turned back to him with an abundance of gleaming teeth. "Sir, will you be wanting to discuss anything while you finish your breakfast?" Michael, his mouth full, shook his head. "Then I'll step out in the yard for a breath of fresh air, sir."

Michael swallowed. "Don't breathe too deeply. We leave in a quarter hour."

"Sir." Spry saluted and exited with haste.

By the time Michael finished the stack, his chin was only tingly. Enid arrived with more coffee and flapjacks, passed a critical glance over his chin, and nodded with approval. "By the bye, your man's in Mr. Morris's yard jabbering with the servant girl." She slid the flapjacks before him.

Michael suspected she planned to fatten him up. Good luck. "Spry and I met Molly yesterday. Did I understand her correctly that your mistress, Mrs. Chiswell, is in South Carolina?" Enid nodded. He munched another mouthful of breakfast. Chiswell. Yes, that name was familiar. Maybe he'd run into her in Charles Town. "Visiting relatives, perhaps, in Charles Town? I might have met her there."

"No, not in Charles Town." Abruptly, Enid gnawed her lip, and her shoulders sagged. "Er, might I ask, sir, have you any recent word of the British Legion?"

Hair on the back of his neck rose. Hell, yes, he'd had recent word of the Legion: defeated in the South Carolina backcountry two weeks ago. He forced reserve into his expression. That furtive look in Enid's eyes haunted him. Why had she asked about the Legion?

Then it hit him like a pugilist's punch. "Your mistress had business with them?"

Enid nodded, twisted her hands in her apron. "I haven't received a letter from her since early December." Her head tilted, plunging her face into shadow.

He set down his coffee cup and studied the housekeeper. Whatever her lady's business had been, if she'd managed to catch up with the regiment, she wouldn't have been present in the chaos of that battle mid-January. Mrs. Chiswell would probably return to Wilmington any day now. "Enid, see here, you know the post. Unreliable, at best." He rose and spread his hands. "I haven't heard from my sister in Yorkshire for months. But I can tell you that about five weeks ago, I delivered some dispatches to the Legion."

Chiswell. Michael scratched his head a moment. Had he met her back then? His memory vibrated. He suspected that he had—but *where*? "At that time, the regiment was encamped at Daniel's Plantation. If your mistress was there, I assure you she was quite safe. And if Colonel Tarleton received movement orders, he'd send all the ladies to safety in Ninety Six or Winnsborough." At least, he hoped that would have happened. "Why did she visit the Legion in the first place? Does she have kinfolk among the corps?"

A shudder raked Enid. She lifted her head and pressed her hand to her mouth for a second. "I'm not supposed to say, but the truth will out, now that the deeds of those curs Badley and Prescott have come to light. We were out of money, you see. She's a journalist. She went out there to write a story about the Legion, earn some money."

Disbelief rippled Michael. He shook his head. "That's absurd. A publisher would have to be daft to send a woman on such an assignment."

"Aye, that's Mr. Badley, sir. He published a magazine here in town. He tried to keep the secret that he and his attorney had stolen Mrs. Chiswell's money years ago. The assignment wasn't a real assignment, although my mistress thought it was at first. Mr. Badley just wanted her stranded in the backcountry, where the odds were greater that she'd be killed."

Michael stared at Enid, the burn of anger and revulsion in his stomach. Whoever this Badley creature was, he hoped the court system strung him up from the highest tree. The son of a dog was blighted with the same set of morals as Fairfax.

Chiswell. The sensation that he'd met her intensified. "I presume your mistress traveled with friends and in a large group?"

"Yes. She took the Pearsons with her and Mr. Quill, but—"

"Enid, I'll be frank with you. Travel on those backcountry roads is difficult, even under the best conditions. In inclement weather, often couriers cannot get through. Mrs. Chiswell may not even have made it through to the Legion. And if she did make it through, soon as sentries learned she was a journalist, they'd have turned her away. Like many commanding officers, Colonel Tarleton has no time for journalists—unless they can advance him politically, of course."

"That was the trick, you see. She hid what she was doing. No one knew except the Pearsons, Mr. Quill, and—and—" Enid crammed a knuckle in her mouth.

"Then what would have been her legitimate reason for being in camp? Would she have claimed to be an officer's mistress?"

Enid's eyes implored him. "Rhiannon, Arawn, spare us! She pretended to be the sister of a lieutenant in the Seventeenth Light Dragoons, visiting her 'brother' in camp while he trained the Legion's cavalrymen. Do you know any officers in the Seventeenth Light, Mr. Stoddard?"

Michael's breath stuck in his throat, as if he'd been rolled up and smothered in a carpet. He couldn't stop the widening of his eyes. "Er, I know a few." Only *one*, actually.

"Well, this one isn't right in the head. No conscience. *Evil.* I begged my mistress not to go with *him*. No story was worth his company."

Flapjacks in Michael's stomach solidified in a swell of horror. Evil. Lieutenant. Seventeenth Light. This couldn't be. The coincidence was too great.

Enid read his face, and her expression collapsed. "Gods. You must know Lieutenant Fairfax, too."

Michael's jaw dangled. *Lieutenant Fairfax.* What devilry was this?

Rapping on the front door reverberated through the house like the sound of musket fire. The servant gasped and pressed a hand to her chest. Michael's gaze riveted to the dining room doorway.

Pluck returned to Enid's voice. "Now who might that be? It's not yet eight o'clock." She scurried from the dining room.

Michael's pulse hopped about as if he were on a battlefield. He paced around the table twice. When he peered out the side window, he only half-saw Spry lift a shirt from a laundry basket and hand it to Molly at the neighbor's clothesline.

Mrs. Chiswell, the lady of the house, had vanished into the backcountry of South Carolina with Lieutenant Fairfax and the doomed British Legion. Christ Jesus. Far from being on her way home that moment, she could be dead. Or worse, since Fairfax was involved.

Chiswell. Memory swept him back to Saturday morning the thirtieth of December. He and his informant, that damned double-spy in the dusty hunting shirt, Adam Neville, were walking through the Legion encampment's marketplace together. And although Michael hadn't let on to Neville about the personal angle to his presence in camp, he sensed that the ranger knew he was looking for a way to kill Fairfax without implicating himself, especially if he could make the corpse disappear. Knew it and found it hilarious. Oh, the smirk on Neville's face when he'd told Michael that Fairfax was twenty miles away, in Winnsborough.

Neville had grabbed his upper arm and spun them both around to face a pretty gentlewoman with hair the color of honey. She'd obviously been following them. She gabbed twaddle about wanting to interview Neville, but instead of looking at the ranger, she'd used every second of that stolen moment to take a measure of Michael. Those eyes missed nothing. They were the eyes of a journalist. The ranger had dismissed her, then. *Good day, Mrs. Chiswell.*

Enid's voice in the doorway cut through and shredded the memory. "Mr. Stoddard, you've a visitor."

Michael, who'd been looking out the window, composed his expression and faced the housekeeper. No way was he telling her what he knew. She'd be beside herself with worry. He made his voice calm. "A visitor—a soldier from the regiment?"

"No, sir. It's Miss Salome Ward. She says she must talk with you about her sister and brother-in-law. Shall I show her to the parlor?"

Michael's eyes widened. Salome Ward. His pulse settled into a calmer rhythm. "Yes, thank you, Enid."

The Welshwoman returned to the front door to admit the visitor. He let himself out back, into the clear, frosty morning. "Spry!" His assistant pivoted and doused a courtship smile. Michael jerked his thumb toward the interior of the house. "Inside, right away."

"Sir!"

Michael pivoted on the back step, glimpsed his own reflection in window glass, and paused to rotate his head back and forth. Well, now, that was a pleasant surprise. The concoction that drenched Enid's linen rectangle had soothed the irritation on his chin.

Spry stomped his shoes on the step near Michael. "Business, sir?"

Fate had dropped into Michael's lap an interview with the gorgeous sister of Julia Garrity. "Yes. In the parlor right now." He squared his shoulders, and he and his assistant entered the house as a team.

Chapter Eight

FROM THE FOYER window, Michael studied the polished two-seater chair parked in the street before the house. The pair of horses had been groomed well, and the driver, liveried in brown, waited in his seat without restlessness, a professional. Memory of the furnishings in Julia Garrity's bedroom returned to Michael. When it came to a taste for luxury, the sisters were two of a kind.

Enid fidgeted near the closed parlor doors. From the glitter in her eyes, Michael recognized that if he didn't establish some boundaries, the servants' grapevine would spread details of his investigations over town and foul the process of solving each one. So after he motioned for Spry to go on in, he caught her gaze with his. "This is *business*, Enid." He stepped into the parlor and shut the doors behind him.

When he pivoted, a woman at the fireplace glided around from warming gloved hands. Her hat, tied beneath her chin with ribbons, quivered with a riot of feathers. Dark curls burst from her lacy mobcap, and the bodice of her wine-red polonaise gown was taut over impressive curves. The portrait of Salome Ward hadn't done justice to her beauty. Michael swelled his chest and smiled. "Good morning."

Her lips pinched. "I'm Miss Ward, the sister of Mrs. Garrity. Send in Major Craig's investigator immediately. I must speak with him about my sister and brother-in-law." Her glare scraped over Michael's chin. "I don't have the time to waste with two puppies."

Puppies. All warmth left Michael's chest, and he clamped his jaw. The portrait had captured Miss Ward's willfulness quite well. He made a stiff bow. "I'm Lieutenant Stoddard, Major Craig's investigator, madam. This is my assistant, Spry. There are no puppies in this room. And since I've no time to waste, either, I shall press straight to the point. You've been sheltering your sister, Mrs. Garrity, on your farm since Saturday, have you not?"

Her cheeks pinked. "I have not!"

"Then where is she?"

She stamped her foot. "I haven't the slightest idea. Ask my brother-in-law." Her nose jutted into the air. "He's tried to kill her several times."

Interesting, if true. And if a lie, what was Miss Ward's game? For several seconds, Michael studied her, considering what to ask her first. "When and where was the last time you saw your sister?"

"In October. I visited her in her home."

Three months ago. "Where do you live?"

"On the family farm. It's about an hour from here."

That much tallied with what Mrs. Overton had said. However, now that he'd met Salome Ward, he found it hard to believe that Gabriel Garrity would intimidate her into staying away, as Mrs. Overton had implied. Was Miss Ward covering up additional visits? If so, why? "When was the last time she visited you on your farm?"

"Last summer."

"The two of you live only an hour apart, yet you visit each other only once every three months?"

She frowned. "It's that brute of a husband she married. He hates me. It discourages our attempts to visit more often."

Michael still didn't believe it. And what a charming family. "You said a moment ago that Mr. Garrity has tried to kill your sister. Why do you believe this?"

Her eyes widened into a rude stare upon Michael. "Because when I was here last October, I *saw* him put his hands around her throat, and I *heard* him swear that he was going to strangle her to death! Only by the intervention of Mrs. Overton and myself was Julia's life spared. What further proof do you need? Arrest him!"

That was certainly a strike against Gabriel Garrity's credibility. "Why does he want to kill her?"

She rolled her eyes. "He's a crude beast. He knows he's beneath Julia's station, and it angers him. I warned her about him before she married, but she didn't listen to me. Do you know that she has to beg him for clothing? The animal doesn't appreciate her."

Recalling the luxurious bedroom in the house on Third Street, Michael doubted whether even the gifts monarchs bestowed upon their mistresses would satisfy Julia Garrity. He decided to prod Miss Ward with his top theory. "It sounds as though he's deeply angered at being cuckolded."

"Oh, you're so right." She pushed her lips out and studied her nails. "I encouraged her to pursue that affair."

Michael's eyebrows rose. What a shrew. He composed his expression. "When did she begin seeing her paramour?"

"In October, right before Mr. Garrity killed Chipper."

Shock popped Michael like a blanket full of static electricity. Fresh in his memory, he heard Mrs. Overton's summarization of Chipper's death: *It was an accident.* The head cold sure had dulled his wits. He felt like a buffoon.

Feathers fluttered in Salome Ward's hat. She glanced from Spry, who stood at the front window, to Michael, and she smirked. "Yes. He killed the dog.

Betty Overton tells everyone that Julia's terrier died in an accident. Naturally, that addlepated housekeeper protects Mr. Garrity. He employs her. But I was there that night. Julia's husband allowed that horrid bulldog of his to make a meal of poor little Chipper."

Michael's belly again felt like a brick. Horror from an old memory twitched in his cheek. When he'd been about ten years old, his mother's young cousin had sought sanctuary in the Stoddards' home, terrified of her husband. She claimed he'd threatened her verbally almost the entire duration of the marriage, and she ran away when he bludgeoned her cat to death. Her husband wooed her back. Six months later, he bludgeoned her to death, just like the cat.

Violent people often visited their rage on animals first. Strike another blow against the gunsmith's credibility.

"If it were up to me, that dog would be shot. No telling when it'll attack a human."

By Gabriel Garrity's own admission, the bulldog had already taken a bite out of a burglar. The gunsmith harbored a dangerous dog, a third strike against him.

"Ugh, Trouble, what a name for a dog. In five seconds, Chipper was reduced to a shredded, lifeless mess. I'm afraid I quite lost my supper. Serves my brother-in-law right that Julia's found a *real* man. From what she tells me, her husband has problems in that area anyway."

Michael suspected that if Garrity had problems with his equipment, he'd had some assistance arriving in that state. "Have you ever met her paramour?"

She smiled like a cat full of cream. "Yes."

"What's his name?"

"Paul."

"Paul. What's his family name?"

"You know, I'm not sure I ever heard it."

"Describe him."

"Crooked nose, but handsome. Early thirties. Light brown hair. Wears a wig sometimes. Blue eyes. Tall. Big-boned. Big *hands*. I like big hands on men." She licked her lips, her eyes cold. "I told him so, when Julia was in another room for a moment."

She'd described the man in the sketch—one of Garrity's customers, according to Mrs. Overton. And either the gunsmith had outright lied to Michael when he described his marriage as "affectionate," or he lived in a fanciful dream he'd created for himself, denying the reality of violence and violated trust in his marriage. Michael studied how emotion ran through Salome Ward's face and carriage. "You sound a bit envious of your sister for the attention that her handsome paramour lavishes upon her."

"Envious?" Her laughter sounded bitter. "I have money, Mr. Stoddard. I can find handsome attention, if I choose to do so. And I do choose to do so, when it pleases me."

The lady protested too much. She wanted Paul Paramour for herself. Michael paced the length of the parlor and back again. "Where were you this past Saturday morning, between ten-thirty and noon?"

Her interest slanted to the ceiling. For a few seconds, her right forefinger twirled a brunette curl. "Drinking coffee with my neighbor, Mrs. Collier, at least part of that time. Probably in transit back to my farm afterwards."

So she had an alibi. That didn't necessarily absolve her of complicity in her sister's disappearance, but for the time, he decided to move on. "Where did your sister first meet this Paul fellow?"

"She said he was one of her husband's customers."

"You mentioned that she has to beg Mr. Garrity for clothing. What's behind his reluctance to supply her with such?"

Her tone crackled with condemnation. "I told you, Julia married beneath her. Her husband is stingy, plus I get the impression that he cannot manage his money well."

Michael formed a picture in his head of Gabriel Garrity, forever short of money for trying to please a selfish wife, in debt so deep that he never blinked an eye when approached by rebels about repairing stands of arms. In truth, the rebels likely transacted their "big deal" with him while the Committee of Safety was still mismanaging Wilmington, well before the Eighty-Second's flotilla sailed into the Cape Fear River. But financial difficulties didn't excuse a man trying to strangle his wife or killing her terrier with his bulldog. The motive for those acts appeared to be Garrity's discovery of his wife's affair.

"Miss Ward, am I correct in assuming that the Garritys have had marital problems for some time—well before last October?" She nodded. "Then did it not occur to you that by encouraging your sister to have an affair, it would intensify the problems?"

"How dare you blame that beast's actions on Julia or me?" She took a step toward him and jutted her chin. "He's having an affair, too!"

Triumph streaked Michael's veins. He lifted his chin. "Is he now? Tell me of it."

"According to Julia, he visits his lust upon some Frenchwoman reputed to be a witch." Her exhalation quivered. "Vulgar. Just like him."

To Michael, it sounded like tit for tat. What in the world had attracted Julia Ward and Gabriel Garrity to each other in the first place? Maybe his business had been more robust once upon a time, and she'd been enticed by his income.

And what an interesting complication, that Esmé Delacroix might be tumbling in the hay with the gunsmith. In his head, he moved the "witch" to the top of his list of interview subjects.

"Miss Ward, did you drive into Wilmington just for the day, or are you staying somewhere in town?"

"I'm staying with my friends, the Baxters, just up the street." She propped both hands on her hips. "Well? Are you going to arrest my brother-in-law?"

"I'm going to question him again."

"You'll take me with you, of course."

Michael stared her down. "*You*, madam, will go to the Baxters' home, and I shall inform you later of the outcome of my meeting with your brother-in-law. If you've questions of me in my absence, leave them with Mrs. Jones, the housekeeper here."

"He'll lie through his teeth if I'm not there to dispute what he says."

Michael smiled. "Do you imagine I've never been lied to before? Miss Ward, I understand your concern for your sister, but it sounds as though you and Mr. Garrity do not engage with each other in a civilized manner. I order you to stay away from his shop and house while I'm investigating your sister's disappearance."

"But—"

"If you violate my order, I shall have you arrested and conducted to Wilmington jail."

Her expression contorted, and her lips peeled away from her teeth. "You— you wouldn't dare throw me in jail!"

His eyes narrowed. "Don't try me, madam."

"What would a pimply-faced boy like you know about finding a missing woman? Major Craig obviously left you behind because you're incompetent!"

In Michael's estimation, she'd crossed the line from "witness" to "waste of time." Before his more uncharitable sentiments uncorked, he strode from her and opened the doors. Just outside the parlor, Enid dusted the dust-free banister, close enough to have heard everything. He pivoted in the doorway and faced Miss Ward, still in the parlor. "Thank you for stopping by to express your concerns. We shall contact you as soon as we've information of interest to you. Good day."

Enid retrieved Salome Ward's cloak from the rack and handed it to Michael, just as if they'd rehearsed the act many times before. He held the cloak open for the brunette. Enid opened the front door for her.

She scalded Spry with a glare, swooped past him, yanked the cloak from Michael, and flounced out the front door. Then the housekeeper closed the door and let out a slow breath. Leaving the parlor doors open, Michael walked back in and joined his assistant at the window to watch the chair roll off.

Major Craig obviously left you behind because you're incompetent! Michael flogged himself mentally for evidence he'd overlooked the previous day. No telling what other clues he missed. He'd have to do far better today if he expected to progress in the investigation.

Spry said, low, "Maybe Mr. Garrity killed his wife, sir. He could have strangled her last week and hidden the body." The private grimaced. "Sir, I hope he didn't turn Trouble loose on her like he did on Chipper."

Without a doubt, Salome Ward's testimony was damning. Throughout history, adultery had provided a prime motive for spouses who murdered, and Julia Garrity's indiscretion had incensed her husband into killing her dog and trying to strangle her. Nevertheless instinct nagged Michael. "I'm not convinced that he killed her, Spry. It's too easy an explanation for her disappearance."

"Well, sir, I supposed she could have run off with her sweetheart, Paul."

"Indeed. But what doesn't fit about that theory?"

Spry mulled in silence a moment. "A comfort-loving woman like Mrs. Garrity wouldn't have run off without packing some clothing, sir."

"Correct. If that's what happened, we need to find a credible witness to whom Julia Garrity confided plans of leaving in a hurry, or a plausible reason why she'd leave without packing for a journey."

"Sir, did you get the impression that Miss Ward was enamored of Paul?"

Michael laughed, short, with no humor. "He tickles her fancy, all right."

"Doesn't that give Miss Ward a motive to dispense with her sister, making her a suspect?"

"Correct again. And don't forget that we've yet another suspect in this investigation."

Spry frowned. "The French witch, sir?"

"Now, now. According to Mrs. Duncan, Mrs. Delacroix is a misunderstood recluse, not a witch. But thanks to that bit of hearsay from Miss Ward, we must now question her, too. If she's having an affair with Mr. Garrity, she's Mrs. Garrity's rival. If not for affection, then for money."

"Sir." Spry's frown deepened. "I feel like a hound that caught the scents of twenty rabbits at the same time. Building redoubts is a good deal less complicated than solving crimes."

Michael was unsure what to make of his statement. "Having second thoughts about this business?" He shoved disappointment aside. Investigative work wasn't for everyone, he was the first to admit, even if there was a good deal about Spry that he liked as an assistant.

The private eyed him sharply. "Second thoughts? No, sir, at least not yet. Well, not as long as the work doesn't get boring."

If the matter of Julia Garrity's disappearance were like other investigations Michael had solved, soon enough his assistant would be buried in dead leads that not only bored but frustrated him. Again, Michael kept his mouth shut about what he knew, and he nodded. "Well, we've plenty of work to do today, Spry. First of all, we need four men to accompany us for another visit to Mr. Garrity's shop. Recruit them, and have them ready at the barracks when I meet you there in a quarter hour. This evening, we'll need ten men to come with us when we attend Mr. Spivey's footwashing sermon. And all of us will need horses."

"Horses?" Spry shook his head. "We don't have twelve horses, sir. At least not *riding* horses. Major Craig took all but two or three of those."

"Yes, I know. So we'll have to make do with what horses we have."

"But *workhorses*, sir?" Spry laughed, short. "We'll be quite a sight straddling those broad backs."

"No doubt, but we'll return to camp after dark. In the event of an ambush, even workhorses will give us an advantage over men afoot."

"Yes, sir."

As soon as the private had exited out the front door, Michael motioned the housekeeper to step into the parlor with him. "Enid, unless I specifically request otherwise, feed Spry in the kitchen from now on." Spry would be closer to the food that way.

One of Enid's cheeks dimpled. "I'm sorry about that, sir. It's just that last night, I found out that Spry knows a sailor who knows my uncle back in Aberystwyth. Isn't that amazing? Here we are, all the way across the Atlantic, and—and—yes, sir, I shall feed Spry out in the kitchen."

"Thank you. And I appreciate your opening this house to my assistant and me. We shall likely see future use of the parlor for confidential discussions with witnesses."

"Then I shall keep it tidy for you, sir."

"Even more important than that—" He pinned her with his gaze. "—I don't expect any details you happen to overhear from witnesses to find their way out into the street. If they do, Spry and I will relocate to a residence that offers more privacy."

She nodded, her expression solemn. "You can rely on me to keep quiet, Mr. Stoddard, sir."

Chapter Nine

AT MAJOR CRAIG'S headquarters on Third Street, the adjutant informed Michael that the night before, Crown forces had surprised Young's militia at Heron's Bridge—despite advantages that the drawbridge gave to the rebels on the other side of the Northeast Cape Fear River. The Eighty-Second captured eight prisoners and scattered the militia. Soldiers found provisions and arms at the abandoned rebel camp. They destroyed the drawbridge and cast a cannon into the river. Smart work for one night.

The major and his small army of a hundred infantrymen, sixty marines from the transport ships, artillerymen, and a handful of dragoons would remain in the area another day or so to search for vessels the rebels had used to evacuate most of their supplies and ammunition upriver from Wilmington. News of their delayed return relieved Michael. It meant he'd have more time to work on the Garrity investigation and look into Elijah Spivey's organization.

At the barracks, Spry pointed out the ten volunteers for that evening's excursion to the Bethany church. Then Michael, his assistant, three privates, and one sergeant—all armed—marched to the gunsmith's shop on Front Street. Their arrival drew the attention of spectators, who kept their distance out in the street. Michael sent two soldiers to guard the rear door of the shop, in case Garrity or his craftsmen decided to bolt that way, and stationed the other two men on the front porch. He informed all four men that he didn't want to be disturbed while questioning the gunsmith.

From the din on the inside, the "big job" was in full production. The front door was locked. Michael whacked on it several times before sounds of smithing tapered down, and he heard something being dragged across the floor. A container to conceal repaired stands of arms, perhaps? A sweaty-faced Gabriel Garrity yanked open the door, another faux smile in place for them. "Good morning, Lieutenant. How may I help you today? News for me or more questions?"

"Yes." Michael swept his arm to encompass their audience, twenty or so civilians by then. "I doubt you want your neighbors privy to these details, so let's step inside, shall we?"

"Excellent idea." Garrity noticed the other soldiers on the front porch then, and his smile faltered a second before he regrouped. "Morning, fellows." He tugged the door open wider, again inviting Michael and Spry into his overheated shop.

While the gunsmith secured the front door from within, Michael swept his gaze over the shop interior. On the floor, skid lines terminated in a covered crate tucked beneath a table. The crate hadn't been there the previous day. Before he left, he'd open it.

Garrity motioned the two soldiers past craftsmen at work, to the back of the building. "Step in here so we can talk privately." He gripped the door handle to the storage room.

The bulldog! In expectation of forty pounds of Trouble, Michael's muscles tensed, and his hand clapped the hilt of his dagger. But when the door swung inward, no slathering beast lunged out to maim them. Michael relaxed and frowned. "Where's the dog?"

"I give him a change of scenery every now and then. Plus, I had the feeling you lads would be back with news of Julia, so I made room in here for us to talk. I even rounded up chairs."

Michael's blood burned. After they left yesterday, Garrity had gone through his shop and cleared out materials that suggested he was repairing large amounts of weapons. Another investigator—one whose head wasn't fogged in a cold—would have arrested the gunsmith yesterday on the mere suspicion of weapons trafficking.

In the next instant, Michael realized that had he done so, he probably wouldn't have uncovered Garrity's full cache, and Garrity might have wiggled out of trafficking charges based on the small amount of materials impounded. The gunsmith's fulsome smile confirmed Michael's realization. Garrity had convinced himself that he was the more clever man. He was overconfident. That meant he'd show his hand. All Michael had to do was wait for it. His blood cooled.

The gunsmith shut the door and parted heavy drapes to light the room's interior. Michael saw lumber stacked floor-to-ceiling against one wall, along with iron bars and boxes of pre-assembled locks. It was all as Garrity had described the afternoon before. From dust patterns on the floor, Michael could see that larger crates like the one beneath the table in the shop had recently occupied the room. The rotten egg odor of ignited black powder, to be expected from muskets and rifles that had been fired, permeated the room. And someone had done a hasty job of sweeping up a powder spill.

"Have a seat." A magnanimous smile on his face, the gunsmith heaved himself upon a stool and indicated two ladder-back chairs nearby.

Michael signed for Spry to remain standing. He positioned his own chair so he could watch the door, and Garrity would have light from the window in his eyes. "Mr. Garrity, I'm curious. When we spoke yesterday, not once did you mention your wife's little terrier, Chipper. There's a shrine to the dog in your back yard. Do you ever trip over it?"

Garrity shrugged. "I'm a busy man. I seldom have leisure to spend time in my back yard."

He'd seen the shrine. His callousness rammed Michael's senses, and the words with which Miss Ward had described her brother-in-law leapt to memory: *brute, crude beast, animal, vulgar*. With no difficulty, Michael imagined the gunsmith unleashing his bulldog on the terrier. "How did Chipper die?"

"An accident."

"You're lying. You turned your bulldog loose on him."

"What?" The gunsmith scowled. "I did not! Where did you hear that claptrap? Is that what my housekeeper told you?"

"And you made another omission yesterday, when I inquired about your wife's kinfolk living nearby. You didn't mention her sister, Salome, who lives not far away."

Garrity growled. "That conniving shrew! She drove up here and told you I loosed Trouble on Chipper, didn't she? Why, if I get hold of her, I'll—I'll—"

"You'll do what, sir? Strangle her? Is that what you did to your wife?"

"No! I love Julia! I've never hurt her!"

"Never, despite your sister-in-law's testimony that you put your hands around your wife's throat and would have strangled her had not she and Mrs. Overton intervened?"

"Are you going to believe those two women over me? Mrs. Overton's wits are addled, and that shrew Miss Ward has always hated me." He thrust his jaw toward Michael. Forgotten, Spry slipped in closer behind him, at the ready. "You have no motive for me to harm my wife. By god, you're trying to pin a crime on me because you're a shoddy investigator who is unable to discover what really happened to my wife. That's it, you're incompetent, a failure! That's why Major Craig left you behind!"

Spry, scowling, stepped forward. Michael caught his eye and shook his head quickly to halt him from advancing. Then he clamped his teeth at the insult, so like Salome Ward's retort in the parlor.

A chill washed over him from memory. Come to think of it, Lieutenant Fairfax had said something similar. But Fairfax might be dead, killed at the Cowpens. He straightened his shoulders at the thought.

All of a sudden, the gunsmith sat back hard, his rage draining away. "Wait a minute. This talk about strangling—have you found Julia dead, strangled?"

Sweat beaded Garrity's forehead. Was he hiding something besides weapons trafficking? Michael ignored the gunsmith's question and allowed his own dialogue to slip into the past tense. "Oh, but you did have a motive for harming your wife. She was having an affair with your client, Paul. Enraged with jealousy when you discovered the affair back in October, you attempted to strangle her." Michael rose and backed a few steps from Garrity. "Shortly afterwards, still maddened, you set your bulldog upon her terrier and had it kill the other dog."

Garrity's face had ruddied, and his freckles stood out. A moan issued from him. "You've found her body, haven't you? Ah god, ah god."

"Where were you between ten-thirty and noon on Saturday?"

"Here, working! I told you yesterday."

"Which of those men out there can verify that?"

"None of them. I was alone in the shop that day because of what was happening with the government transition."

"So you truly don't have an alibi."

"I—I don't know."

"You need an alibi for that time, Mr. Garrity, because from where I stand, it looks as though you had the opportunity to go home, strangle your wife, and dispose of her body while the whole town was looking elsewhere."

"No! I didn't kill her! I love her!"

Arms crossed, Michael walked over to the window and peered out. Behind him, the gunsmith's breath rasped. His horror seemed genuine. He wasn't following the script, breaking down and confessing to murder.

Michael felt as if he'd stubbed his toe on a couch in the dark. Where the hell was Julia Garrity? His back still to the woman's husband, he decided on another approach. "To what location did you transfer all the rebels' broken firearms that were in here yesterday?"

A rumble issued from Garrity. His tone darkened. "I don't know what you're talking about."

Time to dance the fast reel of bluffing. "Did you not hear the news, then?" Michael whipped about and snarled victory at the gunsmith. "Major Craig triumphed against the rebels last night at Heron's Bridge. Young's ragtag militia is disbanded. We captured and interrogated a number of prisoners. And several of them know you, Mr. Garrity."

Was that a flinch beneath the gunsmith's glower? "What of it? I sell and repair firearms all day. A man has to earn a living, doesn't he? I don't talk politics with customers. All I care about is whether their money is good."

"Oh, that's right. Major Craig told me you claim to be neutral. Well, you really should have paid more attention to your customers' loyalties. The prisoners who spoke of you mentioned seeing an order signed several weeks ago by the rebels' governor in North Carolina, Abner Nash, authorizing payment to you for the service and repair of stands of arms. For someone who professes neutrality, you conduct business with some prominent rebels. Do you expect Major Craig to ignore that?"

Garrity broke eye contact. "You're a liar. Or the prisoners are." He hung his head. "I don't see what this has to do with Julia. She's dead, isn't she?" His fists pounded his thighs. "Go ahead and tell me."

Thrill over the game of bluff and deception wound up and vibrated inside Michael's soul. He pitched consolation into his tone, along with the past tense again. "From many accounts, your wife was a demanding woman. She constantly badgered you for new clothing, new hats, was never satisfied with your gifts. Business slowed for you. You gave up going to White's Tavern with your friends because you ran out of money. And to make matters worse, to rub in your face her belief that you couldn't do anything right, she found a paramour."

Garrity's cheek twitched. He clenched his fists tighter. Michael pressed on. "Last month, when the rebels offered you a deal repairing their weapons, you lunged for it. More money than you'd had for a long, long time. Your chance to make things right with Julia."

Head still bowed, Garrity dragged his sleeve over his nose. "I couldn't make things right with her. I lost her."

"How many broken stands of arms did the rebels send you to repair?"

"I didn't kill Julia, Lieutenant. You must believe me."

"Have they paid you in full?"

"No. Damnation, no. And I *didn't* kill Julia!"

"Such extreme effort on your part to recapture your wife's favor, and she had the gall to spurn you. If I'd been you, I'd have been heartbroken enough to—" Michael saw Spry's head jerk in warning toward the door and a swell of commotion out in the shop.

Before either soldier could move, the door whammed open. Salome Ward burst in brandishing a cane, her glare seeking Garrity. "You murdered my sister!"

The cane arced for Garrity's temple. He sprang sideways in evasion, toppling his stool. "Come and get it, you lying shrew!" He fumbled a broken board off the top of a crate and lunged for her.

Spry tripped him and sent him sprawling into sawdust and black powder on the floor. Michael batted the cane from the woman's hand. She turned on him, and he grappled with her, feathers up his nose, until he got her limbs pinned. "Let go of me!" she shrieked.

Restrained by Spry, Garrity lay prostrate on the floor, the board out of reach. Michael rotated his head to discover most of Garrity's craftsmen crowding the doorway in amazement. When he recognized two of his soldiers in the crowd, he felt his scowl rake from his eyebrows to his chin. "I told you men we were not to be disturbed!"

Awkwardness jerked the jaw of one private. "The lady said she had evidence that proved Mr. Garrity murdered her sister."

In Michael's peripheral vision, Miss Ward reprised her cat-full-of-cream smile. He glared at the gullible redcoat. "Get in here and hold her secure." He eyed the other soldier. "And you fetch the other two men. We've a search to make of this shop, starting with that crate under the table out there." He couldn't miss the nervous glances exchanged among craftsmen. "And none of you leaves this shop until I say so."

With Salome Ward transferred to the restraint of a soldier, Michael helped Spry haul Garrity to his feet, then straightened his uniform. He allowed himself a few breaths while the raucous ride of reaction in his blood slowed. Then he shifted a gaze full of disgust between the sister and husband of Julia Garrity. "You've behaved like crazed apes instead of civilized adults. I hesitate to turn you loose on the townsfolk in such a state. So you're both under arrest. Let's see if a little time in jail doesn't restore your manners."

Chapter Ten

THE COVERED CRATE beneath the table held seven complete stands of arms. Michael's promise of clemency sent the tongues of Garrity's craftsmen wagging. They confessed that about three-dozen complete stands of arms could be found in a warehouse at Dock and Front Streets. However none of the workers knew the identity of Garrity's customer, and the gunsmith refused to answer more of Michael's questions.

The procession up Market Street to jail, advertised by Gabriel Garrity's curses of the Stoddard lineage and Salome Ward's wails about abuse of women, acquired an impressive following of merchants and traders from surrounding shops plus those who happened to be out and about on errands, like goodwives, slaves, and apprentices. Behind bars, Miss Ward wept while her brother-in-law mocked Michael through the grate on his cell door: "What were you doing before you got knighted as an investigator, Stoddard? Working inventory, and counting shovels? You think I killed my wife. Some investigator you are."

Michael signed the jailer's official documents, and before he'd taken four steps from the building, attorneys for Garrity and Miss Ward descended upon him and demanded release of their clients. They smelled of ink, paper, and musty tomes. He snarled both men down. "Disorderly conduct, armed assault upon a witness, assault upon officers of the law, impeding the progress of an investigation. In Mr. Garrity's case, add weapons trafficking with rebels. For Miss Ward, add trespassing. If you don't like it, draft your favorite piece of legal rubbish and buff Major Craig's arse with it when he returns to town. I've weapons to confiscate and a missing woman to find." He flung his arm through the air, and they backed from him. "Out of my way."

He stomped out to where Spry, the sergeant, and the three privates awaited him. Beyond them stood a crowd of the curious. Michael exhaled hard, purging his lungs of lawyers, and addressed the sergeant. "Go to the warehouse. Impound the weapons you find there, including any partial stands of arms.

Business records, too, if you find those."

"Sir."

From the corner of his eye, Michael noted with satisfaction the attorneys vanishing into the crowd. "Also, a bulldog named Trouble is likely guarding the cache. He's suspected of violent acts upon men."

"Yes, sir." The sergeant gripped his musket. "I shall take care of the beast before we enter."

Michael thought of the hound he'd had as a boy. Conflict throbbed in his temple. The men must be protected, the cache must be seized, yet—"Sergeant, wait. Obtain some scraps from a butcher. Try placating the dog with food first. Maybe you won't have to shoot him." The sergeant hesitated, and Michael frowned. "Those are my orders, Sergeant. Don't kill the dog unless you must."

He dismissed the four soldiers, and he and Spry watched them march back down Market Street. His assistant sighed. "What's next, sir?"

Michael cocked an eyebrow at him. "Are you bored yet, lad?"

"No, sir." Spry grinned.

"Good. We've the Garritys' driver and gardener and Mrs. Overton's son, Ben, to question. Odds are that at least one of them saw Mrs. Garrity in her yard Saturday morning and noticed a detail that'll help us with this investigation. If not, we shall question neighbors. Come along."

They headed for Market Street. Garrity gave his parting shot from a barred window in jail: "Stoddard! You're incompetent. You cannot find a tick on a pig's arse, Stoddard."

Incompetent. Memory swept Michael back almost eight months to that copse of trees in Georgia. By daylight, he'd brought a witness from Alton to identify the dead Spaniard. The woman had seen him the night before, when he was still alive. Unfortunately he, the woman, and the dead Spaniard weren't the only ones there at the scene of murder.

***

Michael tramped down underbrush, shoved aside vines, and led the witness into cool gloom past a tethered horse. Eyes still adjusting to shade, he removed his cocked hat and swabbed dank hair off his forehead with his kerchief. A rustle among moldy leaves nearby startled him, and he blinked at the outgoing investigator, who rose from a crouch beside the Spaniard's sheet-covered body. "Lieutenant Fairfax, I didn't expect to find you here. What brings you this way?" He dropped the hat back on his head.

Fairfax straightened. Like Michael, he was in his mid-twenties and of medium height, but he outweighed Michael by twenty-five muscular pounds. With his queued russet hair and handsome face, Fairfax reminded him of a smirky gamekeeper he'd known back in Yorkshire. "I'm solving murders and appreciate your leaving the premises before you destroy evidence. Sir."

For a couple of seconds, Michael gaped at him, unable to believe Fairfax's boorishness. A backward glance revealed the civilian woman's blush. How rude of Fairfax to speak that way, especially with the lady in attendance. He closed the distance to the other man and swelled his chest. "I was given charge of this investigation at one o'clock. You and your commander have been transferred from this garrison. Sir."

He saw the way Fairfax's gaze raked mockery over the pimples on his chin, torn open with the morning's shave. The faint smile that appeared on Fairfax's lips didn't reach his eyes. "How unfortunate. Sir. I presume you've skill solving crimes?"

What the hell? Of course he had skill. "I've tracked down burglars and livestock thieves."

"Capital. Such depth of experience should stand you on firm ground in the realm of violent death."

Humiliation scorched Michael's cheeks, compounding the flush stamped there from the summer sun. He angled his jaw. "And you've skill solving crimes of violence?"

"Four cases of arson, three abductions, five murders. I no longer count the burglaries and livestock thefts."

***

"Son of a bitch," Michael muttered. He fervently hoped that Fairfax had never left that battlefield in South Carolina.

"Sorry, sir, I didn't catch that."

Michael rolled back his shoulders. "Never mind." He gazed ahead.

And there was Enid Jones trotting toward them up Market Street, her petticoat clenched aside to free her legs, her other hand gripping her shawl about her shoulders. She smiled. "Mr. Stoddard!" When she reached the two of them, she took a few seconds catching her breath. "How you fellows do move about! But I'd no trouble finding you. News of the arrests has already spread over town." A gleam in her eye, she edged toward Michael. "Happy to hear you made good on your promise to that snappish wench." She pulled a note from her pocket and thrust it at him. "This arrived about a quarter hour ago. I recognized the messenger as one of them rebels and thought you might want to read the note sooner than later." She winked at Spry. "Shall I make an apple tart for dessert tonight?"

The private patted his stomach. "We might be late for supper. Likely after dark. We've business northwest out of town."

"Ooh. I shall keep the sweet warm for you, then, don't worry."

One of them rebels. No sign of the correspondent was on the outside, so Michael broke the seal and unfolded the note. His gaze shot to the sender: Mrs. William Hooper. God's foot, the wife of William Hooper, a signer of the Declaration, had sent him a message. *Anne* Hooper, if he recalled her name correctly from the list Major Craig had given him.

He read: *I have information of Mrs. Gabriel Garrity that may assist your efforts to learn her whereabouts. Please call on me at my house on Third*

Street at your earliest convenience.

He passed the note to Spry. "Thank you, Enid. An apple tart would be welcome tonight."

"Luck with the day's business, sir." She curtsied, then strode back down Market Street.

Spry read the note and handed it back to Michael, his expression blank, indicative that he didn't recognize the name. Michael said, "William Hooper signed the Declaration of Independence, Spry."

A low whistle emerged from Spry's lips. "To Third Street, then, sir? What will you do with his wife and family?"

His assistant hadn't been privy to the previous day's conversation with Major Craig. "Listen. Cultivate their trust."

"Hunh. Interesting concept, sir. Isn't it a bit late in the game for us to be doing that, though?"

The quirkiness of the situation sent a ripple of humor through Michael. "Don't you see? She made the first move, Spry."

***

In the yard outside the plain, wooden building on Third Street that housed William Hooper's law office, two tall, muscular young fellows inquired their business. Then they escorted Michael and Spry inside to a tiny parlor, its simple but well-made furniture illuminated by daylight. The four men stared at each other in prickly quiet broken only by the serpentine hiss of coals in the fireplace.

In less than a minute, a small, plain-faced woman in her mid-thirties entered, her gown simple but well-made, like the furniture in the parlor. She paused beside the two young men from the household. "I'm Mrs. William Hooper."

Her gaze tracked to Michael's epaulet before she bobbed a curtsy—neither the obeisance of a servant nor the showiness of an aristocrat, but the shade of salutation he'd grown to recognize as unique for American women of the merchant class. Bemused at her absence of airs, he bowed, followed by Spry. Then he introduced the two of them.

"Thank you, Lieutenant, for such a prompt response to my note—"

"Mama, look, I finished the birdhouse!" A ten-year-old girl skipped part way into the parlor with a little wooden birdhouse in one hand. When she caught sight of the two soldiers, her eyes widened, and she skidded to a halt. After a gasp, she ran behind her mother.

As one, the young men from the household took a step forward, closer to mother and daughter.

Anne Hooper extracted her daughter from behind her and looked her straight in the eye. "It's a beautiful birdhouse, Elizabeth, and I shall be delighted to help you select a tree for it in the yard. This moment, I must talk with these gentlemen. Wait for me outside the parlor with Dan and Rob."

The girl's gaze darted to the soldiers. "Yes, Mama." She curtsied and hurried out, followed by the two young men.

Anne Hooper shut herself into the parlor with Michael and Spry. If being enclosed with two enemy soldiers caused her fear, her face revealed none of it. For all her demureness, she possessed a spine of steel.

"Please be seated." She indicated a couch and sat across from them on a chair. "I heard yesterday that Julia Garrity has been missing since Saturday, and her husband had contacted Major Craig for assistance in locating her. I've known Julia for several years and am responding to Mrs. Duncan's request for information to assist your search."

Michael had asked for a credible lady, and the widow of a loyalist had referred him to the wife of one of the fifty-six signers of the Declaration. While he could conceive of several reasons why Mrs. Hooper might lie to him, he could imagine no reason why Kate Duncan would do so, unless she were spying for the rebels, and he'd seen no evidence of that. He decided to trust Mrs. Duncan's judgment. "Thank you, Mrs. Hooper. What information do you have for us?"

She hesitated, as if selecting what to say. "Julia is a gregarious woman who delights in the high events of society." Humor brushed her lips. "She would probably be ecstatic if there were a ball or party every week in Wilmington. Her husband is focused on his business and trying to provide for her. He couldn't care less about society. They are, I fear, sadly mismatched."

Her lips parted and shut a few times, as if groping for words. "I'm worried for her, and so I must trust that you are discreet with what I'm about to tell you. In October, she visited me at Finian, the family estate southeast of town, and told me she'd begun a liaison with a fellow named Paul Greene."

Michael's shoulders straightened, his interest keen. *Your General Greene*, the note had read. This Paul Greene fellow certainly thought the world of himself, borrowing the rank of Nathanael Greene.

"I counseled her against it for a number of reasons, but she pursued the relationship and seemed to enjoy herself." Disapproval tensed Mrs. Hooper's lips. "And she enjoyed cuckolding her husband. Two weeks ago, she told me that she and Mr. Greene had discussed leaving town together. I advised her against doing so. I strongly suspect that she ran off with him Saturday, during the confusion of the day." She sighed as if divested of a heavy load and sat back on the couch, brown eyes soft with concern.

Michael listened to the fire's song and the silence of Anne Hooper for a moment. "Madam, thank you for the confidence you've expressed in us. You have our assurance that we shall treat your information with great discretion. In the course of our inquiries, we have already encountered references to Mr. Greene and his liaison with Mrs. Garrity. The question of their departing town together, as you suggested, is relevant.

"However, one fact leads us to believe that perhaps they didn't do so. If Mrs. Garrity were to leave town with a paramour, we'd expect her to pack a valise or portmanteau, yes? But the Garritys' housekeeper claims that none of her mistress's clothing is missing, and the portmanteau and valise are still in the house. Knowing what you know of Mrs. Garrity, can you provide an explanation for why she left in such a great hurry that she didn't even pack a change of clothing?"

The bob of Anne Hooper's head was vigorous. "Mr. Greene has friends among the Committee of Safety. It's no great secret that the committeemen were ill-prepared for the arrival of Major Craig. They left town at the last possible minute."

"Are you suggesting that Mr. Greene left with Colonel Young?"

"Yes. I suspect he did. They all departed in a great hurry Saturday morning, with almost no time to bid families farewell. Some didn't even pack a valise." She lowered her gaze to her lap for a moment, as if remembering her own circumstances, then tilted up her chin. "So you see why I think Julia may not have taken a change of clothing."

For the sake of the lady in the chair opposite him, he inclined his head in agreement. The theory of a rushed departure fit with the context of the note, but something still nagged him about the note itself. "By now, you've no doubt heard the news that Major Craig scattered the militia posted at Heron's Bridge. Do you believe Mr. Greene was among that militia?"

Mrs. Hooper pressed a hand to her heart. "I—I don't know. Oh, heaven, what if Mr. Greene took her into a battle situation?"

"For her sake, I hope he did not. Some of Young's militiamen were killed in the action."

She gulped. "Julia mentioned to me that he has property in Craven County, near New Berne. Perhaps they went there. According to her, he also has money and is able to provide for her comfort."

If Paul Greene had the funds to supply his mistress with a new wardrobe, Julia Garrity may very well have run off with him Saturday morning on a whim, minus a change of clothing. "Where is this property near New Berne?"

Again, she shook her head. "I don't have more detail. I wish I did."

Michael didn't relish the thought of riding several days to New Berne and combing the area for the property of Paul Greene, especially when he had no strong evidence that Julia Garrity had fled there. Surely he could unearth more productive leads in Wilmington. "Can you provide me with a description of Mr. Greene?"

"I've never met him. Julia said he has light brown hair and blue eyes, a longish face, and a sort of crooked nose. And he's tall and lanky, not stout, like her husband."

Her description sounded like the fellow in the charcoal sketch and the "handsome entertainment" of Salome Ward's fancy. "What is his business?"

She flicked one hand. "I don't know. Julia likes to be mysterious sometimes."

"Have you received any messages from her since she disappeared?"

"No."

"Contact me immediately if you do or if you remember anything else that Mrs. Garrity may have told you about Mr. Greene."

"I will. Find her for us, Mr. Stoddard."

"I shall do my best, madam." At his glance to Spry, they both rose. "Thank you for your time."

She preceded them to the front door, then opened it and eyed Michael up and down. "I must say, you aren't at all how I thought you'd be."

His eyebrows lifted. "And what did you imagine?"

"I was certain you'd question me over my husband." Her word "question" had a biting inflection, as if she'd meant to say the word "torture." She angled her chin a fraction, her gaze never leaving his.

Michael exhaled annoyance. "Mrs. Hooper, Major Craig charged me with protecting the safety of Wilmington's civilians. I'm trying to locate a missing woman who lives down the street from you. I've found no indication that your husband was involved in her disappearance. I don't need to question you about Mr. Hooper." He bowed, unrepentant over the frost his tone had carried. "Good day."

Chapter Eleven

OUTSIDE, MICHAEL'S BREATH huffed with exasperation. Less ruffled, Spry caught up with him as they strode out into the street, headed for the gunsmith's house. "They're watching us from the windows right now, sir. Expected us to pinch the silver, I wager."

Michael bared his teeth. "Sack and pillage, time-honored traditions of our brethren in uniform."

"You cannot blame her, sir. You're probably the first redcoat she's ever met who has manners."

"Manners." Michael snorted. "All right. From Mrs. Hooper's account, Mrs. Garrity as much as admitted that she planned to run away Saturday with her paramour."

Spry regarded him. "Sir, can we trust Mrs. Hooper? She's a rebel, the wife of a signer."

Trust. Michael rolled his head from side to side, trying to loosen neck muscles. His instincts again insisted that he should trust the witness Mrs. Duncan had chosen. "Mrs. Hooper believes that what she told us is true."

"Ah!" Spry's eyes glinted. "You aren't convinced that Mrs. Garrity ran away, are you, sir?"

"I feel like I'm missing something, Spry, and it has to do with that note we found near Chipper's grave. Maybe we should inspect the Garritys' back yard again, and—"

"Hullo, Mr. Stoddard?" A woman's voice called from behind them. "Are you Lieutenant Stoddard, the investigator?"

He and Spry turned about in the street. A gig approached them, its driver a plump brunette. When she pulled the gig up beside them, Michael took in her features: early thirties, pretty face taut with concern. The quality of her wool cloak and leather driving gloves bespoke her as one of Wilmington's more prosperous merchants. He gave her a perfunctory nod. "Good morning. Yes, I'm Lieutenant Stoddard. How may I help you, madam?"

She looked him over and laughed, short. "My goodness, Mrs. Duncan was correct. You *do* have an honest face."

In his peripheral vision, Michael saw Spry smile at him. Recalling the way his assistant had teased him the night before, he made sure his expression was professional. "Did Mrs. Duncan send you to me?"

"Oh, yes, and I've been driving around town in search of you. I'm Mrs. Richard Farrell. My husband is the tobacconist at Market and Second. I must speak with you."

Richard Farrell. Tobacconist. Michael's eyes widened, and he and Spry traded glances. This lady was Alice Farrell, the sister of that owlish astronomer nine miles south of town, the woman those rebels had been calling for when they attacked the estate—and Michael had completely forgotten to check on her well-being. "I'm pleased to make your acquaintance, Mrs. Farrell. I had the good fortune to meet your brother, Mr. Carlisle, on Sunday morning."

She frowned. "You met Godfrey? How did that happen?" Her gloved hand rose briefly to her lips. "Oh, no. Is he all right?"

"Well, we—"It would be both ungentlemanly and unnecessary for Michael to tell her the details. He puffed out his chest and cleared his throat. "My patrol and I chased a group of rebels off your husband's estate."

Her eyes widened, and she placed her hand above her heart. "R-Rebels? Are you sure they were r-rebels?"

Spry chimed in. "Oh, yes, and great cowards, too. Took one look at our bayonets and fled."

"Everyone at the house is safe, madam, including Mr. Carlisle."

"And your brother tells us that he's found a new comet." Spry grinned.

Mrs. Farrell's laugh wobbled with uncertainty, then her shoulders sagged. "Thank you. The—uh—post has been disrupted for a few days. We'd worried about him."

"Holding his own against the stars, madam." Michael gave her a nod. "So you wish to speak with me. Is this in reference to a crime that's been committed?"

Her brow puckered, and her attention flicked away. "Uh—well—uh—" She clenched her hands, trapping the reins between them.

Her need didn't sound pressing, and there were people to be questioned there on Third Street. "I shall be glad to visit you at the tobacco shop after noon today or early on the morrow."

She whipped her gaze back around to his, the bloom faded from her cheeks. "N-No. Oh, no. This afternoon we've stock to unload at the shop. The morrow is the first of February and thus may be too late." She grimaced and lowered her voice. "This is about the missing woman, Julia Garrity, and that—that vicar of the Bethanys."

Michael felt his expression freeze. Mrs. Garrity and Mr. Spivey in the same sentence, and not for the first time. "Very well. Where shall we talk? My assistant Spry and I have a full schedule this morning. Accept my apologies in advance that we must make this brief."

"Then meet me at the tobacco shop straight away. The apprentices won't arrive for another half hour." Biting her lip, she snapped the reins for her horse, and the gig clattered toward Market Street.

Moments later, when Michael and Spry arrived at the tobacco shop, identified as such by the figure of an Indian painted upon the swinging board in the front, Mrs. Farrell was out back with the horse and gig. The soldiers mounted steps to the porch and waited for the tobacconist's wife to open the front door. Michael glanced at his watch and leaned elbows on the wooden rail to study the passersby on Market Street.

A post-chaise driven by a Negro in a homespun wool coat and breeches pulled up before the office of a land agent next door. As soon as he halted the vehicle, the short, tubby man jumped out to assist the exit of the sole occupant, a willowy woman in a wool cloak and ribboned hat. Then he climbed back into the vehicle to wait for her.

Michael walked to the nearest edge of the tobacconist's porch, intrigued by the liquid movements of the lady as she ascended the steps to the agent's office. Spry scuffed over to join him. Then Mrs. Farrell opened the front door of her shop. "Do come in, gentlemen." She spotted the woman next door and stepped out onto her porch for a wave. "Good morning, Mrs. Delacroix."

Her gloved hand already on the door handle, the other woman turned and nodded with grace. "Good morning, Mrs. Farrell."

So that was Esmé Delacroix, the "witch" from Saint Domingue. In that first instant, the English culture bred into Michael's brain stodgily judged her too tall and gangly for beauty, like a fruit tree never pruned and gone leggy. In the next moment, his blood vibrated to the Caribbean rhythm that drenched her voice, and leapt at the smooth, radiant rum-gold of her skin, the eyes and hair the color of dark chocolate—long hair braided down her back like a sinuous stream in a jungle.

She vanished into the office of the land agent. Michael blinked, then shook his head. Woolgathering. The head cold must still be scrambling his brains. Yet he spotted a semi-daze in Spry's expression, too.

Mrs. Farrell sighed. "Poor dear. She's been trying to sell her property since last summer, when her husband died, so she can move back to Saint Domingue. But housing sales are down, and she's stuck here. Imagine how wretched, being trapped in a country not your own, unable to return to your kin. Oh, bother my prattle, Lieutenant. You're in a hurry. Do come in."

Just inside the door, the smell of cured tobacco greeted Michael's nose, along with the more elusive scents of molasses, vanilla, lemon and verbena, and bergamot. As his eyes adjusted to the dimness, he saw shelves filled with snuffboxes and clay pipes, rolls of thread tobacco, earthen crocks of snuff, and boxes of cheroots. His gaze shifted around. Mrs. Farrell had placed three stools to one side of the showroom. Sitting on one of them, her face placid and her back straight, was Kate Duncan.

His eyes widened. "Mrs. Duncan, I wasn't expecting—" He glanced at Mrs. Farrell, then back to her.

"Good morning to you, too, Mr. Stoddard. And you, Spry." She pursed her lips at him—full lips, just as Spry had reported the night before, and a rosy color that matched the hue of her wool polonaise gown. Spry's other observations of her had been accurate, too. A flush sprang from beneath Michael's neck stock and sparred with his earlobes. He must have been half-dead the day before to have not noticed how comely she was.

He cleared his throat and swung his attention back to Mrs. Farrell. "Madam, I received the impression that you wished to speak with me privately."

The tobacconist's wife took a seat on the stool beside Mrs. Duncan and, for a second, tilted her head toward her. "I asked her to be here with me." She tapped the empty stool in invitation, then folded her hands in her lap.

Without another word, Michael settled upon the remaining stool and faced her. Behind his right shoulder, Spry took up position.

Fine lines around Mrs. Farrell's eyes contracted, giving her a haunted look. "In December, when Spivey first opened the doors to his church, many people from Wilmington rode out to attend services. They were curious about the Bethanys. Mrs. Garrity and her sister were among those who attended services several times."

Michael's attention perked. Earlier that day, Salome Ward claimed she hadn't seen her sister since October. His suspicions had been aroused even then that she was lying. Why had she lied?

"It doesn't surprise me that Mrs. Garrity and Miss Ward went to those services, Lieutenant. The Bethanys claim to have women among their clergy. The Ward sisters have always been outspoken on the innate abilities of women. And neither of them is particularly easy on men."

Now that was an understatement. Michael tried to imagine Julia Garrity or Salome Ward serving others in a clerical capacity. The picture refused to come together in his head. "Did they join the congregation?"

"I don't know. However they did visit more than once."

He searched for another angle. "Is the name Paul Greene familiar to either of you?" Both women shook their heads. "Mrs. Farrell, what else can you tell me about the Bethanys?"

"Townsfolk have returned from the sermons with stories about women who wash the feet of congregants as part of the service." A sneer plucked at her lip. "These women are considered Spivey's special handmaidens, authorized by the church to minister to laypeople. So in addition to being trained in ministry, they wash feet."

Michael had attended the Anglican Church until he'd grown bored of all the black and white at age sixteen. The permutation of backcountry folk religion in America baffled him. One thing was certain, though. Elijah Spivey was no Anglican vicar. "Does Mr. Spivey wash feet?"

"Oh, yes. During the service held the final Wednesday of the month—that would be tonight's service—he supposedly consecrates new handmaidens by washing their feet. Then he sends them out into the congregation to wash the feet of others, singing hymns while they do it."

Weird as it was, the mental image of hymn singing females stroking the glistening feet of congregants fired Michael's blood and nudged his groin. Only in America could an entire religious movement be founded upon an act mentioned in but a few passages of the New Testament, in the books of Luke and John, in which people washed each other's feet with oil, tears, or water. He heard Spry clear his throat, as if with incredulity. "Is Mr. Spivey the only one who's allowed to wash the feet of these handmaidens?"

"Yes."

"Not an equitable arrangement." Michael's memory merrily populated the slippery footwashing fantasy with a selection of young ladies from his past. Then, impatient with the intrusion from memory, he refocused his attention on Mrs. Farrell. "What do you think of his church?"

Her expression hardened, and she spat her words. "I haven't visited. I know Elijah Spivey. When I was fifteen, he had his cap set on me, even though I'd met my Richard by then and fallen in love. I told Spivey I wasn't interested in him, but—" The pace of her words slowed. "Sometimes, I'd catch him following me home from market." Her voice lowered in volume, as if molasses had trapped her tongue. "Or watching me from across the street."

Her gaze dropped to her lap, but not before Michael noticed it brush over Spry. Again he marked the shadows on her face, almost gauntness. She had more information to divulge—personal information—but she struggled to voice it before two men, both total strangers. That was when he realized why Mrs. Duncan was there.

An honest face. Perhaps Alice Farrell would find her personal story easier to divulge if he were the only man in the room with her. He shifted on the stool, aimed his attention for the front door. "Spry, er—" He scratched behind his ear. "Who's the merchant on the other side of the land agent? Find out for me."

"This moment, sir?" Spry paused an entire two heartbeats. "Oh. Yes, sir."

Gratitude over Spry's discernment eased from between Michael's lips in a quiet stream of breath. Mrs. Farrell's gaze tracked the private to the door. Some of the tension about her eyes faded when the door closed on his exit.

Michael relaxed his shoulders and placed palms on his thighs, hoping to project receptivity. Mrs. Farrell picked a piece of lint off her gown, licked her lips, and smoothed wrinkles in her petticoat. He waited.

"There was a fall festival." She brought her gaze to meet his. "A group of us rode in a hay wagon. Richard was home abed with a cold. Several girls my age had come, along with some boys. And Spivey. I didn't pay him much mind, as we were singing and passing around some cider." She averted her face and rubbed her upper arms, as if cold. "We were just enjoying ourselves, as young people will do. The fathers of three girls were in the wagon with us, so I felt safe."

Michael flicked his gaze to Kate Duncan. She sat relaxed, lips parted, brow smooth. Her torso was angled to the woman beside her, to shore her up. Mrs. Farrell had chosen her Second well.

Mrs. Farrell rubbed the back of her neck. "I-I've never been sure what happened. The cider became brandy. I-I began to feel sleepy, even though I didn't drink much brandy b-because it had a strange taste to it." She squirmed on the stool and studied her lap, where her hands twisted and tugged. "Spivey and another boy and girl offered to walk me home." She blinked around a shimmer of tears. After taking a deep breath, she clenched her fists. "S-so hard to remember. It's almost not like a memory, but a dream instead, v-very f-foggy, as if it didn't happen." She sucked in a breath. "But afterwards, there could be no doubt."

It sounded like laudanum or something else had tainted Mrs. Farrell's brandy. Michael swallowed. Kate Duncan, the inner edges of her eyebrows pinched upward with empathy, had leaned a few inches closer to the tobacconist's wife.

Mrs. Farrell's voice wavered. "The other boy and girl vanished." A tear inched down her cheek. "I-I remember lying on my back in the cold grass, and Spivey's hand was beneath my petticoat. I remember him delivering me home that night. The next morning, there was blood on my shift, but—but I didn't remember being hurt. "She hugged herself." I—I know what must have happened that night." More tears slid down her cheeks, and she dashed them away. "I j-just cannot remember. Thank heaven I didn't end up with child because of it! And thank heaven Spivey told no one. I'd have heard of it by now if he had." She hung her head and wept. Mrs. Duncan's hand went to her shoulder, then rubbed her back.

Michael's lips pressed together. Elijah Spivey was a predator. He'd stalked Mrs. Farrell and consumed her innocence.

Innocence. Consumed. Memory groped at him from ten years past: dusty summer twilight coating the inside of Lord Crump's mews, and the falcons settled for the night. Lydia shook out her curly blonde hair and leaned against the doorjamb, blocking the exit. Fingers of her left hand toyed with the loosened neckline of her silk shift, and the gold shimmer of her wedding band wove a figure eight above her gown's bodice in the gloom. *There you are, my pet! How I've missed you since last summer. Time for a new lesson in love...*

Michael slammed back the memory and wiped his palms, suddenly sweaty, on his trousers. A hell of a time to think of Lydia. Dwelling on her was never productive. Yet the parallel was obvious.

He returned his attention to the woman sitting before him, who'd paused in her lamentation. Mrs. Farrell had no clear memory of the incident. There had been no pregnancy. And Spivey hadn't gossiped about the deed. That meant no criminal charges could come of the episode. The injustice of it scorched Michael's gut, made him understand the delicacy and respect that Mrs. Farrell was due. He said low, "Did Mr. Spivey press his attentions upon you after that incident?"

"Oh, yes, more than ever." A snarl caught her lips. "But I was certain to never again be alone with him. Richard finally threatened him, and he ceased bothering me." She sniffed. "A few months later, he left North Carolina."

"Have you told your husband of the incident following the hay ride?"

She gave him a sharp look. "No. Do you think me a fool? Richard and I are very happy."

He wondered whether her secrecy was a mistake, but he didn't say so. "Has Mr. Spivey contacted you since he returned to town?"

"Oh, dear God!" She bit her lower lip and swiveled away from both Michael and Mrs. Duncan. "I cannot. I cannot!" She shook with fresh sobs.

Mrs. Duncan wrapped her arms about her in a brief hug, then worked a handkerchief into the woman's tight fist. "It's all right. I'm here for you, Alice. You can trust Mr. Stoddard. But if there's more to this nightmare, you need to tell him everything. Maybe he can keep another woman from being hurt. That is why you broke your silence after all these years, isn't it?"

Still sobbing, Mrs. Farrell nodded. While she blotted her eyes and sought control, Michael studied her "Second." *You can trust Mr. Stoddard.* Mrs. Duncan spoke up for him after having talked with him for less than a quarter-hour the previous night—and how had such trust come about? Warmth fluttered in his chest.

After a minute or so, Mrs. Duncan straightened on her stool, and Mrs. Farrell sniffed a few more times. Her shoulders sagged, and she wrung the handkerchief in her lap. "Last Wednesday, early, Spivey came in when no one else was here. He invited me to church, said he wanted me for his handmaiden." Her expression screwed up. "I told him to leave and never return. He said he'd pray for me. For *us.*

"Why not leave the past alone? I never wished to see him again." The pitch of her voice hiked. "For a week, I have relived all those foul pieces of memories. They haunt my sleep, and—and, my God, what if he tells Richard what happened? I cannot even remember most of it!"

The word "it" echoed in the shop before it faded. Michael sat in silence with Mrs. Farrell's pain like hot grapeshot in his heart. His tone softened. "Madam, what happened to you was deplorable."

She blotted her eyes and face with the handkerchief, unable to meet his gaze. "I—I suspect he's done something of the sort to others. He's attracted to women with dark hair and dark eyes. I've heard that his 'handmaidens' all have dark hair and dark eyes."

Women with the features of Julia Garrity and Salome Ward.

"I doubt they're all participating willingly. He serves wine at his services, and—" Mrs. Farrell winced.

Elijah Spivey sounded like a worthless addition to the Wilmington community: plying women with drugged wine and taking advantage of them while they were insensate. Michael would love to see him sharing Gabriel Garrity's jail cell. But where religion was involved, he must make certain that his case was solid. Otherwise, his actions would come across as religious persecution. The colonists, particularly rebels, owned Jesus in a way that Anglicans simply couldn't fathom.

Michael glanced between the two women and kept his tone soothing. "I don't wish to presume, but do either of you know whether Mr. Spivey is married?"

Mrs. Farrell's features rippled, and she finally looked at him again. "Hah! You might say he has a congregation full of wives."

"I told you he was a lizard," said Mrs. Duncan, her chin hiked.

Mrs. Farrell sneered. "He's just like one of those sheikhs from Arabia."

Teal would laugh at such a comparison. Why did Spivey need to be married when he could rabbit his way amongst the womenfolk, extending to them the carrot of priesthood? He caught Mrs. Farrell's eye. "Madam, I appreciate how difficult this must have been for you to speak with me today, and I thank you for coming forward with the information. Your timing is excellent. I'd planned for a patrol from the Eighty-Second to attend the service tonight anyway, just to see what it's about. But now we've something specific to look for."

Her shoulders hunched. "Be careful, Mr. Stoddard. Spivey commands a gang of about twenty henchmen."

Twenty. That was the number of men that his patrol had chased off the Farrell estate—and those men had been calling for Alice Farrell. A chill found the base of his skull. "Thank you for the warning, madam. Until I resolve these issues with Mr. Spivey, I'd like you to remain in the safety of Wilmington and not venture back down to your estate." She nodded. "And if he bothers you again, notify me immediately. My assistant and I are staying on Second Street, at the home of Mrs. Chiswell."

"Oh, yes, sir." She pointed to Kate. "She told me that. And—and there's one more detail I need to make sure you know. He's bothering Mrs. Delacroix, too."

Michael stiffened, recalling Mrs. Overton's talk of Spivey ridding the area of a witch. "Bothering, as in unwanted affection, or threats of bodily harm?"

Mrs. Farrell shrugged. "She's been a customer of ours for many years. We talk about odds and ends when she comes in. Two weeks ago, she purchased a small quantity of unflavored tobacco, as she does regularly. I believe she uses it to honor her spirits—"

"Her spirits? One moment. Are you saying that Mrs. Delacroix practices witchcraft?"

Mrs. Duncan rolled her eyes. Mrs. Farrell dismissed the notion with a wave of her hand. "No more so than the Indians do. They burn tobacco in their religious ceremonies. It must be sacred in Saint Domingue, as it is with the Indians here. But while she was in, she mentioned a heightened eagerness to sell her property because Spivey had ridden to her house, pressuring her to join the Bethanys. He apparently acted in a way that caused her to call upon the assistance of a man-slave and evict Spivey from her house.

"Next morning, she found a wooden cross posted in her front yard, about four feet tall, painted with red letters that spelled 'Christ Jesus' and 'salvation.' If Spivey is behind that, he must be stopped, Lieutenant. Not everyone in this town subscribes to his flavor of faith. Who might he mark next for persecution?"

"We'll see what we can do."

Kate Duncan cocked her ear toward the back of the store, then rose and carried her stool to the counter. Michael heard what she'd detected; in the rear of the store, apprentices had arrived and were shuffling around. Mrs. Farrell dabbed at her eyes again and allowed Michael to assist her to her feet. "You're such a good man."

Guileless, too. Never would he scheme to murder a fellow officer. He smiled with a flash of teeth. "What time do Wednesday evening services begin?"

"Five o'clock."

"And what is Mr. Spivey's appearance?"

"Almost your assistant's height, but with a good deal less meat on his bones. My age. Blond hair, balding quickly." Derision heated her laugh. "Almost like Benjamin Franklin's hair."

Just as randy as Franklin, if what Michael had heard about him were true. From the back of the store, a man's affable voice called out. "Alice, you in here?"

"Yes, darling, I'll be right there." With haste, Mrs. Farrell shoved the handkerchief in her pocket and showed Michael to the door.

From the porch, he spotted Spry returning from a walk down the street. He swiveled back to Mrs. Farrell. "What is the direction to Mrs. Delacroix's house?"

"About four miles from town off the Sound Road. The drive to her property is off to the right of the road. If you reach Finian, William Hooper's estate on the Sound, you've ridden too far." The corners of her mouth lifted. "Thank you, Mr. Stoddard."

Chapter Twelve

MRS. DELACROIX'S POST-CHAISE had departed during the meeting in the tobacco shop. Although Michael hadn't expected the Frenchwoman to wait around for his questions, the day was growing more hectic, and missing an opportunity to speak with her added to his busyness. He scuffed down the porch steps and met Spry at the bottom.

"We've a tinsmith and a shoemaker on the other side of the land agent, sir." His assistant eyed the front door of the tobacconist's shop before lowering the volume of his voice for Michael. "And sir, Mrs. Delacroix rode off two minutes ago looking mighty worried."

Michael matched Spry's low tones. "That isn't good. Mrs. Farrell told me that Mrs. Delacroix recently repulsed Mr. Spivey's unwanted affections with the aid of her slave man. There's also some sort of connection between Mr. Spivey and the Ward sisters, Julia and Salome. And years ago, Mr. Spivey forced unwanted physical contact upon Mrs. Farrell, assisted by drugged brandy. Apparently, he hankers in a most ungentlemanly fashion after women with dark hair and dark eyes. Plus—" Michael sighed, hard. "—those men we chased off the Farrell estate Sunday were likely Mr. Spivey's henchmen."

Spry's mouth made an "o." "I take it he isn't Anglican, sir."

"A slug wearing a collar is more Anglican."

"Yes, sir."

Michael counted off the connection on his fingers. "Mr. Spivey and Mrs. Delacroix. Mr. Spivey and Mrs. Farrell. Mr. Spivey and the Ward sisters." Possibly Gabriel Garrity fit into this mess, too. He pondered the door of the land agent's office. "You said Mrs. Delacroix looked worried when she left a few minutes ago. Let's see what we can learn about her visit from that agent."

They walked next door, entered the office, and halted just inside the doorway in surprise. Boxes and papers were strewn over the floor. Some of the papers looked like pages from contracts. Had Esmé Delacroix done this?

At the front counter, a sallow, bewigged man in his late thirties was sanding a transaction entry in a journal, his movements jerky, his lips pressed together so hard they were pale. Michael closed the door and avoided stepping on papers. "Good morning, sir."

"I don't care who you are or what you want." From behind the counter, the bewigged man blasted them with an expression of loathing. "You walk right back out that door. Animals! Haven't you already harassed me enough this morning? It'll be days before I have my listings back in order!"

In an instant, Michael understood what had transpired. Even though the agent had surrendered on Sunday and been paroled, he'd been identified as a rebel sympathizer, his business marked by Major Craig for special monitoring. Soldiers had come calling first thing in the morning to sniff around. The agent had resisted them, with predictable results.

"Are you deaf? I said get out of here. Leave me alone!"

His attitude invited plenty more inspections from the Eighty-Second. Michael motioned Spry forward, and together they approached the counter. "A little cooperation might ease the scrutiny on you—"

"Cooperation—after all this? Kiss my arse!"

"No, thank you. I'm Major Craig's investigator, Lieutenant Stoddard. This is my assistant, Spry. Whom do I have the pleasure of meeting?"

The agent sneered. "Criminal investigator. Oh, yes, I've heard all about you." Lace fluttered at his wrists as he stashed the journal on a shelf below, out of their reach, and he kept his hands out of sight. "Come to arrest me, have you? I'm a neutral. A good number of us are neutrals in this town. Do you plan to arrest everyone who doesn't bow and scrape to King George? Won't be much of a town left, if you do."

Michael didn't like the way he kept his hands fidgety beneath the counter. What was he hiding back there? Did he have a weapon? With a slight motion of his head, he indicated for Spry to ease around one end of the counter while he ambled around the other end. "I haven't come to arrest you. Not this moment, at least. Mrs. Delacroix just visited you. What was the nature of her business?"

The agent snarled at him. "A client confidentiality agreement prevents my divulging that information. And no one except employees is permitted in this area. Stay out."

Michael continued straight for him, stopping less than two feet away. The view allowed him to confirm that the man wasn't hiding a weapon below the counter. "We're investigating a criminal action. That renders your confidentiality agreement void."

The agent's snarl deepened. "Mr. Stoddard, is it? Well, I don't recognize Major Craig's authority to investigate actions, criminal or otherwise. And you cannot simply stomp in here, demand information, and expect to get it. I value my clients' business."

He truly was an ass. With casual interest, Michael glanced around, caught Spry's attention. The three of them were alone in the office. "Perhaps it hasn't occurred to you that a vitriolic attitude makes you appear more culpable."

"'Vitriolic attitude.'" The agent mimicked Michael's accent while spanking dust off a sleeve of his velvet suit. "Look at the mess all over my office. I was civil to those soldiers. But you don't want cooperation. You're barbarians."

His lips pursed. "Do you expect an innocent civilian to watch his business be vandalized without developing a vitriolic attitude?"

The man's pent-up fury created a charge in the air, like the crackle of a keg of black powder, just before it blows. Michael relaxed, alert. "What makes you think the Eighty-Second doesn't want your cooperation?"

The agent's hands compressed to fists at his sides. A vein bulged at his temple, and he leaned toward Michael, lips clear of his teeth. "Because you brutes enjoy arresting and abusing civilians!" A fist shot out.

Michael's forearm deflected the punch for his jaw. He pounced on the agent, twisted one arm behind his back, and shoved him facedown upon the counter. The older man tried to writhe away, like a bass on a fishhook. "Calm yourself, sirrah!" Spry closed in, ready to assist, but Michael had pinned the side of the agent's face on the counter, skewing his wig. "You can forget about jail. You're withholding information and impeding a criminal investigation. That'll earn you space on a prison ship. Is that your choice?"

"Let go of me! You're ruining my coat! What the hell do you want from me, you dog?"

"Mrs. Delacroix placed her property for sale through your office. Her safety may be compromised. Out with it. Why did she visit you this morning?"

"To—to see whether there were interested parties. Ow, you're hurting my nose! I think it's bleeding!"

"Not yet." Struggling with the effort to keep him pinned, Michael jammed the man's nose to the counter. "You're as eager as she for the money from a sale. If there were any interested parties, you'd rush out to her house to tell her, not wait for her to come to you. Now, let's have the real reason for her visit, or I turn this big fellow loose on you."

"She lowered the sale price of her property."

"Why?"

"Ow! Wanted to sell it faster!"

He gave his arm a wrench. "Why?"

"Didn't feel safe in Wilmington!" The agent sobbed. "Owwwww!" Michael hauled him up, heaved him away, and backed around to the front of the counter, where Spry joined him. The agent regained his balance and fingered his face with indignation, dark hair frizzed out from beneath his wig. "You broke something inside my nose!"

Michael would have loved to oblige him. Instead, he straightened his coat. "On behalf of His Majesty King George, we thank you for your cooperation in this investigation."

"You bastards, throwing your weight around, I'm going to take this up with Major Craig."

"Be my guest. Splendid of you to recognize Major Craig's authority. Good day."

"Rot in hell!"

Not until he and Spry had reached Market Street, on their way back to the Garritys' house, did Michael's blood cease simmering from the altercation. He hadn't exactly set the best example for Spry on how to gain a civilian's cooperation. In fact, the show of physical force more suited Fairfax's personality. The comparison hiked his irritation, cranked an edge to his voice. "Did that pustule ever take aim on us?"

Spry sounded pleased. "Hasn't got the stones for it, sir. Why didn't you arrest him? He was asking for it."

"Because a man who's all hot air and no stones would delight in playing the martyr behind bars while his attorney pesters Major Craig hourly. The last place that agent wants to be is submitting to business inspections and intrusions, day after day, from 'animals.' So I'll make sure that he gets more inspections this winter than a dog has fleas in the summer."

Spry chuckled, then sobered. "Mrs. Delacroix's situation is unenviable, sir. It sounds as though the only way she'll have enough money to return home is by selling property. And for certain, the disorder she found in her agent's office didn't bolster her confidence that it would happen."

"No one is investing in land right now. Everyone is waiting for conditions to improve."

"She has the look that Mr. Spivey fancies, sir. Dark hair, dark eyes."

"Yes, I admit to concern for her. We shall pay her a visit this afternoon."

"Sir, do you supposed that when Mrs. Delacroix spurned the preacher, it infuriated him into labeling her a witch?"

"Could be. 'Nor hell a fury like a randy preacher scorned.'" Michael drew out his watch, checked the time, and sighed, fretful. He needed about six extra hours in the day.

"If Miss Ward's story is true, sir, Mrs. Delacroix and Mr. Garrity are having an affair. But I don't see how tubby, freckled Mr. Garrity is any improvement for Mrs. Delacroix over a scrawny preacher without a decent head of hair."

"Perhaps the lady will enlighten us as to the selection process employed by the fairer sex."

Spry scratched his head. "Yes, sir. I don't understand that process."

Without mirth, Michael laughed. "Not to worry. Half of humanity puzzles over it." And two or three years earlier, he'd finally stopped puzzling over it himself, given up wondering *why*. Why a married woman seven years his senior, the wife of a visiting nobleman, had sneaked from the manor every evening during the summers of his fifteenth and sixteenth years to tumble with Master Stoddard, Lord Crump's falcon handler.

"When are you going to speak with Mr. Garrity and Miss Ward again, sir?"

"When they've sat in jail long enough to be truthful with me. While Mrs. Farrell talked to us, did you pick up on the fact that Miss Ward lied earlier about when she'd last seen her sister?"

After pondering a moment, Spry snapped his fingers. "Bust my buttons. Yes, sir, Miss Ward said October, but Mrs. Farrell said December."

"Exactly. Any guesses why Miss Ward lied?"

Spry cocked an eyebrow. "No, sir, but I cannot imagine Mrs. Garrity or Miss Ward washing feet. Maybe their interest in the preacher is about something other than religion."

Michael fervently hoped Major Craig didn't return before he'd resolved the absurd, dangling ends on the two investigations. Or were they two halves of one investigation?

As if reading his thoughts, Spry said, "Sir, I cannot help but wonder whether Mr. Spivey knows something about Mrs. Garrity's disappearance."

"Intriguing to ponder that sort of connection." Michael mused. "I wonder about something else. Surely Mr. Spivey allows men to hold positions in his church. Is Paul Greene one of his elders? Wardens?" Exasperation hissed from him. "What title does he give to men in service to his church?"

His assistant eyed him, all innocence. "Minions?"

The pun elicited a groan from Michael. "You're wasted in the Army, Spry. You should take up juggling—"

"And become a fool, yes, sir. My older brother has often told me so."

"All right, your next career, then. Meanwhile, the Bethanys' service starts at five—" They took the corner onto Third Street. "—so I plan for us to arrive early, while we've daylight to look around, question the preacher, and—hullo, there, what's Master Overton's rush?"

Ben Overton, son of the Garritys' housekeeper, was scampering in their direction. The boy waved his hands and put on a burst of speed. "Come quickly!" He drew up before them panting, his expression distorted with alarm. "My mother. Not well. Locked herself in the house." He took a deep breath. "She's got a loaded pistol. She may hurt someone!"

Michael and Spry followed the youth. By the time they reached the Garritys' house, several neighbor women and their servants had clustered out front with hungry, curious faces, as if the house were a dock, and a Chinese junk full of silk and spice and sailors with almond-shaped eyes had just tied down there after being blown halfway around the world.

A middle-aged man in rough woolen breeches and coat stood at the front door. "Mrs. Overton." He knocked. "Come on, now, open the door for Sam." He knocked again and turned, perturbed, spotting the arrival of Michael and Spry.

Puffing, Ben told the soldiers, "That's Mr. Mayer, Mr. Garrity's driver." He gulped air, and his chest expanded. "Mr. Hiller the gardener went around back, tried to get in the door there, but—" He grabbed for another breath. "Mother's locked it, too."

"Mrs. Overton." Mayer faced the door and spread his hands. "I know you're listening. Come now, what harm have I ever done you? Let me in, please."

Michael, with Spry following, had passed the low fence into the yard when he noticed a drape on a window beside the door jerk aside. What looked like the barrel of a pistol pressed to the glass. Horror spiked his reflexes. "Take cover, everyone!" He leapt the fence and hit the dirt behind it, Spry half a second later. Glass shattered, and a pistol report preceded the whiz of a ball just above the fence near Michael's head. Gathered neighbors shrieked. Michael roared, "Get away, all of you!" People scattered.

"Shit!" Spry uncovered his head. "She fired a bloody pistol at us, sir!"

Mayer the driver jumped to their side of the fence, dragged an astounded Ben down out of sight, and hunkered near Michael. "What in hell is wrong with the woman?"

Ben moaned. "Mother. What's happened to my mother?"

Betty Overton's voice rang from within the house. "The witch was in town today! My mistress came to me in a dream last night and warned me to beware. The witch has cast a spell on you, Lieutenant Stoddard. You have been blinded! You have been cursed!"

Chapter Thirteen

NO ONE RESPONDED. The housekeeper's voice grew shrill. "Do you hear me? You have been cursed! And I know how to use this pistol, Mr. Stoddard!"

"Yes, I know you do," said Michael under his breath, his heart hammering.

"Christ Jesus," muttered Spry. "Does she want us to gather firewood and burn the witch, sir?"

Terrific. One day after Major Craig left town, Wilmington plummeted into the Inquisition. On his stomach, Michael rose, supported himself on his elbows for a look around. Alerted by the pistol shot and barking dogs on Third Street, neighbors previously unaware were meandering their way, curious. He had to keep them away, or someone might get shot. Plus a second middle-aged man had inched his way from around back of the house, for the time hidden from Mrs. Overton's sight. Hiller the gardener, no doubt.

Michael faced the house. "Mrs. Overton, your son is out here. So are Mr. Mayer and Mr. Hiller and your neighbors. I know you don't want to hurt any of them, so let's talk peacefully. Put the pistol down, and—"

The pistol presented at the window again. Heart smashing his ribcage, Michael ducked just before she sent another ball skimming the fence over his head. The second round of neighbors screamed and ran for cover.

"I won't speak with anyone who's under the witch's spell!"

Talons of terror scraped the inside of Michael's chest. The well-being of these civilians was his responsibility. Furthermore, a patrol of soldiers would arrive at any moment to investigate the pistol shots, giving Betty Overton more targets. How was he going to pull the fuse from this situation?

"What's this about a witch?" said Mayer. "Can she be blathering about Mrs. Delacroix? What does she have against her? I just drove Mrs. Garrity to visit her last Thursday afternoon."

"You did?" Startled from his indecision, Michael scrutinized the driver's face. His heart ceased thrashing about. What had happened during that visit?

Had Mrs. Garrity confronted Mrs. Delacroix with her husband's infidelity?

Mayer shifted, resituated himself. "Certainly." Odd. The driver didn't seem at all disturbed by the memory. Michael must question him about it. But not that moment.

The pistol waved in the front window. "Did you hear me, Mr. Stoddard?"

"Yes, Mrs. Overton." He studied what he could see of the Garritys' house and yard. "I completely understand your reluctance to consult with anyone who's influenced by a witch. But I need to talk with you, so tell me what I must do to convince you that a witch doesn't have me under a spell, and that I'm not blinded."

"You arrested Mr. Garrity and Miss Ward. You must release them from jail."

Mayer snorted. "Oh, good show, madam."

Spry said, "Checkmate, sir?"

When hell froze. Michael's temples throbbed with irritation. Lord Crump's gamekeeper used to play him in just such a manner. How he loathed being manipulated.

He tamed the wild thump in his veins and lowered his voice. "Spry, you and Master Overton herd neighbors into their houses until we resolve this. If a patrol from the regiment shows up, don't hesitate to use their help. Mr. Mayer, chat with Mrs. Overton. Keep her talking about household minutiae, going to market, cleaning the parlor—anything except witches and the Garritys."

Spry's face tensed. "And where are you going, sir?"

"Ostensibly, to let Mr. Garrity and Miss Ward out of jail. But I plan to come in through Fourth Street and see if I can get a window open—"

"Mr. Stoddard, there is no Fourth Street," said Ben, his expression and tone plaintive.

The lad was correct. Michael had forgotten how small the town was. "Well, then, I shall come in through the foliage beyond the back yard, gain entrance to the house while Mrs. Overton is talking with Mr. Mayer. Let's hope Mr. Hiller over there stays put until I've need of him."

Mayer's tone was dry. "In other words, you're lying to Betty, and I'm supposed to cover for you, all the while my employer remains in jail. Where's my next meal coming from? It's coming from that fellow you threw in jail this morning. God save the King, my arse."

Michael leveled a stony glare on him. "My first priority this moment is disarming that woman in there so she doesn't hurt anyone. Your civic duty is to assist me in that endeavor. If you don't comply, and she kills or injures someone, you're responsible." He watched sullen resignation supplant the man's impudence. "Now, any idea how many pistols she has?"

"No. I didn't know she had a pistol. You realize that she could have a few muskets, too. After all, Mr. Garrity is a gunsmith."

"Mr. Stoddard." Ben pressed his lips together briefly to stop their trembling. "Maybe she doesn't have but the one pistol, owned by my father. Mr. Garrity doesn't bring customers' firearms into the house, and he keeps his own two sets of pistols in a locked chest in his bedroom." The boy's eyes beseeched Michael. "Please don't hurt Mother. My father is long dead, and you've arrested my master. Mother's all I have left here."

"I shall do my best." Vulnerability tore at Michael: his own vulnerability,

Ben's, the neighbors'. He rolled to a crouch and elevated his voice. "Mrs. Overton, I accept your terms. I'm leaving now, headed to jail to fetch Mr. Garrity and Miss Ward. Don't shoot me when I stand. Otherwise, we shall resolve nothing."

Lightheaded with fear, legs trembling, he stood and presented his head and torso a target for the woman in the house. His movements slow and deliberate, he walked to the street, an even clearer mark, then headed back toward Market Street. He felt Mrs. Overton's gaze on him until the intervening houses blocked her view.

Relief had no opportunity to claim him. He almost ran into a patrol of soldiers, come to check on the pistol shot. Quickly he explained the situation, and he ordered them to take up posts as close to the house as possible while staying out of sight of the front window.

Then he strode to where Fourth Street would be, if Wilmington grew someday. Counting the backs of houses, he arrived at the Garritys' house. He scaled the fence without ripping his trousers and dropped into the Garritys' yard.

Skulking past their stable and Chipper's grave reminded him a bit of creeping through woods and hoping to catch Continental sentries off guard. He glimpsed the gardener hugging shadow at the side of the house. From out in front, he heard the driver rambling about having one of the horses on the team re-shod. Michael tiptoed to the back of the house, found the door barred from within, and tugged on each window. One slid up part way before it jammed. After stripping off his coat to prevent snagging buttons, he dropped it and his hat inside, exhaled, and squeezed himself into some sort of storage room beneath the staircase. Spry, all two hundred pounds of him, would never have made it through the space.

Coat and hat donned again, he padded to the door and inched it open to avoid a squeal of hinges. A few steps out, and he found himself before the barred back door at the opposite end of the foyer from Mrs. Overton, who knelt before the window she'd broken, peering out at Mayer and his babble, and clenching the pistol in her right hand. While her attention was occupied, he eased the bar off the door and set the plank of wood out of the way, on the floor.

From concealment beneath the stairs, he studied the fifteen feet that separated them, disheartened by a lack of cover except for a small table with a vase. His hands began trembling. Nothing for it but to proceed.

Halfway to her, still tiptoeing, Michael realized from the way her shoulders shook and she gasped air that she was weeping. Outside, Mayer was reminiscing about a Yule party more than ten years before. The woman's breathing became raspy. Michael sensed her husband had still been alive at the time. Not a good memory to elicit in her, but Mayer didn't realize that.

Horror tunneled through Michael and almost dissolved his knees when Mrs. Overton braced the barrel of the pistol against her temple. "Peter," she murmured. "Peter." Then her awareness shifted. She whipped about, her back braced against the front door, her eyes caverns of defeat, the pistol still poised at her temple. "Lieutenant, I—I cannot bear this anymore. I have failed."

Oh, damn, no. His chest tightened, and his gaze rooted to her twitchy trigger finger. "How?" He coughed, throat as dry as the King's Highway in

August. "How have you failed?"

She ground the pistol's barrel against her head. Her voice squeaked. "I cannot support myself and my child. I shall be cast out into the streets. No one wants to hire a poor widow."

Alas, too true. She knew the world was round. No way could he sugarcoat his response. He realized his toes were clenched in his boots, tried to relax them, thought of Ben's pathetic plea: *Don't hurt Mother...she's all I have left.* Gods, the world was brutal for people like them, people who, because of their meager finances, had little to look forward to in the future. "Madam, Mr. Garrity and Miss Ward should be arriving at any moment. I signed their release papers." He inched forward. A couple more feet, and he'd be able to jump for the pistol. "You'll be going back to work for Mr. Garrity. Please, give me the pistol."

"Better than living on the streets, I suppose." Her eyes grew glazed. The pistol wobbled in her hand.

The insight whacked him, then, and he wasn't sure why he hadn't put it together earlier, except that perhaps he'd needed to hear Mayer's declaration of fealty: *Where's my next meal coming from? It's coming from that fellow you threw in jail this morning.* These servants weren't loyal to the Garritys out of *love.* He shifted closer, trying not to dwell on what little effort it would cost her to blow *his* brains out at that proximity. "Do you know, that's just what Mr. Mayer told me out there earlier."

Her eyes regained a focal point, but the pistol remained at her temple. "Really? I didn't think he would talk about it."

"The Garritys don't appreciate any of their servants. They—they yell at you, don't they?" She nodded. "They never compliment you on the excellent work you do for them."

"No. Never."

"They just give you insults." Closer, closer.

"Yes."

"Especially you, a widow. They convinced you that your work is inferior, worth meager pay, and you cannot expect to find employment elsewhere." Michael extended his hand. "I know that pistol's heavy. Let me hold it for you while we talk, what do you say?" He saw the muscles in her hand relax a little, but confusion trapped her eyes again, and she firmed her grip on the weapon.

Keep talking. He retracted his arm. "Do you know, when Spry and I were in the parlor yesterday, there wasn't a speck of dust anywhere. I've never seen anything quite like it. It's as if there are two of you."

"I'm so tired all the time, I can hardly rise each morning—" She brooded, and he slipped in a few more inches. "Mayer and Hiller began talking about leaving in October. All the arguing between Mr. and Mrs. Garrity, and the way they would strike each other. The men both have prospects elsewhere. They're waiting for final word from their new employers. Then they'll leave together. Serves the Garritys right, having to hire a new driver and gardener at the same time while I'm still here, faithful Betty, mad Betty." Her lips quivered.

Michael wasn't surprised that the two men had planned leaps to new employment, but reinforcing that detail wouldn't help him reach Mrs. Overton. "October. That's when Mr. Garrity allowed his bulldog to kill Chipper."

Self-pity vanished. Her eyes filled with tears. "Poor little Chipper. So cute, so loving."

"I saw a sketch of him sitting in your lap. He looked comfortable there."

"Oh, yes. I've always wanted a dog like him. He knew it."

Michael detected greater relaxation in her wrist. Now. He lunged forward, slapped the pistol from her hand, and flattened her to the floor. She screeched and bucked beneath him, but he kept her pinned. And thanks to the excellent wax job she'd done on the floors, he was able to slide his leg out and kick the pistol well away from her reach.

"You're still under the witch's spell! She cast a spell on Mr. Garrity and slept with him, and now she has you in her clutches! Only Vicar Spivey can save you!"

"That's welcome news. Spry and I will be attending his service tonight." Stunned, she stopped struggling, giving him the opportunity to haul her to her feet, her wrists pinned together. He hollered out the broken window, "Spry, you there? Mr. Mayer, Mr. Hiller, I could use some help in here. Back door is open."

Footsteps pounded up the walkway, and he pulled the housekeeper away from the entrance, breathing heavily, excitement emptying his blood. "Indeed, madam, we're going to church tonight. I've heard so much about the good vicar that I cannot wait to meet him."

Chapter Fourteen

HILLER THE GARDENER hammered the first nail in a board over the broken foyer window. In the study, Michael pocketed the key to the Garritys' house and, from that room's window, watched Gabriel Garrity's physician drive off in his post-chaise, the Overtons his passengers. Spry and the soldiers from the morning's successful expedition to Garrity's warehouse escorted them.

Ben had mentioned an uncle who lived in New Berne, brother of his mother. Michael thought it prudent for the housekeeper to spend a few days with Garrity's physician, on Garrity's tab, before she departed Wilmington for an extended visit to New Berne. Her brother might not appreciate having the care of a deranged sister thrust upon him, but the community couldn't care for and support someone with an illness of the mind.

And it was paramount that the Overtons start new lives for themselves elsewhere, because Gabriel Garrity wasn't going to leave jail anytime soon. The soldiers had found crates containing several dozen broken stands of arms in the warehouse, along with crates of completed stands of arms. Garrity's transactions ledger for the deal was there, along with business contact information. Although most of the names were encoded, including that of Garrity's direct contact, a few were known local rebels. Michael sent soldiers to arrest rebels named among the gunsmith's contacts. He preferred to have widened the net across more weapons trafficking deals, close the net over more rebels. However, solving Julia Garrity's disappearance was paramount and had forced him to move on the weapons issue.

The sergeant had reported a forty-pound snarling bulldog blocking the soldiers' progression into the warehouse. When threatened a clubbing, the dog backed away but continued to snarl. Then the sergeant offered a bit of raw beef and ordered the men to lower their weapons while the dog partook of the treat. The next thing they knew, the four of them had a tail wagging ally who rolled onto his back and allowed one soldier to scratch his belly while the other three searched the warehouse. Head held high, Trouble had trotted away from the warehouse alongside the cart of confiscated weaponry. Whatever Gabriel Garrity had done to him, it guaranteed that Trouble took his first opportunity to leap into the role of the Eighty-Second's official camp dog.

Hammering from the foyer stopped. Michael ambled out for a look at the boarded window. "That will do well, Mr. Hiller. Wait in the study while I speak with Mr. Mayer."

He crossed to the parlor and closed himself and the driver in. The morning's fire had burned out. Even with drapes pulled back to allow sunlight in, the parlor still felt dreary. The Garritys were an unlikely and unlikable couple, bound together through violence and vanity. If Michael allowed his imagination sway, he could hear mutters of discontent from the corner shadows.

The driver perched at the edge of an overstuffed couch and fidgeted, as if never allowed to sit on furniture. Michael walked over and stood before him. "Thank you for your help."

Mayer grunted. "Help, hah. You jailed my employer. Where do I get my next meal?"

Incredulous, Michael took a half step back. "Your employer has enough physical evidence against him to merit the gallows from certain judges. His wife is missing, and her life may be in peril. The housekeeper has gone mad. Yet all you can think about is a full belly?"

"I'm unemployed as a result of your investigating. You owe it to me to put me on the payroll with the regiment."

"Why should I do that when you've another position lined up?"

Mayer's face reddened. "The devil—I don't have another position lined up."

"You most certainly do, you and Mr. Hiller out there. You'd had enough of the Garritys and planned to walk out on them. I suggest that you secure your next position before sunset today. I guarantee that you won't be driving Gabriel or Julia Garrity around for some time."

"What will happen to the horses?" The driver's lips tensed, rolled inward with frustration. "I've spent a good deal of time with them, maintained them well the four years since Mrs. Garrity received them as a gift from her sister."

At least Mayer cared about horses: something other than himself. Michael pursed his lips. "The Eighty-Second lacks adequate mounts. I assure you that the loan of Mrs. Garrity's horses shan't go to waste.

"And while we're speaking of her—" Michael walked a few steps away. "—you mentioned that last Thursday afternoon, you drove her to Mrs. Delacroix's house. Tell me, how was Mrs. Garrity's mood, headed out?"

"The usual."

"Define 'the usual.'"

Mayer glowered at the fireplace. "The woman is a shrew, Lieutenant, twenty-four hours a day."

"What did you witness of her conversation with Mrs. Delacroix?"

"Nothing. I waited outside."

Michael walked back over to him. "How long was she in the house with Mrs. Delacroix?"

"No more than five minutes."

"And how was her mood when she emerged?"

Mayer hesitated, worked his jaw around. "Smug. Pleased with herself. She said something like, 'That'll teach her a lesson.' She hummed the whole way home."

Julia Garrity had hummed. Perhaps the confrontation Michael expected had indeed occurred between the two women. "Where else did you drive Mrs. Garrity last Thursday?"

"In the morning, I drove her up to see the vicar of that new church. She hummed coming home from that visit, too."

Curious. A few days later, Esmé Delacroix had driven to town and lowered the selling price on her property, citing that she didn't feel safe in Wilmington. Both Julia Garrity and Elijah Spivey had reasons to want the woman gone from the area. In some way, they'd precipitated Mrs. Delacroix's latest move.

Michael massaged his forehead, where some of the cold's stuffiness lingered. How was all this connected with Mrs. Garrity's disappearance? "Between last Thursday and this past Saturday, where else did she direct you to drive her?'

Mayer hunched his shoulders. "Nowhere."

"Mr. Mayer, where does Paul Greene live?" A muscle in the driver's cheek flinched, and he averted his face from Michael. "I know Mrs. Garrity is having an affair with him. I'm inquiring to learn whether he comes here, or she visits him."

"He comes here, sir, during the day, while Mr. Garrity is at work. I've never driven Mrs. Garrity to see him. Besides, I've heard he's from New Berne."

Michael nodded. Anne Hooper had mentioned Paul Greene's New Berne connection. "When was the last time he visited her?"

"Tuesday, a week ago. January the twenty-third."

Michael positioned himself in Mayer's line of view and caught his eye. "When was the last time you drove Mr. Garrity for a visit to Mrs. Delacroix?"

The driver's lips pinched, and Michael threw up his hands. "Come, now. I know he's having an affair, too. In this house, it seems that what's good for the goose is good for the gander."

Irascibility stung Mayer's tone. "If it were me, I wouldn't stray. Stay home and keep the wife happy, you know? Say hullo to your hand when she's not of a mood. But no, she strays, so he strays to even the score, and they both lose." He slouched. "Last Wednesday. Mr. Garrity told everyone he'd be talking with suppliers all morning. Out the Sound Road we drove." He rubbed his chin. "Must have been the fifth or sixth time we drove out there since October."

"How long did Mr. Garrity spend with Mrs. Delacroix?"

"About two hours. And no, I wasn't privy to that conversation, either."

Michael ordered events in his head. Mr. Spivey the preacher visited Mrs. Delacroix on Wednesday the seventeenth and was evicted from her home. Mrs. Delacroix found a wooden cross in her yard the next day. Mr. Greene the paramour visited Mrs. Garrity the missing wife the following Tuesday. Mr. Garrity the gunsmith visited Mrs. Delacroix in the morning on Wednesday the twenty-fourth. Mrs. Garrity visited Mr. Spivey on the morning of the next day, Thursday, and Mrs. Delacroix that same afternoon. On Saturday, rebels left town, and Mrs. Garrity disappeared. Mr. Spivey preached about witches on

Sunday morning. The Eighty-Second entered Wilmington Sunday afternoon. Mr. Garrity reported his wife missing on Tuesday. Mrs. Delacroix lowered the price of her house the next day.

With good reason, Esmé Delacroix was a very frightened woman, eager to escape Wilmington.

Upon further questioning, Michael found that the driver hadn't noticed Julia Garrity in the back yard Saturday morning. The weather was too damp for outside work, so he'd spent that time in the stable waxing wood on the post-chaise and grooming tangles from horses' manes. Before Michael dismissed him, he retrieved the name of his prospective employer, just in case he had further questions of him.

The gardener, Steve Hiller, was a quieter man. Fed up with the constant sparring between husband and wife, he'd also made good his escape from employment with the Garritys and was due to begin his next position the following Monday. Chipper's death in October had precipitated his search for another employer. "I was the one had to dig a hole out there and bury him." His face twisted with disgust. "Nothing left of him except bloody tatters."

Michael imagined Trouble shredding Major Craig's trousers, just because someone had looked at the dog cross-eyed. Trouble as camp talisman might not be good for the military career of Michael Stoddard. "What history does the bulldog have of aggression?"

Hiller shook his head. "None for other dogs, that I'm aware of. I've no idea what made him attack Chipper that night. Mr. Garrity claims the bulldog ripped up a burglar at his shop last fall, but that's never been verified."

Chipper was killed after Mrs. Garrity began her affair with Paul Greene. Michael imagined the gunsmith egging his bulldog on, thinking to make his wife submit to him. But Julia hadn't come from a family of submissive women. Instead, she'd revenged herself by rubbing her husband's nose in her affair. So he'd taken up with Mrs. Delacroix. What a twisted mess.

"How much time does Mrs. Garrity usually spend in the yard at Chipper's grave?"

"A good while, even when the weather isn't cooperating. On Saturday, it drizzled a bit, so she sat out with her parasol."

"You saw her out there, then? What time?"

He scratched his nose, thinking. "Ten-thirty, maybe." He frowned. "Yes, about ten-thirty. You know, a few minutes later, I looked around, and she was talking with someone's slave man."

Michael's awareness riveted on Hiller. "Was this a slave you recognized?"

"Never seen him before. Tall, skinny Negro with a wig, dressed dandy, like the coachman off a plantation near Charles Town. Gloves, lace, hat, polished buckles on his shoes. I've lived here ten years. Never seen a Wilmington slave dressed like that. But there are planters up near Edenton and New Berne, now, who got fancy carriages that a slave all dandied out might drive."

New Berne again. Paul Greene owned property near New Berne. Had he sent for Mrs. Garrity with a carriage Saturday morning? "Did you notice a carriage out front?"

While Hiller thought a moment, Spry slipped into the parlor and waited at the doors, listening. "Not out front," said the gardener. "Farther down the street. Nice carriage, dark wood with lighter trim. The sort of transportation that fits a brazier and a bottle of wine on the inside and keeps them rich merchants warm on a damp day. I didn't give it more notice because I was fighting weeds out back. Gardening won't wait for good weather, you know. That coachman passed her a note of some sort. Next time I looked around, they were both gone."

Michael patted his waistcoat pocket. "I found the note he gave her."

Hiller's eyes widened. "I say, you're rather good at this inquiry business, sir. Where'd you find it?"

"Beneath the bench where Mrs. Garrity had been sitting, while I was searching the area yesterday afternoon. Apparently she dropped it in the leaves there Saturday."

Hiller shook his head again. "Beg your pardon, but I don't believe so. I came through Saturday afternoon, after it quit raining, and raked up leaves in the area. I'd have noticed a piece of paper. Got sharp eyes, I do. So I'm not certain what you found."

The framework upon which Michael had been building evidence in his head swung about. For a second or two, the parlor seemed to shift out of focus around him, an unsettling perception. He blinked to clear the sensation. What *had* he found, if not the note given to Mrs. Garrity by the Negro coachman?

He suspected that the gardener couldn't help him answer that question, even if he showed him the paper. "Mr. Hiller, if you see this slave or the coach again, send for me immediately. Spry and I are staying at the house of Mrs. Chiswell, on Second Street. I believe those are all the questions I have of you now. Good luck at your new position."

"Thank you, Mr. Stoddard."

Hiller let himself out the front door, and Michael raised his eyebrows at Spry. His assistant spread his hands. "The physician gave Mrs. Overton laudanum to calm her, but that's a short-term remedy, sir. She's crazy. Keeps babbling about Mr. Spivey. Laudanum won't help her."

If Michael didn't know better, he'd swear that her derangement was the result of a spell: one wrought not by a witch, but a zealous, womanizing preacher. "A pity physicians don't recognize that and find a substance that does help." He withdrew the note from his pocket and unfolded it. "Mr. Hiller has provided us several interesting leads. You heard him say that he saw a Negro coachman in fine livery hand a note to Mrs. Garrity in the back yard Saturday morning. Later, he supposedly raked the area where she sat without finding this note."

"So he missed spotting it, sir."

"I wonder." Michael reread the note. "Mr. Hiller was of the opinion that Wilmington has no Negro coachmen such as he saw, but that they were to be found up near New Berne."

"Maybe that was Paul Greene's coach sent to pick up Mrs. Garrity, sir. Ben Overton told me he spotted the coach while he was running off to snoop on the government transition."

"Has he any idea who might own it?"

Spry shook his head. "Said he'd never seen it before, sir. And no, he didn't see Mrs. Garrity get into the coach."

Michael's blood tingled. "Neither did Hiller."

"But I wager she did so, sir."

"It appears that way. Before we lock up the house, let's have a look in those chests of Mrs. Garrity's upstairs. I wager she's the type of woman who keeps love letters from men."

They returned to her bedroom and flung back the drapes, flooding the room with sunlight. With both clothing chests opened, the two men lifted out the wardrobe folded within and set it on Julia Garrity's bed.

From the lace, linen, and fine wool gowns, velvet slippers, embroidered pockets, silk shifts, fans, jewelry, and beribboned hats, Gabriel Garrity had spent his fortune and numerous years trying to appease his wife with clothing. Michael wondered why he kept buying her more when it hadn't improved her mood. He admitted that he was just as dense as his fellow man when it came to understanding women, but if *he* were to go a-wooing with gifts, and the woman didn't appreciate the gifts, he'd know that he'd missed the mark. And perhaps it was time to listen to the woman herself instead of continuing the shower of material possessions.

He regarded the portrait of Salome Ward. In natural light, her dark eyes and red lips condemned. Did either of the Ward sisters want men to listen to them? Or did they just want men who obeyed them? How obedient was Paul Greene? From the charcoal sketch of him, he'd looked impudent, not compliant.

Since his assistant was sorting through the art portfolio, Michael dug deeper and found a stack of letters tied with a silk ribbon, every one from Paul Greene. Silently he thanked Julia Garrity for being so predictable. A scan of the contents revealed professions of devotion and lust. He unfolded several letters upon a corner of the bed, opened the note beside them, and straightened. Offhand, he couldn't see major differences between the writing samples. "What do you think, Spry? Were these written by the same hand?"

Spry peered down at the writing. "Looks close to me, sir. If not by the same hand, it's done by someone with a talent for copying handwriting." The private fell silent, and Michael watched him study the note and letters. "See here, on the note, look at the way the letter 'y' is closed, somewhat narrow. Seems to be a wider closure on the 'y' in these letters. But I wouldn't lay money on it."

Michael absorbed the detail Spry pointed out, but he didn't know whether it was significant enough to establish a forgery. "Let's have another look at that sketch of Paul Greene." He replaced the folded note in his pocket and strode to the other side of the bed.

"It isn't in the portfolio, sir."

With a sharp glance for his assistant, Michael reviewed each sketch. The picture of the man they presumed to be Paul Greene was missing from the collection. Damn. Michael pivoted to the fireplace, squatted, and studied the blackened ash within. Using a poker, he dragged a scrap of paper roughly three inches square to the bricks at the front and stood, the paper pinched between forefinger and thumb. At one edge, where the paper had blackened, the top of a sketched periwig was visible.

Spry blew irritation out his mouth in a rush. "Ever-efficient Mrs. Overton."

"We should have expected it." Michael pitched the scrap back into the fireplace and dusted off his hands. "I wonder why she didn't burn the letters, too? On our way out the Sound Road, let's drop them off at the house on Second Street. After we return from church tonight, we'll examine them. Check both chests to make sure I haven't missed any."

Before they were done in Mrs. Garrity's room, they poked beneath the mattress and rugs and behind the hanging portraits for hidden sketches or letters. Finding none, they closed her sketches and wardrobe back into the chests, and shut the door.

Of the three other bedrooms on the second floor, two were guest rooms that, from their stuffiness, hadn't been used in months. The third was Gabriel Garrity's bedroom, austere when compared to his wife's quarters. They flung open drapes and made a thorough search, but there were no letters, either from rebels leaders or Esmé Delacroix. Ben Overton had described the padlocked chest in Garrity's room, but no key was available for unlocking it, so Michael would have to send a locksmith to the house. The fireplace had been swept clean and didn't look to have been used for a while.

Hands on his hips, he surveyed the room. His scrutiny brought him to a bedside table and a candle, or rather a candle and the remains of another candle.

The second candle had burned down to a lump of white wax. Trapped within the wax were three silk ribbons—white, pink, and red—that appeared to have encircled the shaft of the candle before it was lit. The yet unburned candle had no ribbons around it: a big, practical candle meant for providing light. Michael motioned Spry over. "What do you make of this?"

Spry leaned in close and sniffed the melted wax. "Roses, sir." His teeth shone. "That was a lady's candle. What's that liquid at the base?"

Michael touched a fingertip to a small pool of golden fluid. "From the consistency and color, I'd say it's honey." He dabbed the sticky stuff off on his handkerchief.

"Hah. Mr. Garrity had a woman in his bed, sir. I vote for Mrs. Overton."

Michael laughed. "Why Mrs. Overton?"

"Can you imagine the housekeeper allowing something like that messy candle to remain here unless she was part of it? And no way in Hades would she allow 'the witch' up here."

Trapped within the melted wax, the silk ribbons retained their resilient softness, like a heart within someone's ribcage. The candle, with its colors, scents, and textures, whispered a promise of love. Betty Overton, embittered and unbalanced, was an unlikely candidate for romance. Michael felt certain she'd had no part in the candle. But he had a hunch that Spry was correct in metaphor. The candle stood proxy for a beloved woman. Had Gabriel Garrity found love?

Michael retreated a step from the table. What command romantic love wielded in the hearts of people. He'd seen men and women kill for love, even to attain the shape of it, and wondered at the mystery that rode men like Garrity to almost bankrupt themselves in attempt to please a woman. The mystery wasn't housed solely in pleasures of the flesh. That much he knew.

He cleared his throat. "I don't think Mr. Garrity had Mrs. Overton in his bed, Spry."

"Now that I consider it, me, either, sir. You want to take this candle along for evidence?"

Garrity was in jail, his wife missing, his mistress threatened. Whatever his dream had been for finding love, it had collapsed, the shape of it now as unrecognizable as that of the melted candle. Michael took another step back and held up his palms, chest high, toward the table. "No. Leave it be."

Chapter Fifteen

JUST AFTER NOON, firearms resting across their laps, Michael and Spry trotted southeast out of Wilmington on horses the regiment had confiscated from rebels: Michael on a mare named Cleopatra, and his assistant on a gelding. The track they rode was barely wide enough for a wagon and horse team. At a roadblock, three soldiers were conducting inspections of incoming and outgoing vehicles and questioning riders about their business in town. The privates waved Michael and Spry through.

Salt marsh and swamp effaced civilization. The two men bore the scrutiny of buzzards and hawks from the branches of cypress, cedar, and pine trees. Beneath their mounts' hooves, crushed shell and sand rasped like seeds in a dried Indian gourd. Egrets, startled by the intrusion, flapped about. Even in winter, the Atlantic commanded the air, salty on Michael's lips.

Spry finished up his portion of bread and cheese, a gift from Enid when they'd stopped by the house earlier. The two men rode along in amiable quiet for a quarter hour, then veered off the Sound Road south onto a narrower, sandier track. Surrounded by eerie, spicy pine murmur on the path to the Delacroix property, Michael felt the isolation of the place and understood why William Hooper, twice as far from Wilmington at Finian, had moved his family into town. Desperate men banded together, calling themselves rebels when they torched a loyalist's home, or loyalists when destroying a rebel's property. At a horse's gallop, help was more than ten minutes away.

The pines thinned. The men passed substantial gardens planted with herbs and winter vegetables. A clump of pines shaded a small, two-story wood manor in need of a fresh coat of paint. Wood smoke trailed both chimneys. Several smaller wooden buildings behind the manor, including a kitchen and stable, were in greater need of paint. Inside a fence, a skinny cow worried at sparse grass. Chickens bobbed and pecked near the stable.

"Doesn't look like much, sir." In the silence, Spry's voice seemed to boom.

Not much at all, but too much to divest quickly in the economic climate of war. Strange that a man would leave his wife out there so many years to fend for herself. Did Mrs. Delacroix never long for the regular company of other ladies? Michael's lip curled. Irrelevant if Wilmington society shunned her for being a witch. But he hadn't received that impression from Mrs. Duncan or Mrs. Farrell.

A dog barked, followed by another, and in seconds, four lean hounds paced the horses. As Michael and Spry arrived within hailing distance of the manor, a big-boned Negro man with skin darker than any slave Michael had seen stepped out the front door of the house and called the dogs, his words like French, yet not French, drenched in island rhythm: the patois of Saint Domingue. The dogs pranced up to the porch, sat, and yawned, but the Negro's face remained obdurate, his regard of them as coarse as his breeches, shirt, and coat.

Michael waved. "Good afternoon. We're here to speak with Mrs. Delacroix, a courtesy call from Major Craig." He paused. From the Negro's impassive expression, the fellow understood little English. His own French wasn't that good. The death of an uncle at the Battle of Quebec had stymied any enthusiasm he might have cultivated for Gaul. "Spry, you speak French?"

"Not much, sir."

A crow cawed, as if jeering both of them. Michael cleared his throat. "*Bon jour.* Madame Delacroix—"

The Negro spun about and stomped into the house. Michael muttered after him, "I see you've learned social grace from your Parisian masters."

"Beg your pardon, sir?"

"Never mind."

A young mulatto woman in a shawl, short jacket, and homespun petticoat appeared in the doorway and bobbed a curtsy. "Armand says you speak with Madame?" The Caribbean also seasoned her speech.

"Yes, we wish to speak with Madame Delacroix. Is she receiving visitors?"

The woman curtsied again and gestured. "Tie horses there." She indicated the railing around the porch. "Come in. I fetch Madame."

She vanished into the house. After securing the horses, the men removed their hats and stepped into the foyer, where Armand, still unsmiling, blocked their passage, the build of his chest and arms impressive. He extended his left hand. Michael surrendered his fusil without a word. Spry handed over his musket with a grin. "We need to get you on a rowing team, my fellow."

The slave's face displayed no inkling that he'd understood Spry, but his right hand gestured to the unoccupied parlor. The two soldiers entered. Armand closed the doors after them.

Gauzy curtains muted daylight in the room to the level of a verdant, Caribbean jungle floor, the illusion enhanced by the presence of potted plants arranged throughout the parlor, their leaves huge and glossy. Landscape paintings mounted upon walls depicted palm trees, tropical beaches, and hibiscus blossoms. The illumination also tricked the eye into skimming over threadbare spots on rugs, chairs, and a couch. Heat from an established bed of coals in the fireplace intensified the bouquet arising from bowls of dried herbs and flowers. The room's temperature was almost too warm for Michael.

Within ornate, metal cages suspended from the ceiling, two vivid green parrots inspected them. Michael sauntered over to a caramel-colored tabby cat lounging on a footstool below the closest cage. The cat stretched and yawned, flexed a sleek paw loaded with the claws of a hunter, stood, and bumped Michael, demanding to be stroked. The parrot scooted away on his perch and said something in patois with a distinct, derogatory air to it.

Whether the bird's comment was for Michael or the cat, he didn't know, but he cocked an eyebrow at the parrot. "I wonder how long you'd last among those hawks out there?"

Spry snickered at the brazen bird, then dabbed his brow with the back of his hand. "Awfully warm in here, sir."

So unlike Yorkshire or Nova Scotia, that parlor. "Welcome to Saint Domingue, Spry."

The mulatto entered and set a lacquered tray bearing china coffee cups, linen napkins, and a sugar cone upon a low, mahogany table between the couch and a chair. "Madame rest after her visit to town this morning. Armand inform her that you arrive. She ask me to prepare coffee, and she join you soon."

Michael took a step toward her. "And your name?"

"Noisette."

Hazelnut, the meaning of her name, unless Michael was mistaken. She certainly was brown as a nut. "Thank you, Noisette. Are you and Armand the only slaves?" He knew they weren't. Mrs. Delacroix had at least one other slave, the fellow who'd driven her post-chaise that morning.

"No." As if to avoid answering more questions, she curtsied and left, pulling the doors closed with her.

Spry sniffed at a bowl of dried flowers. "Sir, I hope Mrs. Delacroix has more lads like Armand around. This is a long way out from Wilmington."

The parrot near Michael repeated its earlier comment and evaluated Spry as if he were covered in lice. Spoiled creatures. Michael imagined both birds being hand-fed delicacies by a travel-weary sea captain, the half-English John Delacroix.

Or had the Frenchwoman's husband pronounced his name *Jean*?

Michael's senses processed the parlor anew, and he envisioned both birds perched on the massive shoulders of a black-haired Gaul, a bottle of rum in one hand, a cutlass in the other, and gold rings through his earlobes. According to Mrs. Duncan, *le capitaine* was dead, buried somewhere on the property. The lot of a sea captain's wife was to endure her husband's long absences—but not all wives endured those times alone. Esmé Delacroix pulsated with life. She might have tolerated isolation off the Sound Road to hide extramarital affairs from Wilmington's residents.

He wiped sweat off his forehead with his handkerchief. "Yes, this is a long way out, and I want an introduction to the other slaves."

Spry studied him before catching on. "Ah. Yes, sir. The gardener's account of the tall, thin coachman who passed the note to Mrs. Garrity. Mr. Hiller said he hadn't seen any slaves like that around Wilmington. These people do keep to themselves out here."

"Exactly." Although from what Michael had seen, he was skeptical that Mrs.

Delacroix could afford the finery that the Garritys' gardener had described.

The doors opened again, and Armand entered, followed by Esmé Delacroix, her wool gown a forest green that set off the golden hue of her skin. As that morning, she wore her dark hair down her back in a long, single braid, lace upon the crown of her head more a circlet than a mobcap. Pearls adorned her earlobes and throat. Armand remained in the parlor and stationed himself beside the closed doors, his expression unfathomable.

The soldiers bowed. Michael said, "Lieutenant Stoddard, Madame, investigator for Major Craig. And my assistant, Spry."

She inclined her head. "Armand will remain during our meeting. He seeks to assure my safety. I have had recent experience with visitors who compromised it."

"Madame, assuring your safety is the reason for our visit." The cat bumped Michael's leg again, hard. Annoyed, he stepped away from the footstool.

She snapped her fingers once. "Henri." The cat leapt from the footstool and sat at her feet, his fluffy tail swirling over the rug. A dimple appeared beside her mouth. "If Englishmen are bold enough to drink coffee as we do in Saint Domingue, do let us sit and enjoy." She gestured the soldiers to the couch and nodded over her shoulder to Armand.

Michael took a seat on one end of the couch and motioned Spry to sit on the other end. In the chair opposite them, the cat at her feet, Mrs. Delacroix arranged napkins and cups in saucers upon the low table, along with spoons for the sugar. Noisette returned with a china coffeepot, placed it before her mistress, and slipped out.

The coffee poured out the color of common brown mud, and almost the same consistency. Spry lifted his cup to swill the liquid.

"Ah, monsieur. I recommend two teaspoons of sugar. Otherwise, you will swear I have poisoned you." She slid the cone of sugar between their cups.

Spry frowned into his coffee, no doubt thinking of witches and spells. Michael reached for the sugar, hacked a liberal dose into his cup, and stirred it around. "It's made with chicory, Spry. Very bitter."

Mrs. Delacroix awarded him a full smile. The radiance of it distracted him enough to slosh coffee into the saucer with his spoon. The woman wasn't beautiful. She was magnetic. She compelled the marrow of his bones to orient upon her the way the North Star drew the dedication of mariners. No wonder Gabriel Garrity had taken her for his mistress, and his wife had visited her in jealous agitation. Michael sipped coffee, grown a little dizzy due to the warmth of the parlor or perhaps the remnants of his head cold. "Excellent. Thank you, Madame." Beside him, Spry pacified his coffee with sugar.

She caressed Henri the cat, prepared her own coffee, and sat back, sipping. "Major Craig's investigator. The redcoats have been in town but a few days. So. What is it you investigate?"

"The disappearance of a woman, Julia Garrity. The wife of your paramour, Gabriel Garrity."

One of her eyebrows curved up. "To the contrary, I am no man's mistress, especially not that man's."

"His driver informed me that he's driven Mr. Garrity out here to visit you a number of times, starting in October of last year. The most recent visit was a week ago Wednesday, in the morning. Mr. Garrity stayed about two hours."

She nodded. "The driver's account of the date and time of Mr. Garrity's visit is correct. However his master did not share my bed."

Michael set down his cup. "I beg your pardon, Madame. Do you suggest that Mr. Garrity spent two hours with you in a platonic state?"

"He spent barely fifteen minutes in my company that morning. Most of that two hours, he sat here, in my parlor, alone."

He blinked at her, baffled. "Why? Where were you?"

She placed her cup in its saucer on the table and regarded both of them with a level expression. "I was preparing the love charm he had requested of me."

"Excuse me?"

Henri jumped up in her lap, and she kneaded him with long, dexterous fingers. "I have somewhat of a reputation for producing simples, medicines, and charms. People come to me when a physician has failed them, or they need advice for a business decision or love. I charge them for my services. Their money stabilizes my finances while I await the sale of my property.

"Mr. Garrity's wife began having an affair with a man last October. He wanted to woo her back, so he paid me to help him. Last Wednesday, I consulted the spirits and created a candle that I instructed him to burn in his bedroom."

Spry's voice sounded sluggish. "White, pink, and red ribbons around it."

"Ah, you have seen the candle."

Spirits? Love charms? Michael squinted, unable to believe what he'd heard. "Madame, are you saying you're a witch?"

"Do I consult the spirits of Saint Domingue every day and allow them to guide me? Yes. Do I sleep with the Christian devil and ride a broomstick at night? No. I am what I am. Call me what you like."

The cat's purr was the distant rumble of thunder, and he smirked at Michael with green eyes. Michael scratched at his own hairline out of frustration. Never had he expected Esmé Delacroix to be engaged in an activity that might be misconstrued as witchcraft. He'd expected a logical explanation to everything her accusers had said. Discovery that she was indeed involved in a daily activity that sounded like witchcraft changed conditions a great deal. For one thing, it meant that superstitious ignoramuses like Elijah Spivey could claim a legitimate target. For another thing, it opened the possibility that paying clients who didn't get the expected results from Mrs. Delacroix's "magic" might revenge themselves upon her. The woman was living a dangerous life out there by herself.

"The candle you gave Mr. Garrity is on his nightstand. It seems like an ordinary, burned down candle to me. What makes it a love charm?"

"Nothing is ever as it seems on the surface, Lieutenant. Before I could speak with the spirits to incorporate Mr. Garrity's request for his wife's love into the candle, I submitted my tools to the spirits for their intercession. I became their hands, their eyes in creation of the candle. That is what took almost two hours last Wednesday morning."

Michael knew skepticism colored his expression. "Where did you assemble this love charm?"

"In a dedicated shrine on my property."

Before he could rein in his imagination, it delivered the image of a darkened hut filled with noxious smoke from a cauldron that bubbled green slime. *Double, double, toil and trouble.* He shoved the thoughts away. By God, this was the eighteenth century, not a dark age. "Mrs. Garrity paid you a brief visit last Thursday afternoon. What was that about?"

Mrs. Delacroix's gaze lowered to the cat, and she stroked him again. "She insulted me and insisted that I break off the affair with her husband. As I have already said, I am not having an affair with him. When she became physically threatening, Armand encouraged her to leave."

"She isn't the only one whom Armand has encouraged to leave recently." Because the woman continued to pet the cat and avoid eye contact, Michael pressed on. "Elijah Spivey was out here a few weeks ago. Armand threw him out, and the next morning, you found a gift from him on your lawn, a wooden cross." He leaned forward, elbows on knees. "What did Mr. Spivey say to you?"

"He invited me to attend his church."

Michael snorted. "Was that before or after he tried to seduce you?"

Her eyes flashed sudden fire at him. "I am no man's mistress, and I will have nothing to do with that man."

"So you spurned him, and now he's targeting you as a witch. Madame, your property is isolated from help out here. I've seen a great deal of what the irrational can do in a man, especially a man who is stymied at lust. I'm also investigating certain actions of this Spivey fellow, and I would like you to consider taking quarters in town for awhile, where you'll be safe, at least until I can resolve the issues he's stirred up."

She stared stonily at him. "I have not the money to live in town."

"Then I shall find an arrangement for you at a discount—"

"No. Did you hear me? I am not leaving. The spirits will protect me."

In Michael's peripheral vision, he saw Armand flex his biceps. Spirits, yes. He pushed back, sat straight. "Very well. Consider discontinuing your practices that people might interpret as witchcraft until I can resolve these issues."

"No. It has always been a part of me." She studied him a few seconds. "You mock me, Lieutenant. Practical Englishman, you do not believe in spirits, charms, curses, or even the devil. You doubt my gift."

Indeed, Michael had often wondered why humans needed a god of evil when so much wickedness lurked in their own souls. He spread his hands, a jerked motion that belied his exasperation. "Madame, it matters little what I think of your gift. What does matter is that you're in danger out here, and I assure you, that's quite real."

She considered his words a moment. Then her expression mellowed. "You honestly are trying to help me."

"Yes, I am."

"That is kind of you. But you must believe me when I say that my spirits will protect me. They have granted me a vision of destruction wrought upon Elijah Spivey and his church."

Michael rubbed his forehead. He wasn't reaching her.

She inhaled, deeply. "I can see that is not proof for you, so I offer another vision the spirits gave me, this one as I rested upstairs after returning from Wilmington today. You were the subject of this vision."

He squinted at her. "How can that be so? You only saw me for a moment this morning. We weren't even introduced."

"Greeks did not require that the Oracle at Delphi be acquainted with those in her visions."

Fortune telling. Resigned, Michael composed his expression into polite attention. How could he convince her of the danger she was in?

Her hands stilled on Henri, and her eyes lost focus. "The herald who shifts his shape and wears two faces comes within a few days. His news will disappoint you."

"Disappoint me?"

Spry shifted about on the couch. "Two faces, sir? What does that mean?"

Michael said, "Madame, if you meant this to prove a point, I've no idea what you're talking about. Who or what is this herald?"

She ignored both men and drew a shaky breath. "And the shadow..." Her hand on the cat trembled. "The shadow who bathes in blood, he comes."

Despite the warmth of the parlor, Michael felt flesh on his arms and neck contract. Without complete success, he attempted to cast off the sensation. "When and where does this shadow come?" To his ears, his tone sounded stiff.

"You are the one to vanquish him." As with an oracle, it was a one-way conversation. "Fortunately the teacher is here. Learn from him."

Spry stirred. "Sir, what's she talking about?" His voice carried a weird pitch to it, as if a shadow had crawled up his backbone.

"I don't know, Spry." Michael fidgeted. "Madame Delacroix—"

"The shadow is your responsibility. If you do not vanquish the shadow—" Her face paled, and her eyes rolled back in their sockets. Armand sprinted over just in time to catch her, prevent her collapse from the chair. Henri tumbled from her lap, perturbed.

"Noisette!" bellowed the Negro at the closed doors, prompting the entrance of the mulatto.

"Ai, Madame, *mon dieu!*" She rushed forward.

A blend of chagrin, relief, and disappointment wended through Michael. He eased out a pent-up breath and watched while Armand, assisted by Noisette, lifted Mrs. Delacroix into his arms. He'd witnessed the entire routine before among Gypsies on the Yorkshire moors. Sometimes, the fortuneteller faked an epileptic seizure to add drama to her presentation and coax a few more pennies from her clients.

Too bad His Majesty couldn't figure out a way to ship the entire pick-pocketing lot of Gypsies across the Atlantic. They'd do well among the rebels in America, considering how many rebels he'd encountered who were superstitious zealots. And to think he'd started to buy into Esmé Delacroix's routine. Well, she had refined her act to art, possibly assisted by stays cinched too tightly.

He regarded the mulatto and injected calm into his voice. "Noisette, is

Madame ill?"

"The work takes much out of her. She is drained when she spends long hours as the hands and eyes, as she did this weekend—"

"Noisette!" Armand, standing with his limp mistress in his arms, glared at the young woman, who lowered her gaze to her shoes. Armand proceeded to lambaste her in patois.

When he finished, Noisette, head still hanging, said, "Madame rest. You go. I give your weapons. You go."

So much for a chance to see the other servants on the property: Michael and Spry would have to return for that. Their excuse? To inquire into Mrs. Delacroix's health after her fainting spell, of course. "Give Madame our regards. On the morrow, we shall look in on her."

Chapter Sixteen

THEY'D GUIDED THEIR mounts back onto the road and ridden several minutes side-by-side without speaking before Michael snapped his fingers several times near his assistant's ear to disrupt his look of preoccupation. "That was all mumbo jumbo back there, Spry. Haven't you ever seen a fortuneteller act?"

"But this sounded different, sir, like she's really an oracle or something. Herald, teacher, shadow: what does all that mean? How does anyone vanquish a shadow?"

He is your responsibility. Skin on Michael's arms and neck again drew up into bumps. He gritted his teeth.

In Michael's peripheral vision, Spry stared at him. "Sir, the way she said it, I got the impression that the herald, teacher, and shadow aren't strangers to you. Do you know this shadow, sir?"

Memories burst into his thoughts. *Assassins like to kill*, Fairfax whispered. His dagger pressed to Michael's carotid artery, the blade burning, drawing blood.

On the Sound Road, more than half a year into the future, sweat rolled down Michael's temple, and he clutched his throat. Then he shrugged off the memory, returned his hand to the reins, and sat taller in the saddle while silently giving himself a quick, thorough dressing down. Mrs. Delacroix had admitted that she needed money. She'd attempted to reel him in, intrigue him into becoming her paying client with her vague statements. On the morrow, during his visit to her, he expected her to build a compelling case for how frequent consultations with her could enhance his promotion options or some such nonsense.

Aware that Spry had been watching him, he met his stare. "Forget it, man. It wasn't real. What *is* real is that we don't know where Mrs. Garrity is. Nor have we spoken with Mr. Spivey. An oracle named Stoddard predicts disaster for two investigators who don't report progress when Major Craig returns."

"I see your point, sir." Spry's shoulders straightened, and he faced forward. "All Mrs. Delacroix's talk of charms and spirits. Do you suppose she's as mad as Mrs. Overton?"

"Oh, no, she's sane." Michael exhaled his frustration. "I wish we could find a way to protect her."

Spry's mouth stretched into a taut line. "Why, sir? You heard her. She doesn't want our protection. I think we should leave her alone, as she's requested. Let her spirits do the work, sir."

"I doubt Major Craig will condone such action from us. I've seen no sign that she's a rebel or even a rebel sympathizer."

"Then what are we supposed to do, sir—carry her off to Wilmington? Armand wouldn't take kindly to that. I say leave her be. She's a hermit, sir. Let her commune with her spirits for days on end, if that's what she wants. According to Noisette, that's what she did all last weekend."

Was that what Noisette said before Armand silenced her? *She spends long hours as the hands and eyes.* Exactly what did that mean? Had Mrs. Delacroix closed herself up in her shrine at the week's end to produce charms for clients? How much time did each charm take? How many clients did she have?

Up ahead, Michael spotted the sentries and checked the time: nearing two-thirty. After the day's events thus far, he had additional questions for Mrs. Duncan at White's Tavern. "When we arrive in town, take my mare with you. Have the sergeant ready those ten men and their horses for the mission at Mr. Spivey's church. I've an errand to run and will meet you at the barracks within an hour."

"Yes, sir."

***

In White's, Michael occupied a table by himself nearer the fireplace. Only one tavern maid had arrived for work, and Kevin Marsh was helping to fulfill orders for ale and small beer among the other eleven patrons. He breezed past with a tray of drinks for them. "Claret for you again, Mr. Stoddard?"

"Yes, Mr. Marsh. Thank you."

While Marsh was collecting payment from his customers, Michael spotted Kate Duncan gliding his way with a glass of claret. She must have seen him when he first walked in. He sprang to his feet and bowed. She set his wineglass on the table and smiled. "Well, Mr. Stoddard, repeat business at my tavern. This is good."

Indeed, she was lovely. And blonde—after his experience with Lydia, he'd found himself attracted to bosomy blondes. However Mrs. Duncan was petite, not buxom—and that wasn't the only difference. There was something stimulating about her personality. He couldn't quite figure it out. "Madam, will you join me a moment?" At her nod, he pulled a chair out and seated her.

"Your color is much improved today, sir."

"Thank you." He sat and scooted his own chair in. "I took your advice, got a good night's sleep in a warm bed. But I believe my recuperation started with that bowl of chicken soup yesterday. I'm also grateful for your referral to Mrs. Hooper."

Mrs. Duncan nodded. "She's already told me that you and Spry were very much the gentlemen. I imagine that she expected you to interrogate her about her husband's whereabouts. She doesn't know where he is, so she was probably quite nervous in your company."

"I did receive that impression." He drew the wineglass to him.

The twinkle returned to Kate Duncan's eyes. "However, Miss Salome Ward has seen another side of you. Tell me, how goes the search for Julia Garrity?"

He sipped wine, stalling. "Well, now, this is certainly a unique investigation—"

"Hah, you've no idea where to find her yet! I knew it. Kevin swears that she ran off with her beau. If she did, I wouldn't blame her. I wouldn't tolerate a brute like Gabriel Garrity in my home."

A woman like Kate Duncan, secure in herself, wouldn't tolerate most men in her home. Likely her own brother Kevin walked a thin line. "Madam, how much do you and your brother know about Mrs. Garrity's paramour?"

"Very little. Most of the town suspects she's carried on with a fellow since last fall. But Anne Hooper is the one who has her confidence."

He sifted through what Mrs. Hooper had said as well as how she'd said it. From several accounts, Paul Greene had an appeal about him, good looks to make a woman feel daring and adventurous, quite the opposite from Gabriel Garrity. "So your brother speculates that Mrs. Garrity ran off with her paramour." He leaned forward. "But I sense you don't agree with him." She shook her head. "Well, why not?"

"Oh, Kevin's only twenty-two. He might have a good business head about him, but he hasn't a clue when it comes to understanding women. Julia insists on comfort. If running off with this man meant she had to be cold, wet, or hungry, even for a little while, she wouldn't do it. And Saturday was both cold and wet."

Elbows on the table, he steepled his fingers before him. "Suppose her beau provided her a warm coach on a cold, rainy Saturday, and a competent coachman to stock it with a brazier, blankets, a bottle of wine, and bread and cheese. Do you think she might leap into his waiting arms and leave her husband—without packing a valise?"

Mrs. Duncan frowned at him. "Is that what happened?" Michael raised his eyebrows at her, sat back, and folded his hands in his lap. "You have reason to believe it might be so, don't you? Very well, yes, I can envision Julia doing that." She crossed her arms on the tabletop and sighed. "Woe to her paramour. He must now keep her in the style to which she's grown accustomed or incur her disfavor. Not a position for which I envy him."

"Wilmington certainly has its share of idiosyncratic women."

Her frown deepened. "What's that supposed to mean?"

"Earlier today, Spry and I drove out the Sound Road and met the French witch."

"Mr. Stoddard." Mrs. Duncan slapped one palm on the tabletop." Esmé Delacroix is not a witch. She has far more knowledge of treatments and cures for ailments than do most physicians."

"She makes love charms."

"I expect so."

"She also talks with spirits."

"How is that different from what devout Christians do when they bow their heads every day in prayer?"

Discussing religion was usually a losing proposition, so he declined to answer her question. "Who in the area has complained that she's harmed them by making love charms or talking with spirits?"

"Goodness, no one."

"But I hear that she makes Mr. Spivey uncomfortable."

She scowled. "That's because he hasn't a brain in his reptilian head."

"Mrs. Delacroix is isolated out there. Has she ever come into town for one of your women's socials?"

"As a matter of fact, yes, but she's reclusive, so I don't see her very often. For the record, I admire her for not remarrying or becoming some man's mistress, just to ease her finances. She's attempting to live within her means. That's a lesson we should each learn."

He nodded and sat forward. "I've heard that John Delacroix was out at sea a good deal of time. You don't think she missed a man in her husband's absence and took a paramour?"

Chill glazed Mrs. Duncan's eyes and voice. "Mr. Stoddard, exactly what do you expect she missed in a man all those years?"

His stomach sank into his legs. Somewhere in the conversation, he'd taken a wrong turn, hit a sensitive spot with Kate Duncan and gotten her back up. He understood women no better than most men did, however in such situations, he knew it was best to stay quiet and not try to repair his gaffe. Again he comprehended that the woman at the table with him was very different from the women with whom he'd dallied and passed his time in America for nine years. Different on many levels.

"You know what the problem is with this town? The people have tiny, little minds." Mrs. Duncan's forefinger tapped the table for the words *tiny, little minds*. "They hear a rumor about someone, decide it's truth, and gossip about it. I know what they say about me. They call me the Ice Widow. Hah. I was expected to remarry within a year after Daniel's death, not go into business with my brother. But where's my selection of prospective husbands, I ask you? Why, they're in here every day. Gossiping and getting drunk."

Beneath her rant, Michael heard the lament of an intelligent woman who was trapped in a mediocre life. Stuck in a port town of Colonial America, where the most excitement anyone could expect, week after week, was the loading of naval stores and the unloading of the same, old merchants' wares. No wonder Betty Overton's pistol firing display had drawn such a crowd. She'd be the topic of gossip for years after she'd moved to New Berne. And no wonder many residents of Wilmington hadn't immediately disparaged the regiment's arrival. Even if redcoats frightened some residents in town, they were a curiosity, most of them from the other side of a wide, dangerous ocean, men who'd seen something of the world beside pitch production, buzzards in pine trees, and tidal flats.

"Have you nothing to say about that, Mr. Stoddard?" She jutted her nose in the air, as primed for fiery debate as a man in a London coffeehouse.

The gesture so resembled his memories of Miriam that Michael almost laughed aloud. Instead, he channeled his humor into a polite smile. "You sound like my sister in Yorkshire." No sooner did the words leave his mouth then he winced, knowing they were wrong, knowing he should have kept his mouth shut.

White spots appeared on her nostrils. "Your—your *sister*."

His hands fanned air, a lame attempt to erase words. "What I meant to say was that—"

"I know what you meant to say." She scooted her chair back and rose.

Before he was even halfway to his feet, Kevin Marsh whizzed past balancing another full tray. "Kate, Jack Colney's out back with a wine shipment."

"Excuse me, Lieutenant." She rushed away as if he had the Plague.

Michael slumped into his seat, exasperation emptying through his nostrils. "Aye, what a charmer you are, laddie," he muttered.

Three men strutted in, dockworkers from the look of their coarse clothing. They claimed the table beside Michael's, acknowledging him with boisterous smiles. While standing, one caught Marsh's eye. "A round for everyone in the house, Mr. Marsh!"

Marsh drew back, jaw gaped open. "You buying, Peabody? What's the occasion?"

"Got a promotion to dock manager." Peabody sat and, with a flourish, raised his arms over his head.

The tavern exploded with, "Huzzah!" Men sauntered over to shake Peabody's hand or clap his shoulder, offer their congratulations. Kevin Marsh and the tavern maid scampered about to get drinks refilled.

In her hurry, the tavern maid carrying a laden tray bumped into Michael's table and sloshed ale from a tankard on one corner of the table's surface. "So sorry, sir! I'll be back in a moment to clean that up. Here's your wine."

He waved it away, wanting to be completely clear-headed at Spivey's church that evening, and called after her, "No rush on cleaning up here." After all, no ale had splashed on him.

At the next table, Peabody's friends took turns toasting the success of the new manager. His cheeks pink from spirits and salutations, Peabody yielded to their request, brought a folded letter from his pocket, and spread it open on the table. "Out of my light, you bum-kissing scoundrels. All right, how does this sound? 'Notice is hereby given of the excellent service of Mr. Ned Peabody.'" He halted for effect, and his friends thumped the table with approval.

For the ten seconds, Peabody swanked out the letter of recommendation he'd received. Then Michael heard the moist thump of a tankard overturning, and the new manager jumped to his feet in alarm. "Why, you son of a mongrel! Look what you done!"

"Sorry, Ned." The other fellow righted his tankard and began blotting beer off the letter with his handkerchief.

"Get your snot off my letter!" Peabody batted his arm away and dabbed the letter with his own handkerchief. "Bad enough that your beer is all over it. Damn, too late. It's smeared."

Michael craned his neck for a glimpse. Ink on the left third of the letter was blurred and streaked from contact with the spilled beer. Something about the image nudged his brain. Moisture. Ink. Moisture: water, rain.

With piercing insight, he shoved his empty wineglass to the side, reached in his pocket, and pulled out the note that he and Spry had found beneath the bench the day before in the Garritys' back yard, the folded message that they'd presumed was given to Julia Garrity by the Negro coachman in fine livery and dropped by accident. While the fellow at the next table placated the proud Peabody by purchasing him another beer, Michael unfolded his own note and pressed it flat.

Saturday morning, it had drizzled. The sky hadn't cleared, in fact, until Sunday. If Julia Garrity had dropped this note beneath the bench, and it had remained there until Tuesday afternoon, when he and Spry had found it, the damp weather would surely have smeared the ink and wrinkled the paper. He scrutinized the script on the note as well as the paper itself, but he saw no indication that water had ever touched it.

What had Steve Hiller the gardener said? *I came through Saturday afternoon, after it quit raining, and raked up the leaves in the area. I'd have noticed a piece of paper.*

Realization plowed from Michael's scalp to his toes. Mr. Hiller didn't see the note they'd found because it hadn't been there until much later, after he'd tidied the area. Someone had planted the note beneath the bench Sunday or Monday, even arranged dead leaves beneath the bench to shield it. Someone had intended for the note to be found and read without running the risk of rain-smeared ink obscuring the message. And the note was meant to lead an investigator astray, make him believe that Mrs. Garrity had run off in haste with Paul Greene.

Michael dipped his forefinger in the spilled ale and put a drop on the letter's date. Sure enough, the ink smeared with the moisture. He blotted it dry before the smear progressed.

Anger and chagrin shot through him. Had Lieutenant Fairfax been assigned the investigation, he'd have made the connection immediately. He wouldn't have bumbled around with the evidence—

Oh, rot Fairfax. The ruse didn't fool Michael anymore. He replaced the note in his pocket, tossed a few coins on the table, and headed for the exit. Time to find his assistant.

★★★

Michael arrived at the barracks about a quarter hour after a messenger had galloped into town and reported an update on Major Craig's activities. Redcoats had found the provisioning vessels the rebels smuggled out of Wilmington in advance of the Eighty-Second. Soldiers destroyed the enemy's stores and rum. According to the messenger, the major was confident that he'd dissuaded the rebels from future attempts to establish an outpost there at Heron's Bridge or closer to Wilmington.

What excellent news. Outside, Michael and Spry watched a sergeant's inspection of the ten volunteers. Extra crispness in their movements demonstrated their pride and confidence after the news about Heron's Bridge.

Swaggering alongside the sergeant was Trouble, the most ugly bulldog

Michael had ever seen, his coat a mottle of brown and gray, his tongue awag with slobber. The dog's face held even more wrinkles and folds than usual for the breed, prompting Michael's suspicions that Gabriel Garrity had disciplined the poor beast by slamming his face into a wall. Since Trouble also bore whip scars across his back, the face-slamming theory didn't seem too far-fetched.

The bulldog spotted the two of them and bounded over. Spry patted his head, but Michael leaned over and scratched behind his ears. "Listen here, lad. I got you out of that warehouse in one piece. You must promise me not to rip the seat out of Major Craig's trousers. I might lose my job, get transferred to inventory." With a sinuous rotation of his neck, Trouble dragged his tongue across Michael's cheek. Then he strutted back to the sergeant, well pleased.

Grimacing, Michael straightened and swabbed his face with his handkerchief. Perhaps he should introduce Kate Duncan to Trouble. Affectionate and eager to please, not prone to excessive consumption of spirits, all character and no gossip. The perfect gentleman.

Spry said, low, "By the bye, sir, you were right about the mumbo jumbo. Remember that Mrs. Delacroix mentioned a messenger, a herald with disappointing news?" Grinning, he indicated the ten redcoats. "Look at the men. No disappointments here in Wilmington. Our messenger brought news of victory. You might say that Major Craig took a bulldog-sized bite out of those rebels."

"Indeed." Michael clapped his shoulder, then pulled the note from his pocket and opened it. He told Spry his theory about the note and pointed out the date, where he'd blurred the ink. "So if Mrs. Garrity isn't with her paramour, where do you think she is?"

Spry's expression sobered, and he shuddered. "Ah, no sir, I don't like the way this is sounding."

"Me, either. Here's something else to consider. Whoever wrote this note copied Mr. Greene's penmanship well. Where would this person have obtained a sample of his writing?"

Spry looked hard at him for a second. "The love letters, sir. Mrs. Overton."

"Or Mr. Garrity, Spry. He's heartbroken and infuriated over her affair."

"Mrs. Overton's crazy. She's angry with her mistress for the way she's been treated, and she's an excellent shot with that pistol."

"Difficult to imagine a gunsmith not being an excellent shot with any firearm." He and his assistant studied each other. "All right, let's slow down." Michael massaged his temple. "Puzzle pieces are coming together, but we aren't seeing the whole puzzle." He re-folded the note and tapped it on his palm a moment before returning it to his pocket. "There's something else here, another force at work."

"Mr. Spivey, sir. Mayer, the Garritys' driver, said that Mrs. Garrity paid Spivey a visit last week."

"And seemed pleased with herself afterwards. Yes, I remember."

Spry's eyes widened. "Maybe he tried to seduce her, so she threatened him, told him she'd expose his footwashing rubbish as a cover for his seduction attempts."

"Eh." Michael wrinkled his nose. "Then how did he copy Mr. Greene's handwriting?"

"Suppose Greene's one of his church elders. You know someone must have the task of dumping dirty water from all the foot tubs. What better job for a surplus stallion in a herd of mares?"

Michael stroked his chin, thoughtful, then yanked his hand away when he remembered the pimples. But the pimples didn't feel like they owned his face so much anymore. "That certainly explains how Mr. Greene, with property in New Berne, could make himself available so often to Mrs. Garrity. He stays at the church, perhaps helping Mr. Spivey with construction work."

He spied the sergeant approaching, and saddled horses being led from the stables: mostly broad-backed workhorses. At least Cleopatra was among the mounts. "Spry, I've noticed that the civilians here in Wilmington seem to need things to talk about. So let's make a spectacle of ourselves, shall we?"

Chapter Seventeen

THERE WAS NO avoiding the impression that those soldiers who rode the workhorses looked like bumpkins. Michael didn't see the last of the humor in people's expressions until he and the patrol passed the blockade set up for inspections on the road northwest of town. They crossed the Northeast Cape Fear River on a ferry, and he sent a man ahead to scout for the church road, a left turnoff. For the most part, the flat terrain, well-maintained sand-and-shell track, and cleared roadside enhanced visibility. However Michael took note of two areas along the route where nature abetted an ambush.

The scout rode back to report on the turnoff, which they found with no difficulty. As Betty Overton described, the land grew swampier to either side of the drive, vegetation closing around them. After two hundred yards and a third potential ambush location, the party rounded a bend to behold a rundown barn and matching two-story house perched a hundred feet apart on a cleared ridge of sandy soil.

Although the cleared zone was empty of vehicles or mounts, it could easily have parked several dozen wagons and horses. Nothing in the area moved except crows, offering an occasional squawked commentary from the pines. Michael saw no sign of people. Still, it was early yet, not quite four o'clock. He rode forward, Spry behind him. "Hullo! Is anyone here? Mr. Spivey?"

Receiving no response, he signaled the men to proceed. They fanned out, circled both buildings, and converged without spotting anyone.

New pinewood watering troughs had been filled with clean water. Portions of rotted roof and walls on both barn and house had been replaced with new shingles and planks. A large garden bed was tilled but not yet planted. Add to that a huge trash pile, a sand pile with several shovels and overturned wheelbarrows, stacks of new lumber, and a vault. All of it was indicative of recent activity.

The soldiers dismounted. Michael sent four men to the house to look around. To the four who'd be standing watch, he specified that if anyone from the congregation showed up, the soldiers were conducting an official assessment of the facilities. He, Spry, and the remaining two men entered the barn.

Opened doors provided enough light for them to see crates and barrels stacked along both walls in the aisles. Six unlit lanterns hung from hooks in the low beams overhead, and sconces minus candles had been mounted on the walls. A nave of sorts separated five rows of rough-hewn benches. An altar table, pulpit, and two ladder-back chairs designated the chancel area. No crosses, banners, cloth, or paintings. The interior of the barn reeked of mold, worm-eaten wood, and Atlantic Ocean. Dampness enhanced the day's chill and trapped it within, encouraged to linger by the packed dirt floor of the barn.

Behind the chancel, a partition walled off a room from the main sanctuary. An open space gaped where a door should have been. After instructing the men to search the sanctuary, including the crates and barrels, Michael and Spry lit one of the lanterns they'd brought along and retreated into the room behind the chancel.

They stepped up about a foot onto a wooden platform installed in the narrow room. Floor-to-ceiling, shelves stored wooden basins, towels, linen cloths for the altar table, kegs of purple wine, wrapped loaves of bread, candles, and a few tattered copies of the Bible. On a shelf, wrapped in a canvas sack, Spry found two black wool clerical robes. He shoved the sack of vestments back onto the shelf, then sniffed. "Do you smell burned powder, sir?"

"Yes. I wager Mr. Spivey has a firearms cache hidden around here somewhere." Michael stomped his boot on the floor. "Stashed beneath this platform, perhaps."

They searched over the floor twice without locating a way beneath it. Then Spry found a ladder hidden in the shadows at the end of a shelf. Michael craned his neck to study the ceiling. "There's the loft entrance above those shelves. I shall have a look at what's up there."

Spry braced the ladder against the top of a shelf and held it steady for Michael to climb. At the upper rungs of the ladder, Michael pushed the board away that covered the entrance to the loft. Spry handed him up the lantern.

In the cramped space beneath the roof were five wadded sheets of canvas. From footprints in the heavy dust near Michael, several men had recently been through the loft. He lifted the edge of the closest canvas. The concentrated smell of burned black powder sprang out at him. Beneath another canvas, he found a spill of powder and one rolled cartridge, suggestive of but not proving the recent presence of firearms. Damned rebel preachers and their houses of sedition.

Michael tucked the rolled cartridge in his tote sack and eyed his assistant below. "Looks like someone may have stored ammunition and firearms up here. Too bad they aren't here now." Perhaps when the Committee of Safety left Wilmington, it split the weapons cache, sent part of it upriver with Colonel Young to Heron's Bridge and the rest to the Bethany Church, in case they needed weapons to fall back on.

Spry chuckled. "Let's throw Mr. Spivey's arse in jail, sir."

"What, and miss the footwashing? Alas, one cartridge and some spilled black powder are all I found. Not enough evidence against him." The lantern held up, he made a final sweep of the area with his gaze. "If weapons do move through this church, I want to know who else is involved. Mr. Spivey might be a bigger participant than Mr. Garrity."

"Yes, sir. According to our witnesses, Mrs. Garrity's been out here to visit him several times. Do you suppose Mr. Spivey was involved in her husband's recent contract?"

"Possibly. But for now, we must make sure he doesn't suspect that we've snooped in the loft. Otherwise, he might not move weapons through here again."

Michael backed down the ladder part way. Light swept over the very top shelf, where he spied another canvas bag wedged between ceiling and shelf. After handing the lantern down to Spry, he tugged the bag to him and worried the tie open a little way. Folded inside was a bolt of dark fabric—wool, so his fingers told him. Another clerical robe, perhaps.

A sentry shouted, followed by the indignant bellow of another man. Michael and Spry stared at the entrance of the storage room. The private's voice was taut. "That could be Mr. Spivey, sir."

In haste, Michael pushed the bag back where he'd found it. After closing the entrance to the loft, he scampered down. "Spry, replace that ladder in the shadows and come along."

Infantrymen blocked entrance to the barn from outside, muskets held ready. Just past them paced a fellow with blond hair balding like the pate of Benjamin Franklin. "You profane the House of God! Let me in there!" Extravagant theatricality suffused each gesture. He appeared to be in his early thirties and fit in his clothing like a scarecrow who'd lost most of his stuffing. From witness descriptions Michael had received, the man had to be Elijah Spivey.

A second man stood about ten feet away, arms crossed calmly over his chest, booted feet shoulder-width apart. He sported a powdered periwig and finer clothing. From his rugged handsomeness and crooked nose, Michael guessed that he'd at last found Paul Greene.

What luck. Two men he wanted to question.

Michael stepped past his men, followed by Spry. The balding fellow's eyes widened when he spotted them, and although he continued to pace, his vocalizations rose like the climax of a sermon. "How dare you set foot on this property and enter a house of worship uninvited? Thus saith the Lord God, 'I will shortly pour out my fury upon thee, and accomplish mine anger upon thee: and I will judge thee according to thy ways, and will recompense thee for all thine abominations.'" He glared at Michael and Spry, squared off with them, and narrowed his eyes. "Ezekiel 7:8."

Michael, with Spry at his side, took a position that allowed him to keep an eye on both men. He smiled and addressed the blond man. "'Blessed are the peacemakers: for they shall be called the children of God.' The Sermon on the Mount."

"Peacemakers, bah." He glared at Michael's epaulet. "You're the man in charge here?"

"I am, sir. Good afternoon. Lieutenant Stoddard, at your service."

"If you're at my service, I demand an explanation for why you're carousing around inside my church without permission."

Michael heard the tension underlying his indignation, the suspicion that he might be arrested. "Are you the minister here?"

"Yes, I am. Vicar Spivey." He took a deep breath. "This is an outrage, Lieutenant. I leave my property for a mere hour, and when I return, I find a dozen redcoats pilfering the house of God! We are peaceful here at this church, sir, humble servants of the Lord. I assure you we mean to cause no trouble with Major Craig."

"That's encouraging to hear, Mr. Spivey, and I do apologize for giving you a fright just now. We're on a courtesy call from Major Craig. And my men and I are all good Anglicans here, eager to attend your service this evening. Oh, don't fret. We shall remain in the back so as to not distract your flock. As for our business in the church building, we merely conducted an inspection of the premises to ensure that you're in compliance with regulations issued by Parliament."

Spivey's lips puckered as if he'd bitten into a lime. "Regulations? I don't have to comply with any regulations."

"To the contrary, Major Craig now commands the territory for the Crown. You'll find that we operate in a much more efficient manner than the Committee of Safety."

The preacher's eyes narrowed. He drew back a bit, and his gaze made a furtive dash toward the barn. Michael's spirits sank. Spivey had guessed that they'd found evidence of his trafficking.

How could Michael pull the wool over the preacher's eyes? Instinct told him that his reputation as Craig's criminal investigator hadn't yet reached Spivey. Desperate to allay his suspicions, Michael cast the net of his imagination wide. "You see, I'm a safety inspector, Reverend." Spivey's brows lowered, so Michael continued. "A safety inspector is a special engineer assigned to the Eighty-Second. As soon as I return to Wilmington, I shall draw up a list of violations that I found on the property and send it to you, along with a copy of Parliament's latest act passed for houses of worship. You'll have thirty days to comply with the standards."

True, the regiment had a selection of engineers among the men, but there was no "safety inspector." Michael glanced at Spry and bit his tongue to keep from guffawing. His assistant attempted to disguise his astonishment at the pretentious nonsense his commander spun. "And, ah, the first offense for non-compliance is usually a fine of ten pounds. Subsequent offenses incur elevated fines and incorporate jail terms and eventual seizure of the property for the Crown's use."

Spivey licked his lips, and his expression sagged. Michael guessed that his fears of being arrested and having operations interrupted had been supplanted with the expectation of facing long-term, crippling sanctions on his enterprise from a hostile government. "Mr. Stoddard, the Church of Mary and Martha of Bethany is poor, in its inception, with few resources to effect construction repairs or pay fines."

"I understand, sir." He resisted looking at Spry, so he wouldn't be tempted again to laughter, and pretended to contemplate the trees just beyond the cleared zone. "Of course, we do regard cooperation in a good light. If you work with us, we're much more likely to be lenient for a missed deadline at correcting a violation."

"You mention violations. What violations are these?"

"As I said, you'll receive the full list with my report in a few days." Spivey clenched his jaw, and Michael realized that the preacher wanted an example. Michael dug deep into his mental bag of horse feathers. "That trash pile out back, for example, is too close to the buildings by at least one hundred feet."

Spivey snorted. "I don't see how a trash pile matters."

Blast, how did a trash pile matter?

"Yellow fever and malaria, Mr. Spivey," said Spry.

Bless Spry for the nudge. "Yes, this area is prone to malaria and epidemics of yellow fever." Michael squared his shoulders, having found his footing at last. "Come summer, the trash pile presents a breeding ground for contagion. If your congregants catch yellow fever, they'll threaten the health of everyone in Wilmington. So you'll need to relocate all the garbage."

Spivey's eyes glazed. Michael felt his own momentum pick up. "By the bye, Mr. Spivey, how many people are in your congregation, on average?"

"Fifty. Sixty."

"Regulation two paragraph seven stipulates proper illumination for a church interior, a minimum of two hanging lanterns per ten congregants. You have six currently, making you short by four lanterns."

Spivey frowned. "We use wall sconces during services to ensure enough lighting."

"Actually, wall sconces fall under another sub-section of the regulations document and aren't considered a substitute for adequate overhead illumination."

Up until then, Spivey's companion had remained silent, although Michael was aware of his attention on the conversation. He walked over and clamped his hand on Spivey's shoulder. "Elijah, let me handle this. What is it you really want with us, Lieutenant?"

Sharp fellow. "I don't believe we've been introduced, sir."

"I'm Vicar Spivey's cousin, Mr. Greene."

Spivey's *cousin*, ah, yes. There did seem to be a faint resemblance between them. Michael allowed the surprise of name recognition to color his expression. "Mr. Greene. How excellent that I have both Mr. Spivey and Mr. Greene together. You see, I need to question both of you about Mrs. Gabriel Garrity from Wilmington. I know from the testimony of other area residents that both of you have her acquaintance." He bored his gaze into Greene. "So. Where shall we sit and talk?"

"I'm afraid we don't have time to talk right now." Greene's upper lip curled. "We must prepare for a worship service that begins in less than an hour. Return on the morrow at ten o'clock, and we shall answer your questions then."

Michael mirrored Greene's disdain, amazed that Spivey's cousin thought him so naive. "We can do this one of two ways, Mr. Greene. We can talk now, before the service, and be finished in good time for your preparations. Or you and your cousin can journey back to Wilmington under our escort this afternoon, and your congregants won't have a worship service this evening. Your choice."

Chapter Eighteen

HANDS CLASPED BEHIND him, Michael strolled past the preacher, who sat on a bench inside the barn. Closing the barn doors for privacy, and for the purpose of isolating Spivey from his cousin, had plunged the interior into gloom. Overhead, all six lanterns were lit, but in Michael's opinion, they could use far more lanterns to keep congregants from tripping on each other. "Mr. Spivey, when was the last time you spoke with Mrs. Garrity?"

Spry hovered behind Spivey. From the corner of his eye, the preacher noticed him and sniffed. "Why do you want to know?"

"Allow me to clarify a point. I don't expect you to answer a question from me with a question. Otherwise, we shall be here quite a while, and you shall be canceling your service this evening."

"You cannot possibly be Major Craig's safety inspector."

Michael halted his stroll, crossed his arms, and scowled. "No, I'm not his safety inspector. I'm his lead investigator for criminal activity. His safety inspector marched with him to Heron's Bridge. He's actually a personable, easygoing fellow with an excellent sense of humor, while I'm an irritable lout who gets a bellyache around uncooperative rebels. But I volunteered to inspect your church in his stead, and I wager that I found twice as many violations as he would have found. I can make life very unpleasant for you, Mr. Spivey, and I won't ask for your cooperation a second time. When was the last time you spoke with Mrs. Garrity?"

Spivey glowered at the floor. "She visited this church on Sunday the third of December."

"For what reason did she visit?"

"She attended the first service."

"Who was with her?"

"No one."

At Michael's curt nod, Spry yanked Spivey's right arm around and pinned it to his back, wrenching it upward. Spivey squawked with pain and writhed for release but found himself trapped. "Burn in hell, you demons! I've done nothing wrong!"

Michael uncrossed his arms and stalked over to stand just out of reach of the preacher. "God doesn't much favor liars, sir, and you've just lied to me several times."

"She did come to my first service, I swear it!"

"Who was with her?"

"Her sister and her housekeeper."

As he suspected, Salome Ward had lied about the last time she'd seen her sister. He wondered why. He nodded. "Good. I like hearing the truth. Let's hear more. How many times have you seen Mrs. Garrity since then?"

"Six, m-m-maybe seven."

"Sunday services only?"

"No. A couple of Wednesday services, too. Sometimes she was joined by her sister, and sometimes by her housekeeper." He groaned. "Please, release my arm. I've lost feeling in my hand."

"Do you need my assistant to flex your arm further to recall the date of Mrs. Garrity's most recent visit?

"The morning of Thursday the twenty-fifth of January, I think. She was alone that day."

"Why did she visit you on a non-church day, alone?"

"She wanted my counsel about an affair of the heart. I-I cannot speak more detail. I must keep the confidence of—" He let out another squawk.

"Sorry, sir," said Spry. "I must have squeezed him too tightly."

"Her husband," gasped Spivey, "took a mistress—Mrs. Garrity was angry—wanted to kill him."

What an intriguing new twist, if Spivey could be believed, and Michael thought he could by that point. He knew Julia the shrew, and Julia the adulteress, but this was his first introduction to Julia the murderess. He should have expected it. If she pulled off the murder of her husband without being found guilty, she'd be free to marry her paramour. Had she attempted to murder Mr. Garrity Saturday, while the transition in government distracted all of Wilmington?

He signaled Spry to release the preacher, who tried to rise, but Michael shoved him back onto the bench. "How did you counsel Mrs. Garrity to deal with her husband?"

Spivey shuddered, flexed the fingers of his right hand, and worked his right shoulder gingerly, as if the parts no longer fit together well. "I-I reminded her that murder is a sin, and I encouraged her to read Song of Solomon."

Michael commanded his gaze. "Song of Solomon? A curious choice, considering that Mrs. Garrity detests her husband. And you're aware of that, so you suggested that she read the most erotic love poetry in the Bible because she's having an affair with your cousin. You've encouraged their affair because the Ward sisters have money, and how did you put it earlier? 'The Church of Mary and Martha of Bethany is poor, in its inception, with few resources to effect construction repairs or pay fines.' Sir, you're a master of the art of hypocrisy."

Spivey gripped the bench. "How dare you slander me?"

Michael spread his hands. "You don't need my help at slandering yourself. You're doing an excellent job of it all on your own."

Spry intercepted Spivey's lunge at Michael and shoved the preacher back onto the bench with far less delicacy than Michael had done seconds earlier. A snarl erupted from Spivey. "You baseborn scoundrel, I'm going to report you to Major Craig."

Michael grinned. "Who do you think sent me out here to investigate you? While we're having such an enlightening conversation, tell me how you advised Mrs. Garrity to deal with her husband's mistress."

"I told her to stay away from the woman."

"You told her that because you planned to deal with Mrs. Delacroix yourself. You made an attempt at ravishing her, and when her slave cast you out of the house on your arse, you resorted to threats. She's now a witch to be driven from the community."

Spivey drew a raspy breath. "That woman is practicing black magic and sleeping with the devil!"

"Please don't insult my intelligence. The witch laws were repealed decades ago."

"The Bible stands, no matter the decade. 'Thou shalt not suffer a witch to live.' Exodus 22:18."

"'But I say unto you, Love your enemies.' Reverend, if you purport to preach Christianity, you must pull your head out of the Old Testament. I haven't yet heard you quote Jesus. And I believe my men and I really do need to stay for the services tonight so I can ascertain just what sort of divine love you're advocating for your congregation." Michael drew his lips over his teeth in a gesture that couldn't be mistaken for humor. "If anything ill happens to Mrs. Delacroix, you're at the top of my list of suspects."

"Lieutenant, let me go. My congregants will begin arriving within minutes."

Mrs. Farrell's years of anguish returned to Michael's memory, and his pulse thumped around. What a ball of slime he had sitting on the bench before him. How he wished the preacher would give him good reason to punch him. "So after Mrs. Garrity confessed this highly charged, intimate matter to you last Thursday, you slept with her."

Spivey's cheeks reddened. "I did nothing of the sort!" He flinched, seeing Spry bend toward him, and spittle gathered on his lips. "Ask Mrs. Forbes! She was a witness the entire time."

"Who is Mrs. Forbes?"

The preacher bared his teeth. "The church's Manager of Education."

Manager of Education? What the hell was that? The conviction grew in Michael that the Bethanys had no male leadership besides Spivey and Greene, and the preacher had turned over church operations to his women congregants. What a unique but bizarre idea. He regarded Spivey anew: a scrawny stallion who'd figured out a masterful way to lure mares to him. "I'm sure you've heard by now that Mrs. Garrity disappeared last Saturday. Where is she?"

"I don't know."

"Where were you last Saturday morning?"

"In my house, praying for God's guidance on my upcoming sermon."

"Who witnessed this?"

"No one. I was alone all morning."

The preacher had no alibi for the time that Julia Garrity disappeared. Michael nodded to Spry, and Spivey found his arm twisted again. "Let's think through this, sir. Your cousin has been amusing Mrs. Garrity since last October, and he knows that she's been telling her sister all sorts of intimate details about their lustful encounters. Miss Ward is fascinated with Mr. Greene—"

"I don't know what you're—arrgghh, you're torturing me!"

"Torturing? Beg your pardon, sir—Spry, are we torturing this gentleman?"

"No, sir. If we were torturing him—" Spry gave Spivey's arm a shove, and the preacher choked with pain. "—he'd be bleeding, or bones would be broken. Or his guts would be hanging out. Or his arm would be ripped out of its socket. Aye, those were the good old days, when we were allowed to draw and quarter, sir."

"M-m-monsters!" Spivey's face was pale.

Michael regained his attention. "So. It's more difficult to get money from Mrs. Garrity than from her unmarried sister. You and your cousin abduct Mrs. Garrity, murder her, and dispose of the body. Miss Ward needs consolation. Mr. Greene steps onto the stage and claims her heart. They're married, and the church is blessed with a substantial sponsor. Did I miss any details?"

"A—A lie! Haven't s-seen Mrs. G-Garrity since Thursday!"

Spry cranked the arm further. Spivey sobbed and shook.

"Perhaps your cousin acted on his own?"

"D-Don't know—ask him!"

"I shall." At Michael's signal, Spry released the preacher, who hugged his abused arm and rocked himself. "Thank you for your cooperation in this inquiry, sir. No further questions for now, but don't be surprised if we're back on the morrow."

★★★

His shoulders thrown back, one fist cocked on his hip, Paul Greene regarded Michael from the bench his cousin had occupied, his gaze unwavering. "Make haste with your questions. Congregants have started gathering."

Michael flicked his attention to Spry, at the ready behind the bench, before resuming a study of Greene. The sketch Mrs. Overton had destroyed of him had blazoned out his self-confidence and authority in charcoal. Michael got the impression that Greene was really the brains behind the operation. Not only was he more handsome than his preacher cousin, he was more resilient and assured. That meant the arm twist behind the back might not generate the kind of results Michael needed from him.

"Mr. Greene, you don't strike me as the sort of fellow called to the clergy." Michael waited for a response. Greene said nothing, just continued to regard him with a closed expression. He didn't even fidget.

Very well, that prod didn't work. What would rile Greene and make him divulge information? Michael rethought his angle. Greene oozed a controlled and supercilious self-confidence. A man like him had to be smug over his prowess with the ladies. "So. You're the fellow who's been amusing Mrs. Garrity for three months. How did you meet her?"

"She was in her husband's shop the day he sold me a brace of pistols."

"What a lucky man you are. I've seen the portrait of her above the fireplace. Must be difficult to keep up with a woman like that. Not sure whether I'd even try. I cannot blame you for, you know, the *problem*."

A wrinkle appeared between Greene's brows. He leaned forward. "What problem are you talking about?"

Hah. A chink had appeared in Greene's armor. Michael waved his hand. "Forget it. Likely just idle gossip among women. As you know, I'm investigating Mrs. Garrity's disappearance. When did you see her again after your rendezvous last Tuesday?"

Greene drew back, then frowned. "How did you know about that meeting?"

"Mrs. Garrity confides in her sister. Most of it is true, although some of it I suspect to be embellishment. You know how merciless ladies can be when we don't measure up."

His eyes bulged, and he stabbed a forefinger at Michael. "Damnation, I don't have a *problem*, you got that, Lieutenant? I measure up well and good, so I've always been told. Miss Ward lied to you, gave you some of that *embellishment*." He crossed his arms over his chest, straightened his shoulders, and jutted his chin. "I'd gladly have met with Julia Wednesday, Thursday, and Friday, too, but she was too busy. She's been far too busy lately."

"Too busy." Michael let the echo hang in the air and nodded at Greene gently. Then he cocked an eyebrow at Spry. "It sounds as though Mr. Greene doesn't know about Mr. Lloyd."

"No, sir."

"Mr. *Who*?" Then Greene scowled. His lips sealed over the suspicion that his mistress had been cuckolding more men than just her husband.

"As I said, sir, ladies can be merciless. What did your slave tell you happened after you sent him to fetch Mrs. Garrity Saturday morning? Did she send him away with an insult? It sounds as though she'd already made plans for a rendezvous with another gentleman."

"I don't know what you're talking about. I didn't send anyone to fetch Julia Saturday morning."

Michael unfolded the note and turned it toward him. "Explain this."

Greene read the note and shook his head with a sincere expression of perplexity. "I didn't write it. I don't know where it came from. Where is Julia?"

Michael replaced the note in his pocket, propped hands on his hips, and studied Greene. "You tell me."

Greene's eyes hardened with challenge. "What makes you think I had something to do with her disappearance?"

"Your cousin told me that Mrs. Garrity had plans to murder her husband and his mistress."

Disbelief ripped through Greene's face. "Why would she do that? Did she fancy she'd marry me afterwards?"

"No. She planned to marry the other fellow." At Greene's gape, Michael added, "Remember, she complained to her sister of your problem."

Greene slammed the bench with both fists and cursed in a very un-preacherly manner. "What does she expect of me? It only happened once, but the tart had the nerve to compare me to that husband of hers."

Behind his back, Spry covered his mouth with his hand. Stifled laughter emerged as a cough. Michael adopted what he hoped was an expression of sympathy. "That's bloody cruel of her, especially after all those detailed love letters you've faithfully written her."

The volume of Greene's voice rose. "She promised to burn them!"

Maybe Greene wasn't as smart as Michael had presumed. "Women never destroy love letters, sir."

"That crazy housekeeper must have let you have them." Greene's forefinger wagged again. "Julia insisted that I write her twice a week. Every Monday and Thursday, I've posted her a letter. I'll tell you something else. She's obsessed over that French witch, jealous to the point of wanting to run her out of town. And I don't blame her."

"You also believe Mrs. Delacroix is a witch?"

Greene clamped his jaw in defiance and glared.

Michael paced a few steps away and tamped down the aggravation that splintered his concentration. Witches. Were all these people daft?

He spun on his heel and walked back to stand before him. "Before this afternoon, I hadn't heard anyone except the Garritys' housekeeper complain about Mrs. Delacroix operating in the traditional negative capacity ascribed to witches: cursing, blighting, and so forth. In my opinion, Mrs. Overton's credibility is questionable."

"Mad Betty," Greene muttered.

"Do you really believe that Mrs. Delacroix has supernatural powers?"

He growled. "You decide. Two weeks ago, my cousin paid her a visit." He sneered at Michael. "A *courtesy call*. He asked me to ride with him. That slave of hers threw him out on his bum."

"Yes, Armand did so because your cousin attempted to ravish the lady. Oh, save your breath defending Mr. Spivey. He's already admitted to the deed. What's supernatural about having a servant evict a scoundrel from the house?"

"Because she cursed him afterwards. And she cursed me, too, though I'd not touched her."

"Jolly well for her. And I shall tell you what I told your cousin. If anything bad happens to Mrs. Delacroix, you and he are my top suspects."

"You dog, you don't understand. She cursed our—my—"

"Ah, and that's when your *problem* started." Behind Greene, Spry doubled over and coughed. With iron control, Michael restrained himself from guffawing and focused on Greene. "Mrs. Garrity mocked you for it and compared you to her husband, and to repair your honor, you abducted and murdered her. Where's the body?"

Greene radiated belligerence. "I won't confess to a crime I didn't commit. I already told you I had nothing to do with her disappearance, and I don't know where she is."

"Where were you last Saturday morning?"

"Running errands for the church and picking up supplies."

From outside the barn, Michael could hear the murmur of voices: men, women and children. Spivey's congregation had arrived and awaited admission. Paul Greene appeared sincere in his denial of wrongdoing, but did he know something about Julia Garrity's disappearance? Irked, Michael decided to try one more strategy to trip him.

"All right, sir, I believe you. Perhaps you can see the direction from which I'm approaching my inquiries. From the evidence I've collected, it appears that someone abducted Mrs. Garrity from her back yard Saturday morning. This person knows her well, knows her routine, and knows how to slide beneath her guard. I've wracked my brains for ideas how the culprit might accomplish such a feat, but I don't know Mrs. Garrity. You, however, know her very well. Assist me in constructing a possible sequence for this abduction. If you were to abduct Mrs. Garrity, how would you do it?"

Greene stared at him as if he were a creature from another world and sneered. "I wouldn't abduct her, you ass."

A loud banging on the barn door fragmented Michael's concentration, followed by Spivey's blast of indignation just outside the barn: "Mr. Stoddard, it's ten minutes after the hour! I insist that you allow me to begin the evening service!"

Instinct told Michael that Paul Greene didn't possess knowledge of Mrs. Garrity's disappearance. He might even have a solid alibi. He fought to keep his shoulders from sagging. He had several more suspects, two of whom he'd rounded up in jail. On the morrow, he'd have to tighten down on matters, question all of them again.

"Very well, Mr. Greene. You and your cousin may conduct the service. I shall likely have further questions of you on the morrow, so don't leave the area." Without waiting for Greene's response, he strode for the door to unlatch it and let church begin.

Chapter Nineteen

A FEW MINUTES after six o'clock that evening, at the front of the church, Spivey lifted outstretched hands to his flock, beatific peace wreathing his expression. "My sisters and brothers, let us go forth in the name of Christ."✱

Behind him, and to his right, Greene intoned a prompt for the people, appropriate response for the end of an Anglican service: "Thanks be to God."✱ The fifty-three congregants mouthed the response.

They'd needed each and every prompt Greene had delivered, Michael recognized at the back of the barn with his men. From the confusion of Spivey's flock, a group already subdued at the presence of twelve soldiers, he suspected that not a one of them had ever before attended an Anglican service. At the last minute, Spivey and Greene had switched to a proper Church of England service.

Quiet weeping had come from four plump brunettes on the front bench, the only attendees wearing white kerchiefs on their heads. (Had they expected to be inducted into Spivey's secret order of handmaidens that night?) The towels and wooden foot-washing basins had remained stored in the room behind the chancel. Michael felt certain that out of spite for the regiment, and to disappoint twelve infantrymen who'd anticipated experiencing an exotic ritual—and especially to punish *him* for disrupting their routine—Spivey and Greene had omitted the footwashing ceremony from the service. Thus did they ensure that nothing controversial occurred during the service to warrant a follow-up visit from the regiment.

Spivey and Greene, both dressed in the dark robes from the storage room, rushed the flock out the door. Congregants' wagons, chairs, and horses disappeared within ten minutes. Having no excuse to linger, Michael and his men headed back to Wilmington, loaded muskets across each man's lap. He deferred reports from the four soldiers who had searched the house until later, when the party wasn't occupied with a safe return. Even though a moon almost at first quarter aided their passage, night provided far too much advantage for an ambush party.

The rebels had the sense to wait until the soldiers gained firmer ground on the road before launching their attack. About twenty of them emerged on horseback in a cluster from behind one of the bends in the road. Their pistol fire sporadic, they issued bloodcurdling Indian-style yells as they charged.

Three horses of the Eighty-Second shied and whinnied with the sudden commotion. Their riders brought them back under control. Hearing the whine of a ball past his ear, Michael ordered his men to fire at will straight into the approaching party.

Musket fire pocked the dark. Rebels yelped in pain and shouted. In the clearing smoke, Michael saw some men struggling to manage their frightened horses while others succumbed to panic.

The faltering rebel offensive fed the fire in Michael's blood. He drew his sword and tilted back his head, so his command wouldn't be swallowed in the clamor. "Eighty-Second, advance!"

The soldiers charged their opponents. Shouts of confusion became screams of fright. The rebels scattered east and west into the swampy wilderness ahead of them, no order to their flight. Wounded men clung to their horses.

Rather than giving chase by night across terrain familiar to foes, Michael halted the charge to inspect damages. Two infantrymen had been nicked with musket balls but were capable of controlling their mounts. Michael pressed the patrol back to Wilmington.

In his estimation, other than selecting a reasonable spot for ambush, the rebels in the encounter had exhibited no seasoned fighting experience. They'd provided a large target and hadn't anticipated a turn of the offensive. From reports thus far, Major Craig was encountering a similar resistance, disorganized and weak. But this corner of North Carolina had been almost devoid of war for five years, and with his own eyes Michael had seen how fiercely rebels fought elsewhere. It wasn't wise to underestimate the rebels.

The infirmary in town was set up at one end of the stables. There Michael learned from the head surgeon, Clayton, that the two men scraped by musket balls would be fit for duty within a day or so. He thanked the soldiers for their courage and service, exited the infirmary with Spry, and finally heard reports from those men who had searched Spivey's house. All four reported that the place was filthy. However they'd uncovered nothing that could be used against Spivey, such as weapons or ammunition.

Michael and his assistant left the regiment around eight o'clock. Neither spoke while they walked in the cool darkness for their lodgings on Second Street. Two dogs barked at them, then hushed as soon as they passed.

The seclusion of the Bethanys' church—ten miles northwest in the wilderness—made it an ideal spot to transfer weapons from one party to another. Michael pondered how he might discover other links in a trafficking chain. He wasn't hopeful about finding enough to arrest Spivey on his follow-up inspection. Spivey didn't come across as an inherently stupid person, especially after the way he'd manipulated the format of his church service on such short notice.

They arrived at Enid's house. Candles were lit inside. On the front walkway, they paused to sniff the air. Michael's stomach grumbled. "She said she was going to bake an apple tart, Spry."

His assistant grunted. "It's apples I smell, sir, with butter and cinnamon."

Michael pointed toward the side yard. "We'd better wash up first, or she won't let us anywhere near the food." Mother hen.

They ambled around the house and emerged in the darkness of the back yard. Spry sniffed again. "Mmm. Lights on in the kitchen, sir. Enid was baking while we were getting shot at."

They walked past the front stable door, headed for the rear. "She was probably baking while we were listening to Mr. Spivey's drone at the pulpit, too. Remember to thank her, lad."

Movement in Michael's peripheral vision was his only warning. A man with a kerchief concealing his lower face barreled from behind the stable into Spry. His fist slammed the private in the stomach, sprawling him on the ground.

Another masked man darted for Michael, but Michael had his dagger ready. He gouged the other man's upper arm with it. His opponent howled and staggered back, clutching his arm. "You shit!" Neighborhood dogs barked.

A third man came from behind and wrenched the dagger from Michael's hand. The injured man's fist jutted out and smacked Michael's cheekbone. Pain exploded through his head, and a million stars poured into the back yard.

He flung up his forearm. It blocked the next punch at his face. He tore the kerchief down below his attacker's chin to reveal a familiar face. Then the man behind pinned his arms, leaving him open to the man with the injured arm, who pumped a blow to Michael's gut. "You didn't learn earlier tonight! Stop persecuting the Bethanys!"

With a sudden bawl of agony, Michael's captor released him, enabling Michael to evade another punch and crack the injured man in the nose. He pivoted to spot Enid chasing the man who'd pinned him, herding him off the property by jabbing him with a pitchfork. She screeched. "Out of here, varmint!" Neighborhood dogs ramped up the volume on their commentary.

Nose streaming blood, the man with the injured arm swung at Michael again. He dodged, delivered a fist to the man's gut. Then he grabbed him by the coat and flung him straight at a returning Enid who screeched again and chased after him with her pitchfork.

Michael dragged an unmasked man off Spry and kneed him in the groin, off-center, but still potent enough to extract a wheeze of agony from him. The second man on Spry, who'd also been unmasked, spotted Enid with the pitchfork and fled, leaving the attacker who'd been kicked in the groin to shamble his escape from the housekeeper.

Battle frenzy emptied from Michael's blood. He breathed heavily. His stomach and the left side of his face pulsated with pain, but he bit back a groan to give his assistant a hand up from the ground. "You all right, Spry? Still have all your teeth?" He fingered his face and flinched at a goose egg decorating his cheekbone. At least his jaw was operable. He'd have been infuriated if a broken jaw had kept him from eating Enid's apple tart.

"Yes, sir." Spry rotated his shoulder, scooped Michael's dagger off the ground, and presented it to him. "Those rogues on me were in the congregation tonight."

"Yes, and I recognized one from the raiding party at Mr. Farrell's estate last Sunday."

Spry whistled, low. "After we talked with Mrs. Farrell this morning, I suspected there was a connection, sir. They were trying to kidnap her and bring her to Mr. Spivey. Those worms."

"Exactly. Mr. Spivey's minions have attempted to abduct a civilian, and they've now assaulted two officers of the law."

Spry grinned and clapped his hands together once. "Yes, sir. Looks like we're arresting Mr. Spivey on the morrow."

"And throwing his scrawny bum in jail."

They both turned and spotted the return of the bobbing, victorious pitchfork. Spry snorted. "Sir, do you get the impression that Enid's used that thing on someone before?"

Michael laughed. "Indeed, and I want to know where to find a hundred warriors like her."

***

In the dining room, the clock on the mantle chimed ten at night. Michael's left cheekbone throbbed despite Enid's mustard poultice, and his chin tingled from another application of her pimple treatment. He'd hoped that they'd find a clue for the investigation among Greene's love letters to Julia Garrity, so he and Spry had spread them out on the table. But after reading for half an hour, the lurid, lusty encounters smeared together in Michael's head, and he gave a huge yawn.

The yawn transferred to Spry. Then the private's eyes bugged at the content of a letter in his hand. "Oh, wait, sir. Here's one description I missed earlier. 'Even the thought of laying my whip to your smooth arse and sucking the welt drives my cocke to near bursting.'" Puppy-like exuberance frolicked over Spry's face. "This bugger could earn a living writing for magazines in London."

Michael winced from his bruises. "Better keep your voice down." He pointed upstairs. "Enid's got good ears."

He pushed back from the table and reevaluated the letters, golden by candlelight. "Greene claims he posted to Mrs. Garrity every Monday and Thursday. If the post were running smoothly, she'd receive a love letter every Tuesday and Friday. Greene corroborated what Mr. Mayer, the driver, said about Tuesdays being their rendezvous days. We've already noticed that his Monday letters confirm their meeting for the next day. Let's look for other patterns. The passage you just read. What was the date on the letter?"

"The sixteenth of November, last year, sir."

Michael calculated backwards. "A Thursday letter. Sort all the Thursday letters in one pile by you, and I shall sort Monday letters." They shuffled letters to create two piles. "Now order them chronologically within the piles, the newest letters on top." They fell silent to read again.

After a few minutes, Spry said, "Sir, Thursday seems to be his day to recapitulate the highlights of their Tuesday encounters."

"Hmm. On Monday, he confirms their meeting for the next day, and he also feeds her a tease about what he plans to do with her at their next encounter." Michael fingered a newfound scalp bruise, then shuffled letters. "Are you missing any Thursday letters?"

"No, sir. Looks like he wrote her every Thursday, starting in October."

"I'm missing a letter dated Monday the twenty-second of January. That's Monday a week ago. I have his letter from this past Monday, the twenty-ninth. Mrs. Garrity had been missing two days by then, so I doubt she read it." Frowning, he sat back and allowed his gaze to drift to a shadowy corner while twiddling his thumbs in his lap. "But the seal was broken on that one. *Someone* read it."

"Mrs. Overton, sir?"

"I'm not convinced. Look through your pile for a Monday letter from the twenty-second."

Spry searched, and after a moment, glanced up at him. "It's not here, sir."

Michael thumbed his stack of letters again. Bemused, he grabbed a candle, bent over, and scanned the floor, but the letter hadn't dropped from the table. "That letter's missing, Spry." He straightened, grunted at his achy stomach, and returned the candle to the table. "Can you recall anything significant for this investigation in the events of Monday the twenty-second?"

"Not that I can recollect, sir."

Michael drummed fingertips on the table and returned his gaze to the corner. "We untied the packet of letters on Mrs. Garrity's bed this morning. I opened a few of them there."

"Yes, sir, comparing handwriting with that in the note from the back yard. But you didn't accidentally drop a letter in her bedroom. I came around behind you after you'd bound up the packet again and made sure there were no letters on the floor or under the bed."

The same conscientiousness and curiosity had led Spry to find that escape tunnel on the Farrells' estate. Out of all the privates in the regiment, Michael was now certain that he couldn't have chosen a better assistant than Spry. He gave him a crooked smile. "Lad, you've earned your pay for the week."

"Thank you, sir. Maybe Mr. Greene didn't post a letter to her on the twenty-second."

"Mr. Mayer confirmed their rendezvous on the twenty-third. Mr. Greene has clearly enjoyed his sport with Mrs. Garrity. I cannot imagine him forgetting to remind her about any upcoming encounter. If we presume he did indeed post a letter to her on that date, either it was lost in the post, or someone removed the letter from the packet."

Spry stomped a foot with disgust and pushed up from the table. "Mrs. Overton—bah! She beat us to it again, sir. The remnants of that letter are probably keeping the remnants of Mr. Greene's portrait company in Mrs. Garrity's fireplace."

Michael rubbed his eyes, scratchy with fatigue. "I agree. Which suggests that in Mrs. Overton's judgment, the content of the missing letter was incriminatory in a manner far worse than what's in these remaining letters."

"Her judgment?" Spry's expression contorted like that of a man with a mouthful of moldy bread. "The woman's mad, sir. Who knows how her judgment functions?"

Michael stood and collected letters. "Of all our suspects, Mrs. Overton was in the best position Saturday morning to either abduct Mrs. Garrity or assist in her abduction."

"And she has a motive for wanting to dispense with her mistress, sir. She's angry with the way she's been abused by the Garritys for so many years, and she feels trapped as their servant."

"She also has no alibi for her whereabouts late Saturday morning. Yes, Mrs. Overton is highly suspect." Michael bound the letters, thoughtful. "But what about her means?"

"The Negro coachman, sir."

"Yes, Spry, but who is he, and who is his master?"

"Looks like that's our key right there, sir, finding this coachman."

Michael couldn't have agreed more. However, weary as they both were, he doubted they'd make further progress until they'd had some sleep. He dismissed Spry for the night, retired upstairs, and secured the correspondence in his room. Then he unpacked a portable desk his uncle Solomon, the blacksmith, had given him before he left Yorkshire.

Not until almost midnight did he finish detailing the day's events in his journal. The candle at last blown out, he lay back in bed. But his face throbbed, and excitement from the day gyrated in his mind. Sleep didn't find him for at least an hour, and when it did, dreams spun him to the aftermath of a battlefield.

***

Unearthly stillness claimed the soldiers lying on the field. Michael walked among the fallen, knowing that all of them shouldn't be so still and quiet, that some should be writhing and shrieking in agony, moaning in delirium and shock from their injuries. Yet when he looked closer, none of them even appeared injured. No blood, no torn or broken limbs, no decapitations.

It didn't take him much longer to realize that every fallen soldier had dark hair, and every uniform bore an epaulet. He knelt beside one man lying prone, rolled him onto his back, and recoiled at the corpse's facial features. His own sightless eyes entreated the sky, his expression twisted with unnatural torment, his mouth frozen in a soundless scream.

He'd seen that expression before, and the recognition nearly pitched him backwards. He steadied himself and closed his eyes. Then he blinked and gawped.

A different corpse lay below him, that of the murdered Spaniard. The stench of the decomposing body coated his nostrils and tongue. Gagging, he recoiled to flee the scene. But from behind, he received a brutal push back down to his knees.

A hand gripped hair on the back of his head and pressed his face close to the flayed torso of the Spaniard. "Smell it, Stoddard. Stinks, does it not? And it's right beneath your nose."

With a twist of his shoulders, he punched at the gloating face of Lieutenant Fairfax. Fairfax blocked him. Michael squirmed for better leverage. Fairfax slammed him back to his knees. Michael opened his mouth and formed the words to curse him. No sound emerged, as if he were being choked.

"Ah, poor Stoddard. Yes, that's the worst part about it. No matter how hard you struggle, you know you'll remain powerless and silent—about me, about a shadow. In the mean time, look there, it's all beneath your nose. But you don't want to see it now, just as you didn't want to see it in Alton. Red wool fibers beneath the Spaniard's fingernails. Red, from a red coat, from my coat. You didn't want to see it, a fellow officer who'd tortured and murdered. You won't see it now, even though it's beneath your nose."

✶✶✶

Michael thrashed himself to heart-hammering wakefulness. Clutching at his throat, he sat up in bed and gasped for breath. In the corner of the room stood the black outline of a dragoon in the Seventeenth Light. With a scream that reverberated through the house, Michael leapt from bed, his bare feet shocked by the cold floor.

He was still panting, crouched, a dagger in his hand, when Enid tapped at his door. "Mr. Stoddard, are you all right in there?" She continued speaking through a yawn. "I heard you holler."

The dragoon in the corner dissolved into shadow. Michael straightened and re-sheathed the dagger. Sheepishness trickled through him. "Sorry to awaken you, Enid. I—er—it was a leg cramp."

"I've a poultice for that too, sir."

"Yes, yes, in the morning. Thank you. And good night."

He crawled back into bed, realized he still carried the sheathed dagger, and set it on the bedside stand. Another goddamned nightmare. A lucky few soldiers who'd been active in battle never suffered such nightmares, or so he was told. Others endured them far more often than he and drank to numb the horror.

His pulse slowed. Sweat on him cooled. Then details of the nightmare crept back into his head.

Shadow. In the nightmare, Fairfax had labeled himself a *shadow.*

The shadow who bathes in blood, he comes. He is your responsibility.

Michael's pulse tripped. Could Esmé Delacroix have been talking about Fairfax? No, no, that was absurd, sheer coincidence. A French fortuneteller from Saint Domingue couldn't possibly know about Michael's nemesis.

He shoved aside her words and yanked his thoughts back to the nightmare's blatant message: that he was powerless to change orthodoxy. The British Army would never execute one of its officers, a son of the aristocracy, for torturing and murdering Britain's enemies. What lunacy it had been for him to ride those dispatches out to the Legion encampment back in December, imagining he'd find the opportunity to kill Fairfax on his own. And Adam Neville, the scout he'd trusted to help him locate Fairfax in the hinterlands? He was a double spy. Michael had been so foolish to trust him.

His only sensible course was to give up his desire to kill Fairfax before it got *him* killed. Or executed.

As he drowsed, Esmé Delacroix's words snatched away sleep. *You are the one to vanquish him...the shadow...is your responsibility.*

Wide-awake, he stared at the ceiling. Darkness in his room loomed more absolute. He pulled the blanket to his chin. No longer caring whether it earned him eternal damnation, he wished Fairfax dead at the Cowpens. And for the sleepless remainder of the night, he couldn't escape the sense that he'd hidden a message for himself within the tangled skeins of his nightmare.

Chapter Twenty

FIRST THING THURSDAY morning after breakfast, Michael and Spry returned to the barracks. Tongue wagging in delight, Trouble pranced over to greet them, received a round of petting, and tagged along. In the infirmary, the two wounded men rubbed the dog's belly while informing Michael that they'd be released for light duty later that morning. When Michael found the sergeant and requested another ten men for a raid upon Spivey's church, the sergeant scratched behind Trouble's ears and apologized that he couldn't pull together so many men and a cart until after ten o'clock, due to their engagements in other assignments.

Trouble capered off in the company of the sergeant. Michael watched them go. That bulldog got fondled more than a man's mistress.

Carrying firearms, he and his assistant rode past the sentry post and out the Sound Road on the horses they'd had the day before. Their follow-up visit to Mrs. Delacroix wasn't just to inquire after her health and meet the rest of her household. After the reception they'd encountered the previous day from the Bethanys, both men were concerned for the safety of people living so far from help.

Beyond town limits, Spry grew reserved, and after some prodding, he admitted that he hadn't slept well. Although all but traces of Michael's head cold had vanished, he felt far from refreshed after his nightmare, and the black-and-blue knot on his cheekbone ached. He faked a smile and dumped pragmatism into his tone. "Come on, Spry. Being in a fistfight will do that for you."

"Yes, sir. Er, no, sir. I had a nightmare about bloody shadows."

A chill scurried Michael's neck. "Hail the power of suggestion."

"Sir, maybe you should ask Mrs. Delacroix what she meant about a shadow bathing in blood."

Michael's pulse skittered with aggravation. He relaxed his jaw. "So she can charge me money to read my fortune and predict calamity? No, thank you."

"Are we so certain she can tell us nothing of Mrs. Garrity's disappearance, sir?"

What would it take to quiet Spry over the mumbo jumbo? Michael allowed his aggravation to sour his tone. "Do you suggest that we employ her as some sort of spiritual guide to find Mrs. Garrity's location?" He envisioned how far a requisition for such services would move before it and his credibility were bayoneted. Of course, were he a senior officer sneaking through the purchase of a token of affection for his mistress, he might encounter success. Spry, bless him, hadn't been in the Army long enough to observe that mechanism in action.

The corners of Spry's mouth sagged. "No, sir."

"Good. I believe we shall gather enough evidence to figure out what happened without calling upon Mrs. Delacroix's spirits."

They arrived at the Frenchwoman's house about nine-thirty. Thin smoke rose from the chimneys, but nothing else in the vicinity moved. The skinny cow was absent from the fenced field, as were chickens from the yard. Despite hollered greetings from Michael, Armand didn't venture out the front door to scowl at them, and no hounds appeared.

Michael saw the reflection of his own concern in Spry's expression. They rode around back. Past the barn and slave quarters, they found a footpath through woods of pine and cedar. They dismounted and walked their horses forward, firearms in hand. Despite patchy sunshine, the air grew colder. Within a minute, Michael, who was in the lead, halted. "Do you hear that?"

Spry nodded. "Singing, and drums. Sir, I know this will sound daft, but I have the feeling someone's watching me. When I look over my shoulder, no one's there."

"I've the same feeling." Michael's skin had been crawling with it since they'd left the front yard, as well as with the sense that they ventured where they weren't welcome. He expelled a breath and continued forward. In a moment, he heard Spry follow.

They emerged in a clearing raked clean of pine needles, leaves, and debris. What appeared to be a small family graveyard occupied the clearing, nine crosses marking nine graves, some of them well older than a decade. Singing in patois and drumbeats stamped with a distinct Caribbean rhythm were much louder there. Through trees on the other side of the clearing, Michael spied a wooden, one-story building, which he presumed the source of the music.

Spry stepped around him, closer to the most recent grave. "John Delacroix, it says, 1731 to 1780. Must be the grave of Mrs. Delacroix's sea captain husband. Three of these graves have single names on them. Slaves, perhaps? But these five small graves—"

"Infants," Michael said without needing to step closer. An ocean apart, they appeared the same as that of his stillborn niece, Miriam's first child. His mouth filled with the bitter taste of loss. He had a vision of Esmé Delacroix with no one for company but slaves, birthing one stillborn baby after another across more than two decades while her husband was out to sea, unable to console her.

He swallowed and walked around the graveyard opposite Spry. Pine needles and tree debris were piled just outside the border. He presumed that Mrs. Delacroix observed a custom from Saint Domingue that dictated keeping each grave clean, and she had directed a slave to rake the graveyard regularly and toss debris on the pile.

As he neared the pile, about six feet in length, he spied what appeared to be burned fabric mixed in with the top layer of pine needles. Beneath the debris, he also spied fresh dirt. He bent closer for a look.

"*Arrêtez-vous!*" From behind them, a man's deep command to halt froze the air.

Michael and Spry turned about to face him at the same time. He kept himself partially concealed by the trunk of a pine tree, but he was well over six feet tall, with black hair and broad shoulders. He aimed one pistol in his steady right hand at Michael and held another pistol in his left hand. Michael dropped the reins of his horse and raised his hands slowly, elbows bent, chest high, in his peripheral vision seeing Spry do the same. The drumming and singing, now at his back, strove for a climax. "Good morn—"

"*Les mousquets.*" The giant Frenchman flicked the pistol in his right hand, indicating that they were to throw down their weapons. The soldiers complied. In French, he also ordered them to drop their cartridge boxes and sit ten feet from their firearms.

"Have a seat, Spry."

"I'll get my arse wet with dew, sir."

"Better than having your brains spattered with lead." Michael lowered himself cross-legged to the wild grass and pine needles, trusting that Cleopatra wouldn't stomp on him while she nibbled grass. His nerves hopped from the eldritch setting.

The Frenchman continued to watch them. His partial concealment also masked his expression, making it difficult to read whether he anticipated shooting them. Michael slowed his breathing, sought calm.

The music and singing wound down. He cranked his head around in the direction of the wooden building. In less than a minute, the driver of Mrs. Delacroix's post-chaise strolled from the other side of the building out to the graveyard, accompanied by Armand. Both slaves halted upon seeing the soldiers. The driver scurried back for the building. Followed by the driver, Esmé Delacroix emerged in the short jacket, petticoat, and shawl of a lower-class woman who performed manual labor. At the edge of the graveyard, she paused, hands on hips, to survey her guests.

Behind her clustered her slaves—Noisette, Armand, the driver, one middle-aged Negro woman, and an elderly Negro man—each staring with curiosity and some trepidation. Did the gathering represent her entire household? No one Michael saw could have been the tall, slender Negro in splendid livery who'd passed a note to Julia Garrity.

He released an unhurried breath, but relief didn't arrive. The Frenchman, who he sensed wasn't a member of Mrs. Delacroix's household, nevertheless still had a pistol aimed at him. Madame didn't look pleased to discover two redcoats lounging in her family graveyard during her morning commune with the spirits; in fact, as she strode to him, her eyes were cold, her jaw set.

Without rush, so the Frenchman wouldn't be tempted to squeeze the trigger, Michael stood and bowed. Icy dew had seeped through his trousers and stiffened his arse. He pasted a smile on his mouth.

"Mr. Stoddard, you and your assistant are trespassing."

"So that fellow hiding over there has informed us, and I do apologize." Drawn up to her full height, she was taller than he by at least an inch. He wondered how tall her sea captain had been. He also noticed the sheen of sweat on her upper lip. Communing with her spirits must have involved physical exertion.

"You were taken ill yesterday afternoon during our visit. Spry and I rode out this morning to make sure you'd recovered." Recovered she did appear, cheeks and lips flushed with health. A reward from her spirits, he supposed, for acting as their hands and eyes.

Acting as their hands and eyes: what *did* that mean?

"Why did you not wait on the front porch for me?"

Truth breezed from Michael. "We saw no one about the premises and wished to ensure that you and your household hadn't come to harm." He swept his scrutiny over all the slaves. "This is your entire household?"

"Yes. And as you can see, we are safe." Her frown deepened upon a closer look at his left cheek. "Which is more than I can say for you. What happened to your face?"

He held her gaze. "Clumsy. New living quarters. Walked into a half-closed door."

"Elijah Spivey struck you. The spirits told me."

Lucky guess. He'd implied the day before that he planned to visit the preacher. Still, cold teased his bones at her seeming omniscience, while across the graveyard, Spry, who'd also risen, dangled his jaw open in surprise at her announcement.

Determined to ignore the issue of fortune telling, he pushed onward. "Madame, yesterday afternoon, my assistant and I and a number of soldiers visited Mr. Spivey, insisted that he cease his attacks upon you, and informed him that Major Craig would hold him personally responsible should any ill befall you."

"Confronting him was foolish." Her mouth twitched, tightened. "Mr. Spivey is a dangerous man with many connections. Do not attempt to engage him again."

He frowned. "If I can find him, I intend to arrest him today. And I ask you to reconsider. Please move temporarily into town."

"No." She mirrored his frown.

Was she mimicking him, dismissing him? He tightened his jaw a second, at a loss for how to reach her. "Why not? You have everything to gain from the protection of the Eighty-Second. Do you misunderstand my concern?" He punched his palm once. "Mr. Spivey is a fanatic. Until he's in jail, he may try to kill you!"

Her chin held steady. Her eyes remained remote. "Let him try. I am unafraid. I have told you that the spirits will protect me here. But also—" She swept her arm toward the graveyard. "—my family is here, as you have no doubt noticed. I will not leave them."

"When you sell your property and return to Saint Domingue, they'll stay here."

"No. I will take them with me."

After a flinch of revulsion that he was certain his expression betrayed, he apprised her anew. Not that he thought her plans logical—different cultures, different values—but that explained why she needed so much money to leave America. She'd be carrying nine coffins back to Saint Domingue. And he could blather to her for hours about her safety, but she wasn't going to leave her property.

His shoulders sagged, and his gut tightened. He truly couldn't help her. "Very well, Madame. But I shall send a patrol out here several times a week to check on you. You needn't fear that they will interrupt or harass you. I simply wish to ensure that during the remainder of your time in this land, you aren't persecuted by Mr. Spivey. Please don't hesitate to send for our assistance if he escalates his aggression toward you."

She studied him a moment before her expression softened, and he glimpsed her smile. "You are a good man, Mr. Stoddard, understanding far more than that for which you give yourself credit. You know that lust can be a cavern of unkindness. But love—ah, do not mistake love and vulnerability for limitation. Allies come from love, from vulnerability. In this world, allies help us combat shadows."

Shadows. Jove's teeth, not that again!

She broke eye contact with him and addressed the giant behind the tree in French so rapid that Michael only picked out a few words of what she said. The man lowered the pistol. She summoned Armand forward, and her inscrutable gaze returned to Michael. "Retrieve your weapons. Armand will escort you back to the drive. Good day."

***

On the ride back, Esmé Delacroix's closing comments clung to Michael like cobwebs, even though he tried to slough them off as fortuneteller rubbish. From Spry's babble, those comments had fed his growing conviction in what appeared to be an otherworldly element in the investigation. "Yes, sir, if it was me, I would have asked her to explain what she meant by 'combat shadows.' She handed you the perfect opportunity to find out more about that blood-bathed thing. Sir, don't you want to discover who this devil is and when he's coming? You're supposed to vanquish him. Surely you want to know how, sir. And don't tell me a shadow that bathes in blood can be vanquished just by ignoring him."

Michael kept his mouth closed and his awareness on the road. Bad enough that Mrs. Delacroix had to bring up that shadow business again, but this time she'd thrown in an admonition: *But love—ah, do not mistake love, vulnerability, for limitation.*

Love and vulnerability.

The summers of his fifteenth and sixteenth years, Lydia had almost drowned him in a lustful "cavern of unkindness." For several years after he entered the Army and shipped to the North American colonies, he smelled her perfume everywhere, astray and lost in that cavern, his companion wanderers the beguiling, willing wenches who could spot epaulets from miles away. A year ago—or had it been longer?—he'd awakened one day weary of all those wenches.

Miriam, at her most annoying, nagged him in her letters to supply her with a sister-in-law. She didn't know the harsh existence dealt to women and children who followed the Army. Even if he had money, how could he plunge a wife into such turbulence?

Besides, if he truly meant to kill Lieutenant Fairfax—if he found a way for the murder to never trace back to him and earn him execution—Fairfax, while still alive, would exploit any weakness he revealed in himself. A deep connection with a woman would prove both limitation and liability.

And yet nine graves, nine crosses. If anyone knew vulnerability, it was Esmé Delacroix, who'd lost all her loved ones and lived alone, stranded in a strange land. The Oracle from Saint Domingue considered the vulnerability of love such a strength that she ignored the menace of Spivey and lingered in North Carolina, tried to sell her property so she could return the remains of loved ones to her native land.

Michael roused himself, brought his attention to Spry, who repeated a statement he'd made: "Sir, I don't think the coachman who gave Mrs. Garrity a note last Saturday was one of Mrs. Delacroix's slaves."

"I don't, either. None of them fits the physical description. And it wasn't that Frenchman with the pistol, either." Who *was* that Frenchman?

"Maybe she was hiding the slave."

"I don't believe she was." Michael sighed. The dead leads were piling up. "On the morrow, we may as well start searching farther north, toward New Berne."

Wilmington was abuzz with military activity when they rode in. Major Craig and his men had returned from Heron's Bridge with prisoners. And a ketch had docked bearing Phineas Badley, captured in the Bahamas after he'd escaped Wilmington back in November, a fugitive for defrauding Enid's mistress and murdering several people. Jail was a busy place that morning.

Soldiers flagged Michael down with the message that Major Craig had called him in. The announcement sounded portentous. Michael was aware that he had little substantive to report and too many loose ends floating around. Spry kept quiet at last, sensing that fewmets would soon hit the wind.

Outside the house on Third Street, Michael sized up the queue of men waiting to talk with the commander. Sure he'd be delayed at least an hour, he gave Spry his weapons and Cleopatra and sent him off to locate the sergeant and assemble ten men, along with a cart, for the raid on Spivey's church. Right after his assistant rode off, the provost's guard motioned Michael up the steps. "You're next, Mr. Stoddard."

A few men eyed him with a new look: annoyance. Perhaps they presumed he'd become Major Craig's favorite. But most men in line knew better and drew away when he passed them. Craig possessed a healthy set of lungs, and the bellow of him reprimanding someone in the study permeated the steps and porch, provided all the entertainment of a public flogging. A hundred jagged edges formed on the remnants of breakfast in Michael's gut.

The front door opened. Face colorless and expression stiff, the criticized subordinate swept past Michael on his way down the steps. Then Michael heard Craig's bellow, like a beach of broken, spiky coral on bare feet: "Where the devil is Mr. Stoddard? I saw him out there. Tell him to shake a leg!"

Michael's throat shrank three sizes as he reached the front porch. He ducked into the study and saluted. The major, his face as stiff as the marble likeness of a Roman senator, refused to return the salute straight away, forcing Michael to hold the address while his commander plowed a visual condemnation over the bruise on his lead investigator's cheek.

Craig grudged a salute at last and strutted around to his chair at the table. Michael removed his hat. "Welcome back to Wilmington, sir, and congratulations on your—"

"Stand there." Craig indicated a spot before his table, then sat. "If I need my boots shined, I shall call my batman."

Michael stepped forward at attention, hands sweaty, the seat of his trousers clammy damp. Beside Craig's chair sat Trouble, his brown-eyed gaze fixed on the major and full of adoration. The bulldog never looked at Michael.

Craig's lips tightened for an instant. He lowered his hand to the top of Trouble's head and stroked compulsively. "Where is Mrs. Garrity?"

"I don't know, sir, but I suspect that she—"

"I don't care what you suspect. You've had almost two days to find her, and I want that woman found. I don't see what's so difficult about it. After all, you managed to find Vicar Spivey with no problem whatsoever."

Vicar Spivey. That didn't sound good. Michael's mouth desiccated. The contents of his stomach became an irate porcupine.

"Just before his service last night, you tortured him. Looks like he gave you a bit of a fight."

"No, sir, that isn't the way it happened."

"The vicar has filed charges of assault against you and Spry. I interviewed three of the men you took with you to his church yesterday. They reported that for their encounter, he was cooperative and conducted himself with dignity."

"He isn't Anglican, sir."

"Oh? All three soldiers tell me the service was an Anglican mass and contained no controversial practices or messages. Furthermore, two of the three men were involved in a search of his house. They found nothing there to indicate that Vicar Spivey aids and abets the rebel cause."

"Sir, Spry and I found evidence suggesting that weapons and ammunition have been stored in the loft of the barn used for Mr. Spivey's church services."

The major sat taller, and his eyes glinted with interest. "What sort of evidence?"

"The area behind the chancel reeks of burned black powder. I found powder spilled in the loft, where I also found an unused cartridge."

Craig growled. "That's hardly enough evidence to stand up in court, and you know it." He petted Trouble with ferocity and briefly picked up a piece of paper on his table. "A Mr. Horatio Bowater has also filed assault charges against you and Spry." Craig interpreted Michael's expression. "His name isn't familiar, eh? He claims that you entered his office yesterday morning, forced him down to the counter without provocation, and bruised his face."

Michael counted silently to five. "Does Mr. Bowater have witnesses to this act?"

"Three witnesses, in fact, who claim they stood in the shop and watched it happen, too terrified to render assistance."

"Sir, I assure you that no one was in the shop except Spry, Mr. Bowater, and myself. Mr. Bowater was identified as a rebel sympathizer. Rebels have been known to bear false witness against the King's men."

"Of course, but there's the matter of a bruise on Mr. Bowater's face, which I myself saw." His gaze scoured Michael's own battle damage again. "Thus contributing credibility to his story."

"The three witnesses are lying."

"That remains to be seen. Yesterday morning, you arrested Mrs. Garrity's husband after revealing that he was repairing stands of arms for the rebels. Is he involved in her disappearance?"

"Possibly."

"Possibly?" Craig pressed forward, his eyes blazing. "Why don't you know for sure? Almost two days to complete this investigation. What is so difficult about finding the woman?"

"The investigation is convoluted. Mr. Spivey is involved with her to some degree, as is his assistant and cousin, Mr. Greene, who has been having an affair with Mrs. Garrity, and a fortuneteller woman named Mrs. Delacroix who lives off the Sound Road and may be having an affair with Mr. Garrity." Michael winced. It sounded absurd.

Craig squinted at him. "Is Mrs. Garrity's sister, Miss Ward, involved in her disappearance? Don't say 'possibly' again. Unless you can tell me 'certainly,' I want her released from jail today. Her attorney rode out to Heron's Bridge yesterday to protest her incarceration and badger me to liberate her."

Jail was, indeed, a busy place that morning. Michael imagined several dozen men crammed in one cell, while Julia Garrity's sister had the other cell to herself, and comprehended his commander's motive for ordering her release. Jailer Caldwell needed more room.

Craig crashed both fists upon the top of the table. "Mr. Stoddard, you have acquired a reputation of using excessive and unnecessary force. How will that encourage loyalists to cooperate with us?"

Michael said nothing. The left side of his face pulsated. His buttocks felt frostbitten.

The major sat back and glared. "I reiterate. I've a depot to establish in Cross Creek for Lord Cornwallis. A supply base to set up here and defenses to fortify within this town. All with very few resources." Strain in Craig's voice told Michael that he needed to put the inquiry behind him. "Our tactics at Heron's Bridge only slowed down the rebels, Lieutenant. There are hundreds of them out there. I don't have time to track down one missing civilian. Are you capable of finding Mrs. Garrity?"

"Yes, sir."

"Then do so. If you fail to find her by this time on the morrow, you and Spry are dismissed from the investigation. I shall assign someone else to finish it and assign *you* to work inventory until I can figure out what to do with you. Any questions?"

Damnation. Working inventory with the quartermaster's obsequious assistant: a fate worse than death. "No questions, sir."

"Dismissed!"

Chapter Twenty-One

ENCASED IN THE chill of Craig's criticism, Michael exited the house and trotted down the steps. Scorn seeped from men in line like a humid, sticky cloud. Each of those who'd heard the reprimand was thanking his lucky stars that his own arse hadn't been blistered.

Spry was nowhere to be seen.

Unless Michael wanted to be entombed in inventory, he had twenty-three hours and fifty-nine minutes to find Julia Garrity, so he'd best start batting the brush for her. He strode to the street, then realized that one of the camp boys was running toward him on Market Street, calling his name and waving a note. "Mr. Stoddard, sir, hold up! A message for you!"

Michael walked out to meet him, and while the boy caught his breath, broke the seal on the note and read: *Spivey harassed me again this morning, beg your help, Mrs. Farrell.*

The cloud of moroseness hanging over Michael from Major Craig's reproof blew away. Spivey had been rutting after Mrs. Farrell again. Michael jammed her plea in a pocket and extracted a penny from his purse. The lad's eyes lit at the coin. "Find Private Spry immediately. He may be talking with a sergeant about mustering some men. Tell him I said to make haste to Farrell's tobacco shop at Market and Second. I shall expect him there."

"Sir!" The boy grabbed his tip and sprinted off. A penny had guaranteed the "immediately" portion of the message to Spry.

Michael strode one block to the tobacconist's shop. After all Mrs. Farrell had endured, he hated to imagine that dog of a preacher forcing new depredation upon her. And the gall of Spivey to file assault charges against him and Spry. What an ass. He looked forward to jailing him.

At the tobacco shop, he vaulted up the steps. A mellow-faced man with straw-colored hair exited from the opened front door and met him on the porch. "Are you Lieutenant Stoddard?"

"At your service, sir."

"Richard Farrell." They shook hands. "Come in. Something's upset my wife, and she claims you're the only one who can help her. Do you know what this is about?"

"I do, sir."

"Very well, then." Bewildered, Farrell led him inside, then cupped hands around his mouth for a shout toward the back of the shop. "Alice, Lieutenant Stoddard is here!"

She emerged from the workroom, a handkerchief wadded in her hand, her face blotched from weeping. "Oh. Oh." She sobbed, oblivious to the curious stares of apprentices from the doorway to the workroom.

"Aw, honey." Her husband went forward and took her in his arms. "Hush, dear."

No way was she going to discuss what had happened while her husband and apprentices listened. Michael joined them and said, "Mr. Farrell, where may I speak with your wife privately?"

"Our office in the back. It's a bit untidy right now."

"Take us there. I'm expecting my assistant, Private Spry, shortly. Please bring him back when he arrives."

Farrell installed his wife and Michael in a cramped office with a single window and closed the door on them, perplexed but trusting. Vulnerable. The fellow adored his wife with the same kind of quiet, stable devotion he'd seen in his father's love for his mother, and his brother-in-law's love for Miriam. As he settled the brunette upon a chair, he realized that whatever happened, Richard Farrell would stand by his wife. Limitation? Hardly.

He pulled up a stool opposite her, sat, and was quiet. She dried her eyes, closed her fist over the handkerchief, and stared at her hands. "About eight this morning, I came in to write some drafts for invoices." She trembled. "I must have left the back door unlocked, and that's how he got in. I heard footsteps and looked up. Spivey was standing there in that doorway, leering at me."

She wrung the handkerchief and lifted her teary gaze to him. "Gods, sir, I was terrified by the heat in his eyes. I—I grabbed that scissors over there, on the desk, but before I could rise, he knelt on both knees before me, spread his arms wide, and—and he said that confession was food for the soul, and he'd been starving for so many years, unconfessed."

"Unconfessed, Mrs. Farrell?" Was that even a word?

"Yes. Unconfessed to ravishing me all those years ago." She bit her lip. "He—he admitted that he'd drugged the brandy during the hay ride and ravished me in a meadow!"

What a fool Spivey was. Both Alice Farrell and Esmé Delacroix could witness against him. No telling how many other women he'd violated or attempted.

Alas for Mrs. Farrell and the journey she must make in her heart. Compassion for her swirled in Michael's soul. "What happened after that, madam?"

"On his knees, there in the doorway, he proceeded to describe exactly what he'd done to me, in shocking detail, how he'd ravished me not once but thrice that night because he was so ruled with lust for me, and I lay senseless, unable to respond. And then, oh, that ogre, he claimed he still lusted for me every day because I'd never returned his affection, but God forgave him—*forgave him*—because he'd confessed, and his heart was eased at last. He said that for that reason, I should forgive him, too."

Her swollen eyes entreated Michael. "I cannot forgive him! I have lived for years haunted by pieces of memories from that night, never knowing for sure what had occurred. His confession reawakened the pain in my soul as if it had all just happened." A shudder rocked her shoulders. "I feel violated again, used horribly, unclean. Yet he spoke as though my burden should be lightened by his confession, and he—he told me that I would burn in hell if I didn't fall upon my knees with him that moment, pray with him, and accept him as my brother."

Haunted. Violated. Used. Unclean. Lydia's voice whispered in Michael's mind: *Come, my pet, don't deny me. I dream of your winsome, dark eyes all year round.* Nauseated, he pushed back the intrusion.

At a light tap on the door, he rose and admitted Spry. His assistant assumed a stance at the closed door just inside the office, arms crossed over his chest, silent.

Michael sat again, and his gaze met that of the tobacconist's wife. "How did you get rid of him, Mrs. Farrell?"

For a second, she clapped her hand over her mouth. "God forgive me, Lieutenant. I rose up with the scissors and stabbed him in the arm and told him to never, ever come near me again."

"Good. Which arm?"

"The left upper arm." She gasped. "Oh, no, I'm not going to jail for stabbing him, am I?"

Considering Spivey's talent for twisting truth, he might try to contort the incident to his favor and file an assault charge on Alice Farrell, too, but Michael saw no reason to alarm her with the possibility. He straightened on the stool, resolved that Thursday, February first, would end with Spivey in custody. "Go to jail for defending yourself against a scoundrel? Not if I have any say in the matter."

She pressed hands together in gratitude. "Oh, thank you. You are truly a good, kind man, not at all like what that odious Bowater next door says about you, and—oh, my, what happened to your face, Lieutenant?"

"Walked into a half-open door."

She scowled. "Spivey did that to you, didn't he? You said yesterday that you were going to have a word with him, and he must have punched you. You poor dear." She bent toward him and brushed her lips over the goose egg, availing Michael of an exquisite view down her bodice and the scent of her perfume. He imagined Spry's eyes widening with envy.

"My goodness." Mrs. Farrell subsided into her chair, blushing. "I apologize. That wasn't very proper of me, was it? I don't know what came over me."

Spry said in a bland tone, "Not to worry, madam. In the name of justice, Mr. Stoddard suffers improprieties far more devastating."

Michael laughed. Healthy pink crept to Mrs. Farrell's cheeks, and she chuckled. "I say, you aren't married, are you, sir? We really should find you a lady friend."

He stared at her, baffled, panicked. "Why? And who is 'we?'"

Her smile grew sly. "For dinner parties, you know. And 'we' are the Wilmington ladies who gather for coffee."

Of course, she was in that group, too. He scrambled for a change in topic. "What—what did Mr. Spivey do after you stabbed him with the scissors?"

"He fled."

"Excellent. Where are the scissors?" She gestured to the desk. "Keep them safe. We may need them."

She clasped her hands, as if in prayer. "I would like to put all of this behind me."

Well he knew. But it was never a simple task to do so. "Of course you would. Know that we shall address this issue with Mr. Spivey today. If matters go well for us, we'll jail him, and he won't ever bother you again."

A long breath of relief eased from her. Her brow smoothed. Taut lines around her mouth faded.

"Can you recall any details about this morning's unfortunate encounter that might assist us in apprehending Mr. Spivey?" At her blank look, he added, "For example, did he mention where he might be spending time today?" Sarcasm whipped a corner of his mouth. "In the event that you had a change of heart and needed a partner at prayer."

"Ugh." Her lips contorted. "No. He said nothing of the sort."

"Well, then, we shall be about the business of removing Mr. Spivey from the community. Thank you for the confidence you've placed in us. Henceforth, when you're in the shop alone, do make certain the doors are secured." He stood, swiveled for the exit, then turned back to her. "One more point. Your husband knows something is amiss. Tell him about your history with Mr. Spivey. Now."

Her head bowed, and she hugged herself. "No—oh, no, I dare not tell him. We've been very happy."

"Madam, this situation is a keg of powder sitting too close to flame. At any moment, your background might emerge. Would you rather Mr. Farrell heard it first from a gossip in a tavern?"

Her voice trembled. "I don't know. I'm afraid—"

"Afraid of losing your husband's trust and affection? Do you not see how much the man loves you?"

"He trusts me."

"Yes, after all these years, he trusts you to be forthright about difficulties you see coming so the two of you can manage them as a team." He watched her shoulders cave and softened his voice. "If I were he, I would want to hear the story first from my wife, my partner in life. The stark truth, before it's embellished with vulgar sensation. Tell him now." He thought of his parents holding hands, and of his sister's husband stroking her cheek. "Consider it a contribution to your marriage."

Mrs. Farrell lifted her head, her eyes wide. Then her regard of him altered, as if the light from the window had shifted about, painted another dimension upon him. "Very well. I shall do it." She hiked her chin.

When she emerged from the office, she managed a pretty smile for her husband, who hugged her in relief. He walked Michael and Spry out, thanked them, and shook their hands. The two soldiers clomped down the stairs and stood at the edge of the street for a moment. Spry eyed Michael up and down. "Sir, you realize your days as a bachelor are numbered."

"Pffft."

"What did Major Craig say, sir?"

Michael pulled out his watch. "He said we have just a little over twenty-three hours to find Mrs. Garrity."

"Find her or what, sir?"

"Or I'm transferred to inventory. He didn't specify what would happen to you. So, let's fetch our raid party and cart and pay Mr. Spivey a visit."

The door to the land agent's office swung wide, and the dandy agent stepped out onto the front porch of his shop, his expression a mask of malicious glee. "There you fellows are. My, I feel sooo safe with you patrolling the streets."

"Who stuck a splinter up his arse, sir?" muttered Spry.

"That nockhole filed assault charges against us and claims three witnesses to the act," Michael said under his breath before mirroring the agent's grin. "Good morning, Mr. Bumwater. How does your face feel today?"

The agent's humor shriveled. "That's *Bo*water, not *Bum*water! Correct yourself, or I shall have a chat with my attorney about slander!"

"Retained an attorney, have you? Costs a good bit of money. You must be overcharging clients or underpaying taxes. Either way, it's something we're happy to investigate and regulate." Bowater demonstrated an uncomplimentary finger gesture, stomped back inside, and slammed the door.

The soldiers grinned and headed for the barracks. There Michael posted an arrest warrant about town for Elijah Spivey: wanted for one count of ravishment and two counts of attempted ravishment. Then he headed northwest with Spry, ten soldiers, and a cart. En route to the church, he realized that releasing Salome Ward from jail had slipped his mind. Oh, well. Another few hours of incarceration wouldn't kill her.

They reached the Church of Mary and Martha of Bethany around noon, as high, thin cloud fingers grasped for sunlight. Michael set two sentries before the bend in the drive. Then he, Spry, and the remaining eight soldiers surrounded the barn and house with caution, in case armed rebels had holed up inside. Nothing human moved in or around the buildings. A search after they gained entrance to both buildings confirmed that no one from the church was about.

Michael posted more guards, lit a lantern, and entered the room behind the chancel. A section of floorboards had been torn up, exposing gravel, a couple of knapped musket flints, and a small pile of black powder. The weapons and ammunition had lain there the day before, and the two soldiers had walked over them, distracted by the possibility of a cache in the loft and by Spivey's return.

Disappointment chewed at Michael's gut. Spry rechecked the loft and verified the absence of weapons. Michael's hopes for success fizzled.

As Spry descended the ladder, he sniffed, grabbed the canvas bag on the top shelf, and handed it to Michael when he reached the bottom. "Did you notice this yesterday, sir? Smells like roses."

So it did. Michael shook his head. "That bloody head cold knocked out my nose. We'll have a look at the sack after we search the house."

Outside the barn, he hooked the bag onto his saddle. When he and Spry entered the house, a moldy, briny odor greeted them. Solidified grease from fried bacon filled a skillet set off to the side of the fireplace, contributing the stink of scorched pork to the interior, along with more subtle smells arising from boiled coffee grounds and half-burned cornbread. Coals in the fireplace had been extinguished, rather than banked. Spivey hadn't expected to return soon.

For light, and to air the place out, Michael opened the front and back doors and both windows and sent Spry up the ladder to check the loft. On the ground floor, he searched jars on the mantle, plunged his hand into a sack of cornmeal to see whether Spivey had hidden anything inside it, dumped out a sack of apples, poked behind fireplace tools and stacked pots and pans, and pried at replaced boards with his dagger to determine whether Spivey had installed any false walls or floors. But the preacher was far too wily to have left damning evidence behind.

The task of searching the bed shoved against the corner he saved for last, reluctant to handle the dirty linens. Quilts and sheets were examined and shoved aside. Beneath the straw mattress, he found a long, rectangular piece of lace.

Spry called down, "A man's been living up here, sir. Mr. Greene, I suppose. There's a mattress and quilts and extra clothing. Some of it's fine clothing."

Michael realized that he'd extracted a lady's scarf from beneath the mattress. Unfolding it released the scent roses, like whatever was in the canvas bag. "Mr. Spivey's hidden a lady's tucker beneath his pillow."

"Huzzah!" Spry clomped down. A grin raked his face at the sight of the tucker.

Michael folded it up and closed it into his haversack. "Finished in the loft?"

"Yes, sir. Not much to see."

"Very well. Let's close up the place for now."

Spry pulled a window shut. "Inconsiderate of the preacher to have missed his own arrest."

"Don't worry. We'll nab him." But as Michael shut the doors, a hollow expanded in his soul where his confidence should have resided. He didn't know where to find Spivey. Furthermore, plenty of locals with no love for the preacher detested the British and the war and would refrain from passing along tips for his capture, even bypass a monetary reward, or hide Spivey, just to frustrate Major Craig and the regiment.

Back at the horses, he loosened the drawstring on the canvas bag. "Let's have a look at what's in here now, while the lighting is good." He drew out the bolt of wool, noting additional garments at the bottom of the bag, then spread the wool wide across the side of his mare. That was when he realized that the fabric was a woman's polonaise gown, cut for a lady with a full figure, crafted from high-quality wool. Daylight blazed it the hue of deep red wine or cranberries. Cranberry red. The hair on the back of Michael's neck stood up. Where had he heard that phrase?

"Beautiful," said Spry. "Where did a pauper the likes of Mr. Spivey find the money to afford a gown like that? Hmm, turn it over, sir. Seems to be torn along the back."

Michael flipped it over and heard Spry suck in a breath at the same time he did. The back bodice of the gown was slashed from the top to below the waistline. He dug into the bag and extracted a pink wool petticoat, also slashed at the waistline. He spread the petticoat atop the gown. By then, his actions had attracted several soldiers, who gathered around and stared at the garments in puzzlement, especially after he draped a fine, linen shift over the petticoat. A jagged cut matching the slash to the bodice of the gown marred the bodice of the shift.

Lace identical to that of the tucker he'd found beneath Spivey's mattress trimmed the sleeves of the shift. Astonished, he surveyed all the clothing. No blood that he could see. Why ruin such fine garments? Why hide most of them in the barn and keep the tucker beneath a pillow? Where was the woman who fit the clothing?

The color of the gown—cranberry red. His memory at last provided the reference, that of Mrs. Overton standing over Julia Garrity's clothing chest two days earlier in the bedroom. *All my mistress's clothing is in here except for the clothing she wore on Saturday: a pink petticoat, and a cranberry red gown.* He jammed his hand back in the bag and withdrew what remained—embroidered pockets, stays, a pair of ladies' silk stockings and garters, and shoes with silver buckles. The sight of it all sent a surge of disbelief through him.

"Sir, that's Mrs. Garrity's clothing, isn't it?" Spry's voice cracked with shock.

"I suspect so."

"How can we confirm it?"

"Mrs. Overton. She said Mrs. Garrity had been wearing a gown that color on Saturday."

"What's Mrs. Garrity's clothing doing out here, sir?" Spry's face paled. "The way it's ripped, like it was cut off her." His breathing grew ragged. "Spivey, that dog—he ravished her. He shoved the garments atop that shelf where he didn't think anyone would ever discover them. But why did he keep them at all?"

"Maybe the sick mongrel wants to be able to look at the clothing again and again, remind himself of his fun. That's also why he slept with the tucker close by, where he could smell her perfume." Michael expelled a sigh of exhaustion. "Ah, but this clothing is circumstantial evidence."

Spry opened his fists. "Yes, but where is Mrs. Garrity?" He swept a glance over the area. "For god's sake, sir, I hope the preacher hasn't tied her up naked out here somewhere. It's the dead of winter!"

"Quiet, Spry. Let me think." He scrutinized the clothing again before performing another search of the sack. "There's no cloak or parasol. We know Mrs. Garrity had a parasol with her in the back yard. On a drizzly, cold morning in January, surely she'd have worn a cloak."

Spry squinted at him. "So her captor forgot to put the parasol and cloak in the bag, sir."

Michael's thoughts danced with potential explanations. "Possibly. If Mrs. Overton gives us a positive identification on this clothing, I'll upgrade the warrant on Spivey to include abduction. I wager he isn't going to be able to explain this clothing away."

"Sir, Mrs. Overton may have been part to the crime. She may have given Mrs. Garrity the confidence she needed to step into the carriage with that coachman."

Michael loaded clothing back in the sack. "True. But then who afforded the coachman and his fine livery? Neither Elijah Spivey nor Betty Overton."

"Mr. Garrity? Miss Ward? Mr. Greene?"

"We shall see."

Chapter Twenty-Two

BENEATH A HIGH overcast a little past one o'clock on Thursday afternoon, the patrol returned to Wilmington. Michael sent the rest of the men on to the garrison. He and Spry rode straight for the home of the physician with whom Mrs. Overton was staying. The butler seated them on a couch and brought the former housekeeper to the parlor.

When she slumped in the chair facing the couch, Michael noticed that her face had lost color. Her vacant expression and listless hands bespoke a sedative dose of laudanum in her blood.

She spoke as if in a dream. "Mr. Stoddard. Doctor says I'm to be moved. To my brother's house in New Berne." A crease developed between her brows, as if thinking had become difficult for her. "I wish to return to work. When might that happen?"

"That's a discussion you must undertake with your brother."

"No, not my brother. Not in New Berne. Here in Wilmington. I haven't been feeling well. But I must work. My husband is dead. I'm a widow. My employers are Mr. and Mrs. Garrity. Where are they?"

"Mr. Garrity is in jail, madam. I arrested him for contracting with the rebels to repair their weapons. I've something to show you." He rested the canvas bag on his lap and withdrew the gown, careful not to reveal the damage. Despite the influence of laudanum, her eyes widened with recognition, and the fingers of one hand clenched her tucker at her throat. "Yes? Where have you seen this gown before?"

"On my mistress."

Well, that settled it. Circumstantial evidence weighed in that Spivey had taken a role in Mrs. Garrity's abduction. "When did you last see her wear it?"

"In the back yard. She was sitting beside Chipper's grave." Her gaze clouded. She clasped her hands in her lap and focused on the gown. "I—I believe Colonel Young and his men left town that day. I've forgotten the exact date."

"It was Saturday, the twenty-seventh of January."

Her bewilderment wandered to his face. "What is today's date?"

"Thursday, the first of February." He folded up the gown, returned it to the sack, and handed it to Spry.

Mrs. Overton brushed fingertips briefly to her forehead. "I have lost a day or two. When did Mrs. Garrity return, that you obtained her gown?"

A mind befuddled with laudanum was still capable of matching cause and effect. He'd anticipated the query from her. However, he could supply no answer that wouldn't serve to unbalance her further, so he parried aside her inquiry. "I cannot answer that question right this moment. However, I have a question to ask of you regarding the love letters from Mr. Greene that Mrs. Garrity keeps in her chest—"

"You know of those letters?" Mrs. Overton's expression darkened. "Why, you snooped! For Mrs. Garrity's eyes only. Her personal property. How dare you!"

Michael maintained a mild tone. "The correspondence has been of benefit in this investigation."

The housekeeper pouted. "Don't care what you think is beneficial. You shouldn't read her letters. Neither should Mr. Garrity."

Mr. Garrity? Michael and Spry exchanged a glance. For a second or two, Michael wondered whether Julia Garrity had thrown salt into the fatal wound of her marriage by allowing her husband access to the letters. "Mr. Garrity reads his wife's love letters from Mr. Greene?"

"I caught him." Again, she seemed to struggle with concentration. "At least, I think so. Last—last Tuesday evening."

"Tuesday the thirtieth?"

She deliberated. "No. Earlier. Tuesday a week before. I have lost days somehow."

Spry whispered, "Tuesday the twenty-third, sir. Isn't that the letter you said was missing?"

Indeed, it was. "Mrs. Overton, did Mr. Garrity remove a letter from the chest that day?"

"I—I saw him thrust something into his pocket. I asked whether he'd taken a letter. He denied it." She chewed her lip. "He said, 'I'll have Julia's heart again.' I think he lied about stealing a letter."

If Betty Overton's testimony could be trusted, Gabriel Garrity had made a cryptic statement that could be interpreted several ways, including as a threat. Michael had to know the level of Mrs. Overton's involvement. He cast aside evasion. "We have evidence that Mrs. Garrity was abducted Saturday morning."

The housekeeper's pale eyes widened, and her gaze shot to the canvas bag. "How did you obtain her clothing?"

She'd expressed interest in recovery of the clothing, rather than in the whereabouts of her mistress, as if the abduction wasn't news to her. He decided to proceed on that line of reasoning. "We also have evidence implying that you assisted her captors."

The housekeeper shrank in the chair and covered her throat with both hands, her eyes like those of a possum startled by torchlight. "I—I did not."

Michael softened his tone in attempt to gain her confidence. "I'm finding our evidence difficult to believe. Granted, you're angry with the Garritys for treating your poorly and paying you such a pittance all these years, but you don't seem the sort of person who would conspire to injure another person."

"No. No, I wouldn't do that!"

"That's why I suspect that when you convinced Mrs. Garrity to accompany the coachman Saturday morning, you thought you were helping her in some way. You had no idea that she would come to harm."

She squinted at him, as if sharpening her vision compensated for lack of comprehension. "Coachman?"

"Yes, the Negro coachman dressed in fine clothing. He came to fetch her about ten-thirty from the back yard. Tell me where I can find him, or tell me the name of his master or employer, and I shall ensure that your name is mentioned favorably with the judge when this inquiry comes to court."

Panic flickered in her eyes. "Don't remember a Negro coachman."

He drilled his gaze into her. "Where were you between ten-thirty and noon on Saturday?"

"In the house. I told you that."

"Who can vouch for your whereabouts after your son left?"

A muscle in her shoulder twitched, jerked her head. "No one."

He allowed accusation to flood his tone. "You have no alibi for that time. You assisted her captors with her abduction, did you not?"

She trembled. "No! I didn't help with her abduction. The last time I saw her was in the back yard. I never saw a coachman with her."

"The gardener, Mr. Hiller, saw him, and both he and your son saw the fine coach parked a short distance up the street. Who sent the coachman?"

Her muscles twitched again. "I know of no such coachman."

Frustration at his inability to reach the housekeeper expanded within Michael. More harshness leaked into his voice. "Very well, Mrs. Overton, I shall inform you that we have direct evidence implicating your friend, Mr. Spivey, in foul play with Mrs. Garrity. Your mistress is still missing. That gown we showed you earlier? We found it hidden in the Bethany church. We found her matching tucker stuffed beneath the preacher's mattress."

He scooted to the edge of the couch, hands gripping his knees. "Is it not true that Mr. Spivey hired the coachman to abduct Mrs. Garrity? Tell me the truth about the preacher and what he did with Mrs. Garrity. I have enough evidence to arrest you as an accomplice in her abduction."

Mrs. Overton pressed both hands to her cheeks, mouth agape. "No. Vicar Spivey wouldn't abduct anyone!"

"We have the testimony of two women in the area who say he tried to ravish them. One of them he did abduct. I think he abducted your mistress with your help and ravished her, and now he's holding her prisoner somewhere."

Mrs. Overton rocked herself. "Not true, not true, no, not true. The vicar is a man of God." She froze in her chair and stared at the floor, then whipped her gaze to Michael and scowled. "Not Vicar Spivey—it was the witch! The witch abducted her. The witch kills her husbands and lovers and bathes in their blood."

Ye gods, not "the witch" again. Michael reeled in his impulse to roar in Mrs. Overton's face. "Mrs. Delacroix has no slaves resembling the coachman who was seen with Mrs. Garrity Saturday morning. Furthermore, her post-chaise bears no resemblance to the carriage that Mr. Hiller described. If she were truly involved in your mistress's abduction, why did we find Mrs. Garrity's gown in Reverend Spivey's church, and not somewhere on Mrs. Delacroix's property?"

For several seconds, Mrs. Overton worked her mouth, as if her mind groped for an explanation to support her belief. Then her eyes lit. "Why, she flew the gown there, Lieutenant. In the dark of night. Of course. That's how she did it." Her mouth hung open, giving her a demented appearance.

He studied her, unable to fathom the irrational. "'Flew the gown.' You mean that she transported it over on a broomstick?"

"Exactly!" she breathed.

With a sigh, Michael sat back on the couch beside his assistant, who'd bowed his head at Mrs. Overton's explanation. He should have known the housekeeper would blame everything on Mrs. Delacroix. At least she was consistent.

He might never know whether Mrs. Overton was involved in Julia Garrity's abduction. She was just too crazy. How much time had he just wasted questioning her? And how many hours did he have left before Major Craig yanked the position of lead investigator from him?

Mrs. Overton slid to the edge of her chair, her smile doused. "Arrest the witch. And I now think that Mr. Garrity should stay in jail for stealing that letter. Nobody should get away with stealing."

Mr. Garrity, hmm. Perhaps their time with the housekeeper hadn't been a complete waste. It would be interesting to hear the gunsmith's account for why he'd taken that particular letter. Michael had been meaning to have a chat with him anyway, now that he'd cooled off in jail a day. Who knew, but maybe he'd cast some light on Spivey's contraband business?

Michael stood, and Spry pushed up from the couch after him. "Thank you for your time, Mrs. Overton. You've provided some insight into the investigation and answered all my questions for now. We may return with more questions. If I were you, I'd use the time between now and then to consider the events of the past few days and see whether you've forgotten to tell us any details. Good afternoon."

***

Before heading over to visit Gabriel Garrity, Michael and Spry returned their horses to the regimental stables, and Michael revised the warrant on Elijah Spivey. The number of people who'd tolerate the presence of a suspected abductor and rapist in their midst had to be quite small. Somebody somewhere, would divulge the preacher's hiding place.   ·

Inside the jail building, Michael discovered three men from the Eighty-Second blocking the men's' cell. He looked around for the jailer. "Mr. Caldwell, are you here?"

Caldwell stepped from his tiny office and opened his mouth to speak, but a screech erupted from the other jail cell. "Stoddard! Is that you?" Salome Ward's face pressed to the grate in the door. "Let me out of here, or I'll have you kicked out of the Army!"

"Shut up, you shrew!" Garrity flung himself at the door of the opposite cell. "Living in hell would be easier than this past day, listening to your whining and ranting."

Michael elevated his voice over the barrage of exchanged insults. "Stop the fighting, or I shall arrange for the immediate transfer of both of you to the belly of a prison ship!" He strode to Miss Ward's cell.

Her upper lip curled at the sight of him. "My attorney says you have no choice but to release me today."

"Is that so?" Michael hoped he mirrored her sneer. "Your attorney's a bloody liar. So are you. You told me you haven't seen your sister since October, but you two have actually slipped away together numerous times since then to chat with Mr. Spivey. Why lie about it? What is it you're doing with him that requires secrecy?" Her eyes seethed through the grate, but she said nothing. "Fortunately, madam, I don't need your cooperation. I found out that you and your sister have been plotting with Mr. Spivey to murder Esmé Delacroix. And that's why I won't be letting you out of here today. Good day, Miss Ward."

He spun on his heel and marched out just ahead of Garrity's howl: "Burn in hell, you damned she-demon! You've been scheming to kill an innocent woman!"

"Not true! Lies! Not true!" Salome Ward's shrieks drowned out whatever else Garrity said. Caldwell grimaced, and Michael crossed his arms and waited just out of sight of the cells. Within seconds, the tone of her shrieks altered. "Lieutenant! Come back! I need to talk with you!"

Restraining victory from pinching his lips, he swept back in and paused a moment before the gunsmith's crowded cell. "You fellows on the bench in there, make room for Mr. Garrity. Mr. Garrity, have a seat well away from the door, and don't give me cause to suspect you of snooping on my conversation with your sister-in-law." When he was certain that the gunsmith had moved away from the door and sat down, he leaned against the other door. "Talk. Keep your voice down."

Words spilled from her in a sensuous murmur. "Julia and I have been discussing giving money to Vicar Spivey to help the church grow. Last week, she changed her mind."

"Why?"

"She's been concealing her true wealth from that beast in the other cell. She doesn't want him knowing how much money she has at her disposal."

At the ring of truth in her confession, Michael stomach churned with disgust. "I see. She enjoys bleeding him for her luxuries."

"Bleeding?" Scorn tinged her voice. "Hah. A husband is supposed to provide for his wife."

"You're absolutely right." He could envision neither his mother nor his sister treating a man in such a way. "How did Mr. Spivey take the news that your sister wouldn't give him money?"

"He did seem upset, but he said that he'd pray for her to change her mind."

Upset enough to abduct and harm Julia Garrity? Michael wondered whether her own sister had inadvertently funded her abduction by supplying Spivey with money. "Perchance did you donate money to the church?"

"Yes, earlier this month, and Vicar Spivey was very grateful, but I hope you can now see why I lied and didn't mention my other meetings with Julia."

"Indeed." He grappled with gloom. "Thank you for setting the record straight. Good day."

He'd almost reached the jailer's office when her panicked, elevated voice sought him. "Wait a moment! Aren't you going to release me?"

He called over his shoulder, "I shall consider it."

"Gah, you woman hating beast!" The thunder of her cell door being kicked several times echoed through the jail. "You tricked me! Villain, baseborn cad!"

Michael headed outside, where Spry waited. Caldwell followed him out and said, "Sir, you must release Miss Ward to house arrest. I need her cell for male prisoners." He rubbed his temples as if he'd developed a headache. "And all she and Mr. Garrity do is hurl insults at each other. I've had drunks in jail with better manners."

Discouragement spiraled into Michael. "Very well, I'll sign the release document. Those soldiers inside—are they there to stop Mr. Garrity and his sister-in-law from killing each other?"

"Er, no. Our sudden abundance of rebel prisoners is a bit more than my lads and I can manage. And when I locked up Phineas Badley earlier today, I found out how many people in Wilmington wanted to kill him before his trial."

Michael didn't envy Caldwell his job. "As soon as Miss Ward is released, transfer Garrity to her cell, alone. I require some amount of privacy when I question him, and for a few hours, I want him isolated from the prisoners captured at Heron's Bridge."

"Yes, sir. If you'll step inside, I already have Miss Ward's release document ready."

Michael released the she-devil to house arrest at the home of her friends, the Baxters. The only positive aspect about the moment when she exited jail, accompanied by two soldiers, was that she didn't linger and taunt either him or Garrity. Michael waited in the office while the jailer and his men transferred Garrity to the cell Salome Ward had occupied. For the gunsmith to divulge what he knew about Spivey, Michael suspected that he required far more incentive than the absence of his sister-in-law from jail. And as Michael headed back for Garrity's cell with his assistant, he hoped he'd gathered enough incentive.

Chapter Twenty-Three

MICHAEL AND SPRY entered the cell to find Garrity lounging on the wooden bench bolted to the wall. "Bugger yourselves," said the gunsmith. His glower slithered into a sneer. "Lieutenant, someone decorated your face right smartly, I see."

Michael took the sack of clothing from Spry and heaved it to Garrity. "Is anything in there familiar?"

Scorn transitioned to puzzlement when the gunsmith pulled out the gown. "Looks like Julia's clothing. Say, what happened to the back?" He set the garment on the bench and pulled out the petticoat in disbelief. When he noticed the rip in the back of the shift, a moan tore through him. "Julia! Oh, hell, is she all right? Where is she?"

"We were hoping you could tell us."

Garrity picked up the shift, examined it more closely, then flung it back atop the pile of garments. His sneer returned. "You arse pickers. You're trying to fool me. You fetched her clothing from the house and cut it to make me think she's injured or dead. Well, I've seen how much people bleed from knife wounds. There isn't any blood on this clothing. Like I said, bugger yourselves." He crossed his arms and sat back, impassive.

Michael directed Spry to retrieve the sack and garments. When the private returned to stand by the door, Michael said, "According to Mrs. Overton, these garments are what your wife wore on Saturday."

Garrity said nothing.

"We found her clothing at the Church of Mary and Martha of Bethany." He paused to let the news sink in. "You know your wife is having an affair with Mr. Greene, the assistant there. And judging from your nonchalance, you've been expecting my query about the affair."

"Find that scoundrel and interrogate him. He had plenty to do with her disappearance."

"I'm not convinced he did. But his cousin Mr. Spivey has a history of abduction and rape. We have a warrant out for his arrest: one count of rape, two counts of attempted rape, one count of abduction, one count of attempted abduction. Your wife's clothing was hidden in his sanctuary, and her lace tucker was beneath his mattress. Why none of it was destroyed, I'm not certain, so all I have is speculation. Speculation that a rapist disguised as a man of God appealed to your wife's desire to see women taking more active roles in the church." A gust of amusement left Garrity. Michael continued. "He arranged transportation for her visit to his church Saturday morning, overpowered her while she was there—"

"—slashed Julia's clothing off her, had his way with her." Garrity's mouth contorted. "That's the story you want me to swallow? Julia would have fought him. If he were cutting her clothing while she fought him, he'd have cut her. There's no blood on the clothing. You're grasping at straws. Like I said yesterday, you're a shoddy investigator. You cannot find my wife." He slapped his knee and hooted. "Major Craig's going to fry your arse!

"Julia ran off with Paul Greene to New Berne. An idiot could see it. You're even more stupid than an idiot. Idiots in red coats are what the King has dumped on America. God save the King!"

A growl revealed Spry's big teeth by lantern light. Michael saw him bunching muscles in his neck and shoulders and gripped his upper arm to stop him from barreling forward and battering Garrity. Not that he didn't long to pound the tar out of the gunsmith, too, but yielding to the impulse would have wasted precious time.

When he was certain Spry had himself under control, he released his assistant and inhaled to ease the pummel of his pulse. "Since you're aware of Mr. Greene's recreation with your wife, tell me the name of the Negro coachman he sent to pick her up at ten-thirty Saturday morning. Mr. Hiller your gardener saw him, and both he and Ben Overton caught a glimpse of a handsome, enclosed carriage waiting to carry your wife away."

"I don't know what you're talking about." Garrity sniffed. "I've never seen Greene with any transportation except a horse."

"It rained Saturday morning, Mr. Garrity. Would your wife have ridden pillion on a horse in the rain?" Doubt crept into Garrity's eyes. Michael pushed onward. "Her abductor lured her from her yard with the promise of a plush, warm carriage. I think someone other than Mr. Greene sent the carriage." He paused, searched for reaction. "As I said, Mr. Spivey has a history of abducting and ravishing women. He also prefers women with dark hair and dark eyes, like your wife. I suspect that he used church money to hire the coach and driver. Then he abducted and ravished her."

"Shut up slandering Julia!" Garrity gritted his teeth.

"He cut off her clothing." Michael stepped past Spry, his movement deliberate, as if he were circling Garrity. "And he kept her clothing as a memento." Color fled the gunsmith's face. "You can help me catch this mongrel."

"No, I—I don't know how."

Garrity looked sick to his stomach. Michael realized he'd dangled him too far over the edge. That moment, he had to yank him back from grinding away over what Spivey might have done to his wife. Besides, evidence against Spivey as Julia Garrity's abductor and rapist was circumstantial and might not stick. On the other hand, if he could link the preacher firmly with weapons trafficking—

"Tell me what you know of the weapons smuggling. Mr. Spivey stores weapons and ammunition at the church for rebels. He approached you last October to repair stands of arms. He was the go-between, never named in your records book. You know his business partners and the routes the weapons take. He's now gone to ground. Tell me where to find the hole he's crawled into."

The gunsmith slouched. "I don't remember. It's been too long." He lay back and flung the inside of his elbow across his eyes. "Julia, ah, Julia."

"Mr. Spivey's holding her prisoner somewhere. It's winter. She hasn't any clothing. Help us find the fiend that's hurt your wife."

Garrity jerked himself back to a sitting position. "Take me with you." He sniffed again. "If I see landmarks—houses, farms—I might remember where he and I conducted business."

Michael's fist clenched with impatience. How green did Garrity think him? If they let him out of jail to assist their capture of Spivey, the gunsmith would do his best to escape.

He relaxed his hand and pitched consolation into his voice. "Releasing you isn't an option. What I hope is that after we leave you alone in here, without the distraction of your sister-in-law's taunts, you'll meditate upon your dealings last fall with Mr. Spivey and the rebels. When you remember pertinent details, you'll send word to me. Oh, I fully realize your spite for me. But you're doing this for Julia. She's a prisoner, tormented. At this point, I believe you're the only one who can help her."

He took a step toward the door before pivoting back around to study the morose gunsmith. "One more query, sir. You'd been reading the letters Mr. Greene sent your wife. Almost two weeks ago, Mrs. Overton saw you steal a letter from your wife's chest. The one that's missing is dated Monday the twenty-second of January. Where is it? I suspect that the content may provide a clue to your wife's abduction."

Garrity remained quiet so long that Michael believed he wouldn't answer. Then he heaved a sigh. "I don't have the letter. I gave it away."

More impatience tugged a frown from Michael. "To whom did you give it? Mr. Spivey?"

Garrity sat up and shook his head. "No, not him. You shall think me a fool if I tell you."

Michael sighed. "See here, I'm not in a position to pass judgment upon your motivations or actions. My job is to collect evidence, and where there is probable cause in a crime, make arrests. I leave judgment to judges—and if you so believe, the Almighty."

Garrity concentrated on the stone floor. "I gave the letter to Mrs. Delacroix."

Astonishment flooded Michael. Had he heard Garrity correctly? "Esmé

Delacroix, off the Sound Road?" Garrity's head bobbed once.

The scaffold for evidence in Michael's head swung about with an almost painful jolt. Could the Frenchwoman have used the letter to forge Greene's script in the note, assist her in abducting Julia Garrity? Certainly. But Mrs. Delacroix didn't fear death, so he doubted Mrs. Garrity's insults were a strong enough motive for abduction. And to expect a widow of strained means to hire an elegant carriage and the services of a professional coachman—no, he didn't see it.

The gunsmith lifted his chin. "I know what you're thinking. You're thinking I've been having an affair with her, since Julia's having an affair with Greene. But I'm faithful to my wife. Mrs. Delacroix, she works with herbs, she makes love charms, she claims to talk with spirits and receive guidance for her clients. Some people call her a witch. I don't believe in witches.

"But I've visited her several times since October, paid her to consult her spirits and advise me, because Julia was growing more and more distant from me. I got desperate. A few weeks ago, I asked Mrs. Delacroix to make me a love charm, something to call Julia back to me. She said that love charms were among the most complex, powerful spells on the earth. She asked me to bring her something that both Julia and her lover had touched, so I went into the chest and took the most recent letter she'd received from Greene, and I gave it to her."

"What happened to the letter?"

He hung his head. "She said she consumed it in the production of the love charm. Took her about an hour and a half. She presented me with a white candle and ribbons on it, instructed me to fill the base with honey and burn it at my bedside. I told you it would sound foolish of me."

Foolish? From Garrity's confession, Michael realized that he himself had never been in love with a woman, never felt the intensity of longing that compelled men to perform actions that they believed irrational, out of desperation to regain a woman's love.

Ice slithered the length of his backbone again. He related to Garrity's obsession well enough. Obsession had driven him to crave Lydia for years. Obsession had also driven him to ride dispatches out into the South Carolina hinterland in hopes of finding and killing Lieutenant Fairfax.

Wasn't there something hideously out of kilter and warped within his soul that in his lifetime, he'd never experienced tender love to displace his obsessions?

He dragged in a deep breath, disturbed at his own thoughts. "Many of us stand on a limb when we've grown desperate. Mrs. Delacroix corroborated your story about the love charm and your relationship with her. I suppose a man does what he must do."

The gunsmith said nothing and continued to study his hands, so Michael motioned to Spry, walked to the door, and rapped on it. "Jailer!"

Keys jingled just outside the door, and Caldwell swung the door open. Spry exited.

"Lieutenant." Michael paused in the doorway to regard Garrity. The gunsmith's larynx shivered with a gulp. "Mr. Spivey hates Mrs. Delacroix. He's afraid of her. He believes she can curse a man's staff, make it wither. I think he may try to kill her."

Garrity's announcement came as no surprise. "Thank you for the warning, Mr. Garrity. And as I said earlier, if you recall where Mr. Spivey might be hiding, send for me. That information could help save lives."

Caldwell followed him outside the jail. "Mr. Stoddard, a message arrived from the regiment. Major Craig requires your presence at his headquarters immediately."

Michael's stomach tensed. The words "requires" and "immediately" felt inauspicious—but what to do about Garrity in the interim? He waved his hand toward the jail. "Leave Mr. Garrity in there alone for a while longer. If he decides to talk, don't wait to seek me out."

"You'll be in town?"

"For the next hour or so, I suspect."

"Very good, sir."

Michael and Spry set out for Major Craig's headquarters. After they'd walked a quarter minute, Spry cleared his throat. "The message didn't sound promising, sir."

"I hope he doesn't change his mind about the twenty-four hours he gave me earlier. I anticipate that our gunsmith will search his soul and provide helpful information soon."

At the house on Third Street, just beyond the soldiers and scouts queued for an audience with Craig, civilian men and women milled about. White kerchiefs covered the heads of several women. The group ceased talking and regarded the two soldiers with narrowed eyes and frowns. Michael grabbed the canvas sack from Spry. Shoulders squared, he strode past the civilians and bounded up the steps as if what awaited him at the top was good news.

The guard rolled his eyes and pushed open the front door. "Sir, Mr. Stoddard has arrived." He held the front door open for Michael. "Go in. He's expecting you."

In the study, Craig sat behind his table, the bulldog's head resting in his lap. Occupying the only chair opposite the table from them was a stern-faced woman about forty years old who measured Michael's advance with wintry, blue eyes. He was certain he'd seen her among congregants at the service the previous night.

Craig returned his salute. "Mr. Stoddard, this is Mrs. Forbes from the Church of Mary and Martha of Bethany."

She pursed her lips at Michael. Her name was familiar. He combed memory in effort to place her.

"Lieutenant, she's the church's Manager of Education."

Manager of Education—of course! According to Spivey, Mrs. Forbes had been privy to the preacher's conversation with Julia Garrity a week earlier. Michael wanted to question her.

"And she described how you and your patrol obstructed their mass last night."

Michael stared at his commanding officer, then snapped his scrutiny to Mrs. Forbes. Satisfaction slicked her smile. She'd certainly manipulated the truth.

Craig dislodged the dog and balled both fists on the table. "Mr. Stoddard, I do not have time to field problems created by inappropriate actions between my officers and civilians. You will cease using the law to fulfill personal grudges! Is that clear?"

Chapter Twenty-Four

ANGER FIRED THROUGH Michael, and he whipped his gaze back to Major Craig. "In what way do you believe that I have used the law to fulfill personal grudges, sir?"

Across the table, the carved ivory of Craig's facial features exuded winter. "Are the charges you leveled against Vicar Spivey grounded? Ravishment. Mrs. Forbes speaks for the congregation in saying that Vicar Spivey never treats the women of his church with anything but the deepest respect.

"And abduction." Craig lashed the word against Michael. "Mrs. Forbes says this charge is preposterous, that Vicar Spivey and Mrs. Garrity have a cordial relationship with no indication of disagreement or animosity."

"Sir, I have questions of Mrs. Forbes—"

"Mr. Stoddard, if you want those charges to stand, you have some explaining to do." Craig pushed back in his chair. Trouble nosed his thigh happily. "On what do you base these charges?"

Smugness twisted the Manager of Education's lips. She tapped her foot in expectation.

Damn! Michael had seen this before: senior officers too preoccupied with higher strategy to attend to details, and making decisions based only upon the first pieces of information they received. He must regain his authority.

He pinned his gaze on the major. "Sir, I will provide you with that information. But out of desire to protect witnesses, I insist upon addressing this matter in a private audience with you." Confirming that Mrs. Farrell and Mrs. Delacroix had named Spivey as a perpetrator might incur a backlash from the preacher if it were done before his capture and arrest.

"Protect witnesses?" Mrs. Forbes jammed her nose in the air. "What about protecting the reputation of Vicar Spivey? You've slandered him! If these witnesses speak the truth, they have nothing to fear. God is on their side."

Her excitability clawed at Michael. He forced it away, refused to look at her full on, and pulled his response from the calm well of logic. "God is on the side of those who employ wisdom. Major Craig, I see no wisdom in sharing the identities of these witnesses with Mrs. Forbes."

"Stop stalling, Lieutenant. Out with their names."

A foul taste invaded Michael's mouth, and his stomach wrung at the thought of divulging to a hostile party the names of two women who deserved the Crown's protection. Major Craig didn't trust him. What did it take to earn that trust? Jaw tight, he said, "Mrs. Richard Farrell and the Widow Delacroix."

"*Mrs. Delacroix?*" Mrs. Forbes leapt to her feet, teeth bared, and gawped at Major Craig. "Mrs. Delacroix isn't a credible witness at all. She practices witchcraft! The town is terrified of her. You see, Major, I told you the charges were hogwash."

Michael rammed back his fury at the cost of feeding the ache in his stomach. "Mrs. Forbes's information about Mrs. Delacroix is incorrect, sir!"

"You scoundrel! You've labeled me a liar!"

Craig frowned at her. "He didn't label you a liar at all, madam. And you will refrain from insulting my officer. Resume your seat and contain yourself, or I shall end this audience." She huffed back into the chair, and Craig regarded Michael. "Witchcraft, bah. What is Mrs. Delacroix's position on this issue?"

Michael steadied his galloping pulse. "On Wednesday the seventeenth of January, Mr. Spivey and his assistant and cousin, Mr. Greene, called upon the lady. Mr. Spivey attempted to force his affections upon her. Out of fear for her own well-being, she ordered one of her slaves to evict Mr. Spivey from her house. Mr. Greene has corroborated the story."

The woman from church expelled a breath. "Preposterous!"

"Mrs. Forbes, you will cease from commentary while I question my officer. Mr. Stoddard, what of the other witness, Mrs. Farrell?"

"She's the wife of the town tobacconist. She informed me yesterday that Mr. Spivey entered her shop unbidden early one morning in December and attempted to woo her. She rebuffed him. This morning, she asked for protection after he again attempted to force his affections on her. This time, she had to stab him in the upper left arm with a scissors to rid herself of him. Mr. Spivey knows her from their youth, sir. He confessed to her that he once drugged her drink, and while she lay insensible, he ravished her."

A strangled cough emerged from Mrs. Forbes. Craig's gaze darted to her before fixing back on Michael. "And the abduction charge?"

"Two abduction charges, actually, sir." Michael explained how Spivey's men had attempted to abduct Mrs. Farrell from the estate nine miles south. Then he laid the canvas sack on Craig's table, earning a whine and some serious sniffing from Trouble. "We identified clothing in this sack as that of the missing woman, Mrs. Garrity. It's what she was wearing when last seen on Saturday." Craig peered into the sack but didn't remove anything.

"Sir, the garments are slashed, as if a knife was used to rip them off the wearer. Spry and I found the sack during a search of the Church of Mary and Martha of Bethany. It was shoved almost out of sight on a top shelf in a room behind the chancel. In Mr. Spivey's living quarters near the church, I found a matching tucker beneath his mattress. He has no alibi for the time of Mrs. Garrity's disappearance."

Major Craig turned to Mrs. Forbes, whose lips were almost white from containing outbursts. "Explain how the sack wound up in your church, and the tucker beneath your preacher's bed."

Indecision and perhaps the first inkling of doubt quivered in her hands and lips. "I cannot, except to suggest that your investigator and his assistant planted everything to falsely incriminate Vicar Spivey. I myself have never seen the sack before this moment."

Craig's regard of her cooled. He returned the sack to Michael. "You said you had questions of Mrs. Forbes, Mr. Stoddard. Proceed."

"Thank you, sir." Michael slid the sack to the ground near his foot and faced the woman. Her self-righteousness flogged him, sending hope through him. He'd seen people trip over their self-righteousness. How precariously was she balanced? Would she stumble in Major Craig's presence? "Madam, I offer you the opportunity to clear Mr. Spivey's name. When and where was the last time you saw Mrs. Garrity?"

"Last Thursday at the church." The corners of her mouth contracted, as if she were fighting a smirk over the memory.

"With whom did she visit, and what was the nature of the visit?"

"Vicar Spivey. Mrs. Garrity discussed personal matters with him."

"Mr. Spivey corroborates your statement and claims you were privy to their conversation. Tell Major Craig what they talked about."

"I'm not at liberty to divulge details of Mrs. Garrity's private life."

"I shall fill in the details for Major Craig, then." Michael took a step toward her. "Mrs. Garrity and Mr. Spivey discussed how to murder Mrs. Delacroix."

Mrs. Forbes gasped, and her eyes widened. "That's a lie!"

"Mr. Spivey quoted to me from the Bible, 'Thou shalt not suffer a witch to live,' thus declaring his intentions for Mrs. Delacroix." Michael turned to Craig. "He wanted her murdered because she spurned his affections, ridiculed him, and cursed his manhood the night she had her slave evict him. Mrs. Garrity wanted her murdered because she mistakenly believed Mrs. Delacroix was having an affair with her husband. Thursday afternoon, after her meeting with Mr. Spivey, Mrs. Garrity drove to Mrs. Delacroix's house and threatened her with murder if she didn't give up the affair."

Mrs. Forbes beat her fists in her lap. "Lies!"

"Last Sunday in church, Mr. Spivey preached about driving out the witch from the community. A few days later, Mrs. Delacroix came into town to lower the price of her property in effort to sell it faster, confiding in her land agent, Mr. Bowater, that she feared for her life."

Mrs. Forbes bolted up from her chair, her fists knotted. "You animal! All you know from your battlefields is murder. You presume that Vicar Spivey would stoop to the crudity of murder, outright kill a witch to rid us of her, when economic ruin is far more—"

She broke off too late. Michael glared at her, saw her expression emblazoned with the realization that she'd just sprawled upon her face and betrayed Spivey. One of her eyes quivered with repressed horror. "Economic ruin, is it, Mrs. Forbes? So that's what Mr. Spivey, a man of God, schemed with Mrs. Garrity for Mrs. Delacroix. Slow, economic ruin."

"You—You're putting words in my mouth."

Craig stirred. "Oh, no, madam, we haven't misunderstood you at all. A campaign of slow, economic ruin sounds like a far worse fate for a 'witch' than a quick murder."

Michael watched her gaze dart between them and said, low, "Mrs. Garrity originally offered to provide Mr. Spivey with monetary assistance for his campaign against Mrs. Delacroix, but then she retracted her offer, leaving him in a financial pinch, angering him. Where is Mrs. Garrity, Mrs. Forbes?"

Her gaze jumped for the window. "I don't know." Her brow creased, as if she truly didn't know.

"Where is Mr. Spivey?"

She rubbed her shoulder. "I-I don't know. With these charges leveled against him, he's left the area, gone into hiding." She squared her shoulders and addressed Craig, her voice more steady. "I remind you that your investigator has disrupted our church. Our *Anglican* church. He's clearly a vain man seeking to vent personal frustrations upon others and secure your favor. I demand that you retract the charges. They are groundless."

Craig evaluated her. "Now that I've heard Mr. Stoddard's analysis and explanations, I doubt the charges are groundless. I also doubt whether you're consistently providing congregants with Anglican worship up there in that church."

The ache in Michael's stomach subsided. At last, Major Craig had heard what he had to say. But at what cost? He'd exposed Mrs. Farrell and Mrs. Delacroix.

Mrs. Forbes gaped. "You cannot be serious!"

Craig fixed her gaze with his. "Mrs. Forbes, I'm temporarily suspending all activities at the Church of Mary and Martha of Bethany, pending an investigation into the nature of the services provided there."

"*What?*"

"If you have contact with Mr. Spivey, I suggest that you encourage him to turn himself in for questioning. The sooner the better, for if he's innocent of these charges, we shall dismiss them quickly and release him. Your cooperation with the regiment will facilitate the return of your worship services."

"And who decides the validity of Vicar Spivey's statements?"

Craig stood, his expression stony. "Our audience is concluded. Good day, madam."

Mrs. Forbes granted Major Craig the barest curtsy and ignored Michael as she flounced out. Perturbed, the major scrutinized Michael a moment before resuming his seat. Then he lowered his voice. "I'm now satisfied with your progress in the inquiry. Bring it to a close as quickly as possible. The longer it goes on—" With a jerk of his head, he indicated the direction of the front steps, where the Bethanys had gathered. "—the more time you give them to inject superfluous information into the investigation and muddy the water."

"Sir." Michael couldn't have agreed more. Relief would have soared through him, but for the weight of his concern for Mrs. Farrell and Mrs. Delacroix. "We must provide the two ladies with protection."

Craig squinted at him. "Mr. Spivey is that dangerous while he's trying to hide?"

"Oh, yes. His approach on Mrs. Farrell this morning after she'd already repulsed him in December indicates that he's ignoring her rejections. Not to sharpen the blade too well, sir, but if neither she nor Mrs. Delacroix is alive to testify against Mr. Spivey, the charge of ravishment becomes smoke."

Craig nodded once, a sharp motion of agreement.

"Last night, during my party's return trip from the church, Mr. Spivey's men ambushed us. Fortunately they scattered as soon as we showed them the offensive. Later, a smaller delegation of his men mounted a personal attack upon Spry and me in Mrs. Jones's back yard. Several men had been present at the attack upon the Farrell estate last Sunday. They warned us to cease persecuting the Bethanys." Michael touched his left cheek.

Craig's interest darted there. "How long will these women require guards, Mr. Stoddard?"

The commander of the Eighty Second didn't have the resources to guard the women for more than a day or two. If Gabriel Garrity didn't come through with the lead he needed, Michael might spend weeks searching for Spivey. He might never find him. And Spivey might make good on his intentions for the two women during that time.

Quite clearly, Michael had to wrap up the investigation within the next day. But he had a hunch that if Spivey were going on the offensive, it would be during the next day anyway. "Through Saturday morning, sir, unless I arrest Mr. Spivey sooner."

Craig gave him another nod. "I shall make it so."

When Michael emerged from the meeting, he noted from the porch that all the Bethanys were gone. He trotted down the steps and walked out to meet Spry, who'd waited for him near the street. "Any word from Mr. Garrity?"

"No, sir." The private's lips tensed. "Those Bethany congregants certainly were angry when they left." His gaze searched Michael's face. "I take it we're still assigned to the investigation, sir?"

"Yes, but the pressure to solve it now isn't coming from Major Craig. It's coming from Mr. Spivey. I fear he may attempt to murder Mrs. Farrell and Mrs. Delacroix."

"Yes, sir. They're witnesses against him."

"Major Craig will shortly send out soldiers to guard the ladies through Saturday morning. But I want this investigation closed before Saturday."

"Understood. Where shall we go next, sir? Shall we lean on Mr. Garrity to improve his memory?"

"I wager he's expecting that of us, so let's give him more breathing space." Michael studied the sky. The overcast had lowered a bit. Perhaps they'd have rain that night. "Let's head to the infirmary."

"The injured men have been released already, sir."

"I know it. I want to borrow the surgeon's table for a closer look at Mrs. Garrity's garments."

***

At the infirmary, Michael took advantage of a wooden table, seasoned with dried bloodstains but otherwise clean, to spread Julia Garrity's garments upon it, the gown and chemise flipped over to display the backs. The surgeon, Clayton, meandered over from cleaning equipment. "Who would take a sword to such fine clothing?"

"A sword? I presumed a dagger did the damage."

The surgeon bent closer to study the edges of rips in the fabric. "Not a knife. Something with a wider blade. Short sword or cutlass, perhaps. The strokes seem too broad for a knife. And clean, too. No one was wearing this clothing when it was sliced."

Michael imagined that the surprise on Spry's face must match his own. "What makes you believe that no one was in the clothing?"

"Look here. Very little fraying around the edges of the cuts." Clayton hesitated. "Perhaps I presume, too. Someone may have been wearing the clothing when it was cut, but if so, she didn't struggle."

"She was unconscious," said Spry, "or dead."

Clayton smiled with suggestion. "Or cooperative."

The thought of any woman lying still while Spivey cut a fine gown off her kindled a burn in Michael gut. He swallowed hard to dispel it and turned the gown back over so the front faced them. "Look." He pointed to dirt smudges on the bodice that he and Spry hadn't noticed before. "Unless her clothing was dragged through dirt, this implies that she was lying prostrate on the ground at one point."

"In such a position," said the surgeon, "the clothing could be cut without much difficulty."

Spry plucked a couple of pine needles from just inside the bodice. "Longleaf pine. Too bad it grows everywhere around here. Otherwise we might have a better idea where she was when the clothing was damaged."

Michael bent over for a closer look. Caught in wool fibers beside where the pine needles had lodged was a dark hair. He extracted it completely and stretched it out upon an adjacent empty cot, a single strand of hair more than three feet in length.

The surgeon straightened. "This woman has quite a head of hair."

Michael frowned at Spry. "Do you remember Mr. Garrity describing the length of his wife's hair to us the other day?"

"Sir. Middle of the back, I believe he said."

Performing a quick estimation of the distance between the two other men's heads and the middle of their backs told Michael that the strand of hair they'd found was at least a foot longer. "I don't think this is a strand of Mrs. Garrity's hair."

"Miss Ward's, then, sir. We let Mr. Garrity examine the gown while he was in the cell she'd just vacated, and he set it upon the bench beside him. The gown must've picked up a hair."

"Good thinking. But is Miss Ward's hair is this long?"

Spry pondered the strand. "No, sir, I don't believe it is."

Clayton clapped his hands together once and grinned. "Good show, fellows! Looks like you found yourselves a clue. Someone with very long, dark hair has some explaining to do."

The image of long, black hair like a river down Esmé Delacroix's back ignited Michael's memory. His heart skipped a beat in astonishment. He gaped at Spry and saw his own insight reflected in the private's eyes.

The person who had some explaining to do was the "witch" from Saint Domingue.

Chapter Twenty-Five

ESMÉ DELACROIX. MICHAEL thanked the surgeon and folded up the clothing in haste, eager to step outside, where he and Spry could confer about the discovery. They exited the infirmary and walked away from the stable, into the privacy offered by a public street.

Spry spoke first. "I got suspicious back there in the jail, sir, when Mr. Garrity was talking about the missing love letter."

Bloody hell, why hadn't Michael listened to his instincts when he'd been questioning Garrity? Because he was a sentimental fool and hadn't wanted to believe it?

Spry worked through the logic aloud. "The missing letter to Mrs. Garrity was dated the twenty-second. It was the letter that Mr. Garrity gave Mrs. Delacroix to make the love charm. Suppose Mrs. Delacroix used it to forge Mr. Greene's handwriting and signature for a compelling summons for Mrs. Garrity. She also created another note, the one we found under the bench in the Garritys' back yard, to misdirect an investigator into thinking that Mr. Greene and Mrs. Garrity had run off together."

Michael had flogged himself in his dream with the jeering apparition of Lieutenant Fairfax. Right beneath his nose, indeed. Garrity's taunt echoed in his head: *You're a shoddy investigator*. Why hadn't he seen the connections earlier? Had he been so obsessed with the satisfaction he'd derive from arresting a weapons-smuggling rebel that he'd overlooked clues left by a murderess? His shoulders ached, as if he carried weight that bent him double.

Spry kept talking, his words all logical. "And if Mrs. Delacroix deliberately wrote the note to throw us off her track, it makes sense that she also would have planted the torn clothing in the church, to frame Mr. Spivey. That mangy preacher makes such a convincing abductor and rapist, it's hard to believe the bugger could be innocent of harm to Mrs. Garrity. But if Mr. Spivey isn't holding Mrs. Garrity prisoner, where is she?"

"Dead." As soon as he spoke the word, he knew it was true. "Mrs. Delacroix has no need for Mrs. Garrity."

The finality in Michael's tone dragged a sigh from his assistant. "How, sir? There's no blood on the clothing." He shook his head. "I don't believe Mrs. Garrity would have held still while Mrs. Delacroix's sword was ripping her clothing. Oh. Begging your pardon. I presumed she was conscious. Well, then, when and how would Mrs. Delacroix have transported the clothing to the church without anyone seeing her at the church, especially Mr. Spivey or Mr. Greene?"

"She'd have done so Saturday night, while heads were turned toward the change in government." Michael mused over Noisette's cryptic remark: *She is drained when she spends long hours as the hands and eyes, as she did this weekend.* Had Esmé Delacroix gone into some sort of trance with her spirits to murder Julia Garrity? Surely maintaining such a trance for hours was impossible. Perhaps she'd given the task of hiding the clothing in the church and Spivey's house to the capable Armand. "She might also have planted the note in the back yard Saturday night or early Sunday morning."

"Who was the coachman seen by Mr. Hiller, sir? And where did the fine carriage come from?"

Michael stopped walking, the reminiscence of Mrs. Duncan's filtering back into his memory from two days earlier: *When he was in port, they'd ride to town in a splendid carriage...I haven't seen the carriage for a good ten years. They replaced it with a more practical conveyance.* Yet another clue that he'd brushed aside. He faced Spry. "The Delacroixs had such a carriage ten years ago. Mrs. Duncan at White's Tavern remembers seeing it in town." Breath rasped from him. "Dressed in livery and a wig, Mrs. Delacroix might attain the illusion of being a Negro coachman if she could contrive to temporarily darken the skin on her face and hands."

"Yes, I can imagine it, sir. Maybe she waited until Wednesday to visit Mr. Bowater in town and drop the selling price on her property because she had to allow whatever dye she'd used to wear off. But Mrs. Delacroix's motive—I'm still not clear on that. Did she kill Mrs. Garrity because the woman insulted her, threatened to expose an affair with her husband? Or maybe Mrs. Garrity told her that Mr. Spivey and his church were planning to kill her?" Spry coughed into his fist. "From what little I know of Mrs. Delacroix and her household, I cannot see them rattled by ridicule or cowed by a death threat."

Spry was correct. Ridicule and death threats wouldn't daunt Mrs. Delacroix. That was why he'd been dismissing clues about her all along.

However at the meeting with Major Craig, Mrs. Forbes had supplied him with the Frenchwoman's motive for murder. She'd been threatened with slow economic ruin. Combined with her inability to sell her property in a timely manner, it prevented her return to Saint Domingue with the remains of her loved ones.

Michael rolled his shoulders back and filled the private in on the conversation with Mrs. Forbes. "We may now decipher Mrs. Garrity's smug attitude after her visits last Thursday to Mr. Spivey and Mrs. Delacroix. She'd gotten through to her rival, convinced her that she and Mr. Spivey were a real and imminent threat to her household."

"Are you saying that Mrs. Delacroix felt she had no choice but to murder Mrs. Garrity and frame the preacher for her murder?"

Michael rubbed his eyes, grainy from sleeplessness and remnants of the head cold. "The best person to answer that question is Mrs. Delacroix."

Spry's expression saddened. "Suddenly all the puzzle pieces feel as though they fit."

"Yes, it's what happens when you've hit upon the correct solution."

"Sir, Mrs. Delacroix is no common felon. With the threats of Mr. Spivey and Mrs. Garrity, and the fact that the government was in transition, she probably felt she was backed into a corner. I wager she wouldn't have stepped outside the law otherwise. Most of us are the same way."

Mrs. Duncan and Mrs. Farrell, respected businesswomen, admired Esmé Delacroix. And they and Mrs. Hooper held Julia Garrity in enough esteem, despite her faults, that they'd been forthcoming with helpful information about her. If Mrs. Delacroix had murdered Mrs. Garrity, the revelation would flabbergast the community.

Almost, Michael could agree with Spry's argument. Except that if the logic they wove that afternoon was correct, Mrs. Delacroix had committed deliberate and self-serving acts of evil. Since the previous summer, he'd been unable to regard a premeditated, violent crime without thinking of what Lieutenant Fairfax had done in Alton. "I agree that most of us wouldn't kill another person unless backed into a corner, Spry." Cold resolve paved over his emotion. "But if Mrs. Delacroix *plotted* these crimes, she took criminal intent a step farther than what most of us would have done. Not only did she scheme the murder of Mrs. Garrity, she figured out how to plant evidence that would implicate Mr. Spivey for it."

"Ah. Yes, sir." Spry's jaw tightened.

"It explains how she could claim her 'spirits' would protect her from harm, how they granted her a vision of Mr. Spivey and his church destroyed. There was no witchcraft involved. She knew how everything would play out."

From the reluctance in Spry's expression, Michael sensed the way his assistant flinched from their next step. His voice was quiet but firm. "If we're to prove beyond a doubt that murder and abduction have been done, Spry, we must find Mrs. Garrity and the carriage. Are you with me on this?"

The private's head lifted. "Sir. Yes, sir. I'm not happy for it. I want to find Mrs. Garrity alive and throw Mr. Spivey in jail. But I'm with you." He pressed his lips together, signaling his frustration. "If Mrs. Garrity is dead, her body could be anywhere in the Cape Fear."

Michael envisioned the recent mound of leaf and tree debris beside the family graveyard on the Delacroix property. "It could be, yes, but I've an idea of where it may be."

"And the carriage, sir?" Spry caught himself. "Several buildings on the Delacroix property are large enough to hold a carriage. We never searched them."

"Exactly."

"So now we ride out to Mrs. Delacroix's house, sir?"

"With a patrol of soldiers. No point in arguing with Armand or those hounds." He pivoted in the street and headed back for the stables. "Let's go."

***

The two men assigned by Major Craig to protect Mrs. Delacroix hadn't yet left town, so Michael included them in his patrol, bolstered it with six additional men, and commandeered horses for all eight plus himself and his assistant. While the men underwent a brisk weapons inspection with Spry, Michael dashed off a note to Craig of his intention. By three o'clock, the party of ten had cantered out of Wilmington, weapons loaded and ready.

While still on the Sound Road, less than a mile from the drive to the Delacroix property, Michael sniffed the air, startled. "Spry, do you smell that?"

"Yes, sir, like someone's burning refuse."

"No one lives out here except—" Michael squinted in the direction of their destination. Just visible against the gloomy sky was a column of smoke, not unlike the smoke he'd seen rising from the Farrell estate last Sunday. Comprehension blasted him, and he kicked his horse into a gallop. "Ah, bloody hell! Come on, lads!"

The party reached the Delacroix property just in time to witness the final wall of the main house collapse inward and release a storm of sparks, heat and smoke so intense that Michael was forced to withdraw the patrol back near the garden for safety. At first, he did little except gape, his stomach roiling with horror, loss, incredulity, and regret. Every man beneath his command stared at the destruction with disbelief. They could do nothing for anyone who had been in the house.

The herb and vegetable garden had also been destroyed, trampled by horses not from his patrol. The garden had been a major food source for the household. Esmé Delacroix hadn't torched her own homestead.

Through smoke, he saw intact buildings on the property. Hope seesawed through him. Perhaps Mrs. Delacroix and her people had taken refuge in one of the undamaged structures.

He ordered reconnaissance around the house. There was no sign of the cow or chickens. However within a minute, they found two hounds, shot dead. On the ground outside the intact barn, they found the other two dogs, Mrs. Delacroix's driver, and the elderly man. The patrol dismounted to check for survivors. All were dead.

Beside both men lay bloody machetes. His eyes watery with smoke, Michael knelt beside the old man. His body and that of the driver were pocked gory with musket balls. The men must have hacked at their assailants before being brought down, their courage born of desperation, for multiple hoof prints around the bodies revealed that the slaves had been well outnumbered. They'd never had a chance of escaping the butchery.

And was this butchery of Spivey's making?

Fury poured through Michael's veins. Easily, he could imagine Spivey commanding his men to kill "the witch," mobilizing the same force of men who'd ambushed the Eighty-Second the previous night, the same men who'd tried to kidnap Mrs. Farrell from her estate. Michael glared at the ground between the old man and him, envisioning the preacher on the site, personally directing his men, rather than awaiting the outcome at some distant location. Michael also imagined Spivey savoring the screams, the wild-eyed terror, the stench of blood and black powder, and the agonized writhe of moribund humans: Spivey, plunging his senses into the full experience of neutralizing his enemies, just as he'd sought to neutralize another enemy, Alice Farrell—

Recognition staggered Michael. No, Esmé Delacroix and Alice Farrell weren't Spivey's enemies. They were his *sport*.

Four weeks after Fairfax flayed his Spanish victim alive, Michael had been Fairfax's sport. Michael had persisted in wondering over Fairfax's motive, even after Captain Sheffield had warned him off: *War achieves a queer mastery over some men. Were I you, I wouldn't dig too hard for his motive.* But Michael's curiosity created an opening, allowed Fairfax to lure him to the copse near Alton. And there the monster had gloated his motivation for torture and murder.

★★★

"You've falsified a message from my commander and wrongly detained me." Michael reached for his reins, the biscuits and bacon in his stomach curdling at the thought of being isolated with a murderer. *"Good day."*

"Stoddard, don't be such a stump." Fairfax dismounted, an unearthly twinkle in his eyes, and strolled toward Michael leading his horse. *"Captain Sheffield's at peace with your circumstantial evidence, with your conclusion that the Spanish assassin's partner killed him. But you—you're still wondering about a motive, aren't you?"* Fairfax's teeth flashed. *"Superb. Always tie a motive to a crime.*

"Think like your quarry. It isn't an assassin's nature to trust anyone. If the slightest detail seems amiss, one assassin assumes he's been betrayed and falls upon the other. It's that simple."

Instinct warned Michael the lunge was coming, but he didn't parry it in time and found himself slammed against the nearest oak. The twenty-five extra pounds of muscle on Fairfax subdued his resistance inside of five seconds. With their chests heaving together, the twinkle in Fairfax's eye metamorphosed to an archangelic radiance that suffused his expression.

"Assassins like to kill," he whispered. *"One incapacitates the other, and with him at his mercy, he recalls how a man looks at him right after—"* He pressed his dagger to Michael's carotid artery, and not for all the strength of his own teeth grinding terror could Michael dislodge the blade from burning into his skin. *"—right after he's slit his throat."*

"God damn you to hell!"

"Oh, yes, Stoddard, it's that pivotal second before the victim loses consciousness, when he realizes his attacker is the instrument of his death.

You've seen it when you've shot men. They beg you for life and damn you to hell. You're their creator and destroyer."

Michael should have fled when he had the chance. Now he would beg and damn. "You murderous, bloody bastard!"

"But a man dies, and the moment flees, and the only way to recover it is to kill again." Fairfax's breath covered his face like a kiss. "Does it make sense yet? How glorious if you could protract the moment when you become divinity, make it last several hours, taste, smell, and hear mortality. How witty if you could implicate others in the process. And this location is isolated. No one hears the Spaniard's agony. No witnesses."

Michael's larynx bobbed, a grunting, torturous gulp that conveyed his horror and comprehension.

A chuckle like the greeting of a canebrake rattlesnake emerged from Fairfax. "Ah, I see you understand at last."

The sear of metal retreated, as did Fairfax's weight against his chest. Michael staggered away massaging his nicked throat, his own blood on his thumb. He heard mockery supplant the rapture in Fairfax's voice. "Did you enjoy the lesson on motives, Stoddard?"

★★★

Michael's fingers on his own throat trembled. He lowered his hand to his side and balled his fist. The only reason Fairfax had let him leave the copse alive was because he'd contracted with local bandits to kill Michael on the road to Augusta that afternoon. But Michael had anticipated the bandits, just as he now anticipated—

Horror bolted through him. Gods, no! He sprang to his feet, vaulted over the corpse, and signaled his closest men. "You four ride with all haste to the tobacconist's shop at Market and Second and reinforce the ranks by which Mrs. Farrell is protected!"

"Sir!" They scrambled for their mounts. Within seconds, they'd galloped from the property, headed for the Sound Road.

"The rest of you!" Michael's gaze took in Spry and four other soldiers. "I want survivors!"

Over by the barn, Spry hauled open the door, the crash of it muted through smoke. "Halloo!" The private stopped short, staring, as Michael did, at a barn empty of horses, livestock, and cowering Delacroix household members, its sole occupant a fine, lacquered coach, dark with pale trim.

Smoke smarted Michael's eyes, bitter, like the taste in his mouth. He pivoted, raised his voice. "Halloo! Is anyone here?" But only the crackle of famished flame on timber answered from the remains of the house.

He, Spry, and the men remounted their horses to search the area, calling for Mrs. Delacroix, Armand, and Noisette. They discovered the middle-aged woman slave killed on the path to the family graveyard, likely during flight. Farther along the path, at the entrance to the cemetery, lay Noisette, face down in the pine straw and grass, blood drenching her short jacket. One of the mulatto's hands twitched, as if she grasped for earth.

Michael and Spry dismounted, rushed to her, and eased her over. Frothy blood trickled from her mouth. A musket ball had penetrated one of her lungs, a fatal shot.

Spry elevated her back slightly and supported her. She blinked at Michael without recognition, likely beyond clear sight. Nevertheless, he fought to wipe from his face and voice the certainty of her impending death, present her with a neutral tone. "Noisette, it's Lieutenant Stoddard. Who did this to you?"

Her face contorted with pain. "Preacher."

"Mr. Spivey—the man who harassed Madame a few weeks ago, and Armand threw him out?" Her head quivered a nod.

For three seconds, he fantasized the preacher's scrawny neck between his hands. The heat of primal justice flooded his veins while he gouged Spivey's windpipe with his thumbs—held fast while Spivey clawed at him, unable to communicate except with bulge-eyed, choking terror. How would the preacher spend his final seconds of consciousness: praying for deliverance, or cursing the redcoats?

Noisette's groan recalled him. He leaned closer to her and said, "How many of his men were here this afternoon?"

"Many." She licked her lips and left a pinkish film on them. "Twenty?"

The same size party that had attacked the Farrell estate and ambushed the soldiers during their return from church the night before. "Did you see Mr. Spivey's cousin, Mr. Greene, here today?" She shook her head, confirming Michael's suspicions. Unlike those twenty henchmen, Greene wasn't Spivey's minion. Nor had Michael perceived in him the intense hatred and fear that Spivey had for Mrs. Delacroix.

The four other soldiers converged on them, dismounted, and stood in silence. Michael glanced at them. They shook their heads. One private said, low, "We found no one else, sir."

Michael returned his attention to Noisette. "Where are Madame and Armand?"

"Defend house. Muskets."

"Shit," whispered Spry.

Spivey and his jackals had torched the manor, trapping Mrs. Delacroix and Armand inside to fire at their foes in futility. Michael hung his head a moment, overwhelmed by Spivey's senseless, self-serving actions before the mulatto emitted another groan, this one weaker. She wouldn't be alive much longer. Perhaps he could give her some semblance of peace.

"Noisette, I promise that Mr. Spivey will pay for his wretched work here this afternoon. But I must have your help. I know that Madame took the life of Mrs. Garrity, and—"

"*Non*, not Madame." Noisette struggled to firm her voice. "She of the scarred face and sharp dagger. Vengeance Mother. Warrior lady. Give children strength to face obstacles."

For a few seconds her meaning escaped Michael. Then comprehension sifted into him, although he could scarcely believe it. "Are you saying that one of your spirits from Saint Domingue killed Mrs. Garrity?"

"*Oui*. Madame call her, become her eyes, her hands. Poison in wine. In c-carriage."

Arctic cold penetrated Michael's ribs, and he remembered Armand silencing Noisette in the parlor the day before, when the mulatto had hinted of the event. The previous Saturday, Esmé Delacroix had placed herself into a trance, somehow embodied characteristics of a warrior spirit from her homeland, and disguised herself as a Negro coachman. Her portrayal, along with the forged letter, had been convincing enough to lure Julia Garrity into the coach, where poisoned wine awaited her. "Where is the coachman's livery that Madame used last Saturday?"

"Burned. He die years ago." Pain clenched her face.

Michael glanced across the cemetery. Smoke shifted, revealed the pile of yard debris. The burned fabric he'd spotted there that morning must be a remnant of the livery. Mrs. Duncan had ceased seeing the Delacroix's magnificent coach in Wilmington so long ago because after their coachman died, the Delacroixs had decided on a more practical conveyance.

The mulatto coughed blood filled with bubbles. Michael took one of her hands in his, flinched at how icy it was. "Noisette, where is Mrs. Garrity's body?"

"Cemetery." Her voice weakened.

"Beneath that pile of debris?"

After another feeble nod, Noisette struggled for breath. "Vengeance Mother remind Madame...this morning...the investigator will know what she do. Madame still fight."

Vengeance Mother. "Why did Madame call upon Vengeance Mother, not another of your spirits?"

"P-protection. No government. No justice."

It was as Spry had suggested. More disappointment and loss scalded Michael's soul. For years, Esmé Delacroix had lived with the ineptitude of the Committee of Safety. But even rebel frontier justice had abandoned her a week ago, exposed her to the scheme of human predators. Molly the laundress's gushed declaration two days earlier sprang to memory: *We need you.* If only the Eighty-Second had arrived in Wilmington the week before, they might have—

"*Bienvenue, maman.*" The grip of physical agony had smoothed from Noisette's face, and she focused on something beyond Michael's shoulder.

He swiveled around in surprise, wondering if Esmé Delacroix had somehow escaped the inferno of her home. He saw no one except soldiers. But Noisette was staring at *something.* "With whom are you speaking?"

"Vengeance Mother. Forgiveness Mother." Noisette rotated her gaze almost straight overhead, as if to look at someone standing beside her, and lifted her hand. "*Oui, maman,*" she whispered. Then her hand dropped, and her body sagged against Spry, the spark of life forsaking her eyes.

Chapter Twenty-Six

A SMOKY GUST of winter scraped over Michael and Spry, dead leaves chuckling in a demented swirl about them and the body of Noisette. Michael folded the mulatto's hands over her breast, closed her eyes, and stood. Spry eased her body to the ground and pushed himself to his feet.

For a moment, all six soldiers remained silent. The ruined house continued to crackle. Michael ordered his thoughts.

He assumed that Mrs. Delacroix and Armand had died in the fire. All four slaves he'd seen with them that morning were dead. He wondered briefly about the Frenchman. Although he felt certain the giant wasn't a member of the Delacroix household, he was clearly an ally. Who was he? Why hadn't he been there to help defend the property?

After striding past his men, he paused five feet from them to regard the cemetery, then faced them. "We shall move the bodies of the dogs and the Delacroix household members inside one of the undamaged buildings overnight to keep scavengers off. I shall request a burial service for them here, in their own cemetery." And back in Wilmington, if Gabriel Garrity weren't immediately forthcoming with details about where Spivey was hiding, he'd charge him as an accessory in the murders of the Delacroix household.

Spry gazed among the trees, toward the incinerated manor. "The house will burn into the night, sir. No one will be able to approach the ruins and search for Mrs. Delacroix and Armand until at least the morrow."

Michael glanced in the direction of his gaze. "Assuring Mrs. Farrell's safety and capturing Mr. Spivey and his men are our priorities right now. Other searches must wait, including the search for Mrs. Garrity's corpse. I believe Noisette's testimony that it's in that debris pile over there. But we don't have time to verify that. It's obviously protected from scavengers, so there it shall lie awhile longer."

"Do you also believe Noisette's testimony that her mistress and Armand were in the house, sir?"

"I'm not sure I understand your implication, Spry."

"Noisette admitted Mrs. Delacroix's role in Mrs. Garrity's death, sir. What if she believed that her mistress and Armand had escaped being trapped in the fire and also escaped Mr. Spivey's band? Might she have lied to protect her mistress from capture, delay our search for them?"

"That's why we shall search the ruins of the house for their remains after the timbers cool. If they died in the fire, we shall find what's left of their bodies." He squared his shoulders and addressed all the men with him. "For what it's worth, I've seen many people die. Only one of them chose to speak falsehood on his deathbed. However skillful we become at lying while we're alive, when we stand face to face with our Maker, we're disinclined to lie that final time.

"All right, lads, we've bodies to secure from scavengers and a murderer to track down. Let's hop to it."

***

Upon his return to Wilmington, Michael learned that Spivey hadn't menaced Mrs. Farrell. It could only mean that he was lying low after murdering the Delacroix household, biding his time until the heat on him dissipated. Michael didn't plan to give him that time. His next stop was the jail.

Caldwell hung a lantern on a hook inside Garrity's cell and enclosed Michael and Spry with the gunsmith. Garrity sat in much the same spot as when they'd left him hours earlier, but this time he submerged a flash of curiosity in his eyes into sullenness at their arrival.

Garrity had misconstrued his civility earlier as weakness, an error easily corrected. Michael kept his voice low, although he felt a muscle in his cheek quiver with fury. "Mr. Garrity, where's Elijah Spivey?"

Shadow swallowed the gunsmith's smirk, but it seeped into his tone nonetheless. "You know, I've thought about it all afternoon. I seem to have forgotten anything that might be of help to you. My dealings with his group were months ago."

"That's odd. Two days ago, I distinctly recall you telling me that 'a plantation owner south of here' gave you your big job. Mr. Spivey's hiding on that plantation, isn't he? Which plantation?"

Garrity gloated from the shadows. "What time is it getting to be? Mucking jailer hasn't fed me since dawn."

Michael swept forward, wrenched him off the bench, and shoved his back to the wall. Surprise whooshed from Garrity. To preempt the gunsmith's swing at him, Michael stomped his instep and pinned his shoulders to the wall, his face inches from Garrity's bristly, unshaven cheek. "Your wife is dead, you son of a whore! She was murdered last Saturday. Now so is Mrs. Delacroix, and we've a witness that the preacher murdered her this afternoon."

Breath full of pain rasped from Garrity. "Lying scoundrel! He had no reason to kill Julia!"

"Oh, didn't he? We discovered that she teased him with a promise of money for his church, then retracted her offer last Thursday, pinching his pockets." The intentional misleading brought out the whites of Garrity's eyes. Michael rattled him against the wall again. "He isn't the first man she thrashed over money. Fool, your wife was bleeding you, making you work your fat arse off for her luxuries. All these years she and her sister ingeniously kept most of her money out of your hands and laughed at your struggles. I presume you know who'll get your wife's money, now that she's dead and you're in jail."

Garrity's bellow of rage and humiliation resounded through the cell.

Michael slung him by the waistcoat onto the bench and backed off a pace, beside Spry. "Have a taste of the anger Mr. Spivey felt when she cheated him. *Killing* anger, wouldn't you say? You conspired with him to kill your wife on Saturday."

"No, no, I didn't kill Julia!"

"And you were responsible for Mrs. Delacroix's murder, too, and the murder of her household."

Garrity's eyes became bloodshot knobs of terror. "I've been in this jail cell for a day! I had nothing to do with their murders!"

"You might not have been physically present on her property when she was murdered, but that doesn't absolve you of complicity. Garrity, this is your final chance to tell us what you know. If you don't help us find that preacher, we've enough evidence to see you hanged alongside him for every one of those murders." The rasp in Garrity's throat changed to choking noises. "A plantation owner to the south. Out with it. Where's Mr. Spivey hiding?"

"West of—west of the first Davis homestead southbound. But don't take the main road along the Cape Fear. There's another road, less traveled, to the west of it. And there's a track that runs off of that. A quarter-hour ride due west on the track, and you'll come to the plantation. Well, there's not much to the plantation. Mostly just a house."

"Who owns it? Spivey?" When Garrity shook his head, he pressed him. "How many men does he have?"

Garrity's head rattled again. "Not sure now. Paul Greene had about thirty back in October. Together he and Spivey have more now. They've been recruiting."

Up until last week, when the Eighty-Second arrived, the local climate had been excellent for recruiting rebel weapons smugglers. "Where are sentries posted?"

"On the main road at the Davis turnoff. If you take that parallel road I mentioned, you miss the first sentries. In October, they had sentries posted every half-mile westbound to the house."

Michael crossed arms over his chest. "Where are the smuggled weapons hidden?"

"Everywhere. Some might be there at the house, but they're spread among houses across the Cape Fear. And they change locations often."

The regiment might not find every one of those caches, but all Michael needed was some of the weapons that night. "What's the terrain like around the plantation house?"

"Swamp and sand, much like up yonder at the church. The house is built on a rise."

A desperate rebel who knew the swamp could vanish into it in the dark of night and hide for a long while. Fortunately, loyalists scouts were just as familiar with the area—scouts like Teal, who Michael had spotted several times in Wilmington after the occupation. If the raiding party had Teal's help in maintaining stealth until the plantation house was surrounded, Spivey's chances of wiggling away again weren't good.

Spry said, "Sir, it really is too bad we didn't have his information this morning."

"I agree. It might have saved lives in the Delacroix household."

Garrity popped forward on his bench, alert to their implication, his expression taut with fear and incredulity. "You said I wouldn't hang if I helped you!"

"Did I say that, Spry?"

"No, sir."

"The judge examines evidence and decides whether you hang, Garrity. I hope you've been truthful with us about the plantation house. You see, there's one more woman's life at stake. If you've misled us, and harm comes to her, you'll really see my unpleasant side."

"I haven't been out to the plantation in almost four months!" The gunsmith flapped his hands. "They may have changed everything!"

"For your sake, and for hers, I hope they haven't changed a thing."

★★★

Men from the regiment hoisted the sentry off the ground and roped him in line at the rear of seven other prisoners, all with wrists bound behind them and mouths gagged: sentries who'd been posted along the westbound track to the plantation. "Well done, lads," Michael murmured to his dark-cloaked soldiers.

He squinted ahead on the dirt track, trying to resolve detail in a night made inky by overcast and clumps of trees and brush bordering the path. Soldiers of his party and captured sentries appeared as blobs of gray against a grayer landscape, almost indistinguishable from foliage unless he was right upon them. His hand, held a foot before his face, was pale, his wiggling fingers almost disembodied. He couldn't see frost hanging in the air from his breath.

But poor visibility wouldn't delay rebels from moving contraband, so the Eighty-Second wouldn't delay its raid.

Skin along the sides and back of his neck trembled and shrank, as if brushed with freezing mist. He glanced at the sky. The precipitation held off. He directed his attention southward, visited again with the impression that they were watched—not unlike the sensation he and Spry had experienced that morning on the Delacroix property. He'd sent Teal out a second time to scout land south of the road, make sure no one was following them.

His voice hissed out. "Spry!"

The tallest gray blob dislodged from a cluster of others and moved closer to him. "Sir."

"Any sign of Teal?"

"No, sir."

Exasperated, one fist on his hip, the other wrapped around his fusil,

Michael presented himself south and listened. A wet breeze tickled sighs from pine needles and whispered over frost-blasted foliage. Except for a distant owl's hoot, the eerie, empty quiet of winter possessed the wilderness.

The impression of being watched withdrew. His shoulders relaxed. Probably a lone bear had stood out there and observed them, curious but cautious around humans.

The other scout, Ross, padded back to them from the west. His soothing voice was at odds with the information he reported. "A hundred yards ahead, just after the track bends. There's a final sentry posted. Two-story wooden house in a clearing beyond that. Two guards on the porch, a dozen or more men inside, plenty of windows for launching a defense."

Michael thanked him, realized that Teal had found his way back to them, and motioned him over. His footsteps indistinguishable from the brush of the breeze, the Mussulman gazed south and said, low, "Once or twice, I thought I saw and heard something, Mr. Stoddard, but if it is a man, he is very good."

Michael's lips quirked with irony. "Better than you?"

Teal's shoulders straightened. "No, sir. Night this dark and wild creatures trick our eyes and ears."

Night and wild creatures but enhanced the tricks Michael's conscience made, bruised from having failed earlier that day at bringing justice. He nodded his head west, where three soldiers awaited his order to advance and bring down the final sentry. "Follow those three men. After they subdue the last guard on the track, scout around the edge of the clearing where the house sits. Garrity said it's on a ridge. Ross reported its defenses. But I want to know its secrets."

"Yes, sir."

Michael ordered the three men and Teal ahead. Night yawned and swallowed them. He circled the eight roped rebels, paused to glance south a final time, strolled to the front of the column, and stilled the wrist of a soldier whose fingers tapped out a nervous drum drill on his cartridge box. Men shuffled around, cold, eager for action instead of sneaking.

Stealth allowed the ninth sentry to be subdued as easily as his fellows a few minutes later. When Michael and the main group rejoined the advance party near the clearing, they roped the final guard in with other prisoners and prepared for the raid, planned at the barracks, refined with scouts' information. Teal materialized from foliage, and Michael signaled him forward with him.

He crouched at the edge of the clearing to survey the house thirty feet away. By his count, some fifteen to eighteen men moved about within, illuminated by candlelight and lamplight when they passed before windows. From time to time, he picked out Spivey's or Greene's intonations among the conversations within. On the porch, two men hunched over a small table, a lantern and the clatter of dice between them, muskets propped against the wall beside the front door, tankards at their feet.

Teal's soundless, silky drop to a squat beside Michael brought to mind the furtiveness of another scout, one of Thomas Brown's rangers. Adam Neville, that snake, what was he up to now: spying for rebels, or spying for the King? That moment, Michael had no time to ponder it.

"Sir, there is no full cellar here." Teal rotated his face to Michael, eyes glittering, "But it would not surprise me if this house is connected to an escape tunnel similar to the one on the Farrells' estate."

Michael's eyebrows rose. "Where might it emerge?" The Negro shot a glance around the side of the house. "Yes. Good. Have a look, but don't take longer than ten minutes."

"Sir." Teal rose like a deer and slipped between the pines, gone with less sound than the wind's whisper.

In seconds, it was Spry who crouched beside his commander. "All quiet on the track, sir," he murmured. "Complacent up there on the porch, aren't they?"

"Drunk, too."

"Good for them. Better for us. Where's Teal?"

"He's searching for an exit from a possible escape tunnel, like that one you found last Sunday. The next phase of this operation shall start in ten minutes. Pass the word."

"Sir."

As Spry moved off, a branch popped beneath him, but he had the sense to stay low and not panic. One guard on the porch straightened and looked in Michael's vicinity. Then he scratched his head. "Th' hell was that?"

"Cornwallis and a thousand redcoats, you idiot." The second guard laughed, the bray of a donkey. "I'll whip your arse on the next roll."

"Cow piss." The men resumed their diversion.

Michael rose and folded four or five feet back into the foliage, a smile on his lips. The rebel's count was off by 970 redcoats and one general, but his arse would be whipped nonetheless. Even in the dark, he bore resemblance to one of Spivey's apes who'd attacked the Farrells' estate. He touched his bruised cheekbone and looked forward to the rebel's capture.

Hair on his neck froze the second before he discerned a shuffle behind him. Too late, he stiffened. An arm flung across his left shoulder from behind pinned his back to the barrel chest of a giant. A French-accented whisper above his right ear arrived fumed in brandy. "Quiet, English pig." A dagger point pressed Michael's side near his right kidney. "Or you die this moment."

Chapter Twenty-Seven

MICHAEL'S HEART RATE slammed into double-speed. He recognized the voice. His French captor was the fellow who'd held the pistol on the Delacroix property that morning. He whispered, "I didn't realize you spoke English, monsieur."

"Release your weapons and ammunition to the ground."

The hold felt flawless. The Frenchman had been practicing. Michael opened his hand. The fusil sighed against dried ground cover. He followed it with his cartridge box. His hand drifted toward the sheath of his own dagger.

Again, the knifepoint prodded his kidney. "Drop it."

He complied with the dagger. His teeth chattered, and not from cold. He clenched them, aware that he was seconds from sacrificing a kidney to Gaul. The Frenchman must have been stalking them for at least an hour, his scouting ability so smooth that he'd eluded Teal.

Or had Teal betrayed the Eighty-Second to the Frenchman?

Obviously if the giant wanted to kill an Englishman outright, he'd have taken advantage of the pathetic job Michael had performed at maintaining his own guard. Who was this fellow, and why was he there? Were other Frenchmen in the woods with them? That moment did each soldier have a dagger pressed to his back or throat?

Were the French helping Spivey run weapons? What an interesting complication, if so.

"You have done well tonight, disabling sentries without alerting men in the house. You might have fared worse had they been sober. Still, a satisfactory performance for an English pig. It suggests intelligence."

"Thank you," whispered Michael, wondering what in hell the man wanted from him.

A soft belch issued from his captor and bathed Michael with garlic fumes. "You are Major Craig's investigator. You are Lieutenant Michel Stoddard."

He didn't care much for the Gaulish pronunciation of his name. He tested the Frenchman's hold, dismayed to find it sound. For the moment, he was definitely a prisoner. His captor was more massive than Spry, likely capable of lifting him off his feet. "And who might I have the pleasure of meeting?"

"Claude, Monsieur Stoddard. You were stationed in Alton, Georgia last summer."

Michael's scalp crawled. Who was this *Claude*, that he knew so much about him? Had the fellow been monitoring his movements for several months? "Have we met before tonight, monsieur?"

"*Non*, but you murdered my friend. I am curious. How many Frenchmen have you killed, English pig?"

Michael loaded as much courtesy as he could muster into his whisper. "How many Englishmen have *you* killed?" He resisted the temptation to tack, "you French pile of dung," to the end of his sentence.

Claude's chuckle brushed Michael's cheek. The dagger prodded his side again. "Before I slit your throat, I want to know how you killed Jacques."

Jacques. What a good, solid French name. Unfortunately, Michael had no luck bringing to memory a "Jacques" he might have killed. He frowned into the night. If he wanted to stay alive, he'd have to keep Claude engaged. "I don't recollect killing any Frenchmen in Alton, Claude."

"Not in Alton, pig. You followed him from Alton to Havana, Cuba and killed him there."

The crawl in Michael's scalp spread over his body, became a gouge of horror. "Oh, damn."

Claude chuckled again in his ear. "*Oui*, pig, you have remembered. Tell me now."

"Claude, you have me mistaken for another lieutenant." Of all the bloody worst injustices in the world, here he was about to be murdered for one of Fairfax's indiscretions.

"*Non*." The dagger point transferred to the skin above Michael's carotid artery. "You were in Alton—"

"But I wasn't in Havana. That was Lieutenant Dunstan Fairfax—" Michael broke off with a grunt, the sear of knifepoint drawing blood. Fear burned his lungs, scorched each breath as if he'd been running for hours. He blinked, hard, at the smart of sweat in his eyes, each breath jagged. He corralled and centered his thoughts. Jacques. Who was Jacques? Had he met him? "There was—there was a Spaniard murdered in Alton."

"An assassin from *Casa de la Sangre Legítima, oui*. What has this to do with Jacques?"

Michael forced down a swallow, his throat like a pebbly desert. "I was assigned to solve the murder in Alton while Fairfax traveled to Havana with his commander. They were chasing Will St. James." A weather-beaten face with beady, dark eyes materialized in his memory. Jacques. Jacques le Coeuvre? "Yes, I recall now. Your friend Jacques was among St. James's party. After they left Alton, I pieced together that Fairfax murdered the Spaniard, flayed him alive."

"And you did nothing about it. Cowardly pig, protecting your own monster. Were Jacques alive, he would be pleased when I remove your miserable hide from the earth."

Michael gulped. "I-I disclosed everything to my commander in Alton, but justice was denied the Spaniard." Bitterness ate through his whisper. "Fairfax walks free, damn it. No one deserves to die the way that Spaniard did. It was sport for Fairfax."

Claude was silent a moment, the point of his dagger caressing Michael's artery. "Then you have no idea how Jacques died."

"Fairfax shot him. More of his *sport*. In Camden, he tortured to death men in the Ambrose spy ring. Never in my life have I so desired to see a man executed as he." His breath rattled. "But if such is to be accomplished, it won't happen through the courts of King George. Fairfax is from a noble family."

The Frenchman spat his loathing of nobility upon the ground somewhere near Michael's right boot. Savagery carved his whisper out of the night. "What is the regiment of this pustule?"

Michael thought again of Adam Neville mocking him in the hinterlands of South Carolina at the end of December. The scout detested Fairfax as much as Michael did, but all along, his problem with Neville had been that he didn't know how to reach him, what would move Neville to commitment. In contrast, Claude's motivations were clear.

Again, the Frenchman's dagger prodded his neck. Michael gasped for another breath. "You want to slit Fairfax's throat. I don't blame you. But do you feel a slit throat is truly commensurate retribution for the kind of depravities he's committed?"

"Of course not." Then incredulity and interest laced Claude's whisper. "You wish to kill this pig yourself!" He sucked in a breath. "Ah, *pardon, monsieur*, naturally an officer would not implicate himself by validating my assumption."

"Listen well, Claude. I've learned the hard way that one man acting alone will accomplish little against Lieutenant Fairfax. You're going to need help." Michael's knees began knocking. He squeezed his eyes shut, thought of his mother, father, and sister, and three nephews he'd never met. "And if you plan to kill me, you'd best hop to it. But if you do, the death of your friend Jacques may never be avenged."

"*Mon dieu.* You intrigue me. I never thought I would live to hear an Englishman ask for a Frenchman's help." The pressure of the knifepoint vanished from Michael's neck. "I shall consider it, but only if you first show me that you are capable of dispensing King George's justice upon the footwashing Protestant dog in that house."

Claude's arm released his shoulders. Before Michael had time to spring for freedom, the Frenchman hauled him off the ground and heaved him forward, as if he were a sack of grain. With a great snapping and popping of branches and dead wood, Michael tumbled into the clearing, the breath oofing from him, and landed in plain view of Spivey's guards on the porch.

The twitchier of the guards leapt up, musket in hand, overturning the table. "Bloody hell!"

The second man staggered to his feet, fumbling for his musket, voice slurred. "Who's he?"

Michael scrambled up and dashed for protection in the foliage surrounding the track.

"Stop right there, you!" A musket fired, and a ball crackled past Michael's head. "Don't just stand there, Harry, after him!" A bell on the porch clanged.

Foliage shrouded Michael from the house. He shot past Spry and another private, both crouched and partially concealed, and took cover in the brush. "Ready the rope, lads!"

The thump of footsteps, pursuit approaching, became audible. Spry snapped out, "Buchanan, Cunningham, three, two, one!"

The two guards from the porch gained the track, then tumbled through the air and sprawled into the dirt, tripped by a rope stretched taut and knee-height by privates Buchanan and Cunningham on opposite sides of the track. Soldiers jumped out, subdued, and disarmed Spivey's men. Then they dragged them into the brush.

None too soon. Four firearm-laden rebels from the house pounded for the track, backups for their comrades. Up yanked the rope. All four slammed together, cursing, in a heap upon the track. Overpowered and disarmed by soldiers, they were thrust off the track with the two porch guards, to be bound and gagged with the nine sentries.

Still breathing heavily, Michael confiscated the musket, ammunition, and knife of a rebel and sneaked back through foliage to where he'd encountered Claude, but as he suspected, the Frenchman had moved on, and he'd taken Michael's weapons with him. A pity they couldn't lure the remaining rebels from the house and trip them. By then, lights in the house were doused, and every window ledge displayed at least one musket barrel.

Itchy for action, a man in the house discharged his weapon into the clearing. Shot smacked trees to Michael's left. Inside, Spivey lambasted the nervous man to conserve ammunition and stand his ground.

Spry rustled over to Michael and squatted beside him. "What happened to you, sir?"

"Met the Frenchman from this morning. His name is Claude. He took my weapons and tossed me into the clearing. Now we'll have to smoke the rebels out. They've every window watched. Send out the four teams from men not guarding prisoners. Surround the house, make ready, present. Code word: castle." He added, "And watch out for Claude," although instinct told him the Frenchman was observing, rather than participating.

"Sir." Spry rustled back to the track. Ghostly forms of redcoats fanned out into the foliage to cover all sides of the house.

While he waited on Spry's confirmation that the soldiers were in place, Michael used the ramrod on the musket he'd confiscated to verify that the firearm was, indeed, loaded. He also wondered what had happened to Teal and whether the Negro had betrayed them to Claude. Several soldiers crept past him and assumed position just within cover, readying and aiming muskets.

A rebel on the other side of the house fired out. Spivey's voice elevated in ire, overriding his own man's voluble insistence that he'd seen something moving in the trees. With no report back from the six men they'd sent down the track, the rebels were growing edgy.

Spry found his way back to him, crouched beside him. "Men in position, sir."

"Let's give the preacher a taste of the King's finest." Michael cupped his hands around his mouth and hollered, "Castle!"

A volley of musket fire spewed from foliage around the house, followed by the pandemonium of shattered glass, splintered wood, and shouts from within. Before the black powder smoke cleared, soldiers ignited torches and heaved them at the house. Most torches sputtered on the ground, short of the house, but one cleared a window on the lower floor and landed inside, prompting cheers from the regiment.

Michael heard men on the inside yell about powder. Powder? Had Spivey stored powder inside the house? Perhaps he hadn't time to move it to a magazine, where it would be safe.

Denied distinct targets by darkness, the rebels pocked trees with random shot. Except to target windows at will and provide cover for men tossing torches, the soldiers stayed low, moved about, and avoided being shot. The fellow with the excellent pitching arm lobbed another torch in through the side window. Michael heard Spivey's bellow of rage. Rebels continued to fire out of the house, exhibiting no indications of surrender.

Spry fidgeted. "Sir, if we never manage to catch the house afire, they could shoot at us all night. No doubt they have more ammunition than we do."

On the verge of addressing his concern, Michael sensed a presence behind him. He sprang up and whirled, edgy from unanswered questions in his confrontation with Claude, dagger ready for the Frenchman.

The whites of Teal's eyes glittered. "Sir! I found it on the other side of the house, the exit from the tunnel!"

Michael grabbed Teal's upper arm. "Where's that giant of a Frenchman? Is he waiting there at the exit?"

Teal gaped at him, his breath drawn in little gasps. "Wh—what Frenchman, sir? Only one man have I seen back there, and he was escaping from the exit into the swamp!"

Instinct told Michael that Teal's confusion over Claude was genuine. He released him. It wasn't Spivey who the scout had seen exiting the tunnel. He could still hear the preacher orchestrating defense from within the house. Had Teal seen Paul Greene, then? Michael's pulse hopped at the thought of roping up Spivey's smug cousin like a hog. "Spry, you're with me. Lead us, Teal."

Hunched over, the three made their way through foliage and smoke outside the ring of men from the Eighty-Second who continued to fire at will upon the house, despite the return fire. Just inside a cluster of pine trees, the siege of the house ongoing behind them, Teal pointed out a sandy path, pallid in the darkness. "Thirty feet back in that wood, sir. You will find a hinged wooden door on the ground, dead leaves and moss pasted to the top to hide it. Pull it open, and there is a low tunnel. Who is this big Frenchman you mentioned?"

Another cheer erupted from the redcoats. Maybe a third torch had landed in the house. Michael regarded the path. "I'm not sure, but he eluded you earlier."

Protest and consternation emerged from Teal before Michael whispered for quiet. Above the noise of battle, his ears detected a squawk from deeper in the wood, the sound of rusty hinges. "Someone's using the tunnel right now.

Ready with your weapons. After me."

Followed by Teal and Spry, he crept about ten feet down the path, guided by huffing and puffing from straight ahead, sounds of a man exerting himself. He spotted a moving blob, halted, and presented with his musket. Spry, to his right, did the same. Accurate targeting, even that close, was almost a joke in the dark. He hoped the situation wouldn't escalate.

"'Pour out thine indignation upon them,'" the man growled into the night.

What luck. Spivey. And from what Michael could discern, he was alone, jabbering to himself, cocksure that he'd eluded capture.

The preacher shoved the wooden door shut with a hinge-squeak and a whump. "'And let thy wrathful anger take hold of them.'" Brushing off his hands, the preacher straightened.

Michael's teeth bared. "Drop your weapons, Mr. Spivey."

The preacher whipped a pistol from his belt and fired at the same time Michael and Spry discharged their muskets. Spry howled in pain and crumpled. Spivey floundered down the path, deeper into the copse.

Torn between responsibilities, Michael dropped to a crouch beside his assistant, where Teal was already kneeling. "Spry, are you all right?"

"My leg!" Spry hunched over and cradled his left thigh.

Michael could see little of the injury except a dark smear of blood on the trouser material. "Let's see how well you can walk, lad. Teal, help me get him on his feet."

They heaved a panting Spry to a standing position. As soon as he put full weight on his leg, the private grunted and would have collapsed again had he not leaned against Teal. "Ah, damn, it hurts! It's no good, me coming along. Leave me. Spivey's getting away." Spry gritted his teeth. "Bring him in, sir!"

Michael clasped his shoulder, then the shoulder of Teal. "Do what you can for him."

"Sir."

Fury and determination knotted Michael's gut. His discharged musket clenched in his hand, he bolted after Spivey. If the preacher escaped, the Eighty-Second would have to deal with massive amounts of weapons trafficking among rebels and unlimited sedition in the backcountry. The murderer of Esmé Delacroix and her household wouldn't be brought to justice. Alice Farrell would live in danger. And Spry's injury would have been in vain.

On the path, he quickly overtook the preacher, who loped, his breathing harsh, and gripped his side. A musket ball must have found him, too. Spivey darted a look over his shoulder and reached for a weapon at his belt. Michael darted behind a tree half a second before another pistol discharged, the ball shaving bark near his throat. Michael sprang forward and swung his musket.

The butt end clubbed Spivey's back and punched the breath from him. Michael tackled him into a puddle of brackish water. On the way down, Spivey knocked the musket from him.

They wrestled on boggy ground, impaling their coats with pine needles and twigs, each seeking to gouge the other's throat, eye, nose, or groin. The metallic wink of a blade arced toward Michael's face. He batted Spivey's wrist, sending the knife into the bushes, but took a fist in his shoulder, and exhaled with pain. Spivey, on his back and wiggling to escape, bashed Michael's unbruised cheek.

Enraged, Michael found a grip on the preacher's left upper arm. His opponent's bleat of agony surprised but gratified him; he'd grabbed the arm punctured by Alice Farrell with her scissors. He wrenched on it, hard.

Spivey howled, lashed a glancing blow to his jaw. "Damn you, son of Satan!"

Michael blocked a jab to his throat and backhanded him, satisfied to hear a hiss of pain for response. "You murdered the Delacroix household!"

"Burn the witch!" Spivey succeeded in flipping from his back to his stomach and almost bucked him off.

Michael seized him by the hair and shoved his face into the mud. "And you raped Alice Farrell!" He yanked his head up. "And you shot my assistant!"

Spivey coughed. "How dare you strike a man of God?"

"I don't care if you're Christ Jesus, stepped down from the cross! You're going to jail!" He hauled Spivey to his feet by his hair and breeches and cuffed his ear.

Blood and mud glistened on the preacher's mouth, and he wobbled, seeming too dazed for another offensive, but Michael stayed alert. Sure enough, Spivey feinted. Michael was ready for his charge and jammed a knee into his groin. A rodent-like squeal emerged from the preacher. He doubled over, collapsed, and lay in a heap on the path.

Michael snarled down at him, his breath burning in the chilly night, his wounded cheek smarting. "Bum fodder." About twenty feet back on the path, he found rope that he'd dropped, along with his cartridge box. He returned to the unconscious Spivey and bound him like a hog. He straightened and grunted at his bruises. "There you are, Vicar, I cannot have you walking out on your own arrest."

In a heap of dead leaves, he located his musket and loaded it, his hand throbbing and bruised, his pulse still jumpy. Backtracking, he found that Spry and Teal were gone from the vicinity of the tunnel exit, but he was in time to apprehend another rebel hoisting himself out. Michael marched him straight to the men of the Eighty-Second and ordered the man to be bound and secured with his fellows.

After he sent men to fetch Spivey and guard the tunnel's exit in the pine copse, he learned that Spry, his leg quickly bandaged, had headed for the track, assisted by Teal. Tentative relief flooded Michael's chest. If Spry's leg could bear some weight, perhaps the musket ball had missed his femur.

The rebels continued to defend the house, despite a portion of the structure that smoldered. Michael set out for the track through wood smoke and black powder smoke stinging his eyes. He'd almost reached the front of the house when the comet's tail of a pitched torch pierced the murk and disappeared inside. The redcoats sent up a huzzah of victory. Then Michael heard panic and terror electrify voices in the house. When he strained to make out words, horror crawled up his neck. He hollered, "Cease fire, Eighty-Second, cease fire!"

The shot frequency dwindled, and the rebels' words became distinct: "Can't stop it! It's going to blow!" The front door crashed open spewing smoke and coughing, stumbling rebels.

"Men, take cover!" Michael dove beneath a shrub facedown and smashed the palms of his hands over his ears. In that second, he didn't give a damn about rounding up the fleeing rebels.

A massive sizzling and whistling swelled from the house, followed by a deafening explosion that almost knocked the wind from him. Heat belched over the area, as if lightning had struck and fused ground nearby. Cinder, ash, and glowing chunks of wood bombarded the terrain and plunked down around Michael, popping and sputtering.

When the rain of debris ceased, he rose, filthy, unable to see more than a few inches in front of him from airborne dust. His eyes watered, and he coughed. As the ringing in his ears subsided, he pieced together sounds of soldiers around him as they staggered up, coughing, cursing.

"Bloody hell, just like Vesuvius blowing the Romans from Pompeii!"

"Can you believe that bugger stored powder in his house? What an idiot."

"Damn, I'm dry. I hope they've extra rum for us back at the garrison."

Michael brushed at his coat, a sooty, soggy mess, and stepped into the clearing. Little could he see of the house through smoke, but from the fiery glow, he wagered that Spivey's weapons depository was in no better shape than the Delacroix house. A savage but suitable justice.

Chapter Twenty-Eight

BY TEN-THIRTY next morning, Friday the second of February, Michael was back on the Delacroix property after having gotten three hours of sleep in the barracks. He brought with him the regiment's chaplain, another detachment of soldiers, a wagon, canvas, and shovels. Most of the men were assigned the task of digging graves in the family cemetery, a job made easier by an overnight rainstorm that had softened the soil.

Michael, with two privates, set to his first unenviable task of the day: shoveling away the debris pile. About three feet below ground, he located Julia Garrity's nude body, wrapped in her cloak, a parasol tucked in beside her. He ordered the soldiers to enclose the corpse within canvas and transfer it to the wagon for later delivery to the undertaker. Then he sent a private to the Baxters' house on Second Street to transmit the bad news to Salome Ward. He hoped she hadn't defied house arrest and driven back to her farm. Gabriel Garrity was in no position to make funeral arrangements.

Finally he sought the ruins of the Delacroix house for his second unenviable task. He searched among the charred, soaked, but still-warm timbers for the bodies of Esmé Delacroix and Armand. And he found both corpses—blackened and reeking with the distinctive stench of burned human flesh—in what had once been the parlor.

Satisfaction thumbed its nose at him as he rode back to Wilmington in Julia Garrity's escort. Although she'd been dead for at least a day before the regiment occupied the town, he still wished, lamely, that he'd been able to stop the lethal cascade of fear, greed, and revenge. The justice he'd salvaged from the affair felt blighted.

In town, a messenger conveyed Major Craig's order for a meeting. Michael sent the men with the wagon to the undertaker and headed for Third Street. Before he got there, he heard his name called and reined back Cleopatra the mare. Anne Hooper trotted a gig up beside him. His spirits plummeted further at her somber expression. Damn, how he detested being fumed at by a woman. But she wasn't just any woman. She was the wife of a signer, and now she was going to question his motives again.

She tilted her chin up, her eyes frosty. "I heard about Mrs. Garrity."

"My commiserations on the loss of your friend. I regret that I don't have better news for you, and I wish the Eighty-Second had arrived a few days earlier—"

She held up a hand a second to halt the stream of formal drivel, then eyed him square on. Again, he sensed her spine of steel. If Anne Hooper wept for her friend, it would be in the privacy of her home, in her bedroom. "Thank you for your efforts on her behalf. I regret that I hadn't more actively intervened months ago in her mistaken notions."

Dull surprise slid through Michael. She wasn't reprimanding him after all. He selected his words with caution. "Those who have no regrets, madam, are foolish."

"Indeed." The severity in her eyes softened a fraction. "As a representative of the ladies of Wilmington, I would hear from you what plan your regiment proposes to ensure the safety of town residents henceforth."

"I should be glad to oblige you, but this very moment, I'm due for an audience with Major Craig—"

"Not *now*." Her nose wrinkled. "You're covered with a layer of filth and look as though you haven't slept in a week." She didn't smile, but her lips relaxed. "Monday the fifth. Three o'clock in the afternoon. Coffee in my parlor on Third Street."

Astonishment shredded some of the cobwebs in his brain. Major Craig wasn't going to believe this. He bowed his head. "I shall be honored, Mrs. Hooper."

***

"Mr. Stoddard, a surgeon has proclaimed the puncture wound in Mr. Spivey's left arm a good match with the tip of Mrs. Farrell's scissors."

Standing at ease before his commander's table in the study, Michael felt himself scowl. "In my opinion, sir, the lady exercised restraint of heroic proportions. Consider where else she might have stabbed him."

Craig chuckled. "Quite." He drummed fingers on the table, the rhythm synchronized with Trouble's panting. "Unfortunate that Mr. Greene escaped. As for your prisoners from the raid, I may have to parole some of them, as well as some of the prisoners from Heron's Bridge."

Disbelief swirled through Michael. "Sir?"

The major's eyebrow hitched with sarcasm. "Jail is full. I hope that those men out there complete the pen quickly." He rose, drew back the curtain on the nearest window, and gestured across the street.

Michael leaned over the table to peer out the window. In what had been an empty lot that morning, he saw soldiers busy digging holes and unloading rough, six-foot-long wooden posts from wagons. A few posts were already set in holes, revealing the outline of a large, circular stockade for the containment of the Eighty-Second's prisoners. At the rate the men were progressing, they'd have "the pen" finished within a week.

But if jail were already full, and he tracked down more of that weapons trafficking band before the stockade was finished, who would guard the prisoners? The majority of the regiment's men were deployed along the northeast quadrant of town, fortifying defenses by constructing earthworks, redoubts, and an abatis. He straightened. Skepticism compressed his lips.

"I know just what you're thinking." Craig dropped the curtain and reseated himself. "No way to secure more prisoners until the pen is finished, not enough men to guard all the prisoners. Don't let that stop you from arresting rebels who run weapons. I shall secure their parole as a last measure, if imprisonment isn't feasible. And if they take up arms against the King after signing their parole, we hang them on the spot. No trial. Simple. They know the rules."

If the rebels knew the rules, why did so many of them risk execution by continuing to fight against His Majesty? As solutions went, paroling rebels was much like swatting rats beneath a porch with a broom. Michael kept his mouth shut yet again and subdued the urge to blurt out percentages of broken paroles. Craig knew the percentages. And Michael knew the rats would return. No jail—or pen—was big enough.

"I sent a detachment of men out to torch the Bethany church building. One less house of sedition, one less haven for weapons trafficking. I'm pleased that the congregation is disbanded." Craig shuddered. "Women at the pulpit. Very odd, very disquieting."

Michael wasn't certain the Bethanys had been disbanded, but he volunteered no conjectures on the matter, as he knew how irked Craig became when he heard a sentence beginning with the phrase, "I'm not certain..." Instead, he said, "Well, sir, what man hasn't been sermonized by his own mother?"

Craig's countenance clenched with humor. "Ah, you see my point." He eyed his lead investigator up and down. "Your rapport with the wife of William Hooper intrigues me. Keep me informed. And you'll be relieved to know that Mr. Bowater has dropped assault charges."

"Bowater?" Then Michael remembered. "Oh, that pimple of a land agent."

"The inspiration to drop charges didn't originate with him, but he quickly warmed to the idea when exposed to the proper persuasion." Trouble barked once.

How Michael would love to have been a fly on the wall for that. "Thank you, sir."

"Don't mention it. And as for your mysterious Frenchman, I have alerted my superior officers of his presence in the area. He's the assassin Claude Devereaux, also known by the names of Claude Demaris and Anton Devereaux. In the old French war, he was one of Montcalm's scouts, along with Jacques le Coeuvre and several other Frenchmen. All extremely dangerous, proficient with knives and sabotage, excellent marksmen, spies for the rebels." Craig paused, taking measure of Michael with respect. "I'm not certain how you talked him out of slitting your throat. Most men wouldn't have been able to do so."

Michael swallowed, wondering if he'd encounter Claude again. True, he'd captured the "footwashing Protestant dog," but did that mean the Frenchman now had a vested interest in him? Claude had certainly seemed to find vicious glee in precipitating conflict between rebels and redcoats.

In all the business of French spies and rebel weapons trafficking, he didn't want to forget a long-overdue act of justice. Craig could help with it. "Sir, have we a packet scheduled to depart for London anytime soon?"

"Yes. The ship will leave in a week or two. Why do you ask?"

"The scout, Teal, needs to be aboard." Michael summarized the history of Tasheel bin Rasul. "He helped us halt Mr. Spivey's men from raiding Mr. Farrell's estate, and he was instrumental in the capture of Mr. Spivey. From London, his grandfather will be able to transport him back to Mokha. That's why I ask that you arrange for him to be a passenger on the packet."

"Consider it done, Mr. Stoddard. An amazing and tragic story."

Spry was still recuperating in the infirmary, so Michael headed over. As he approached, he saw the surgeon sharpening a bone saw in the sunshine, whistling a merry tune. When Michael spotted the gore on his apron, he gaped, and his stomach lurched. Was Spry going to lose his leg?

Clayton noticed Michael and set down the saw. "Afternoon, sir. How may I help you?"

Michael squeezed back panic. "How are the six injured men?"

"I put three stitches in Cunningham's eyebrow. Damned lucky he was that the falling board didn't strike an inch lower. As for the others—" He shrugged. "Mostly bruises. Fit for duty, even Cunningham. Except for Spry, that is."

Michael glanced at the bone saw. "And Spry?"

"He's a big pussycat, but laudanum cheered him on while I cleaned and bandaged the wounds. If he'd been a slighter man, without so much thigh, the ball might have lodged in his leg, hit bone. And that would have been bad. But it passed straight through." Clayton crossed his arms high on his chest. "We'll see within a day or two how much infection he develops. Heard him groaning awhile back, so he probably needs another dose of laudanum. He's my only customer right now. Might I trouble you to check on him for me while I finish with this saw?"

Breath whooshed from Michael. "It's no trouble at all."

He entered the infirmary quietly. Spry's grunts and groans came from the first stall. Imagining his assistant restless with pain, Michael walked over and peered in. He stared.

Spry lay prostrate on a cot, head on his pillow and facing the wall, a blanket over his legs, while Molly the laundress sat on the edge of the cot kneading his back through his shirt. Spry grunted again. "Oh, aye, right there, it's tight right there. Feel the tight muscle? That rebel was crazed, I tell you. He and I must have wrestled a quarter hour before I got him off me. That's when he shot me."

Michael felt his mood curdle. There lay his assistant, freshly shaven and in a clean shirt—and he was lying through his teeth to persuade a bosomy blonde to nurse him back to health. Michael glanced at the door. Did Clayton know about this?

Meanwhile, his own back ached from wrestling Spivey, and the preacher had tenderized his face two nights in a row. After spending the morning with the remains of Julia Garrity, Esmé Delacroix, and Armand, Michael not only looked but smelled demonic. He'd definitely drawn the short straw for wartime glamour.

Over her shoulder, Molly spotted him. Her eyes widened, and she yanked her hands off Spry. Michael motioned her out. She scooped up an empty basket and exited without a word. He stepped into the stall and propped hands on his hips.

"Molly, don't stop now. Where'd you go?" Spry eased himself over, started at the sight of his commander, and struggled to a sitting position. "Oh, sir, hah hah, afternoon, sir!" His teeth looked bigger than ever, his cheeks pink with healthy color. "Kind of you to stop by!"

"Kind of you to fit me into your busy schedule. Are they treating you well here, Spry? Serving you meals in bed? Serenading you to sleep? You look a bit bored. I might be able to arrange a visit from *all* the ladies of Wilmington."

Spry's smile went lopsided, shifted from one corner of his mouth to the other. "Sir, surely you know that Enid feeds us far better than the Army does. She sent an apple tart with Molly. You want some of it?" He peered beneath his cot. "Hmm, looks as though I ate it all."

Michael relaxed his arms and sighed. "How's your leg?"

"Doc says I'll have impressive scars to show at private viewings." His teeth flashed again. "Throbs a bit. Odd, I don't seem to notice it as much when Molly's rubbing my back."

"So you think I should recommend to Clayton that he allow Molly to rub your back."

"Can you do that?"

"If it'll get you out of here faster."

Spry's eyebrows shot up. "Have we another investigation already, sir?" His eyes sparkled. "I rather enjoy it. Well, not the part about getting shot, and my hat's off to you for dealing with those corpses this morning. But thinking things out, sir, it's like a big puzzle, piecing evidence together. Better than building redoubts, or running messages. Or digging latrines."

Michael snorted, warmed by Spry's enthusiasm, grateful to have him as an assistant. "Then see that you don't linger here." He moved to exit the stall.

"Sir. One thing before you go." Spry lowered his voice in conspiracy. "Make sure you stop by White's tonight. I heard that the men plan to descend upon the tavern to celebrate chasing rebels off Heron's Bridge and capturing Spivey. If you happen to show, you won't pay for any of your drinks."

"Is that so?"

"Wish I could be there, sir. Promises to be quite a party. But I'm stuck here in the infirmary." The corners of his mouth tugged downward. "In pain, you know. Sir."

"With a pretty blonde to rub your back, poor lad. For King and country."

Spry grinned. "God save the King.

Chapter Twenty-Nine

WHILE ENID CLEANED Michael's primary uniform coat and brushed out his spare, he spent the remainder of the afternoon in correspondence, swaggering to his benefactors after the fashion of all junior officers who sought advancement. For the benefit of Lord Crump, who had funded his early career, he boasted of the military prowess of James Craig and the Eighty-Second, and of the skill of Craig's lead investigator and his assistant. He also bragged to his uncle Solomon, the prosperous blacksmith whose infrequent but crucial gifts of bank drafts supplemented the paltry pay of an infantry lieutenant. For his parents and sister, he inquired after their health, his nephews' growth, and the latest news from the locals.

His hand ached from subduing Spivey. Writing and brawling were incompatible. While updating his journal with details of the investigation, he ran out of ink and borrowed some from Enid. When he returned the bottle, the housekeeper, expression dour, pointed out warm water for bathing and the dreaded linen rectangle for his chin.

A full, hearty meal she lavished upon him that evening fortified him for the cheer at White's, courtesy of a tavern full of victorious redcoats. By the time he'd gotten into his fifth beer, the edge had come off his disappointment over the dismal outcomes in the investigation.

And Kate Duncan looked lovelier than ever as she approached his table.

He drained his tankard and scooted it to the table's edge. Then he stood, pulled out the chair nearest his, and bowed. "Will you join me, madam?" She accepted the invitation, and he resumed his seat, eager for talk that wasn't gloomy. "Tell me, how is Mrs. Farrell?"

A smile lit her eyes. "She's always been rather reserved. But when I spoke with her this morning, she was happy, full of life, like a different woman."

Like she'd been released from prison. "I'm glad to hear it."

"The way you handled that meeting with her..." Her voice softened, and she tilted her head to the side. "I see a good deal of what people are like in my business. Perhaps owning this tavern has made me something of a student of human nature. Your integrity is a rare quality, sir."

Michael's lips parted in astonishment over the compliment. His cheeks grew warm. "Well, it—it's a pleasure to be of service, madam."

What was it she'd said to Alice Farrell during the meeting? *You can trust Mr. Stoddard.* How had Mrs. Duncan known he could be trusted? At that point, they'd only spoken for a few moments the night before.

Beer didn't usually impart an abundance of wisdom upon him, but he grasped that somehow in that brief, first conversation, Kate Duncan had understood his character. More than that—she'd recognized his worth as person.

In contrast, Lydia had exploited him solely for her pleasure.

Astounded, he sat back in his chair to ponder the revelation. Then he noticed the downturn to Mrs. Duncan's perfect lips. "Do you have concerns about Mrs. Farrell?"

She shook her head. "No, not Mrs. Farrell." Below the table's surface, she wrung her hands. "You're the investigator. Tell me why Esmé Delacroix murdered Julia Garrity. There should be a motive with a crime, yes? Esmé was self-sufficient. What motive could she possibly have had for killing another woman?"

Most civilians didn't care about details from a criminal inquiry, but the widow seemed interested. He leaned an arm on the table. "Mr. Spivey and Mrs. Garrity had schemed to economically ruin Mrs. Delacroix. Two days before Mrs. Garrity was murdered, she drove out to Mrs. Delacroix's house and flung their intentions in her face. No government of competence existed to protect Mrs. Delacroix at the time. Mrs. Garrity backed her into a corner, so she sought her own justice."

"I see." Mrs. Duncan grimaced. "How could they have been so stupid? Esmé was never helpless."

"No, she was not."

The woman from Saint Domingue had seen her own death coming and walked into it, unflinching, a warrior. For a moment, her voice whispered in Michael's memory: *The herald who shifts shape and wears two faces...the teacher is here, learn from him...the shadow who bathes in blood.* He shook off the fortune telling and straightened in his chair.

"Mrs. Duncan, now that I've answered your question, perhaps you can answer mine. In the cemetery plot on Mrs. Delacroix's property are graves of a number of infants. Either John Delacroix got her with child every time he came home from the sea, or..." Michael cocked an eyebrow to reinforce attention on the anomaly. "Her husband was gone most of the year. I believe that she loved him and that she loved her independence, too. Several times, she insisted to me that she was no man's mistress. But she was a passionate woman, quite attractive. Living out there by herself so many years—was she truly no one's mistress?"

The owner of White's Tavern held Michael's gaze and said, low, "A woman's passion doesn't die just because she's widowed, or her husband leaves her alone for long periods of time. Townsfolk have gossiped through the years that there was another man in Esmé's life. I haven't seen evidence of it, so it's probably just romantic folklore."

He nodded. "From what little I know of her, I cannot envision her in the role of a mistress."

"Perhaps you confuse a mistress—purchased, pampered, and controlled—with a lover."

His eyes widened in acknowledgement of the difference. "I see your point. Well, then, what does local folklore say about her *lover*?"

She glanced at the ceiling. "Oh, he was a pirate, a giant Frenchman, assassin for General Montcalm. A suitable partner, I suppose, for a 'witch.'"

"Ahhh!" Michael grinned as all the weird, dangling pieces crashed together in his head and made sense. Infuriated and grief-stricken over the murder of his long-time lover, Claude Devereaux had unleashed a mutual enemy upon the murderer last night, ensuring Spivey's destruction. Had Michael not apprehended Spivey, the Frenchman would no doubt have hunted the preacher down in the swamp. As for Claude's whereabouts while Spivey and his men were butchering Mrs. Delacroix and her slaves, Michael realized he might never know. But he was certain the assassin's absence hadn't been due to cowardice.

"Mrs. Duncan, I assure you it's no folklore. Mrs. Delacroix's lover is a French assassin named Claude Devereaux. He's quite dangerous, and he's still in the area." He added to her description of him and asked her to spread the word to her brother and employees should Devereaux find a way to slake his thirst in White's Tavern.

Amusement lit her expression. "I believe I helped you with several points of this investigation."

"Well, yes, and thank you."

"Women could be criminal investigators, too." She sat tall in the chair.

"Not likely. Sometimes there's physical peril involved."

She tossed her head. "Physical peril isn't mandatory to solving an inquiry. Intelligence is. And women are just as intelligent as men."

"Of course they are."

"And intuition—women are often credited with having more of it, but I'm sure you use your intuition when you're trying to solve crimes."

"I do indeed use it, madam." He smiled. "But it isn't something I'd emphasize to Major Craig."

"Oh, heavens, no." Elbow on the table, she propped her chin on her fist and observed him a few seconds. "Are you going to tell me what happened to your face?"

The bruises on his face, ah, yes. Swaggering worked for Spry. Might work for him, too. He hadn't forgotten what she said moments earlier: *A woman's passion doesn't die when she's widowed.* Just how frozen was the Ice Widow?

He pressed back in his chair and played for nonchalance. "Oh. Oh, that. A group of rebels jumped me last night, tried to kill me during the raid. Took me several minutes, but I managed to pound the snot out of every one of them." He groaned and leaned forward. "Wrenched my back badly. Tight muscles everywhere."

Suspicion and disbelief pinched the edges of her frown. Then her frown converted to a tight smile. "If that's true, explain why the bruise on one side of your face looks at least a day older than that on the other side."

Intrigued by her powers of observation and deduction, he studied her anew.

"The truth, now." She cocked an eyebrow. "Don't spin balderdash about running into a door or something. You got into fistfights two nights in a row, didn't you?"

The disapproval he detected in her voice stung him a bit, and he recalled the kiss Alice Farrell had bestowed on his cheek—fondly, because the Ice Widow wasn't going to grace him with a similar award for valor. "Rather inglorious, actually. Wednesday night, it was Spivey's men pouncing on Spry and me in Mrs. Chiswell's back yard. Last night it was Spivey himself while I was trying to arrest him."

"*Why* is it that men can do nothing but beat upon each other?" Her sigh weighed of centuries of forbearance.

Insight prodded him. Maybe she hadn't considered her loyalist husband particularly heroic for marching off to Moores Creek and getting himself killed. In that case, a redcoat would impress her even less—especially an officer who risked his life regularly, rounded up murderers, and made Wilmington a safer place to live.

This was one mêlée he'd never win.

He fell back into the flippancy of five beers. "Oh, I don't know. The truth is that most men are brutes, destined to disappoint women. We leave our dirty stockings lying about the house, eat and drink too much, forget to clean our teeth, leer at comely lasses, and expect women to find us irresistible. No sooner than we try to become domesticated when something sets us off, and we cannot resist thrashing each other, trashing civilizations." Gods, how proud Miriam would be of him, apologizing for men.

Mrs. Duncan stared at him a few seconds, then laughed. "Mr. Stoddard, you're even funnier than my brother."

Her *brother*. Oh, well, at least she hadn't relegated him to the status of a boring lout. He leaned toward her, game for silly banter. "I'm also more handsome than he. Here now, envision me without the bruises. Quite the dashing fellow, aren't I?"

As if his words had challenged her, she raked a bold gaze over his face, lowering her stare to encompass the breadth of his shoulders. Their gazes locked.

Tavern laughter and conversation faded. Michael felt as though he was alone with her, sitting on a secluded bench in a garden, and they had just begun a conversation.

Then a serving wench broke the enchantment, set a full tankard of beer before him, and whisked away the empty one. White's Tavern was as noisy, smoky, and public as ever.

"I-I should be monitoring something in the kitchen." Her cheeks pink, Mrs. Duncan moved to rise. He hastened to pull the chair out for her. "Enjoy your drink."

He tracked the retreating sway of her hips. On the other side of the room, her brother had been watching the interchange. Marsh grinned at him. Only then did Michael comprehend that Kate Duncan had enjoyed being flustered by him—and for her to be flustered by a fellow, well, it wasn't a common occurrence.

Not ice at all, that widow. He reseated himself, grasped the tankard, and saluted Marsh with it. Marsh's grin got bigger.

He relaxed back and enjoyed another swallow of beer. Good beer. His gaze slipped around the packed tavern, then spotted a familiar dusty hunting shirt, swung back, and froze. Over the top of his tankard, Michael looked across the room into the dark eyes of scout and ranger Adam Neville.

Suddenly his beer tasted like piss.

He slammed down the tankard, felt himself start to steam. Neville, that Janus-faced son of a jackal. What was he up to in Wilmington? No good, he wagered.

Neville smirked. Michael rose, done drinking for the night, and jerked his head toward the front door. Out. Neville tossed a coin on the table before him, grabbed his battered hat, and followed him into the frigid Carolina night.

Half a block from the tavern, Michael faced him, looking up a bit, for Neville was taller than he. Considering the life he lived, no wonder he looked older and more haggard than Michael. "What are you doing here, Neville?"

Shadows clung to Neville's lean face, framed in dark hair. A gloat creaked across his mouth. "I'm a messenger of doom." He dropped his hat on his head.

On the verge of lambasting him, Michael was hauled up short by Esmé Delacroix's voice in his memory: *The herald who shifts his shape and wears two faces comes within a few days.* His skin chilled deeper than the night. "Explain yourself."

"You've heard about the battle on the seventeenth? I was there fighting, a part of it."

Michael glared. "On whose side?"

The ranger placed his palm above his heart. "How little faith you have in me, Stoddard. The King's side, of course.

"The Battle of the Cowpens. They fought on cattle pastureland, and both sides stomped through fresh cow shit." Neville guffawed. "Do you find universal humor in that, as I do?"

Michael stared down the street, deserted except for two men from the regiment walking their patrol. He didn't respond. Neville was goading him, hoping for a fight. The scout was one of the disaffected, a colonist who reveled in chaos, in frustrating the efforts of both armies. He whipped his glare back to the other man. "Did you lead the Legion into a trap?"

"Oh, not at all." Neville bared his teeth, and his beer breath wafted over Michael's face. "Morgan played far better with the hand dealt him by the weather and the food supply. Tarleton ran his men exhausted. He asked for defeat, so Morgan gave it to him. It's as simple as that."

The authenticity of Neville's explanation sank into Michael's bones. Tarleton was a good cavalry commander, but he was arrogant, and Michael could imagine such a defeat. And yes, knowing of Tarleton's errors...

The herald...His news will disappoint you.

Michael's bones iced. Wait a moment. Was all of this crazy coincidence, or had Esmé Delacroix foreseen the future?

Neville expelled annoyance and backed off a step. "I thought for certain that you'd label me a liar. All your soft living lately has mellowed you. Congratulations on getting yourself boarded in Mrs. Chiswell's comfortable home. No small accomplishment for a toy soldier these days."

Recalling Enid's distress, Michael pinned the scout with a stare. "Did Mrs. Chiswell survive her trip to the backcountry?"

"Oh, yes, saved my life after the battle, in fact. Be a polite lad, and maybe she'll let you continue to board under her roof when she returns."

When she returns. Neville sounded certain of it. Enid would be so relieved to hear her mistress was alive and coming home. Then cold fingered Michael's soul, dragging incredulity behind it. Enid had said that to gain access to Tarleton and the Legion, Mrs. Chiswell had posed as the sister of Lieutenant Fairfax.

The shadow who bathes in blood, he comes.

Damnation! He had no idea who the teacher was, but the shadow was definitely Fairfax. The Frenchwoman had known, it, and he'd dismissed her ability. Loss staggered him.

"Stoddard, you're tepid this evening. Are you ill? You haven't yet asked about our mutual friend." Neville wrapped the word "friend" in antipathy.

"Fairfax survived the battle, didn't he?"

"Correct. And like Tarleton, he now rides in the army of Cornwallis."

He comes. "Lord Cornwallis is coming here, to Wilmington."

"Wrong. He's headed north through the Carolinas." Neville slapped his shoulder with mock camaraderie. "Not to worry. Wilmington is safe from the monster. But *you*, you're in deep trouble, lad. The monster has somehow gotten it into his head that you're a spy for the rebels."

In the first second, primal fear blasted through Michael and hiked his voice. "*What?*" Then he scowled at Neville and steadied his breathing. Surely the ranger was toying with him. "How? Why?"

"I think your visits to the Legion's camp in December made him suspicious. Maybe you should have been honest with him, told him you'd gone out there to catch him off guard and kill him. That might appeal to his sense of humor."

Michael balled his fists and bared his teeth. "You shit. You told him some rubbish about me."

"Not I. Whatever the reason, the damage is done. And you know what he does to spies, to rebels. See that bay gelding over there hitched third from the left? Handsome beast, eh? I got him from one of Fairfax's victims, a rebel spy who could no longer sit in a saddle—"

"You're a traitor and a bloody coward." Michael gripped Neville by the shirt. "You loathe Fairfax as much as I do. Why don't *you* get rid of him?"

Neville whispered, "It's too much fun watching all of you scramble around over his atrocities." He shook himself free.

Michael envisioned a nebulous six-foot-two Frenchman with a dead comrade to avenge. "It isn't personal for you yet, is it, Neville? What will you do when he makes it personal? It's part of why the atrocities are such sport for him." Neville's smile faltered the slightest bit. "Come back here and find me when it does become personal."

The ranger whirled about for his gelding, lanky stride graceful and silent. In disgust, Michael watched him mount the gelding and ride into the night. His posture bespoke a man who'd divested his great load onto another. Damn Neville.

Behind him, a man chuckled like the greeting of a canebrake rattlesnake, like the savage merriment of Fairfax. Michael spun about, his pulse staccato. *There*, behind those three drunks on the porch at White's—the black outline of a dragoon in the Seventeenth Light.

The trio of men toddled from the porch into the street. The dragoon dissolved into shadow. Michael let out a breath he hadn't realized he'd been holding. Then he twisted back, his gaze seeking the direction Neville had taken.

Not to worry. Wilmington is safe from the monster.

No, Wilmington wasn't safe. Nowhere in America was safe while Lieutenant Fairfax roamed unchecked. In the long run, he represented a disaster more vast for Britain than the Legion's defeat at the Cowpens.

And neither were Michael's dreams for his future safe.

At that moment, he realized that was exactly what Esmé Delacroix's unfinished sentence implied: *If you do not vanquish the shadow...* He was the one to vanquish the shadow. Somehow he must find a way to do it.

He strode three steps toward Market Street before stiffening at a noise behind him. Over his shoulder, he saw a cat dart behind a barrel. He continued on his way, his breathing raspy, his pulse aflutter.

Damn Neville for ruining his night.

Finis

Historical Afterword

HISTORY TEXTS AND fiction minimize the importance of the Southern colonies during the American War of Independence. Many scholars now believe that more Revolutionary War battles were fought in South Carolina than in any other colony, even New York. Of the wars North Americans have fought, the death toll from this war exceeds all except the Civil War in terms of percentage of the population. And yet our "revolution" was but one conflict in a ravenous world war.

From late January to mid-November 1781, Crown forces occupied the city of Wilmington, North Carolina. The daunting presence of the Eighty-Second Regiment nearly paralyzed movements of the Continental Army in North Carolina and prolonged the war in the Southern theater. Some 21st-century readers find it hard to believe the actual history: that patriot leaders and the militia abandoned Wilmington's civilians to the Eighty-Second, and those civilians then surrendered peacefully to the regiment. Even in 1781, news of the occupation prompted sarcastic comments from patriot leaders in other states: "6 of the Town's people left it, the rest received the Enemy with 3 huzzas." (John Rutledge, governor of South Carolina) The truth is that the patriot government in North Carolina wasn't organized well enough to mount a defensive against the Eighty-Second. They and the militia had no choice but to flee. Had Wilmington's civilian population—merchants, artisans, seamen, and government officials—attempted to fight the combat veterans of the Eighty-Second, those civilians would have been slaughtered, and their homes sacked and burned.

Major James Henry Craig, the regiment's commander, was short on resources during the entire occupation. Thus he resorted to unconventional strategies that bordered on insubordination, won the devotion of area loyalists (a feat Lord Cornwallis was never able to achieve), and enhanced his garrison's effectiveness. For example, his use of marines from the transport flotilla to supplement the force with which he defeated Colonel Young at Heron's Bridge allowed soldiers of the Eighty-Second to remain in Wilmington during his march on Heron's Bridge and progress on the construction of earthworks for defense of the town.

During most of the occupation, Craig also allowed the wife and family of William Hooper, signer of the Declaration of Independence, to live in Hooper's law office on Third Street. In the middle of the year, Craig permitted Hooper back into town to check on his loved ones. He wined and dined Hooper while he visited, and he allowed Hooper, who must have been on King George's "Most Wanted" list, to leave town without arresting him. Hooper was known for being politically moderate, rather than extreme. As for Craig's motivation for such lenient treatment, when he dealt harshly with patriots like John Ashe and Cornelius Harnett, we can only speculate.

Almost never do we hear of Craig's accomplishments. True, history is written by the victors. But also, the Eighty-Second's triumphs were bracketed and overshadowed by disasters that same year for Crown forces at Cowpens, South Carolina in January and Yorktown, Virginia in October. Had more British commanders adopted Craig's creative, fluid style of thinking, the outcome of the war might have been vastly different. An intriguing cerebral exercise for historians and those who write alternative history fiction.

In 1781, Third Street in Wilmington wasn't yet laid out, although some buildings like Hooper's law office existed on what eventually became Third Street. Because it can be difficult to visualize the strategic military importance of a town with so few streets, I've taken the liberty of granting "official" status upon Third Street.

During the War of Independence, America was far more diverse, culturally and religiously, than what most students learn in high school history class. I created the back story of Teal, aka Tasheel bin Rasul, from histories of several highly educated Muslims who were captured in the slave trade and sold in America. Some of these men eventually returned to their homelands. As for the influence of Islam on early America, Thomas Jefferson studied the Qur'an, and pieces of it may have found their way into his work on the Declaration of Independence.

Colonial-era treasures in cities such as Boston and Philadelphia are well known, but few visitors to North Carolina realize that some houses and geographical features from the time of Craig's occupation remain intact in the historical district of Wilmington. A gem in the city's colonial crown is the house at Market and Third Streets. In April 1781, Lord Cornwallis stayed there while resting his troops in Wilmington after his grueling victory at Guilford Courthouse. The British general described it as "...the most considerable house in town." The Burgwin-Wright House has been beautifully restored and is open for tours.

Dramatis Personae

In order of appearance:

Michael Stoddard—officer of the King stationed in Wilmington, North Carolina. Lead criminal investigator for the Eighty-Second Regiment

Pitcairn—officer of the King

Teal (aka Tasheel bin Rasul)—scout, freed slave

Jackson, Henshaw, Stone, Ferguson, and Buchanan—King's men

Nick Spry—King's man, assistant investigator to Michael Stoddard

Godfrey Carlisle—astronomer, brother of Alice Farrell

Smedes—wainwright in Wilmington

James Henry Craig—officer of the King, commander of the Eighty-Second Regiment

Molly Pepperton—laundress, wench, Spry's sweetheart

Betty Overton—housekeeper for Gabriel and Julia Garrity

Ben Overton—son of Betty Overton

Gabriel Garrity—gunsmith in Wilmington, husband of Julia Garrity

Trouble—a forty-pound bulldog

Kevin Marsh—manager of White's Tavern

Kate Duncan (*née* Marsh)—owner of White's Tavern

Enid Jones—housekeeper for Helen Chiswell

Salome Ward—sister of Julia Garrity

Caldwell—jailer in Wilmington

Anne Hooper—wife of William Hooper, signer of the Declaration of Independence

Alice Farrell—wife of tobacconist in Wilmington

Esmé Delacroix—widow of sea captain John Delacroix

Horatio Bowater—land agent in Wilmington

Mayer—driver for the Garritys

Hiller—gardener for the Garritys

Armand—slave of Esmé Delacroix

Noisette—slave of Esmé Delacroix

Ned Peabody—dock manager

Elijah Spivey—preacher at the Church of Mary and Martha of Bethany

Paul Greene—cousin of Elijah Spivey, paramour of Julia Garrity

Doc Clayton—British Army surgeon

Claude Devereaux—French assassin

Richard Farrell—tobacconist in Wilmington

Mrs. Forbes—Manager of Education at Church of Mary and Martha of Bethany

Ross—scout

Adam Neville—scout, ranger, double spy

Selected Bibliography

Dozens of websites, interviews with subject-matter experts, the following books and more:

Babits, Lawrence E. *A Devil of a Whipping: The Battle of Cowpens*. Chapel Hill, North Carolina: The University of North Carolina Press, 1998.

Boatner, Mark M. III. *Encyclopedia of the American Revolution*. Mechanicsburg, Pennsylvania: Stackpole Books, 1994.

Butler, Lindley S. *North Carolina and the Coming of the Revolution, 1763–1776*. Zebulon, North Carolina: Theo. Davis Sons, Inc., 1976.

Butler, Lindley S. and Alan D. Watson, eds. *The North Carolina Experience*. Chapel Hill, North Carolina: The University of North Carolina Press, 1984.

De Van Massey, Gregory. "The British Expedition to Wilmington, North Carolina, January – November, 1781." MA Thesis, East Carolina University, 1987.

Dunkerly, Robert M. *Redcoats on the River: Southeastern North Carolina in the Revolutionary War*. Wilmington, North Carolina: Dram Tree Books, 2008.

Gilgun, Beth. *Tidings from the Eighteenth Century*. Texarkana, Texas: Scurlock Publishing Co., Inc., 1993.

Hagist, Don N. *A British Soldier's Story: Roger Lamb's Narration of the American Revolution*. Baraboo, Wisconsin: Ballindalloch Press, 2004.

Mayer, Holly A. *Belonging to the Army: Camp Followers and Community During the American Revolution*. Columbia, South Carolina: University of South Carolina Press, 1996.

Morrill, Dan L. *Southern Campaigns of the American Revolution.* Mount Pleasant, South Carolina: The Nautical & Aviation Publishing Company of America, Inc., 1993.

Peckham, Howard H. *The Toll of Independence: Engagements and Battle Casualties of the American Revolution.* Chicago: The University of Chicago Press, 1974.

Schaw, Janet. *Journal of a Lady of Quality: Being the Narrative of a Journey from Scotland to the West Indies, North Carolina, and Portugal in the Years 1774 to 1776.* eds. Evangeline W. Andrews and Charles M. Andrews. New Haven: Yale University Press, 1921.

Tunis, Edwin. *Colonial Craftsmen and the Beginnings of American Industry.* Baltimore: The Johns Hopkins University Press, 1999.

Watson, Alan D. *Society in Colonial North Carolina.* Raleigh, North Carolina: North Carolina Division of Archives and History, 1996.

Watson, Alan D. *Wilmington, North Carolina, to 1861.* Jefferson, North Carolina: McFarland & Company, Inc., Publishers, 2003.

Watson, Alan D. *Wilmington: Port of North Carolina.* Columbia, South Carolina: University of South Carolina Press, 1992.

Discussion Questions for Book Clubs

1. What does author Suzanne Adair do to project an image of the Southern theater of the Revolutionary War in *Deadly Occupation*?

2. What did you learn about the Revolutionary War that you didn't know before you read the novel?

3. What role does the historical setting play in *Deadly Occupation*? How does Suzanne Adair evoke a sense of place? What role does nature play?

4. In a novel of crime fiction, the characters should be put in danger. What makes you worry about the fate of characters in *Deadly Occupation*?

5. For you, what is the most memorable scene in *Deadly Occupation*? Who is the most interesting character in the book? Why?

6. What is your reaction to the inclusion of real historical figures (book examples: Major James Henry Craig, Anne Hooper) as characters in a work of fiction?

7. How does the character of Teal challenge your ideas of the complexity of slavery issues?

8. Do you think Esmé Delacroix was really a witch? Explain.

9. In what way has Michael's concept of women been shaped by his sister, Miriam, as well as by his first lover, Lydia? How do you foresee this changing?

10. What is your reaction to the idea of civilian merchants and artisans surrendering to the Eighty-Second Regiment without trying to fight? Why do you feel that way?

11. In Revolutionary War America, do you think someone could heal emotionally

from the kind of experience Alice Farrell had as a young woman? Explain.

12. Is justice served at the end of the story? Explain.

13. How would the use of modern forensics have changed the plot and outcome of *Deadly Occupation*?

14. How does Michael differ from your ideas of what redcoats were like during the Revolution? In what ways does having a redcoat as a hero challenge your beliefs or teachings? Why do you feel that way?

15. What do you think happens to the characters after the story ends?

Follow Michael Stoddard's journey as an investigator
in Book 2 of his exciting series

Regulated for Murder

A Michael Stoddard American Revolution Mystery

by Suzanne Adair

For ten years, an execution hid murder. Then Michael Stoddard came to town.

Bearing a dispatch from his commander in coastal Wilmington, North Carolina, redcoat Lieutenant Michael Stoddard arrives in Hillsborough in February 1781 in civilian garb. He expects to hand a letter to a courier working for Lord Cornwallis, then ride back to Wilmington the next day. Instead, Michael is greeted by the courier's freshly murdered corpse, a chilling trail of clues leading back to an execution ten years earlier, and a sheriff with a fondness for framing innocents—and plans to deliver Michael up to his nemesis, a psychopathic British officer.

Regulated for Murder, "Best of 2011," Suspense Magazine.

Please turn the page to read the first chapter.

Chapter One

A MESSAGE SCRIPTED on paper and tacked to the padlocked front door of the office on Second Street explained how the patriot had come to miss his own arrest:

Office closed due to Family Emergency.

Family emergency? Horse shit! Lieutenant Michael Stoddard hammered the door several times with his fist. No one answered. He moved to the nearest window and shoved the sash.

Two privates from the Eighty-Second Regiment on the porch with him pushed the other window sash. It was also latched from within. One man squinted at the note. "What does it say, sir?"

Michael peered between gaps in curtains. Nothing moved in the office. Breath hissed from him. "It says that the macaroni who conducted business here sold two clients the same piece of property and skipped town with their money under pretense of family emergency."

"A lout like that wants arresting." The other soldier's grin revealed a chipped front tooth.

"Indeed. Wait here, both of you." Michael pivoted. His boot heels tapped down the steps.

Afternoon overcast the hue of a saber blade released icy sprinkle on him. He ignored it. Ignored Wilmington's ubiquitous reek of fish, wood smoke, and tar, too, and trotted through the side yard. At the rear of the wooden building, two additional soldiers came to attention at the sight of him. The red wool of their uniform coats blazed like beacons in the winter-drab of the back yard.

He yanked on the back door and found it secured from the inside, rather than by padlock. The young privates had no luck opening a window. Michael looked inside, where curtains hadn't quite covered a pane, and confirmed the stillness of the building's interior.

A plume of white fog exited his mouth. He straightened. Ever since Horatio Bowater had grudgingly dropped assault charges against Michael and his assistant days earlier, Major Craig had bided his time and waited for the land agent to supply him with an excuse to take another rebel into custody. A disreputable business transaction presented the ideal pretext for arrest.

And when James Henry Craig ordered someone arrested, it had damn well better happen.

Michael squared his shoulders. By god, he'd nab that bugger, throw his dandy arse in the stockade, where the premium on real estate that past week had risen in direct proportion to the number of guests incarcerated.

Surely Bowater had left evidence in his office. Business records or a schedule. Without facing his men, Michael regarded the back door anew, attention drawn to the crack between door and jamb. "The men sent to Mr. Bowater's residence should be reporting shortly. However, I suspect our subject has departed town." He half-turned toward his soldiers. "Henshaw."

"Sir."

"Fetch a locksmith from the garrison, quickly. Tell him we've a padlock on the front door."

"Sir." Henshaw jogged for the dirt street, the clank of his musket and cartridge box fading.

The other soldier, Ferguson, remained quiet, awaiting orders. A wind gust buffeted them. Glacial sprinkle spattered Michael's cheek. Another gust sucked at his narrow-brimmed hat. He jammed it back atop his dark hair. He and the men would be drenched if they didn't complete their duties soon and seek shelter.

He shrugged off February's breach beneath his neck stock and ran fingertips along the door crack. The wood was warped enough to reveal the metal bolt of the interior lock. He wedged the blade of his knife into the crack and prodded the bolt with the tip. Wood groaned and squeaked. Splinters shaved from the jamb. In another second, he felt the bolt tremble. He coaxed it, one sixteenth of an inch at a time, from its keeper until he found the edge and retracted the bolt.

He jiggled the door by its handle and felt it quiver. At the edge of his senses, he registered an odd, soft groan from inside, somewhere above the door.

But the warmth of enthusiasm buoyed him past it. There was no bar across the door on the inside. The latch was free.

Satisfaction peeled his lips from his teeth. Horatio Bowater was such a careless fool. Had the agent replaced the door and jamb with fresh wood, an officer of His Majesty would never have been able to break in like a common thief.

He stepped back from his handiwork and sheathed his knife. Ferguson moved forward, enthusiastic. Michael's memory played that weird impression again, almost like the grate of metal upon metal. *Careless fool indeed,* whispered his battlefield instincts. He snagged Ferguson's upper arm. "Wait." He wiggled the latch again. Skin on the back of his neck shivered. Something was odd here. "Kick that door open first, lad."

Ferguson slammed the sole of his shoe against the door. Then he and Michael sprang back from a crashing cascade of scrap metal that clattered over the entrance and onto the floor and step.

When the dust settled and the cacophony dwindled, Michael lowered the arm he'd used to shield his face. Foot-long iron stalagmites protruded from the wood floor. Small cannonballs rolled to rest amidst scrap lumber.

The largest pile of debris teetered, shifted. Michael started, his pulse erratic as a cornered hare. With no difficulty, he imagined his crushed corpse at the bottom of the debris pile.

Bowater wasn't such a fool after all.

Ferguson toed an iron skillet aside. His foot trembled. "Thank you, sir," he whispered.

Words hung up in Michael's throat for a second, then emerged subdued. "Indeed. Don't mention it." With a curt nod, he signaled the private to proceed.

Ferguson rammed the barrel of his musket through the open doorway and waved it around, as if to spring triggers on more traps. Nothing else fell or pounced. Michael poked his head in the doorway and rotated his torso to look up.

A crude cage stretched toward the ceiling, a wooden web tangled in gloom, now clear of lethal debris spiders. Bowater hadn't cobbled together the device overnight. Perhaps he'd even demonstrated it for clientele interested in adding unique security features to homes or businesses.

Michael ordered the private on a search of the stable and kitchen building, then stepped around jagged metal and moved with stealth, alone, past the rear foyer. The rhythm of his breathing eased. He worked his way forward, alert, past an expensive walnut desk and dozens of books on shelves in the study. Past costly couches, chairs, tables, brandy in a crystal decanter, and a tea service in the parlor. He verified the chilly office vacant of people and overt traps, and he opened curtains as he went.

In the front reception area, he homed for the counter. The previous week, he'd seen the agent shove a voluminous book of records onto a lower shelf. No book awaited Michael that afternoon, hardly a surprise. Bowater was devious enough to hide it. And since the book was heavy and bulky, he'd likely left it behind in the building.

Wariness supplanted the self-satisfaction fueling Michael. A suspect conniving enough to assemble one trap as a threshold guardian could easily arm another to preside over business records. Michael advanced to the window beside the front door. When he unlatched it and slid it open, astonishment perked the expressions of the redcoats on the front porch. "I've sent for a locksmith to remove the padlock." He waved the men inside. "Assist me."

While they climbed through and closed the window, Michael's gaze swept the room and paused at the south window. Through it, the tobacco shop next door was visible. The owners of the shop kept their eyes on everything. In contrast to Bowater, Mr. and Mrs. Farrell hadn't griped about the Eighty-Second's occupation of Wilmington on the twenty-ninth of January, eight days earlier. *If* they'd happened to notice atypical activity in Bowater's office over the past day or so, he wagered they'd be forthcoming with information.

How he wished Private Nick Spry weren't fidgeting, restless and useless, in the infirmary, while his leg healed. But for the time, Michael must make do without his assistant. He signaled his men to the counter, where Ferguson joined them. "Lads, I think Mr. Bowater left his records book in this building. I want the entire place searched for it."

Michael's hands sketched dimensions in the air. "The book is about yea high and wide. Medium brown leather. Heavy and large. Pick any room to begin your search." He checked the time on a watch drawn from his waistcoat pocket. "Going on three o'clock." He rapped the surface of the counter with his knuckles. "Help yourselves to candles here if you need some light." He replaced his watch and turned to Ferguson to receive the private's report.

"Sir. The stable was swept clean. From the looks of it, months ago. No straw, no dung, just reins and a broken old harness hanging on the side, gathering dust. Dust in the kitchen, too. I found an old broom and bucket and some cracked bowls. That's all."

Flesh along Michael's spine pricked. "My orders, lads. If you believe you've located the records book, don't touch it. Fetch me first."

***

The privates dispersed to search the office. Henshaw returned with the locksmith, a slight fellow about three inches shorter than Michael. Pick in hand, the civilian contractor squatted before the padlock. Michael directed Henshaw to the tobacconist's shop to learn whether the Farrells or their apprentices had witnessed recent unusual activity associated with Bowater.

As Henshaw clanked down the front steps, the locksmith stood and brandished the freed padlock like a severed head. Michael sent him to the back door to assess how to secure it. Then he lit a candle and strode to Bowater's study. One of the privates was already inspecting books and shelves, his examination meticulous, cautious.

Moments later, the scuff of shoes in the doorway interrupted Michael's scrutiny of bills and letters he'd spread open before him on Bowater's big desk. "Sir," he heard Ferguson say, "I believe I found the records book."

Michael swiveled and spotted the bleak press of Ferguson's lips. His tone snapped at the air. "You didn't touch it, did you?"

"No, sir, not after what happened out there. I did as you ordered. Told the others to stand back."

Thank god his men weren't rash. Michael relaxed his jaw. "Good." He caught the eye of the soldier in the study with him and jutted his jaw at the door. "Let's have a look."

In the parlor, soldiers and the locksmith had withdrawn a prudent distance from where a plush rug had been rolled away and three floorboards pulled up. Michael regarded the floor, then Ferguson. "However did you find this hidden compartment?"

"The floor sounded peculiar when I walked over it, so I pulled away the rug and realized that the boards weren't quite flush with the rest of the floor."

"Excellent work." Michael knelt beside the hole in the floor and gazed into gloom.

"Here you are, sir." One of the men handed him a lit candle.

The faint glow enabled him to resolve the shape of a book lying flat about three feet down in the hole. Something lay atop it: an open, dark circle that appeared to contain a smaller, closed circle in its center. Without sunlight, he doubted that even a torch would provide him with enough illumination to identify what lay atop the book.

The gap in the floor howled at him of the cage above the back door, loaded with projectiles. Foulness wafted up from the hole. Like feces. Like death.

No way in hell was he was sticking his arm down there. He rocked back on his heels, stood, and gave the candle back to the soldier. "Ferguson, fetch the broom from the kitchen."

"Sir." He sprinted out and returned with the broom in less than a minute.

Michael inverted the broom, handle first, straight into the hole. As soon as the end of the broom made contact below, he heard a loud clap. The broom vibrated, gained weight. His arm jerked, and he tightened his grip. Men in the room recoiled.

He brought the broom up. Metal clinked, a chain rattled. Affixed to the handle, approximately where a man's wrist would have been, was a metal leg trap used by hunters to snag wolves and bobcats. Its teeth, smeared with dried dung, had almost bisected the broom handle.

A murmur of shock frosted the air. "Damnation," someone whispered.

Revulsion transfixed Michael. His stomach burned when he thought of anyone catching his wrist in the trap. Almost certainly, the victim's hand would need amputation, and the filth on the metallic jaws would encourage the spread of general infection, resulting in slow, agonizing death.

The locksmith coughed. "Mr. Stoddard, sir, I've a question of you."

Michael blinked, broom and trap still in his grasp, and pivoted to the locksmith. The wiry man held a metal chunk that he must have pried off the floor while inspecting the rear door. Hair jumped along Michael's neck when he recognized the metal as a bayonet, its tip broken off.

A muscle leaped beneath the locksmith's eye. "Who designed that trap at the back door?"

"The owner, Mr. Bowater, I presume."

"Sir, with all the valuable property in this building, there's no reason Mr. Bowater shouldn't have secured the rear as well as he did the front, except that he..." The locksmith trailed off. His lips pinched, as if to seal in disgust.

Michael leaned into his hesitation. "Except that he *what*?"

"Inferior workmanship, warped wood on the door. I believe Mr. Bowater intended to lure someone in with the promise of an easy entrance, then kill him horribly in a rain of debris. You've a madman on your hands." The artisan glanced over the redcoats. His empty palm circled air twice, fingers open. "Battle places its own gruesome demands on you fellows. But outside of battle, have you tried to lure a man into a trap and kill him?" He caught Michael's eye.

Michael's expression and body stilled. He held the man's gaze. Winter crawled over his scalp and down his neck. The artisan didn't know, Michael told himself. How could he know?

"You see my meaning." The locksmith raised the bayonet for emphasis. "A decent man like yourself would never set up such a snare."

End of Chapter One

Thank you for purchasing this book. Word-of-mouth is crucial to the success of any author. If you enjoyed the book, please post a review wherever your social media allow (Amazon, Goodreads, etc.). Even a brief review is appreciated.

CPSIA information can be obtained at www.ICGtesting.com
Printed in the USA
LVOW10s1556111115

462081LV00004B/523/P